MIRROR GATE

ALSO BY JEFF WHEELER

The Harbinger Series

Storm Glass

The Kingfountain Series

The Poisoner's Enemy (prequel)
The Maid's War (prequel)
The Queen's Poisoner
The Thief's Daughter
The King's Traitor
The Hollow Crown
The Silent Shield
The Forsaken Throne

The Legends of Muirwood Trilogy

The Wretched of Muirwood
The Blight of Muirwood
The Scourge of Muirwood

The Covenant of Muirwood Trilogy

The Banished of Muirwood
The Ciphers of Muirwood
The Void of Muirwood
The Lost Abbey (novella)

Whispers from Mirrowen Trilogy

Fireblood
Dryad-Born
Poisonwell

Landmoor Series

Landmoor
Silverkin

MIRROR GATE

the HARBINGER SERIES

JEFF WHEELER

47NORTH

Text copyright © 2018 by Jeff Wheeler
All rights reserved.

No part of this book may be reproduced, or stored in a retrieval system, or transmitted in any form or by any means, electronic, mechanical, photocopying, recording, or otherwise, without express written permission of the publisher.

Published by 47North, Seattle

www.apub.com

Amazon, the Amazon logo, and 47North are trademarks of Amazon.com, Inc., or its affiliates.

ISBN-13: 9781503904712
ISBN-10: 1503904717

Cover design by Mike Heath | Magnus Creative

Printed in the United States of America

To Cami

I awoke this morning with the premonition that the emperor's death is imminent. His incapacitation over the last four years has brought a steady host of calamities. There is a sickness rampaging our world, fueled by the machinations of those seeking power. It begs the question of who will be chosen to lead the empire next. Many covet the staggering responsibility and think they are eminently qualified for it. But power is an unwieldy ship.

Vanity comes naturally to all of us. Every human is, to their own mind, the center of all known worlds—the axle on which it all turns. And yet their knowledge is but their own perception of the things around them, and their feelings are inescapably colored by their perceptions of the world's wants and its merits.

Thus is the power of the alchemy of thought. We try to bend existence with our minds. And some are so convinced by their own efforts they deny that there is a source of infinite intelligence, a power called the Knowing that orchestrates the pinwheels of the stars, the majesty of storm clouds, and every tender blade of grass that shoots from the planet. In the past it was called the Medium. Now, the manifestations of the Knowing are called the Mysteries.

It was this power that whispered to my mind knowledge that I could not have otherwise known . . . and a warning of the turmoil that would follow.

—Thomas Abraham, Aldermaston of Muirwood Abbey

PROLOGUE

The prince regent, Willard Richard Fitzempress, had made a habit of reading the gazette called the *Mirror Gate* every morning at breakfast. He had a special set of gloves he used so the ink wouldn't smudge his fingers as he turned the flimsy pages. He had even visited the factory where the popular paper was produced and had received a royal welcome and tour. The smell of the place was odious, and he'd shielded his mouth with a handkerchief to mask the stench, but he had enjoyed observing the artists hard at work sketching the pictures used on the pages. The owner had also introduced him to the people who wrote the different articles—some of whom praised him, many of whom condemned him. He knew *their* names.

Reading the *Mirror Gate* gave him a glimpse of the empire that he did not get from his briefings with the ministers. Humanity was a teeming cauldron of emotions. He was grateful that he lived skyward up in Lockhaven, the hulk of interconnected palatial rock that hovered above the masses lurking in tenements and slaving at factories in the City below. It was only right for the rulers to live above the ruled.

This morning, the picture on the cover of the *Mirror Gate* had him transfixed. An artist had sketched a fanciful piece representing the cholera morbus disease. The picture was of a grotesque man dressed in tattered rags, a food satchel strapped around his shoulder. His pants were pulled up with colored strips of cloth, showing off the festering sores beneath. He wore no shoes, no gloves. His face was riddled with pockmarks, and his sleeves were rolled up past his elbows, highlighting his muscular arms. Two men lay sprawled in the street at his feet—one an aging banker by the looks of him, the other a dockworker whose cap had fallen onto the ground. The wild man was gripping a woman in a teal-colored dress around the waist and forcing his mouth onto hers. The woman's wrap, plumed hat, and gloves all marked her as a member of the upper classes. The eyes of the man, the Cholera Morbus, were fierce and intense as he gazed at the woman in his arms. She was kissing him back willingly, one hand on his chest, the other around his neck.

It was an intentionally provocative piece of artwork. Everyone who looked at the picture would know who the woman was. And everyone either knew someone who had been lost to the disease rampaging in portions of the City or knew *of* someone.

And as he stared at the picture, letting his tea grow cold, he imagined that *he* was the Cholera Morbus, and the woman in the picture was Lady Corinne. Clearly the artist had intended to provoke the readership's sympathy by coloring the woman's dress to match the favored color of the mistress of Pavenham Sky, one of the most respected ladies of the court. The epidemic, which had first broken out a year before, was felling rich and poor alike, much to the alarm of the populace. No one was safe from its deadly grasp. Not even the wealthiest citizens, who dwelled in Lockhaven and the other floating sky manors, were immune. If she were to die . . .

He gazed at the picture, his mind racing, his heart beating faster and faster at the thought of losing her . . . of losing Corinne. Even though he knew why the artist had chosen her image—she was the picture of wealth and class—the feelings made him desperate to see her again, to assure himself that she was safe. For the first time in his life, he was in love.

When he glanced up and looked at himself in the decorative mirror hanging on the wall, he saw his own grotesqueness and hated himself.

He was getting older and losing the vigor he had enjoyed in his youth. Since becoming the prince regent, he had been kept so busy that his body had become disgusting to his own sight. Yet the sight of her in that monster's arms made him wonder. Would she go to him willingly?

A shudder went through him. Such thoughts were dangerous. The lady's husband, Admiral Lawton, was a powerful man—no, *the* most powerful man in the empire, despite his unwillingness to serve in government. Richard had asked him *twice* to serve as the lord high chancellor, but he had refused both times, claiming that his various business interests would have made it impossible to avoid charges of corruption, even if he divested himself of them. His appointment would have brought the admiral—and his wife—into the prince regent's inner circle. In his weaker moments, Richard knew that was why he continued to curry the man's favor.

"Are you done with the gazette, my lord?" asked his secretary, Mr. Case, holding out a white-gloved hand to take it. "Shall I dispose of it?"

"No!" the prince regent said abruptly. He startled himself with the violence of his response. "No," he said in a more temperate tone, "I wasn't finished with it." He glanced at the picture again, trying to quell an inner shudder as the lurid colors washed over him. Those who produced the gazette were experts at stirring the people's emotions. They did so deliberately to keep the people chasing injustices instead of focusing on the causes of them. Most of the gazettes were funded by one of the ministries. Though the *Mirror Gate* was undeniably more independent than most, its contents were still carefully orchestrated. Public content had to be, or the people would rise in defiance as they had on occasion in the past. "Insurrection" was a nasty word . . . to him and his kind.

"On second thought, Case, take it up to my study." He folded the paper and handed it to his secretary, who tucked it unceremoniously under his arm. The prince regent gripped the teacup and took a shallow sip, wincing at how tepid it had become. He'd sat transfixed by the image for longer than he'd realized. "This epidemic, this disease, is truly causing me grave concern."

"Of course, my lord," Case said, always obedient to his whims. "My wife's niece just perished from it, sir."

"Hmmm," the prince regent grunted, the image still fixated in his mind. "Ghastly business."

"Indeed, sir. Do you think . . . do you think it is a sign of a true Blight?"

The prince regent looked at his secretary as if he were daft. "You believe the government caused it? Please, Case, I thought you were more sensible than that. Why would we unleash a plague deliberately on the populace? It's absurd." Of course, there was a Blight Leering, hidden deep inside Lockhaven by the Ministry of Thought and guarded day and night, but it was a jealously kept secret. He had been to look at the stone face himself, had felt the dark magic brooding within it. No one had enacted it. No one would dare.

"*Is* it absurd?" Case asked pointedly, giving him a sharp look. "Could it have come from one of our trading partners, then?"

The prince regent made a flippant hand gesture. "Whenever a contagion begins to affect the populace, we are always quick to attribute it to supernatural causes. Surely the cholera morbus is one of the Mysteries, but it is a Mystery of Wind, and the best objective minds are working to solve the problem. If *Brant Fitzroy* cannot solve the contagion, then we are all of us doomed." The image from the page flashed in his mind again. He squirmed in his chair, wanting to see it again and wishing he hadn't handed the paper over to Case.

The man still looked skeptical. Did his belief represent how the larger population felt? Did they truly think the disease had been unleashed by the government? It was impossible. But people always looked for a scapegoat when there was a terror in the land. Why not look above?

He was growing agitated again. Since he and his wife had separated four years ago, his feelings had been growing increasingly ungovernable. He couldn't abide the woman who was his wife, yet he risked the world's displeasure if he divorced her. They had married to improve their family fortunes on the recommendation of their parents, but he had always been drawn to a certain married lady. No, he must not think of it anymore . . . he had to control his thoughts. The remedy was staying busy.

"What is on my schedule for the day?" he asked Case with agitation, gritting his teeth.

"You meet with the Minister of Law this morning to discuss a possible trade war with the court at Kingfountain. Then you have a sitting with the artist Jacomay, who has been commissioned to do a painting for the new currency. The privy council meeting is set for this afternoon, followed by a state dinner with the ambassador of Naess—"

The conversation was interrupted when the door opened without so much as a warning knock. The prince regent turned, an angry scowl on his face for the intrusion on his breakfast, and prepared to scold the intruder soundly. But the scowl quickly turned to an expression of startled surprise when the prime minister entered, a grave look on his haggard face.

"Lord Prentice! What has happened?" The prince regent pushed his stuffed chair away from the table and rose hastily to his feet. His knees groaned, and the sudden movement made him a little light-headed.

The prime minister advanced and, with only a glance, dismissed Mr. Case. The prince regent watched as his secretary left, the paper still folded beneath his arm. Despite the turbulence of his thoughts, he found himself hoping Case would remember to bring it upstairs. The door shut, leaving the two men alone.

"Grim tidings, Prince Regent," the prime minister said. He smelled of stale sweat, and perhaps a hint of brandy.

"Speak, man! Are we at war? What has happened?"

The prime minister chuckled in a grim humor. "War? Wouldn't that solve so many of our problems. No, Prince Regent. Your father, the emperor, died earlier this morning. He breathed his last at fifteen minutes past five. Doctor Brooke is no doubt scurrying away as we speak, to tell Fitzroy."

The news, delivered indelicately, came as a physical blow, though not because the prince regent would mourn his father. The light-headed feeling persisted, and he found it difficult to breathe. He set his palms on the ornate table to steady himself.

"What does this mean, Prentice? What does this *mean*?"

"It comes as a surprise, for the emperor's health was beginning to improve earlier this week. He couldn't speak or write, but he was no longer bedridden. He would take the air in a sturdy wooden chair fixed with wheels. Not to mention the countless Gifts of Healing he received. All means, both magical and otherwise, were exhausted. And all failed in the end."

"Surely he didn't choose someone this morning to be his heir. Did he? *Did he?*"

"Don't weary yourself, Prince Regent. He did not. He was incapable of articulation. What it means, *Richard*, is that the privy council will now choose the empire's new ruler. And it may not be you."

The prince regent felt the veins in his temples start to throb painfully. The worried agitation in his belly flared into panic. "But Seraphin is only sixteen, not eighteen. She is underage. She cannot be named empress!"

"No, she cannot. Not yet. And as you and I both know, she has struggled to master certain aspects of the Mysteries, even at Muirwood Abbey. The order of our society must be maintained, Richard. At all costs."

The prince regent closed his fist and slammed it on the table. "She cannot because she is *illegitimate*, Prentice! It's no wonder she cannot, her blood is spoiled!"

He watched as the prime minister's eyes flashed with anger. It was an old argument—one they'd never settled between them. His Corinne had opened his eyes to his wife's duplicity and the princess's illegitimacy, yet the others in power refused to see the truth.

"The investigation could never prove that, my lord," the prime minister insisted, echoing his thoughts. "Even the secret one you commissioned without the privy council's sanction. If you continue to pluck on those harp strings, I can assure you that the privy council will bar your right to the throne completely! Do you want to become the emperor or not?"

A watery sickness weakened the prince regent's legs, and he nearly collapsed into his chair. "I'm so close, Prentice. So close!"

The prime minister strode forward and gripped his shoulder firmly. "I came here, Richard, to advise you. If you want to be named emperor, you must appear to have earned it through your own merits. You must be seen as the less *risky* alternative. Your daughter—"

"*Don't* call her that!" Richard quailed, flinching.

The prime minister sighed and released his grip. "The *princess* has been studying the Mysteries for four years at the most prominent school in the empire. Her companion, of *choice*, is that young woman Fitzroy found in the Fells. It is no secret how he feels about the poor. Were he to become prime minister, and I've no doubt the princess would appoint him to that position, I can assure you that our way of life would be compromised. The proper order would be upset. Destroyed. And with sicknesses such as the cholera morbus raging, now is not the time for an inexperienced empress and a misguided prime minister! There are many on the privy council who already see *you* as the less risky option. But they still remember how you tried to sabotage your d—the princess's rights. She may be sixteen and unimpressive in stature, but she still commands sympathy. The populace loves her. They do not love you. I must speak plainly in this. How you react, in this very moment, will be crucial in determining your future and the future of the empire."

The prince regent stared at the table settings, his mind whirling with thoughts. If Seraphin were chosen as empress, he would be ruined forever. She would never forgive him for the way he had treated her since learning of his wife's adultery. But hadn't he hired tutors for her at great expense? And what had she done with his money but waste it daydreaming, climbing trees, and writing fanciful letters to a middling young officer? He was livid whenever he remembered those accursed letters. The young man had refused to surrender the notes Seraphin had written to him. After four years that young man would nearly be finished with his schooling. Soon he would be assigned to a sky ship in the fleet, and Seraphin, no doubt, would make him rise to the greatest heights. Well, if the prince regent had his way, he would have the lad court-martialed for some insignificant offense. Or assigned to one of the most distant posts in the empire.

Yes, he would get his revenge. How dare the privy council accuse him of standing in the way of her education? How dare they insist that she be sent to Muirwood Abbey as if she were truly of the blood?

"Did you even hear what I said?" the prime minister said in a chastising tone.

The man's domineering attitude was becoming grating. He wouldn't confess that his mind had been wandering down dark paths. "What must be done, Prentice? She's a child still, even at sixteen. A willful, disobedient, haughty child. Cannot the privy council see that? She could ruin us all."

"I see that, Richard," he replied smoothly. "If you want to be chosen by the privy council, you must do exactly as I say. Or *both* of us will lose our places."

SERA

CHAPTER ONE

VICAR'S CLOSE

Sera squinted at the iron lamp, willing it with all her might to grow brighter. Each Leering had a face carved on it, and each face held an expression reflecting one of the many human emotions. The little stone face carved into the rock behind the frosted glass was hidden, but no doubt it was smiling mockingly at her. The light did nothing but continue to shine sweetly, innocently, as if completely unaware of Sera's increasing vexation. She screwed up her nose and "pushed" her thoughts at it, trying to make it obey her. *Brighter. Far brighter!* she ordered. She was Seraphin Fitzempress, a princess of the empire. Surely she could manage it. But, no, she didn't even have the power to affect a small stone. It was the bitterest of disappointments that she continued to fail at such simple tasks.

"You're trying too hard."

Her friend and companion Cettie was sitting at the window seat, a book in hand, her dark hair falling over her shoulders. Sera glanced at her, feeling the frustration boil even more. Commanding the Leering stones was effortless for Cettie. Her friend could use them to light the room, cause the hearth to blaze, and produce the scent of daffodils—all while sneezing.

Well, maybe that was an exaggeration.

Sera envied her friend's affinity with the magical aspect of the Mysteries, the power that made manors and castles and cities anchor in the sky like clouds or allowed sky ships the size of whales to sail through the sky. Before coming to the school, Sera hadn't even *known* about whales. But her classes at Muirwood Abbey had taught her many wonderful things about her world—and expanded her consciousness by introducing her to the worlds connected to the empire through magical rifts in the universe. She had learned a wealth of information about the Mysteries of Thought, Law, War, and Wind. The only thing the school couldn't teach her, unfortunately, was how to effectively make Leerings work at her command. That, it would appear, came down to talent.

"Of course I'm trying hard," Sera said with a tone of exasperation. "I'm giving it everything I have. The carving is mocking me. I know it is."

"It's made of stone," Cettie said. "They can't do that."

"This one can," Sera said with a huff. "The only time I *can* affect them is when the Aldermaston is nearby. It's like he gives them a wink or something and tells them to obey me. Otherwise they don't do a thing!"

"He doesn't," Cettie said, shaking her head. She set her book down on the cushion and then turned her head and looked out the window. Her gaze focused, and her nose scrunched in a pretty way. Cettie's nose always did that when she was thinking something over. Sera found it endearing, but her friend hated the way it brought attention to her freckles. These past years, they'd learned so much about each other. While Sera had unburdened herself about her father, who'd attempted to disinherit her, and the less agreeable side of being a princess, Cettie had told her about growing up in the Fells. Her father was a retired dragoon, a military man. He'd had a dalliance with a lady he didn't know, years ago, and Cettie had been the outcome. The girl's deed had been sold, again and again, to progressively worse guardians. Currently, her birth father was married to his landlord's outspoken daughter, and both were fighting with Cettie's guardian, Minister Fitzroy, to prevent him from adopting her. And despite Minister Fitzroy's new wealth and power as the Minister of Wind, they had been unsuccessful at determining her mother's identity. The old housekeeper at Fitzroy's manor, Mrs. Pullman, might know the truth, but she refused to speak to it. She was languishing in a fetid jail in the Fells for her crimes against the Fitzroy family.

Sera sighed. There—she was doing it again. Her thoughts tended to flutter from one idea to another, an incorrigible butterfly that couldn't be tamed. She had tried for four years to learn how to focus, to keep her thoughts directed and not distracted. Four years was a long time to work on a weakness and see so little improvement. Even the breathing exercises that Cettie had tried to teach her didn't work. Her mind just would not sit still. At least she had done well in her classes.

"There's someone watching," Cettie observed.

"That gawky student from the Law classes who likes you?" Sera asked.

Cettie turned and looked back at her, her expression serious. "No. It's a man, not a youth. He was leaning against the building, watching the street. He was looking at our place, I think."

Sera joined her at the window seat, but she could only see the throngs of students passing down the main street from the school to the center of town. "I don't see anyone."

"He's over—oh, he's gone. That was strange. It felt like he was watching us. Oh well. The problem, Sera," she said, touching her arm, "is you're trying too hard. You have to coax the power to do your bidding. To beckon it, like you would a little bird. You do it best when you're gentle. I've seen you do it without the Aldermaston, so I know you can."

Sera bit her lip, her voice lowering. "I'm *trying*, Cettie. I've been here for four years, and I still cannot work the Leerings reliably. If I can't succeed, I will never fulfill my destiny. I may learn every last bit of information about the Mysteries, but an empress must be able to command the Leerings of Lockhaven to defend the people. If we are attacked again, like we have been in the past, people could die. Every book of wisdom I've read says something similar. I understand the principles. Why won't they work for me?"

Cettie rose from the window seat, a look of sympathy on her face. "But listen to yourself. You're *worrying*," she said calmly.

"I know! I cannot turn that part of me off." Sera started wringing her hands and pacing. "I cannot will away the responsibility that may be coming to me. It terrifies and excites me. My grandfather may leave us at any time, and if he does, there's a chance I might be given the crown. There has never been an empress so young before. Not even Empress Maia."

Cettie nodded. This was an old conversation for them, and they each knew their part. "And all your expectations for yourself are tangling your feelings into knots. You cannot force this. It's quite the opposite."

Sera knew her friend was right, but her anxiety was like a muscle she couldn't relax. "I wish there was a way to force it. To command all Leerings to obey me in the name of the future empress!"

Cettie's mouth turned into a solemn little frown. "Don't even tease about that, Sera. Your thoughts are not secret from the Knowing."

She said it in such a gentle, imploring way that Sera felt chagrined. "I'm sorry. You're right, of course. I should be patient, deliberate, thoughtful. It sounds so boring sometimes. I want it now! I fear I'll go mad if I can't ever learn to make the Leerings work. I do try, you know."

"Let's give your mind a rest and take a walk in the village."

"Splendid idea! If you spot the man who was staring at us, let me know, and I'll give him a scolding," Sera said. Cettie knew just how to calm her. Whereas Sera had spent most of her childhood bound to her large, sprawling manor, she now had the freedom to do as she liked. No longer was she forced to climb trees to get a look at the outside world. Even then she'd been limited—the City below had been smothered in fog more often than not, and though she had been able to see most of Lockhaven, the floating portion of the imperial city, from her perch, seeing wasn't the same as experiencing. The schools of learning, the abbeys, were an in-between place. Although they were physically grounded, each of them was separated from the populace in some way. Some, like Muirwood, were on lands surrounded by water. Others, by woods and fences. Yet they taught the magic that made cities hover in the sky.

The girls both grabbed their shawls from the pegs by the door. The small room was so much simpler than Sera's elaborate home. As a princess, she could have chosen to stay at the Aldermaston's beautiful manor, but she had insisted on dwelling with the hundreds of other students in the hamlet of Vicar's Close. The dormitory was so very simple, consisting of a small living room, kitchen, and loft to sleep in—identical to the row of other dwellings comprising Vicar's Close—and yet she loved it. Bunches of dried lavender hung from the walls, adding a sweet fragrance to the air, making it feel more like a home.

It was late afternoon, and the cobbled street bustled with students and those who lived in the community. She could see the spires of the abbey over the wall and felt a wave of nervousness again. Sometimes the beautiful abbey felt like a reminder of her own failures. Linking arms with Cettie, she started walking away from the abbey toward the center of the village. Just being outside lifted Sera's mood.

"It's him," Cettie said with a sigh.

Sera saw him instantly. It was the young man studying the Mysteries of Law, Mr. Skrelling. Of course *he* was the one watching them. Cettie had probably only denied it out of embarrassment. Prior to studying at Muirwood, Mr. Skrelling had worked for Sloan and Teitelbaum, the advocates who represented Fitzroy. The firm had possession of his deed and had sent him to advance his usefulness to them. Even though he had left Sloan and Teitelbaum for the duration of his studies, he continued to work on Cettie's case—the search for her mysterious mother—which he oft used as an excuse to speak with her. He'd been making a nuisance of himself for years, going out of his way to speak to them in his awkward, formal manner.

"Should we turn and go to the abbey instead?" Sera asked conspiratorially.

"We're already walking his way. That would be rude, Sera."

"Isn't it rude of him to accost us every time he sees us?"

"Sera," her friend said warningly.

The young man collided into a bookshop cart as he attempted to cross the street abruptly. The bearded man pushing it railed at him for not watching where he was walking. The young advocate in training rose, dusting off his fine jacket, and started to accuse the driver of gross negligence. He was so discomfited and upset that he didn't see Sera and Cettie hurriedly slip away.

"Did you see that?" Sera said, unable to stifle a giggle. "Mr. Skrelling literally walked into the cart himself and then accused the man pushing it of doing something wrong. I had a class with him last year. He was insufferable, *and* he kept challenging the teacher."

"He *is* rather opinionated," Cettie said, glancing back. "I pity him truly. He doesn't see how he comes off to others."

"Yes, and it is our solemn duty to educate all men on their failings," Sera said lightly. They exited the street into the village square crowded with students. It would be easy to lose Mr. Skrelling there. "All except for that one," Sera said, grinning. She nodded her head to a young man and woman who stood nearby. "Adam Creigh, as gallant as ever. It appears he has been ambushed by Phinia. He has the patience of an Aldermaston," she added under her breath.

"He does indeed," Cettie agreed. "I don't see Anna. He's usually with her and her friends."

Phinia and Anna were the daughters of Cettie's guardian, Minister Fitzroy, and Adam was a boy the minister had pledged to educate. He'd grown into a robust man of eighteen, with ruddy cheeks, light brown hair, and an easy, comfortable smile. Despite his all-too-common tale of woe—his poor father had wrecked the family's fortunes and stooped to selling Adam's deed—he usually seemed in good cheer. And why should he not? Whereas most lost children found themselves legally entailed to scoundrels who'd force them into near slavery, Fitzroy was intent on educating his charge and empowering him to be the doctor he wished to be. And so, even though he was clearly embarrassed by Phinia's attention, Adam was duty bound to smile, and he did. As a good-natured young man, he never deliberately caused offense. All the more reason for them to intervene and save him from his own kindness. That, and her suspicion that Cettie harbored feelings for him—feelings she'd never express because of her loyalty to Anna, who had worshipped him for nearly her whole life. The youngest Fitzroy daughter was also sixteen and had blossomed into a stunning beauty, becoming the darling of the school when she had joined them at Muirwood two years ago.

"Let's save him. Poor soul."

Cettie balked. "I don't think we should interrupt."

"The young man is clearly suffering and seeking an escape from his situation. Come on." A good tug on Cettie's arm won her compliance, and she dutifully followed Sera to the fountain at the center of the main square. Plumes of white water gushed from the hub of the fountain's many Leerings. The ornate sculptures depicted a conflict that had ended centuries before, a commemoration of an event that no one remembered anymore. Sera didn't care much for history. She was more intrigued by the possibilities the future presented.

Phinia saw them approach, and her eyes flashed with irritation at the intrusion.

"Hello, Phinia," Sera said. "What a pleasant afternoon. You look upset. Is something wrong?" She arched her eyebrows innocently.

"Yes, something is *wrong*," Phinia said, a bit of a whine in her voice. "Mr. Creigh is going to work in the Fells after finishing here."

Sera was confused. "Hasn't that been your plan all along, Adam? You've often said so."

"Indeed, Miss Fitzempress."

"How many times do I have to tell you to call me Sera?"

"My feelings of propriety compel me to persist all the same," he answered with an apologetic shrug. "Yes, I do plan to become a doctor in the Fells. It is clear that is where the most help is needed. The City has been struck hard by the contagion over the last year, but nowhere is the spread quicker or more violent than in the Fells. Hello, Miss Cettie." He gave her a small bow, and Cettie flushed in response, poor dear.

"But it is so dangerous!" Phinia complained. "Why not go back to work for Father's mines? The doctor there is getting older; I'm sure he would appreciate your help."

"I could do that, I suppose," Adam said respectfully. But it was clear from his tone that he didn't intend to.

"The cholera morbus is so dangerous," Phinia pressed. "I don't want you to go to the Fells. I know Anna feels the same way. I'm her sister, and I must look after her. Promise me that you won't. You must promise me."

"Phinia," Cettie said. She managed to pack that one word with plenty of meaning.

"Do you want Adam to die?" Phinia said scathingly, unleashing her claws. The oldest of Fitzroy's daughters still didn't fully approve of Cettie, even though her family had become impossibly rich with Cettie's help. Sera suspected she was jealous of all the attention and praise Cettie had rightfully earned. "No one knows the cause of it, but nearly everyone who's stricken by it dies. Those living in the tenements are struck down the most."

"All the more reason," Adam said with controlled patience, "that it needs to be studied by every available doctor. A plague is a Mystery. It can be solved, just like other things." He gave Cettie an admiring look.

Cettie and Fitzroy's discovery of the storm glass, an invention that could accurately predict weather patterns, had brought unspeakable riches to Fitzroy's income. Because he owned Cettie's deed, he was entitled to *all* the profits. Although he wanted to bequeath a significant portion of the wealth to his charge, an annuity that would rival that of any young woman in the empire, he could not do so until she was legally adopted; otherwise her greedy relations could snatch the money away from her before she could spend a farthing of it. The case was tangled and complicated, and it frustrated Sera to no end. But Cettie would certainly not lack for suitors, regardless of the outcome.

"Anna and I could not *bear* it if anything happened to you," Phinia said with exaggerated emotion. "You must reconsider. Cettie, he listens to you. Tell him!"

Cettie flushed again. "I'm sure he is very well aware of the danger, Phinia."

Phinia's eyes flashed with hot emotion.

"I would go to the Fells today if I could," Adam said, stepping forward, "but we all know I must first pass the Test. The breakouts of cholera morbus last for a month or two and then disappear, only to reappear elsewhere. How does it move? Some tenements get decimated, while others, blocks away, remain untouched. Everyone is afraid of it, and people flee as soon as it appears in their community. Does that not increase the risk of it spreading?"

"Isn't the Ministry of Wind studying it?" Sera asked him. This topic did interest her, very much so, and she was certain Fitzroy himself was trying to address it with the best doctors in the empire.

Adam shook his head. "There has been little time to study it. Doctors are working day and night trying to cure those who have it, trying to find the best remedies to treat it. Thousands are afflicted and dying. Every qualified person is needed right now, and here I am living in peace and comfort." He shook his head, clearly vexed by the situation. She sympathized with his motives. She, too, wanted desperately to save her people from the ills of their world.

Phinia reached out and put her hand on his arm. "You mustn't go!"

He looked down at her hand. To touch another person in such a way was a breach of propriety, and she'd clearly done it in an effort to force her will. His eyes darkened with anger, but his voice was still controlled when he spoke to her.

"We attract those things that we secretly fear," he told her. "Some men fear the sight of blood. Some men fear sickness. *I* do not fear these things." Then he looked Phinia in the eye. His anger seemed to soften, though his words were quite clear. "Please do not attempt to infect me with your worries."

And what do you fear, I wonder? Sera asked herself. She was impressed by Adam's self-control, his disciplined mind. If she could only borrow a portion of such a will, she'd have the Leerings heating her bath in a trice.

Phinia's hand dropped away. She looked as if she'd been reprimanded by her father.

Adam looked over their heads, seeing that someone else had joined their small group. "Good day, Miss Fitzempress. Miss Phinia. Miss Cettie." He nodded and then stalked away.

Sera turned and saw Mr. Skrelling standing there, fidgeting. Though it was hardly charitable of her, Sera wished he would simply vanish, or that *they* would. He was tall and gaunt, and though he was dressed in the fashions of the day, his vest was much too big for him.

"Ah, Miss Fitzempress. Miss Cettie. Miss . . . Seraphin? My pardon. I come bearing news of the utmost importance. If you will pardon my intrusion into your conversation, I thought it best to speak to you at once."

Strangely, he wasn't talking to Cettie, whom he normally doted on. He was addressing Sera. Phinia had already sulked off, no longer interested in them now that Adam had gone away.

"What is it, Mr. Skrelling?" she asked, determined to end the conversation as quickly as possible.

"If you do not consider it an impudence?"

"I do not. Speak up, please. What is it?"

"I'm gratified to hear that, ma'am. I would not, under any circumstance, seek to be bothersome to Your Ladyship. To *either* of you," he added, directing a thin-lipped grin at Cettie. Smoothing down his unwieldy dark hair, he turned back to Sera. "Miss Fitzempress, I come to you with news. I will not disclose how I came upon this information, because that is relevant neither to the purpose nor to the point. But if I understand it correctly, and I believe that I do, your grandfather, the emperor, is now . . . well . . . there is no other way to say this except bluntly . . . he is *deceased*."

He may as well have shoved her backward into the rushing fountain.

Everything was going to change.

CHAPTER TWO

THE ALDERMASTON

That Sera should hear such news from a pimple-faced young man in the middle of a crowded square made the surprise even worse. Where was her longtime advocate, Mr. Durrant? Why hadn't she been told straightaway? There was no way to compose herself, no witty retort that flew to the tip of her tongue.

"It can't be" was the only response that fumbled its way out of Sera's mouth.

Of course, she had long understood that her grandfather was ill, *deathly* ill. Four years ago, apoplexy had rendered him mute, powerless, and had put him on a slow spiral toward death. Her father had been named prince regent, for his brothers were so fully in debt that they were too much of a liability to the coffers of state to be bestowed with such an honor. Only one person had the ability to stand in his way and prevent him from becoming the next emperor—Sera herself.

Father had tried every sort of subtle and overt machination possible to undermine her and present her as an impossible choice. It had fallen on the privy council to uphold her rights, which had ultimately led to her being sent away to Muirwood, to receive the education to which her rank entitled her. For goodness' sake, he had even tried to put a *deed* on her! What would he do to try to supplant her now? He was better versed in the laws surrounding inheritance of the crown.

Why was she hearing about it like this?

"No doubt, ma'am, you are surprised by this revelation," Mr. Skrelling said with a head bob.

"How did this information come to you?" Sera demanded abruptly, attempting to make sense of her swirling thoughts.

"As I tried to express, I am not at liberty to discuss the *source* of my information. But I would not have come to you unless I felt absolutely certain that it was true. I am not a gossipmonger, as they say. If I can be of service, Miss Fitzempress, in any manner—"

"Yes, you can get out of my way," Sera said in exasperation, interrupting him. She had to see the Aldermaston, had to know for herself if it was true. An Aldermaston could not lie, and Thomas Abraham was not the sort who would have dreamed of doing such a thing even if he could.

She left Mr. Skrelling standing, openmouthed, in the square and strode back the way they'd come with all the fury her short legs could summon. Why was everyone staring at her? Was it possible they'd all found out before her?

Cettie easily kept pace with her. "I'm sorry about your grandfather," she murmured.

"I hardly knew him," Sera tossed back, probably too sharply. "When I was a child, I rarely visited court. My parents said there was too much intrigue, too much speculation, and so they shielded themselves—and me—from it. I think they did it deliberately in order to keep me ignorant and dependent on *them* for information. My father may have always seen me as a thorn in his side."

And that was what caused her the most pain of all. Sera hated feeling like a fool. She nearly collided with another student and, in her poor spirits, almost chided *him* for being clumsy.

"From everything you've told me about them," Cettie said, staying close by, "they were probably distracted by the faults in their own marriage. How do you think your father will react to the news?"

"He's probably dancing a jig," Sera said. "All the ministries will support him."

"Surely not *all*," Cettie countered soothingly.

"Well, that is true. The Ministry of Wind will support me. At least I hope Fitzroy will. I am eternally grateful for him, Cettie—most of all because he found you in the Fells. I'm not sure what I would do without you." She flashed a grateful smile at her friend as they strode toward the Aldermaston's home, passing the identical dwellings lining the street of Vicar's Close. Each residence featured a brick fence, a small wicket gate, and some sort of ornamental gardening. The students were all required to work at planting and rearing something during their stay, to beautify the street. Some students had trimmed and cut their shrubs into beautiful shapes. Others had neglected theirs entirely. Sera and Cettie had chosen to grow lavender, and as they passed their home, she smiled fondly at it.

"Sera . . . when you see the Aldermaston, remember to be patient."

"I *am* being patient," Sera said defensively, though she did wish she had more of Cettie's calm temperament. "I didn't yell at Mr. Skrelling, did I? How did he know such a thing? Why am I always the *last* person to know things?"

Cettie wisely fell silent.

At the end of the street, they reached the outer wall of the abbey grounds. A tall tower with a crimped archway loomed above them, flanked by the teachers' dorms in the upper story. The ground floor was filled with open arches, which allowed the students to enter the abbey grounds unfettered. Above it all rose the main spire of the abbey, which looked particularly ominous at that moment. Sera did not feel ready for the final examination—what was worriedly referred to as the Test. The final Mysteries were taught in that structure and were not shared outside its walls. Though Sera had started school at age twelve, instead of fourteen, and thus had already been at Muirwood for the customary four years, she did not yet feel like a master. Passing the Test was essential, and yet she was not at all sure a few weeks would make enough of a difference.

Together, Sera and Cettie passed through the closest arched entryway. The abbey grounds were meticulously maintained, and even the mood in the air changed as soon as they passed under the Leering carved into the head of the arch. A feeling of tranquility settled in her soul, one that took the edge off the frantic emotions that usually buzzed inside her. Sera and Cettie loved to roam the wooded grounds to escape the frenzy of their studies. There were rows of enormous, pale-barked trees and copses of oak, and even a small apple orchard. Sera had always been impressed by the care and diligence of the many gardeners who worked at Muirwood. They were always planting new flowers, caring for the lawns, and tending to the trees.

But the familiar grounds could not completely comfort Sera in her present mood. She and Cettie passed the looming abbey, which had stood for generations, and crossed to the Aldermaston's manor, where they were quickly granted entrance. All the staff knew Sera on sight, and while she tried not to abuse her position, she was grateful for it all the same.

"Hello, Miss Fitzempress," said the housekeeper, Mrs. Blake, with a pleasant smile. "It's a fine afternoon; why aren't you out enjoying the spring sunshine?"

"I should like to see the Aldermaston, please," Sera said, a little out of breath.

"He is in a meeting presently. Would you like me to send someone to you when it is finished?"

"It is very urgent, ma'am," Sera said, endeavoring to be her most patient self. She cast an arch look at Cettie, who seemed a little

Jeff Wheeler

embarrassed. At least Sera had remembered to say please, which was the polite and respectful thing to do.

Mrs. Blake simply nodded. "You can wait outside his study, if you please, Miss Fitzempress."

"Thank you." Sera hooked arms with Cettie, and they walked down the corridor together. The walls were lined with wonderful paintings in gilt frames, painted by the masters who had once been taught at the abbey, and each of them told a story from the past. Sera could lose herself in the works—she often did—but today she was focused on one thing: her grandfather. There was a small padded bench outside the Aldermaston's office, but Sera naturally felt more like pacing. Brass lanterns hung from the ceiling, casting light that left no shadows. More Leerings. More reminders of her inadequacy.

"Do you think the Aldermaston knows?" Sera asked Cettie, who had chosen to seat herself on the bench.

"Doesn't he know everything?" Cettie replied with a small smile.

At almost that exact moment, the door to the study opened, and Sera whirled to confront the Aldermaston. She was startled to see Lord Fitzroy emerge first. There was a new weariness about him that was no doubt the effect of his attempts to vanquish the cholera morbus.

"Father!" Cettie gasped, bounding up from the bench and rushing to her guardian. Watching their tender embrace drove a shard of pain into Sera's heart. She tried not to be jealous. She really tried. Even though Cettie wasn't adopted, she still addressed her guardians as her parents.

Sera felt like an orphan.

⁓

The Aldermaston gestured for Sera to sit in the chair across from his. Once she was comfortably situated, she watched Cettie and her guardian get settled on a small settee. The two of them were so close, so dear

28

to one another that it made Sera smile. She *was* happy for Cettie—surely if anyone deserved a loving family, it was her friend.

"I didn't see your tempest. How long have you been here?" Cettie asked.

"I did not travel by sky ship, my dear," Fitzroy answered. He had a kindly voice and very expressive eyes. The look of weariness Sera had observed in him just moments before had been transfigured into one of peace and contentment.

"Then how did you get here?" Cettie wondered. "I thought Muirwood could only be approached by the air."

"You are correct that there are no roads through the woods, no docks for ships to travel here either. By design, it is very difficult to *find* and travel to the abbey. There *is* another way, but I am forbidden to speak of it. You will learn it eventually, I'm sure." He tapped the side of his nose.

"It's another one of the Mysteries, then," Cettie said, shaking her head. "Will I ever learn them all?"

"If any one person can, it is you, Cettie Saeed. Now, I know you are surprised to see me, just as I was startled to find you waiting outside the Aldermaston's study. No one had sent for you. Or you, my lady." He nodded respectfully to Sera, and she bowed her head in return.

"They are probably here," the Aldermaston said in his rich, deep voice, "for the same reason you are, Brant. I think perhaps that news from the empire has found young ears?"

Sera nodded firmly. "Why wasn't I told, sir?"

Cettie gave her a disapproving look and a subtle shake of the head, warning her not to argue with the aged Aldermaston. Sera had no intention of arguing with him. Well, perhaps he *did* deserve a little scolding.

The Aldermaston was a robust man, at least fifty or sixty, with an enormous frizzy beard salted with gray. He wore spectacles that reflected the lamplight, but the eyes behind them were deep and brooding. She had seen him smile and laugh before, but his look was more often serious and probing. It was easy to be intimidated by such a set of eyes, but Sera refused to be. Mr. Durrant, her advocate, had taught her never to explain herself to any man.

The Aldermaston pressed a thumb against the tabletop of his desk. "Your question is fair, Your Highness. But let me pose one to you. Did you not come to this abbey to remove yourself from the distractions of court and the politics there?"

She thought she saw the intent of the question. "Yes," she answered simply, holding her head high.

"Does the knowledge you now have of your grandfather's death heighten your concerns about facing the Test?"

She swallowed. "Indeed, it does."

He gave her a pointed look. "Lord Fitzroy and I were counseling together to determine the appropriate time of disclosure. We both felt that you might be benefited by not knowing for a short time—that it might help you be your calmest self. Of course, now that you are in possession of the knowledge, our deliberations no longer hold value. If you are to be considered a candidate to replace your grandfather—if you are meant to rule—then you must do so on your own merits. Either you will master the power contained within the Leerings of the abbey, or you will fail. I asked Lord Fitzroy to come to Muirwood to personally assist you. He is a patient and long-suffering man, one of the best I have ever known. He has graciously accepted my request to come here and tutor you. I feel that his assistance in this matter will be helpful to you."

Sera's emotions had teetered and changed during his speech. She had come to the Aldermaston feeling outraged that this important news about her family had not been shared with her, only to find out that he was acting in her best interests and trying to assist her in passing the Test. He'd chosen a man she had come to admire and respect to guide her through the process, a man she would want by her side should she become empress.

She found herself stunned speechless again, but the smile that strained her cheeks revealed her feelings on the matter.

"Truly?" Cettie asked, gripping his hands. "You will be staying at Muirwood?"

"I cannot *stay*," he hedged, shaking his head. "But I will come here often and spend time with Miss Fitzempress . . . and *you* and the other girls." Shifting his gaze to Sera, he said, "It is vitally important, Miss Fitzempress—Sera, if I may—that you pass the Test. If your father ascends to the throne, I fear that the people's suffering will only continue . . . mayhap worsen."

"As do I," Sera said emphatically. "I would be honored if you would tutor me, Lord Fitzroy. But what of the sick? Those suffering from the cholera morbus that is ravaging the people?"

"There are many capable doctors trying to discern the source of the infection. I am no doctor myself. All I can do is listen to their theories, examine their methods, and make suggestions. My knowledge is more on the clouds and the weather." He gave Cettie a wink. "I will give you what time I can and sacrifice sleep in order to fulfill my other duties."

Sera simply nodded, moved by his loyalty to her. The Aldermaston cleared his throat, and she shifted her attention to him.

"An Aldermaston must be impartial," the aging man said. "But that does not mean he's a fool. I want what is best for the empire. I hope you approve of my course of action, Miss Fitzempress."

"I do, Aldermaston. And I thank you."

He nodded at her, his forehead crinkling. "I hope you remember this the next time you feel tempted to barge into my study."

CHAPTER THREE
THE MINISTRIES

When Sera had been individually tutored in the past, her studies had largely been confined to a study room, and the boring lectures had always been grounded in abstract theory. Inevitably, her gaze would wander to the windows, and then she'd hunger to be outside. Her lessons with Minister Fitzroy, for the most part, happened outside in the area known as the Queen's Garden, where Empress Maia had once spent time in her youth. It led to all sorts of fanciful thoughts about her ancestor, but she did her best to rein them in and give Fitzroy her attention. Just as Cettie had always said, he was incredibly patient, and he often allowed her to ask questions to help guide their conversations, something that helped her focus. Cettie would sometimes join them in their walks, but she usually gave them privacy.

"What will happen if I do *not* pass the Test within the abbey?" she asked Fitzroy during one of his pauses. "How long would they delay making a decision if that happened? Would it bar me forever from becoming the empress? It doesn't feel entirely fair that my future should hang on a single experience."

"It depends. The privy council cannot wield power indefinitely on its own. Usually, the transfer of power would happen immediately.

They need to make their decision soon, probably in a fortnight or so. Your schooling is nearly over, so it's appropriate for them to wait for that, if not for you to come of age. But as for your other question . . . sometimes our lives *do* pivot on very small hinges. Or rather, very small decisions. I've seen a man die because he was standing two feet in one direction versus another. Is it just that he was stuck by a ball that killed him? That his life was snuffed out for standing in the wrong place?"

"It does not feel fair to me, no," Sera answered, imagining for a moment the horrors of war and wondering what kind of action Fitzroy had seen. She didn't know much about it, but one of their most recent wars had been with a world occupied with the Bhikhu, a race of people who could fly.

"Life is not fair," Fitzroy said soberly. "But whoever promised that it would be? One of the strangest things about life is that we are as much defined by our hopes as we are our secret fears. We are, for the most part, the product of what we think about the most. Our minds are fertile beds, like these flower boxes. What would happen if the gardener did not pull out the weeds? Like this little one," he said, pointing out a small weed in one of the boxes.

"They would grow and overrun the garden eventually," Sera replied.

"Precisely. It takes little effort to pull one up now." And he did so and set it down on the stone railing for the gardener to collect. "But they are much more difficult to remove when their roots grow deeper. There is a tendency within the very nature of all things to degrade. On clear days, the ruins of Sempringfall Abbey can be seen from my estate. People like to wander the grounds there and look at the bones of the abbey. There are a few arches still, but most of the place has crumbled. People who visit there always comment about the structure and imagine what might have caused the desolation."

"Why was the abbey destroyed?"

"It wasn't destroyed, Sera. It was *neglected*. Eventually the decay grew so bad that a roof collapsed. It became dangerous. Rather than spending time and money fixing it, the people who lived there ignored the problems until the entire place was ruined utterly. To reconstruct the abbey would have required enormous funds. A small decision not to fix broken roof shingles led to another decision to put off the problem. And another and another. Eventually, given enough time, there will not be two stones left standing."

"That is an awful story," Sera said. "Fixing the roof should have been a priority. Now the entire structure is lost."

"I understand that someone was hired to fix the roof and the brick-work in the beginning. An accident ensued, and the man who'd been hired was incapable of finishing the work. Eventually the problem was ignored. The same pattern applies to our diplomacy with certain foreign courts and the relations between those who live in the cloud cities and those who live beneath them. It is how our society has reached this juncture. And why you may be so critical to the future of the empire. You cannot stop trying, Sera. And that's what happens when most people fail the Test. It isn't that they can't return and do it later. They won't because they abandon the pursuit."

He paused and gave her a probing look. "I sent Stephen to Muirwood to learn self-discipline. He left here using it to master different dances. He passed the Test, but he may not have learned the most important lessons this abbey teaches."

Sera thought about what he said. Cettie had told her about Stephen and his lack of ambition to do anything beyond rule his father's estate. He intended to inherit Fog Willows and use his position to hold the elaborate balls and celebrations in which his father had no interest.

"So what you are saying, Lord Fitzroy, is that unless I learn to control my thoughts now, in my youth, I will likely not have the self-discipline to do so later?"

"A brick is the softest before it visits the kiln," he answered sagely.

"Is the Test like the fires of a kiln? Does it harden the imperfections we bring to it?"

He looked at her and nodded subtly. "Yes, in a very real sense. It is not impossible to change when you are older, but it is certainly more difficult."

Though she understood his point and, indeed, agreed with it, Sera was feeling more and more hopeless. "I have tried to master my thoughts. I wish I were not so easily distracted."

"If wishes were zephyrs, even beggars would fly."

Sera smiled at the common saying. "Very true. It is a wonder that the entire world hasn't decayed back to the weeds."

"There is always a struggle, Sera. Prosperity can be a scourge as easily as it can be a gift. Some of those who live in the clouds feel they are due their station because of a family fortune or a robust lineage. They resist the need to manage their funds or their property. They fail to invest for the future. And then they fall. There are those down below who manage to amass enough fortune and prestige to purchase the floating manor out from beneath them. And so the cycle goes on and on. Some rise. Some fall. Knowing yourself, and what you want, makes all the difference—even if your dream feels unattainable." He gazed up pensively at the sky. "Even though she lived in squalor in the Fells, Cettie dreamed of living in a manor in the clouds. Is it any wonder that she achieved it?"

Sera looked at him, feeling encouraged once more. "So I need to fix my mind on a goal and then relentlessly pursue it. Even if obstacles stand in the way."

"Especially then. It is almost as if our resolve is being tested. Will we stick to our course even in the face of ridicule or disappointment?" He smiled wryly. "Don't be afraid of the kiln, Sera. You have control over what you bring to the fire to be hardened."

Sera paused by the edge of a flower bed. It was full of dainty blue forget-me-nots. Her heart was heavy with burdens.

"Fitzroy," she said in a soft voice, gazing down at the pretty flowers. "What if . . . what if my father isn't *really* my father? What if the real reason I cannot control the Leerings is because my blood *is* polluted? They say that affinity for the magical component of the Mysteries is handed down from generation to generation. What if . . . what if I'm not *meant* to become empress?"

He stopped his walk and turned back to join her at the edge. "What if there is no cure for the cholera morbus? What if all of us will die from it?"

Her eyes opened wider, and she looked at him worriedly. "Do you believe that will happen, Minister Fitzroy?"

He slowly shook his head no. "But what if I did?"

She licked her lips. "Then you might stop trying to find a cure for it."

"And if we stopped searching for a cure, would one ever be found?"

"Indeed, it would not."

"Isn't it strange, Sera, how so many of our thoughts attempt to persuade us to quit? To fail? To despair of achieving something?" He gave her a cryptic smile. "One would almost think that those thoughts are coming to our minds not from us . . . but from a source that means to do us harm. Are we not always our own harshest critics?"

She looked at him, feeling her heart tingling. A profound truth was being spoken, something that resonated deep in her heart. "I know I am," she answered.

"Then that is the voice you must learn to silence if you are to succeed. Four years ago, my mine ran out of silver. The vein ended abruptly, and my workers had nothing to harvest but droplets of quicksilver. We kept moving forward and finding nothing but bare rock. Worthless rock. I was advised to quit the mine, but before making that decision, I consulted a friend from the Ministry of Wind who was an expert on mining. I brought him out to visit Dolcoath. After inspecting the mine, he confirmed my suspicion that the vein had run out. He said the mine produced plentiful amounts of quicksilver and would continue to, but it was a useless substance. Useless indeed. Thanks to my invention with

Cettie, we have been able to put that quicksilver to good use in helping sky ships avoid storms. That strange metal has made me far richer than the silver mines ever did. That is the interesting thing about life on this floating round sphere we dwell on. The Knowing knew what I did not. We have so much still to learn. And we will, if we listen to the world and its Mysteries and never stop believing in new possibilities."

It was not uncommon for other students to stroll through the Queen's Garden and its environs, but the sound approaching them was of sturdy boots, and, by the volume and cadence, it was several men. Sera turned toward the small arch they had just passed under, and a moment later, three men entered their portion of the walled garden. Two of the three she recognized instantly. The first was Lord Welles, the Minister of War. He had served twice as prime minister when he was younger and had seen success in many battlefields across the empire. He was the man who'd changed her life so many years ago by announcing that her father would be named prince regent upon her grandfather's apoplexy. She'd seen him rarely enough since. The other man she recognized, much to her bafflement, as her former tutor—Commander Falking. When she saw his hat, she remembered the day the wind had blown it from his head, and he had scrambled to recapture it. She and Will had used the opportunity to scamper off into the hedge maze behind her palace. The memory nearly made her burst out laughing, but the diverting portion of that day had been far outweighed by its consequences. Will had been sent away after that, and Hugilde had been banished too.

She shook off the memory and shifted her gaze to the third man. She didn't recognize him at all. It was probably the minister's private secretary.

"Hello, Admiral," Fitzroy said in a cool, measured voice. She noticed his hands clenching into fists as he continued to hide them behind his back.

"Ah, Fitzroy! What are you doing here?" said Lord Welles in surprise, his eyes narrowing suspiciously. The air between the men suddenly filled with tension.

"I could ask the same of you," Fitzroy answered softly.

"I didn't see your sky ship here. Interesting. Well, no matter. I come bearing news for Miss Fitzempress. Of course, you are welcome to hear it as well. No need to depart on my account."

Sera wondered if that last part was a veiled request for Fitzroy to leave. He took the man at his word, though, and remained.

"What did you come to tell me?" Sera asked, walking forward to direct their attention to her. "I have already been informed of my grandfather's passing."

"Of course you have, my lady," Lord Welles said with an understanding smile. "Your father is coming to Muirwood to offer his condolences in person. I thought it might be best for you to know of his plans before he arrives. I believe he intends to surprise you, but I thought that would give him an unfair advantage. And the soldiers under my ministry . . . well, you know they dote on you."

"He's coming *here*?" Sera asked in surprise.

"Of course. There is a matter he wishes to discuss with you. Your mother as well. I'm not the prime minister any longer, so I do not have all the details, but as you know, we've had a long history of conflict with the court in the world of Kingfountain. I've learned that the heir to the hollow crown may be willing to seek a bride from our realm, which could usher in an unprecedented peace between our worlds. Emissaries from Kingfountain may soon be coming to Lockhaven to begin negotiations. Of course, the prince regent will expect your full cooperation and may insist that you come back with him early."

Sera's mouth went dry as Welles spoke. Having studied history and statesmanship at Muirwood, she knew their worlds had indeed collided many times in the past. The relationship between the two realms had always been strained, ever since their inglorious first encounters.

Ships from Kingfountain had passed into the empire through a mirror gate, seeking treasures. The visitors had used a form of sorcery to communicate. They'd pretended, at first, to be from across the sea. But their dissembling had eventually been revealed. They had plundered Muirwood's ancient treasures and, even after all these years, appeared to have no intention of giving them back. The already contentious connection between the two realms had soured further over the centuries, both from deeply entrenched cultural differences and because they frequently vied for trading partners. An emissary from Kingfountain had not come to Lockhaven in over a hundred years.

"But, Lord Welles," Sera stammered. "I haven't yet passed the Test. I can't possibly go back early."

"Honestly, Princess, do you think a few extra weeks are going to make all that much of a difference?"

Sera felt the stab of doubt in her mind, deliberately placed there by Minister Welles. Her agitation was growing by the moment. But she tried to remember what Fitzroy had told her. Her father wished to provoke her, and the best thing she could do was refuse to rise to the occasion.

"Father cannot *force* me to leave Muirwood," she ventured.

"No, he cannot," Fitzroy agreed.

"He has no intention of forcing her," said Welles with a knowing chuckle. "You can surmise that every noble throughout the empire will be keen to send their daughters to Lockhaven to be seen by the Prince of Kingfountain. This is a rare opportunity to share knowledge between our worlds. It's whispered that such an exchange could be mutually advantageous. They certainly guard their secrets as carefully as we do ours, though the timing of their outreach makes me wonder if they haven't heard of Fitzroy's little invention.

"Their religion is still a problem of sorts between us. We both believe in the Knowing, only our understanding is more adaptable. Theirs"—he waved his hand back and forth—"more superstitious. Any daughter of the empire could help usher in a new era of understanding between our two realms, putting to rest some of the bad blood. Water under the bridge, if you pardon the metaphor. Would not the prince regent be seen as unjust to deprive his daughter of the same opportunity? If she comes, it doesn't mean she will be chosen. However, it would be for the best, Princess. But I will let your father convince you. I am here . . . always . . . as a friend." He gave Sera a perfunctory bow.

Sera was intrigued. What Lord Welles said made sense. Not that she was keen to go, but if she had a hand in establishing peace between the worlds, it could be part of her legacy as a leader.

Welles turned his gaze. "Now, Fitzroy, since you are here, may I have a word with you in private with my secretary? I am very concerned about cholera morbus and its impact on the soldiers. If we might step over there"—he nodded to the other side of the garden—"and have a word?"

"Of course," Fitzroy said stiffly. He gave Sera a warning look and gestured for her to stay in the garden. Her father was up to some trick. He had never shown any interest in seeing her at Muirwood. And her visits back to Lockhaven during the summer months were usually spent with her mother. The last she'd heard about her old governess, Hugilde, was that she had returned to her home country. Hugilde had never written to her, likely due to the prince regent's intervention.

She watched attentively as the others moved to the far side of the garden, still visible from where she was standing. She turned as Commander Falking's shadow crossed hers.

"*Ahem*, hello, Princess," he said with a formal cough. "It has been several years since our last . . . visit." He coughed again.

"It has, Commander. It is good to see you again."

"Thank you, ma'am." He looked awkward, worried. He kept glancing over at the Minister of War.

"Is something wrong, Commander Falking?" She was curious why he, of all people, had accompanied Lord Welles.

"Wrong? Nothing. Nothing at all. A fine day. The wind was fair. We shall have a pleasant journey back to Lockhaven, I should think. Pleasant indeed. I am such a clumsy fool I dropped something on my way into the gate. I couldn't find it. Could have landed anywhere, no doubt. I was supposed to give it to you. From a mutual . . . *ahem* . . . friend. Ah, 'tis a misfortune I dropped it. Well, more's the pity. I wish I could have given it to you." He scratched the side of his neck. "Oh, the minister is waving me over. I think he intends to go already. Farewell, Princess. I look back on our time together with fondness. I hope you bear me no ill will."

Sera nearly gaped at his bungling attempt at slipping her a note. She saw it sticking out of the flower bush near the entrance, quite in plain sight. Could it be? Could Will have found a way to reach out to her? They had studied together for a season when she was younger. She'd always looked forward to Falking's lessons because of the handsome young protégé he'd brought with him.

"Indeed I don't," she answered sincerely. "It wasn't your fault. It was all mine."

Her heart burned to start reading it.

CETTIE

It was the harbingers of old who told us they would return. Ships would appear from the sea bearing hosts of men who carried strange weapons yet worshipped the same Knowing. They came as they had come once before, expecting to find our land still inhabited by barbarians. Instead, they found that our civilization had greatly altered under the reign of Empress Maia. They found a city hovering in the sky like in the legends of the emperor-maston Hanokh and his city of Leerings called Safehome.

Both of our civilizations knew of other worlds, but the differences in our beliefs led to conflict. They treated water as sacred and divine. They were appalled by our historic treatment of women, a past which is not shared except deep within the Ministry of Thought. In their culture, women are the ideal—the manifestation of the Fountain.

The harbingers warned us again. The realm of Kingfountain would mount an invasion, their goal to build a tower so high that it might reach the gates of our seat of power, Lockhaven. And so they did.

They came with tools. They came with fleets. And they attempted to build a tower to reach the palace gates. The empress had no alternative but to call on the Blight Leering to devastate their forces. We have been in this conflict, off and on, ever since. They wish to know our Mysteries without training for them lawfully. They consider our religion a heresy. Each time our civilizations clash, the stakes grow higher.

And there are no more harbingers to see the future. There has not been one for eighty years.

—Thomas Abraham, Aldermaston of Muirwood Abbey

CHAPTER FOUR

TANGLED IN THE LAW

Many at Muirwood called her Cettie of the Fells behind her back, and some even insulted her to her face. Mostly these were the jealous ones—the sons and daughters of the wealthiest families in the realm who resented that a young woman from the Fells continually bested them in their studies. Most did not realize that she had helped Fitzroy discover the properties of the storm glass. She preferred it that way. She paid the jealous students no mind, for the friends who knew her best had another nickname for her—Cettie Saeed, which meant "Cettie of the Clouds."

The name reminded her of how very far she'd come. Once, she'd been small and afraid, beset by the nightmarish ghosts that lived in the dark places of the empire. The ghosts had followed her since childhood, one spirit in particular—a tall, malevolent fright with no eyes. There was something about her that attracted them, some part of her she did not understand and did not like, but they had not followed her to Muirwood. Though the old memories recurred in her sleep, it was the only place they could haunt her now. There were protections all around the abbey grounds—a vast interconnected network of Leerings that worked together to shield the abbey. Most of the students did not sense them, but to Cettie, they were as conspicuous as the white and black keys of a clavicembalo—and she knew how to play all the right notes. Though she hadn't told anyone, she felt sure she could disarm the wardings of the abbey. Of course, she never *would*. The wardings kept them safe, and she missed neither the ghosts nor the dreadful anticipation that preceded their visits.

With Fitzroy giving lessons to Sera, Cettie found she had more time to herself. While she adored her friend, Cettie was naturally more guarded and reserved. Being in crowds made her nervous, for they reminded her of the bustle of the Fells. She considered seeking out Fitzroy's youngest daughter, Anna, who had come to feel like a real sister. But although they were the same age, they were two years apart in their studies, and Anna's friends were not very welcoming to her intrusions.

The classes at Muirwood Abbey were rigorous and demanding, and she had learned literature, dancing, mathematics, the tenets of the faith, poetry, and history. After the rigors of the classes were done, students were encouraged to exercise and improve their health. Cettie had found that the hobby she enjoyed most on the school grounds was at the archery butts. For her, there was something soothing about being there. She loved the feeling of tension on the bowstring as she pulled it back. Loved how the practice honed her concentration and focus. The targets were made of coiled rope and were anchored in place at various distances, and in her four years at Muirwood, she had become adept at hitting the farthest targets. Yes, her jealous peers used her "perverse" hobby as another reason to tease her, for soldiers no longer used bows and arrows—they used arquebuses and pistols, the very latest in weaponry. Archery had become nothing more than a diversion for the highborn . . . which she markedly was not. But she refused to let their disapproval of the sport affect her interest. In this and so many other ways, Fitzroy had molded her character.

And so, it came as no surprise to her when she found herself there one evening when Sera and Fitzroy were together in the Queen's Garden. She gripped the stock tightly with one hand and drew another arrow from the small quiver dangling from her waist. Then, raising the bow, she pulled the fletching back toward the corner of her lips and narrowed her focus on a target in the back, imagining it as a Leering beckoning to her. She let the arrow fly and watched breathlessly as it sailed over the nearer targets before sticking into a portion of the coiled rope on the outside rim of the target she'd chosen. The distant thwack made her smile. She drew another arrow and sent it winging as well. It landed closer to the middle than the first. Each arrow made her sink deeper into herself, sharpening her focus, giving her a sense of weightlessness, as if she were an observer of her own body. Every single arrow in her quiver struck the target. After letting the last one loose, she put the longbow on the hook by the shooting stall and waited for the other two girls using the butts, both arrayed in much fancier dresses than hers, to finish their shots.

When they did, all three girls entered the field to retrieve the arrows. The other two ignored her, speaking to each other with their heads tipped together. The smell of the grass and the softness against her shoes made her stay in the moment. She felt calm and peaceful, which was a welcome reprieve from her seething nerves.

Sera was not the only one who felt strained by the prospect of leaving the abbey, though Cettie's anxiety stemmed from a different source. She had no doubt she would pass the Test. Even at this distance from the abbey, she could sense the Leerings inside and, moreover, knew she could tame them. Mastering that part of the Mysteries had come so easily to her. To her ears, each Leering had a distinct sound and melody—one that Sera could not hear.

But at least Sera knew what she would do after leaving the school. Her training was trying to prepare her for a dazzling future as the leader of a vast empire. Cettie was confident that her friend and companion would be chosen over the corrupt prince regent. But what was Cettie's future? Why was that always such a snake's nest of doubt?

After collecting the arrows, Cettie started back toward the shooting stands. Looking up, she saw Adam Creigh waiting at hers, holding her bow in his hands. It struck her yet again how much he'd grown—the boy she'd known had become a man . . . a very handsome and principled man who was also unobtainable. She loved Anna too much to take anything from her—or even to try.

You're just friends, she told herself, *good friends.* Some days Adam could be aloof and distant, but he was always polite and respectful and very solicitous around her. Since they both favored the Mysteries of Wind, they had shared many classes. He, too, was growing more and more nervous as they neared the Test. His wardship to Fitzroy, the man they both admired above all, would be coming to an end, and after leaving Muirwood, he would have to make his own way in the world.

Cettie approached him, holding the arrows out to him like a bouquet of feathered flowers.

"Would you fancy shooting next, Mr. Creigh?" she asked him with an overly formal tone that was meant to be playful. "Is that why you've stolen my bow?"

"I am more comfortable at the arquebus range," he answered with a tone of defeat. He turned the bow around, examining it. "I think they stopped using these on sky ships a century ago."

"I have a difficult time imagining you as a dragoon," she teased, knowing he would never wish to become one.

He flashed her a smile that made her heart tickle, and then handed back the bow. "I was watching you just now, Cettie. You have great powers of concentration."

"Thank you," she answered, taking the bow back from him.

"May I watch you shoot this next round from a closer vantage point?"

"If you wish," she answered demurely, sliding the arrows back into the dangling quiver. She fixed her stance as she had been taught. She found comfort in predictable routines, in making a ritual of the things she did, though sometimes she wished she had a bit more of Sera's spontaneity. As Cettie fit the first arrow to the string, she felt the immediate impact of Adam's gaze on her. The weight of another person's stare made performing any act uncomfortable. Perhaps Adam was doing it on purpose, to test her powers of concentration under scrutiny. Strange how the mind could begin babbling advice as soon as there was an audience. The other two young women at the butts had returned from the field as well, but she cared far more about Adam's good opinion than she did about their potential scrutiny.

Why do you hesitate?

The thought came from Adam, unspoken, but she heard it all the same. Sometimes her powers seemed too intrusive. She could not read people's minds, but she was very sensitive to projected thoughts. Even as a little girl, she had heard the thoughts of the ghosts haunting the tenements. The better she knew someone, the stronger their thoughts came through to her. She knew Fitzroy's mind very well. And after four years with Sera, Cettie could sometimes finish her sentences, a habit she'd forced herself to stop after her friend had admitted it unnerved her.

Because you make me feel self-conscious sometimes, she thought back to him. There was more she could *think* on that subject, but she didn't dare. The last thing she wanted was for him to hear what she would never speak aloud.

Cettie closed her eyes, purging her mind of distractions. She pushed herself and her thoughts into the space of ritual again. Feather up. Fingertips on the rough bowstring. Cock the bow at a slight angle. Draw back toward her mouth. She opened her eyes, narrowing them on the farthest target. When she felt herself a distinct part of it, she released the arrow and felt the slap against the leather guard on her forearm as the strand recoiled. The arrow sailed and struck the center of the rope coil. A bull's-eye.

She nearly allowed herself a self-congratulatory smile. But that would mean giving in to pride, so she refused. Pulling out the next arrow, she loosed that one as well, sinking further into herself with each action. Even with Adam standing nearby, she pushed him away from her thoughts. All five arrows found their marks again. She lowered the bow.

"Astonishing," Adam breathed. "Let me help fetch them." He was about to tread out onto the grass, but she put her hand on his arm to stop him.

"The rangemaster will . . . scold you," she said, dropping her hand instantly. She'd felt a zip of energy go up her arm to her elbow upon touching him.

"Oh, I'd forgotten," he apologized, stepping back. "At the arquebus range, we don't collect the balls." He pitched his voice lower. "And based on how *that* young lady is shooting, I may well need surgery if I wandered out there just now."

Cettie appraised the situation—several arrows had been shot into the ground, and only two had found a target. Even then, it was likely not the target the girl had aimed at. When the other two finally ran out of arrows, Cettie hung up her bow again, and they all headed out into the field together to retrieve the spent ammunition.

Adam walked alongside her. "Has Mr. Sloan or Mr. Teitelbaum made any progress on your case?" he asked her. "I don't think I have asked you in a while."

"Unfortunately no," Cettie replied.

"The Law is such a tangled heap of rope," Adam said with a sigh. "You cannot tell where it starts or ends. Your mother still has not stepped forward, which means she is either dead or unwilling to reveal herself for fear of scandal. If she were dead, then your father could sign the decree on his own, could he not? If the price were agreed upon?"

"That is true," Cettie answered. She felt a flash of impatience and self-pity. There was still so much uncertainty about her adoption. Even if her mother was declared dead, her birth father and his wife would no doubt continue to put up a fight and insist on every possible penny. "Father has done everything he can to ascertain the truth. He has interviewed personally scores of people who were involved in my deed earlier. But as we all know, things just disappear into the Fells. There are clues, snippets, fragments. All have been fruitless so far."

"It must be very trying," he said. "To have your fate hanging in limbo like this."

"I don't care about an inheritance," Cettie said. "It means nothing to me."

"I wasn't referring to that. It's the uncertainty. After four years without answers—answers to what may arguably be a pretty straightforward affair—it must be very trying for you."

Cettie refused to let self-pity govern her, especially when it came to this. However unclear the future seemed, she knew just how lucky she was to have fallen in with the Fitzroys. "He's doing everything he can. Persistence will prevail."

"Indeed. What will you do, then, after finishing the Test?"

They had reached the target and began pulling out the arrows one by one. The first had embedded itself deeply into the core of the target, and she strained as she pulled on it. "Sera said she would ask for me to be one of her ladies-in-waiting whether or not she becomes empress. Alas, I cannot picture myself being comfortable at court. I wish to return to Fog Willows, but that cannot be."

"Why not?" he asked with concern.

"What would I do there?" she asked. "I'm not a member of the family. Not yet. My deed will expire before I'm eighteen. You know how tightly the Ministry of Law controls inheritance. He cannot bequeath any wealth or property on me unless the adoption goes through. I would be a young woman living in his household with no function, no standing. It wouldn't be proper, not that Father would allow that to stop him. I'd willingly be a maid or an underservant, but he refuses to consider it. He hasn't given up hope that he can adopt me legally, but I grow more and more anxious."

"Understandably," Adam said, shaking his head. He offered the three arrows he had pulled from the target, and she returned them to the quiver as they walked back.

"Are you worried about the Test?" she asked him after they'd traveled in silence for a few moments.

"No," he answered humbly. "My worries are more about what happens afterward. I'd like to cure people. But it will take time and means for me to set up a practice. The school provides so many tools and implements for us to use while we are here. I'll need to furnish all of my own. One way of doing so is by joining the Ministry of War for a season. They always need more doctors. But I . . . do not think I would enjoy that life very much. Besides, joining their ranks would require me to purchase a commission, which would put me in substantial debt." He shook his head. "There's no easy way."

"For either of us," she said, nodding. They reached the shooting stall. She looked at him, saw the worries pressing on his brow. "Whatever comes, Adam, whatever happens to either of us, I hope we shall always be friends." She felt her cheeks heat as she said the heartfelt words. "I'm glad you ignored Phinia the other day. I think you are very brave . . . wanting to help people in the Fells."

He looked at her with a serious expression. "And I think you are very brave for having survived them. Because of you, the children who would have died under your last guardian's neglect all survived. All of them have gone to a shelter school. Without your intervention, Joses never would have gotten a job at Fog Willows. I hear he is doing well there."

"Yes, and I miss him," Cettie said. Adam's eyes crinkled slightly at her words.

Her friend Joses had saved her life after Mrs. Pullman's treachery. He'd nearly bled to death after being wounded in her defense, but Fitzroy had used the Mysteries to heal him. He'd been brought to Fog Willows to recuperate and learn a trade. Cettie cherished him as a friend, but nothing more. Did Adam think . . .

Her cheeks were starting to blush. She looked down and was suddenly weary of shooting.

"Can I walk you back to Vicar's Close?" he asked, offering his arm.

"Can we stop by the Queen's Garden first? I'd like to say good-bye to Father before he leaves." She put her hand on his arm. Neither of them wore gloves. Contrary to the fashions and mores of the day, they both had adopted Fitzroy's way of thinking.

When she touched his arm, she felt that energy travel up to her elbow again.

CHAPTER FIVE

HEART SECRETS

Cettie did not find Sera in the garden, but she did notice the tempest hovering over the docking yard near the Aldermaston's manor. It was from the Ministry of War—she could tell by the paint and polish and the uniforms of the attendants guarding the rope ladder on the lawn. Why were they there? Had they come at the prince regent's command? She felt a stab of worry for Sera, but her next thought caught her by surprise. An image of Adam wearing regimentals flashed through her mind, invoking a premonition of dread. She was worried something might happen to him if he served aboard one of the mammoth hurricane sky ships or a tempest. Then again, little though she agreed with Phinia, her guardian's daughter was not wrong—his life could easily be snuffed out by the cholera morbus. She bit her bottom lip, adjusting her arm in his a little closer, as if she could keep him safe by not letting go.

"I wonder whose ship that is," Adam wondered aloud, echoing her first thoughts. "The unmarked ones are usually a sign of secrecy."

"All the ministries have their secrets," Cettie observed. Her own invention with Fitzroy, storm glass, had been kept a relative secret by the Ministry of Wind. They had not revealed the way the contraption worked to anyone—not even the military. It had been Fitzroy's vision that each ship would have its own. But the ministries were locked in an age-old struggle for power that made such a sweeping collaboration impossible, or at least impractical. Instead, Fitzroy controlled a network of people equipped with the apparatuses in various places throughout the realm. These individuals reported readings from their various stations, and the ministry then offered reports of changes in the weather to the other ministries. For a price.

"I wish it weren't so," Adam said with a sigh. "Don't you think all these machinations limit progress?"

Cettie smiled grimly. "Indeed I do. But there is little trust these days. I've heard from Father that when visitors come to Fog Willows, they are watched because many have tried to sneak into his study. Raj Sarin is kept very busy."

"Ah, Raj Sarin," Adam said with a smile. "I miss him. Do you still practice the Way of Ice and Shadows?"

"I do," Cettie said. Raj Sarin, Fitzroy's Bhikhu bodyguard, had taught her the series of fluid movements. It helped her concentrate and had already proven useful in dangerous situations.

"Do you think you could throw me to the ground?" he asked, arching his eyebrows.

She deflected the question lightheartedly. "Why would I even wish to try, Mr. Creigh?"

"Mr. Creigh?" he said archly, noticing her change to the formal.

They passed under the nearest archway leading to Vicar's Close. The shadows dimmed the sunlight and made her momentarily blind. Then she heard Fitzroy call her name.

The two of them stopped at once. Fitzroy was pacing within the web of arches separating the abbey from the village. When her eyes adjusted, she could see his hands clasped tightly behind his back, one of the indications that he was nervous or worried.

"I've already bid good-bye to Anna and Phinia, but I wanted to see you before I returned to Lockhaven," Fitzroy said, placing his hands on her shoulders and kissing her forehead.

She embraced him, holding tight and wishing they had more time together. "Must you go so soon?"

"Indeed I must. I'm sure you noticed the tempest?"

"It was unmarked," Adam said.

"It was Lord Welles, the Minister of War," said Fitzroy with an agitated tone.

A dark feeling entered Cettie's heart. "Are we at war?" She had suspected it would be a ship from that ministry, but the minister himself?

"No," Fitzroy said in a reassuring tone. He squeezed her shoulder and then clasped his hands behind his back again. "He came to see Sera. I'll let her explain it. She's back at the dormitory, waiting for you. While Welles said he was coming to forewarn her, I fear he had other motives. We both know the ministries are not fully transparent with each other."

More secrets. So many secrets stood between everyone. Secrets under the cloak of the Mysteries. Secrets under the cloak of government.

"I will return as soon as I can," Fitzroy said soothingly. "Meanwhile, help Sera prepare for the Test. I've only had a few days with her, and thanks to Welles, she has burdens now she didn't have before. I fear her father's faction is intent on dooming her."

"She would make an excellent empress," Cettie said, and she meant it. She never let anyone else do her thinking for her, and even though she was small in stature, she was fierce in her sense of right and wrong.

Fitzroy's mouth quirked into a smile. "I agree. But her own *father* would do anything to prevent it, and there are other powerful people who would not want a leader so sympathetic to the plight of the poor." He sighed. "I must be off. Word travels quickly in this realm. I'll come soon, before the Test, unless my duties prevent me."

"I love you," she told him, enjoying the feeling of warmth and security that filled her breast when she said it.

"And I you," he said with light in his eyes.

"How is Mother? Is her health still improving?"

"Yes, she joins me at more state functions these days. Your sisters both seem to be doing well."

"And Stephen?" she asked gently, knowing it was a tender subject. "How does he fare at home?"

"I worry about Stephen still. But I trust he will mature."

That was a point of sadness for Cettie. The oldest of Fitzroy's children had not pursued a career yet. His passion had been for the Mysteries of Thought, but he had no desire to become a vicar. He enjoyed writing poetry, but that did not earn him any money. He'd tried working at the law offices of Sloan and Teitelbaum and promptly quit because he found the work tedious. His lack of ambition for anything *but* his birthright made Cettie uneasy. How could he hope to govern an estate when he could not govern himself?

Cettie could see the hurt and disappointment in Fitzroy's eyes. He had tried to raise his son patiently, but his guidance and suggestions had fallen on deaf ears. Fitzroy's own father had ordered him to join the Ministry of War to force his obedience, to separate him from a girl he loved. But Fitzroy was a much more tenderhearted man. Sometimes Cettie couldn't help wondering if his softer approach simply didn't fit his son's need for discipline.

"Well, a tree leans with the wind. But if it is properly staked, it will grow straight." He winked at her. "Eventually. I would appreciate it if you'd give Anna some more of your time and influence, Cettie. I'm happy she's found a place here, but I do worry about all of her friends. They can be distracting."

She loved that he trusted her to act as his helper. To listen to his opinions and counsel.

"I will do my best," she answered loyally.

"Then you will succeed," he said, tapping the side of his forehead. They embraced again, and then Fitzroy shook Adam's hand in a firm, respectful way. "I look forward to hearing about your career, Adam. You will do noble work, of that I have no doubt."

"Thank you, sir," Adam said with a brief nod.

They watched as Fitzroy strode toward the Aldermaston's manor. That was where he went to come and go. Cettie did not understand how he could leave Muirwood that way, but she accepted that she would understand in the future. Some final Mysteries, it would seem, were only explained to those who had passed the Test.

"Sera is probably anxious to see you," Adam said with a smile. He offered his arm again and then led her to the porch of her dormitory. She waited at the doorstep after they bid each other good-bye, watching as he left down the crowded way toward the main square. How easy it was to admire him when he couldn't see her. When the stakes weren't quite so high. Once he disappeared into the masses, Cettie opened the door and went inside.

Sera was pacing, of course. Her cheeks were flushed, and she was holding an unfolded letter in her hand. It appeared she had been reading it over and over.

"Is everything all right?" Cettie asked. Sera startled with surprise. She instantly put the letter behind her back.

"Goodness, I didn't hear you come up the walk," her friend said, fanning herself with her hand. She tried to laugh, but it sounded overly giddy. "I'm so glad you're here. There's much to tell. Did you see Fitzroy before he left?"

"Just now," Cettie answered, watching as Sera moved toward the window seat, still concealing the letter. "What were you reading? Is it from your old governess?"

Why did Sera look guilty all of a sudden? If it had been Sera's old governess, Hugilde, she would not have been quick to hide it.

Sera's look was almost wild. But then her hand dropped, and Cettie could see the letter more clearly. "No." She grazed her teeth against her bottom lip. "It's from Will. Will Russell."

That was a surprise. Cettie had known about Sera's fascination with the young man who had taken lessons with her and her tutor Commander Falking when she was twelve. They had corresponded together, with the permission of those supervising them, until Sera's father found out. He'd blustered about, insisting that Will return the letters Sera had written to him. As punishment for the boy's refusal, he'd practically banished him to the night- and ice-shrouded land of the Naestors to get his schooling in the Mysteries of War. All the letters Sera had received had been confiscated and destroyed. Little wonder she was so keen on keeping this one secret.

"There is a tempest at the docking yard," Cettie said, shutting the door behind her. "From the Ministry of War. My father told me Lord Welles had come with some news."

"Yes, it was Lord Welles *and* Commander Falking." Sera was still pacing, her mood full of energy and wariness. Those emotions seemed to fill the whole dormitory. "Falking brought the letter, but he didn't give it to me himself. He's such a goose. He pretended to have dropped it, although his maneuver was plain as daylight, and anyone could have found it." She stopped pacing for long enough to look Cettie in the eye. "I haven't heard a word from Will in four years. Not since he was sent to the far north for his schooling."

Cettie wanted to read the letter herself, desperately, but she wouldn't ask for it. She listened patiently instead. It didn't take much to persuade Sera to keep talking. The princess folded up the letter crisply and then stuffed it into the pocket of her dress.

"Will said that he's finishing his schooling. He'll likely take the Test before we do. I think they end their curriculum sooner up north, but I'm not certain. Then the ministry will give him his first post. He said he would be coming to the City in the near future. He's nervous, of course. My father may have already forgotten about him, but I doubt it. He can harbor a grudge forever! Will is concerned he may be sent to a distant outpost on another world. That he may never see me again." She shuddered, and Cettie knew what she was thinking. If another war broke out with Kingfountain, the men affiliated with the Ministry of War faced the greatest danger. And it wasn't without precedence for the court of Kingfountain to instigate the trouble. "When he comes to the City, he will bring the letters I wrote him all those years ago. He will give them only to me, not to my father. All he asks is that I allow him to keep one. Just one."

Cettie stared at Sera, feeling the emotional turmoil she was in. They had been so young back then, so naïve, and now they were on the cusp of adulthood, at the age when every decision they made seemed powerful enough to propel their lives in a different direction.

"Are you going to answer him?" Cettie asked, keeping her expression and her tone neutral.

"I don't even know how I could get him a reply," Sera said, shaking her head. "Perhaps it's a poor idea. It's been four years, Cettie. I don't know what . . . if anything . . . he—I don't know! I'm rambling. This isn't the only news. Cettie, Lord Welles came to warn me. He is a very political man. He was the prime minister twice, how could he not be! No doubt he covets the role still. But he came in secret to share with me that my father is coming to Muirwood."

"The prince regent is coming here?" Cettie asked in dismay. She'd never met Sera's father in person, and after all the stories she'd heard about him, she had no desire to do so.

"Yes." Now Sera looked even more nervous. "He wants to send me away. You remember when I took that Mysteries of Law class about the trading we do with other worlds? All that talk of the covenants and laws sometimes got tedious, but I loved learning about other places."

"Yes, everything you told me about the mirror gates *did* sound fascinating," Cettie said, "but why not close them off temporarily? Why risk another war?"

"Because the only way to close them is to destroy them," Sera said. "They're all made from natural rock formations. You've studied the Mysteries of Wind—how long does it take for a natural bridge to form? Thousands of years?"

"At least," Cettie said.

"The Leerings on the gates alert us when something passes through one of them. Still, it wouldn't be smart to leave one of them open near any of our major cities. The ministries destroyed all of those gates years ago."

Sera always came alive while talking of matters of state. It was one of many reasons Cettie thought her particularly well suited to the duties of an empress. "Interesting, to be sure, but how does this relate to your father's visit?"

"Kingfountain has reached out to us again. They want to understand our secrets, how we make the sky cities float and the sky ships fly. Lord Welles thinks they may also have heard about your storm glass, and as you know, that's a secret we don't even share among our own people. You see, a deeper alliance may ensure peace long enough for us to resolve some of our differences and trade some of our most valuable secrets." She bit her lip and winced. "I might as well move along to the point. The prince of the court at Kingfountain is seeking a wife. My father intends to marry me off to him. There, I've said it. Sorry I've been such a goose."

Cettie could see why her friend was so rattled. "A marriage alliance with Kingfountain? Surely it's just a ploy to stop you from becoming empress here."

"Of course it is!" Sera said with a huff. "He'd expect me to give up my rights in this world to become, possibly, a queen in that one. Father cannot force me to leave Muirwood, but it's clear he will do his best to convince me to leave willingly before I've passed the Test. Now that my grandfather is dead, my father will not stop his tricks until I am out of his way."

"And he cannot make you leave?" Cettie asked, coming closer and touching Sera's arm.

"How could he? I have sanctuary."

"Yes, but doesn't the right of sanctuary only apply to someone who has passed the Test?"

Sera shook her head. "A student cannot be forced to leave either. If you pull a cake from the oven before it's done baking, you've ruined it. There are protections and covenants that were strengthened centuries ago under Empress Maia. No, Father cannot *make* me leave. But he's hoping to disrupt my thoughts and throw me off. And now there's this letter from Will . . . I was already having trouble focusing before all this, Cettie. What am I going to do?"

Sera pouted prettily as she fished into her pocket and withdrew the letter. Cettie could almost feel the war raging inside her friend, could sense her desire to keep the letter a secret. To share it with no one, not even her best friend.

"Would you read it?" Sera asked with strained humility, offering the folded paper to Cettie. "I need your help. I need your advice. What should I do?"

It was an excellent letter. Mr. Russell was accomplished in penmanship and articulated himself exceptionally well. There was nothing salacious or provocative in it, but Cettie could see the young man was roiling with ambition. He had not returned those letters to the prince regent four years ago, and perhaps he'd been planning to make this sort of gesture ever since. There was just a touch of flirtatiousness in his request to see her before his assignment came.

It was evident from Sera's wringing hands that she was taken in by the young man. Her feelings were clouding her better judgment.

"What do you think?" Sera asked, looking at Cettie closely, trying to judge her reaction.

Cettie was adept at appearing calm whenever she wished to. She was grateful her friend had trusted her. "It's well written."

"Isn't it?" Sera said enthusiastically.

Cettie thought that Sera's level of interest needed to be tempered. "Sera, you told me yourself he is the son of a merchant who lost his fortune. He has a deed. I don't think the two of you would be a smart match."

Sera bristled. "I don't want to marry him, Cettie. I want to help him."

"Why?"

"Because what happened to him is unfair. His father was ruined through no fault of his own, and now his son must bear the price. And Will also suffers because of what happened with *my* father. It was my fault that he got in trouble. I want to make it right. I feel I owe it to him."

Cettie leaned forward and handed back the letter. "Are you sure that's your true motive, Sera? There are always two reasons people do anything. There's the *real* reason, and then there's the one we think sounds good to others."

From her expression, Sera was taken aback by Cettie's words. She paced restlessly after slipping the letter into her pocket. "I don't think it's fair quoting Fitzroy against me."

Cettie suppressed a smile and lifted her eyebrows inquisitively.

"Well, if you want to know the truth," Sera continued, "I do *like* Will. In truth, I would also like to see him again. I know our lives are very different. But if I'm to become empress, I must understand all of my people. Will gave me a glimpse into a part of the empire I didn't understand before meeting him . . . much like you've helped me understand life in the Fells. I care about him. I wish him well. You know that card game that's so popular these days? Dominion. The person with the lowest rank must forfeit their two best cards at the beginning of the round to the one with the highest, and the other person gives them two cards of their choice. Most people give their worst cards to that person. It helps them maintain their own position while ensuring the other person never rises. The game is designed to prevent people from improving their status, just like our society is. What would happen if the player who needs to forfeit two cards were generous rather than greedy?"

Cettie thought a moment, wanting to be helpful but not overbearing. "I cannot argue that you're not well meaning. The risk, Sera, is that you could give the impression that you feel more than you do. That you might cause a misunderstanding between the two of you. False hope. Tread carefully, Sera. That's all that I'm saying."

Sera brightened and walked up and squeezed her hands. "That's why I have you, Cettie. You help to keep me from making mistakes."

But in Cettie's heart, she wasn't sure the matter with Will was ending. Perhaps it was only beginning.

CHAPTER SIX

GAMES OF CHANCE

Of all the classes taught at Muirwood, Cettie's least favorite was the dancing class taught by Mrs. Ajax. There were always new dances being invented in the City's schools and at Lockhaven, and it was expected for young women to study dance all four years. The result was that there were more girls than boys in the class by the fourth year, and when the music started to emanate from the Leerings hidden behind the wall panels, Cettie was rarely asked to partner with anyone. Though she certainly had an aptitude for dancing, and a passion for it, no young man wanted to be seen standing up with a young woman who'd lived part of her life in the Fells. It only happened when Mrs. Ajax ordered it. During her first year, Adam had often rescued her from isolation.

Sera, of course, never lacked for a partner. Because of her station, she would attend state balls and be required to dance with dignitaries and visitors from faraway lands, so there was extra motivation for her to practice and excel.

Cettie couldn't help but feel the sting, though she didn't wish for anyone else to know, especially Sera, who would undoubtedly try to intervene. To avoid such a scene, she often spent dance class walking from one part of the room to another, trying to keep a smile on her face despite being repeatedly snubbed. The classes reminded her of Fog Willows and how Stephen and Phinia had always taken their dance practice so seriously. The younger Fitzroys cared far more for society's impression of them than their parents did, though that was likely a result of what had happened to their mother, Lady Maren, when she was younger. She'd been shunned after a social fault.

Another dance had started, one of Cettie's favorites—"Sky Ship's Cook"—and she resisted the urge to add a bounce to her step as she walked. The class would be ending soon, which was a relief. From her peripheral vision, she noticed someone approaching her and began to hope that she might get asked to dance after all. Who would it be?

When she turned her head, however, she saw it was Mr. Skrelling. That was odd because he didn't take this class. He had only taken the mandatory one year of social dancing and, from what she'd heard, stepped on a number of feet. His attentions to her were somewhat flattering, but he was always so serious and formal and completely incapable of registering when his presence wasn't desired. It made her feel quite awkward.

"Miss Cettie," he said with a curt, quick bow. He looked agitated.

"Good afternoon, Mr. Skrelling."

"Might I have a private word with you?"

"I don't see anyone standing near us," she answered. She was unwilling to leave the room with him, especially without an escort.

"Ah, yes. That's all as it should be. I would never ask for anything improper. I hope you realize, Miss Cettie, that I take your own interests very much to heart. Indeed, the very heart beating within my own chest pumps with a dual purpose. To sustain my life and to improve yours."

His fanciful little speeches could be tiresome, but she gave him a pleasant smile, still baffled by what he was trying to say. His affinity for long-winded explanations sometimes made the listener rather lose track of the point.

"But I digress. I came because I wanted to tell you something. Not to cause you alarm by any means, but I have a certain"—he sniffed loudly—"penchant for observation. I believe I could safely say I know the face of every student here at the school. Every teacher and underling. And within the domains of Vicar's Close, I could safely own—and this is not a boast—that I know the face of every shopkeeper, every landlord, and every person who normally inhabits the domiciles."

Cettie was still baffled. "I'm grateful that you have such a prodigious memory," she offered. Was he fishing for a compliment?

"If it pleases you to say as much, Miss Cettie. All my powers of concentration, observation, and memory are . . . as you know . . . at your disposal. Such as at the present circumstance. I have noticed, in recent days, someone new to Vicar's Close. He is a man, I would approximate, of thirty years of age. He has dark hair, on the long side. Quite long actually. He wears a gray vest, a blue undercoat, and a gray overcoat. I would call him a merchant, for he resembles one, only I have not seen him conducting any business. He wears a hat usually . . . not the military kind, but a commoner's. His looks, I shall say, are very serious. I would almost describe them as malevolent. He's been watching your cottage."

The last part got Cettie's full attention. She had noticed someone from her window just the other day. She'd noticed the man just before Mr. Skrelling had arrived, and in the excitement of the day, she'd forgotten all about it. "Excuse me, did you say he was watching our rooms?"

"Perhaps I should have mentioned that from the start," Mr. Skrelling said.

"Indeed, you should have," Cettie said. "He's new to the neighborhood, perhaps?"

"He's too old to be a student," he replied. "I've seen him standing at the corner, watching the street, more than once. It's my nature to be suspicious in general. To notice things that seem out of place. The people who live here are friendly in general. He looks . . . not friendly."

"And you are sure he has been looking at our rooms?"

"As certain as I reasonably can be under the circumstances. I thought it proper to warn you and Miss Fitzempress. Naturally, one does not just arrive at Muirwood by road. That's impossible because the area is surrounded by woods and water. But plenty of sky ships have been arriving recently, including an unmarked one from the Ministry of War. He might . . ." He paused and shrugged before finishing. "Be an agent of the ministry. I've been told that there are certain men who spy on their behalf. I don't seek to cause undue alarm, Miss Cettie. You look a little pale."

Cettie *was* worried, but she didn't wish for him to know it. "I am all right, thank you."

"I apologize if I have upset you." His jaw locked, and his lips moved as if he were trying to stop himself from speaking. Then he bowed to her again, turned, and started out of the room. The two rows of dancers were coming back his way and nearly collided with him. With eyes flashing, he turned toward the dancers as if to scold them, but at the last moment he managed to comport himself with dignity and strode out of the classroom.

When the song was finished, Mrs. Ajax gave some more instructions. "Remember, it's turn to the right and clap and then turn to the left and clap. Everyone should clap on the same beat. I heard a little dissonance a moment ago when a few of you forgot the timing. Try it again, please. This is one of the easiest dances. Your performance should be perfect. Remember it starts on nine." She started to clap her hands to mimic the rhythm.

Mrs. Ajax dismissed the class after the second attempt, and Cettie waited anxiously for Sera to join her. Her friend was talking to one of the younger girls—dancing was a class that mixed older and younger students—and Cettie tapped her foot as she watched them, her worry growing.

"Did you not dance today, Cettie?" Miss Fullbright asked with an air of false innocence as she walked by.

"Who would want to dance with *her*?" said Miss Fullbright's companion.

The snubs did not happen every day. But they happened with enough regularity that they made Cettie wary around people she did not already know. Miss Fullbright had a sizable dowry and at least three young men who were actively courting her. She never lacked for partners. Most students were eighteen at the end of their schooling, which meant they were of age to marry and enter society as adults. No doubt, Miss Fullbright planned to do exactly that.

But the young woman's future was as much a game of chance as that card game Dominion. Were the young men interested in her or in her money? Did this one gamble? Did that one overspend? Any one of the three might squander his wife's inheritance on some scheme that would trap the family in the Fells. Any sky manor could come tumbling down to earth.

Such was the fate of a woman whose only ambition was to marry well. There were so many risks at stake. So many games of chance at play. In the present climate, no one's future was secure.

Sera came up breathlessly, a glowing smile on her face. She locked arms with Cettie and guided her toward the door.

"Didn't you dance today?" she asked.

Cettie shook her head no, but still managed a smile. "Mr. Skrelling came by just now."

"I thought I saw him nearly get trampled. I'm sorry, but I couldn't help laughing."

"It *was* rather funny," Cettie said, "but the news he brought to me is not. He came to tell me that a stranger has been watching us at Vicar's Close."

"Watching what?" Sera asked with unconcern. She was already dismissing it.

"Mr. Skrelling thought the man he noticed was watching us. Remember how I noticed someone looking in our window the other day? Let's pay more attention on our way home this evening."

"If anyone is watching us too much, I think it's Mr. Skrelling. Admit it: he's fixated on you. I thought for sure it was him the other day."

"Be serious, Sera. He wasn't the person I saw from the window, but I did get a good look at the man. I'd like to see if I can spot him again."

The outside air was welcoming and warm, and it smelled of grass and flowers. Soon it would be Whitsunday, the end of the school year, when the entire village came to the grounds to dance and make merry. Cettie knew she would dance then because Adam was sure to ask her. He did every year. Mr. Skrelling probably would as well.

"Has he had any luck finding your mother?" Sera asked.

"Mr. Skrelling has been trying to discover her for years. He hasn't quit. Do you think his persistence will be rewarded?"

"What if he's persistent about pursuing *you*?" Sera asked inquisitively.

"I don't think you can make someone fall in love with you," Cettie said. "No matter how persistent you are. There are two hearts involved."

They changed the conversation to a lighter topic as they crossed the grounds before separating to their next classes. This was one of Cettie's favorites—a Mysteries of Wind class involving calculations. Sera did not have a strong head for numbers, but Cettie found it fascinating to learn about the patterns and ratios that were repeated throughout nature. It showed that an intelligent force had organized the worlds and left clues behind to be noticed. Sometimes Cettie felt that the world was like an empty classroom at Muirwood. All the tomes and books had been left behind for them to discover truths and principles, but the master of the classroom was not in the room.

They met up again after their respective classes and proceeded to walk arm in arm back to Vicar's Close. Some boys had doffed their coats and were playing catch with apples from the orchard. Most of the fruit ended up smashed by the end, but there was a jolly feel to the proceedings. As they walked down the street, Cettie kept looking at the various faces they passed, searching for the stranger.

Sera seemed to have completely forgotten, and she was talking about Will Russell's letter again when Cettie picked the man out of the crowd.

He did have a brooding face, a dark look. Was there a scar on the side of his cheek? His arms were folded, and he was leaning against the wall near the main square. Their eyes met briefly. There was no doubt he was staring at her. She looked away.

"Oh, it's Mr. Durrant!" Sera said excitedly.

Cettie, caught off guard, noticed there was another man standing in their yard, the balding Mr. Durrant. Judging from his agitated pacing, he had been there quite a while.

When she looked back to the man at the corner, he was gone.

Cettie felt a strange chill go through her. Something told her he would be back.

SERA

A person is but the product of their thoughts. What I think, I become. The challenge is in the taming of the maelstrom. How easily we fall prey to the thoughts of others. They can spread like a poisoned touch. Too often we unwittingly let the people around us tamper with our minds.

I am morose today. A heaviness is on me that I cannot dispel. Are my thoughts warning me? Is something dreadful about to happen? I sense a menace lurking in Muirwood. I do not know whence this feeling comes. Is it a foreboding of the future? The change in government is a harbinger of ill tidings. No matter which side wins, there will be those who resent the outcome. There will be trouble. I must be vigilant. I sense danger is coming to Muirwood, if it has not already arrived.

—Thomas Abraham, Aldermaston of Muirwood Abbey

CHAPTER SEVEN

PRIVY COUNCIL

Mr. Durrant had become Sera's advocate four years ago, and without his help and guidance, she wasn't quite sure she would have escaped her father's tyranny and found a place at Muirwood. Their visits had become more rare these last years, but she was grateful that he had tied his interests to her future success. He was quick-witted and sarcastic and had a wicked sense of humor. In short, he was exactly the sort of legal counsel one wanted on one's side. And while he was much older than her, at least fifty, he always managed to engage her in interesting conversation. She had not expected to find him standing in the gated porch of her dormitory, pacing like a cat caught in a trap.

Sera knew immediately that some piece of bad business must have brought him there.

As she and Cettie approached the small wooden gate, he came forward to meet them. Cettie was hardly paying attention, looking toward the square as if trying to find someone.

"Mr. Durrant," Sera said with an authoritative tone, "why are you intruding in our little garden? I hope you haven't trampled any of the lavender bushes."

"I thought they were weeds," he quipped in return, his eyes narrowing in an almost accusing way. "I have been stranded here for far too long. You cannot afford me being this idle, Your Highness. You should have come sooner."

"You should have sent word ahead," she countered. "Why are you here?"

"The street is not the proper place to hold a conference." He gestured toward the front door.

Cettie unlatched the gate to let them in, and Sera strode toward the door, feeling her stomach twisting with knots. Her father was coming for a visit, Will Russell had written her, and now Mr. Durrant had come. Didn't crises usually come in threes? Could they not come one at a time rather than all together?

When they reached the interior of their humble dormitory, Cettie immediately invoked the Leerings to bring light and heat. It came so easily to her she was finished in hardly a moment. Pushing aside a twinge of jealousy, Sera turned to face her advocate.

"There. What news do you bring, Mr. Durrant?"

"What have you heard? I'd rather not bore you with redundant information."

"My grandfather is dead, and my father wants to take his place. His strategy is to badger me into going to Kingfountain as the prince's bride, trading me away like a Dominion card."

"Ah, succinct, as always," Durrant said with a morose smile. "Now to the thick of it. You must come with me to Lockhaven at once. Your interests cannot be defended here, at Muirwood, while those who make the decisions are so far away. Your mother is coming here with your father to help persuade you, but she acts on my advice."

Sera put her hands on the table to steady herself. "There is only a short time before my studies end. Surely the privy council can grant me enough time to take the Test?"

Durrant shook his head. "I'm afraid not, Sera. You have spent four years studying at Muirwood. If you are not ready to pass the Test *now*, another few weeks will be insignificant. No, I advise you to return with me to see the privy council in the City. The sides are being drawn. The wagers are being placed as we speak. It is imperative that you return with me lest you be left behind."

"Wagers, Mr. Durrant?"

"I do not mean to make it sound venal, but yes. Wagers are being struck. Vast fortunes will be won or lost depending on the outcome of who is chosen next to fill the throne. Some members of the privy council stand to personally lose or gain by this."

"Pardon me, Mr. Durrant, but that is exactly the definition of venal!" Sera protested.

He shrugged. "It does not alter my recommendation. If you wish to become empress, you need to act as if you have sufficient ambition for it. The opportunity won't be thrust at you. Lord Welles, I think, is a strong supporter of yours. That he came here himself shows this. An admiral's strength in the military comes from the devotion of the soldiers. Most of them are common men who would benefit from your altruism. The Ministry of Law, on the other hand, would not want you interfering in wages."

Sera folded her arms and started to pace. She was sick to her stomach now. "I do want this chance, Durrant. But not for prestige or the power. Not for jewels or ball gowns. I want to be in a position to help all of our people, not just the lucky few who were born to wealth or managed to gain it. The soldiers, the laborers, and the innocent children who suffer for no fault of their own. Lockhaven and the other cities and sky manors will only be part of my empire."

"If you truly wish to help your people, then come with me."

"If I go, won't I lose the protection I have at Muirwood? Could my father compel me to go to Kingfountain to try and . . . try and *woo* the princeling there?"

"He's eighteen, hardly a princeling. Between the two of you, you are the one who would appear underage."

Sera flashed him an angry look. It made her blood boil that she was so short, so small. That she had to face the struggle of her life as a girl of sixteen. "Mr. Durrant, how can this be a good idea? My only hope of becoming empress is if I pass the Test. In my current state of mind, I'm not even certain that I can manage it."

He stepped closer. "All the more reason to come with me. Think of how your actions or inactions will be interpreted. You project confidence even if you do not feel it. There are some—including your father—who are saying that you can't pass the Test because you aren't a true Fitzempress. Prove that you are. Fly to Lockhaven in a tempest and demand to see the privy council. Show them your mettle, Your Highness. You'll gain more converts with your actions than with any fair little speeches. The public's confidence in you is beginning to totter because you have been gone for so long. The people need to see your strength. Your will. *And*," he added, wagging his finger at her in a lecturing way, "you'll have Fitzroy there to continue coaching you. No one can speak louder in favor of your interests than you yourself can. Your presence would speak volumes. I'm afraid that if you delay, it will spell disaster. For us both."

Sera frowned as she paced. "This goes against the counsel of both Fitzroy and the Aldermaston. They both encouraged me to stay here."

Mr. Durrant nodded his head sagely. "Yes, both are men of high principles. Unfortunately, neither is very sensitive to the demands of the world. Clearly you have Fitzroy's support. But if only one of the ministers supports you, I'm afraid that will be insufficient."

Sera stared at him. "What about Lord Welles? He came here to warn me of my father's impending visit. I think he is on my side."

Durrant wrinkled his nose. "I would not trust Lord Welles blindly. There is a reason he has been prime minister twice. The game of politics is already being played, whether you like it or not. Assert yourself,

Sera. You must give the privy council a reason to believe in you. To you, the past four years might as well have been an eternity. But for old curmudgeons like myself—and most of the privy council are fossils, I assure you—the time has passed in but an instant. Many still see you as an impetuous but promising twelve-year-old. No one wants to be ruled by a child."

"I would like to ask the Aldermaston for his opinion on this," Sera said gravely. Durrant had always been very persuasive, and she felt her heart leaning toward his counsel. His words sparked a sense of urgency within her. Delay could indeed be costly. But she didn't wish to make a poorly thought out decision, and the Aldermaston had proven his worth and wisdom on many occasions.

"By all means. I would like to return to the City this evening. While I am here trying to coddle and persuade you, and I mean that in the most respectful way possible, your enemies seek your downfall, and there is only Fitzroy there to defend you."

"And he is capable of doing so," Sera said archly. "If I go, then I would like Cettie to come with me."

Durrant's face went flat. "I wouldn't advise that, Sera," he said, shaking his head. He splayed his fingers and set them on the study table crowded with books and pencils.

"She is my companion," Sera insisted.

"And a charming young woman, to be sure," Durrant said, giving Cettie a respectful nod. "Politically, it would be suicide. But it is your choice."

Sera knew Durrant was probably right, but it pained her to think of stepping away from her friend for political purposes, even if it was only a temporary separation. Silence yawned between them.

"I saw a man outside," Cettie said in her quiet way. "The one Mr. Skrelling warned me about. He was watching our street. He just went away."

Durrant's brow contorted. "What man? What are you talking about?"

Cettie looked worried. "Earlier today, someone mentioned he had seen a stranger in Vicar's Close, someone he believed had been watching our room. I saw him, a man of thirty years with long dark hair. He had a scar on his left cheek."

"That could describe a thousand men," Durrant replied. "Mr. Skrelling worked for Sloan and Teitelbaum before his schooling. Awkward manner aside, he's an ambitious and capable young man. If he saw fit to mention it to you, consider it a sign of his good judgment. An advocate is trained to notice things out of the ordinary. He is trained to puzzle out the possible reasons for them."

Sera felt her alarm growing. The suggestion had seemed so unlikely earlier, when Cettie had mentioned it after dance class. "Why would a man be watching us?"

Durrant gave her a piercing look. "Because it is not improbable, Miss Fitzempress, that one or more of the ministers stands to lose a great deal of money if you succeed in claiming the throne."

Sera watched the sun begin to set from the window in the Aldermaston's chamber. The light streaked through the line of trees on the far side of the grounds, pricking her eyes and making her look away. She imagined Mr. Durrant pacing the small lavender garden in agitation, trampling plants as he awaited her decision. Cettie had volunteered to wait with him.

It was just Sera and the Aldermaston in the office, and he had not taken her news very well. He had removed his spectacles and was fiddling with the rims as he pondered everything she'd told him.

"I feel uneasy about this situation," he said after another lengthy pause. "There are certainly merits to your advocate's arguments. But I've learned to distrust hasty decisions. Something doesn't feel right here. I've been brooding about it all day."

"But my grandfather's death has brought this change," Sera argued, pacing before his polished wooden desk. "It's not Mr. Durrant's fault. I would rather not leave Muirwood at this time, but I'm beginning to feel I must."

"It is your choice, of course. My role is to counsel with you and advise you. In the end, we all must live with the consequences of our decisions. Perhaps you should take more time to think on it . . . reflect on the possibilities with a more quiet mind. Surely another day or two will not affect the outcome?"

"But it might," Sera said. "I don't know if I'm ready to take the Test. I hope that I am. I lack confidence; that much is sure. But haven't you always counseled us, particularly me, that feelings follow actions? If we pretend we are confident, if we act with confidence, we can become confident. The action triggers the feeling."

She almost couldn't see his frown amidst his enormous bristly beard. "In this case are not your feelings prompting your actions?"

She didn't know what to say to that. He was right in many respects. She clasped her hands together, entwining her fingers, and nearly stamped her foot with impatience. Both Mr. Durrant and the Aldermaston had made wise arguments—and they conflicted with each other. "I feel like I should go."

"Then why are we having this conversation?"

"Because I don't want to make a mistake! I still feel like going is the right thing to do, but I also want nothing better than to stay. How can you know what is right when your heart tells you one thing and your head tells you another? I feel so conflicted!"

She valued the Aldermaston's wisdom and experience, but was Durrant right about him? Did his principles cloud his ability to see political machinations clearly?

Again there was a long pause, a deafening silence that made Sera uncomfortable. "Whether or not you heed my counsel, Miss Fitzempress," the Aldermaston finally said in a kindly way, "I want you to know that I will always regard you highly. There is no risk of offending me if you choose not to follow my advice, and I am confident that you will do very well if you are chosen to lead the empire." He set his spectacles down on his desk and then steepled his fingers together. "Whenever I feel particularly rushed or urgent, it is either because my wishes are pushing me toward something or because I am being impressed upon by a higher order of power. I have learned through difficult circumstances to tell the difference between the two. If I feel compelled to act in a way that makes me feel uncomfortable . . . awkward even, then that feeling is almost always, if not always, coming to me from the Knowing. When I've chosen to heed the call, and I always try, it quickly becomes clear to me that there was a higher purpose to it. On the other hand, when I have acted in any degree of selfishness . . . meaning, when I seek a course that will benefit myself and not others, I have usually discovered, much to my chagrin, that I've failed a little test of character." His brows beetled together. "I cannot give you my instincts. I cannot express in words what I've come to learn in my sixty-three years on this world. You will have to make decisions for yourself. If they are wrong, learn from them. Few decisions in life have permanent consequences. That is a gift in and of itself."

His words, his loving manner, had begun to calm her nerves. "Thank you, Aldermaston," she said, feeling her throat growing thick. "I know you cannot make the decision for me. It is mine to make, and I must choose it, even if I don't yet fully understand all of its consequences. What I have learned here has impacted me deeply. I feel that it is my calling to lead . . . and to lead in a way that benefits all of my people, not just the lucky or the rich or the ambitious. I've decided to go. Come what may."

She saw a little twinge in his cheek muscle. But he nodded his head and fixed the spectacles back on his nose. "You will always be welcome back here, my dear," he said. His tone revealed neither approval nor disapproval of her decision.

Perhaps this was the first step of adulthood—made in blindness, leading to an unknown future.

CHAPTER EIGHT

FRIENDS APART

The sun was fading quickly as Sera walked back to Vicar's Close, her mind threshing through the implications of the decision she'd made. She was only partially conscious of the good-natured laughs and voices in the street. She paused at the small wooden gate leading to the yard full of lavender and felt an immediate pang of loss. Vicar's Close felt more like home than the manor of her childhood. She'd known from the start that it wouldn't be permanent. But as she grazed her palm along the smooth edge of the gate, she felt like bursting into tears.

The window of the dormitory glowed with light, and she saw Cettie in conversation with Mr. Durrant, who was holding a steaming tea-cup. Her lawyer was not pacing, as she'd expected him to be, and Sera remained at the gate a moment, watching the two people who had influenced her life in such different ways.

No more putting off the inevitable. She pushed open the gate, and the sound clearly could be heard inside because Cettie turned from the window seat and peered out to see her.

Sera walked past the lavender bushes and paused to break a sprig from one of them. She inhaled the pleasant fragrance and then stuffed it into her pocket before marching up the steps and entering her little dormitory.

"Ah, back from her scolding," Mr. Durrant said with a cynical smile.

"Thomas Abraham would not scold a mouse," Sera answered, shutting the door behind her.

"Indeed he might, if the mouse proved unrighteous. So what did he advise you?"

Sera folded her arms, soaking in all the details of the quaint little dwelling. "He said he would support me regardless of my choice," she answered. "What did you think, Mr. Durrant, that he would forbid me from going?"

Her advocate looked surprised and pleased. "He didn't object?"

"He said he had confidence in my ability to make decisions. And so I have decided. I will go back to Lockhaven and see the privy council."

The look of relief on Mr. Durrant's face made her smile.

"In anticipation of that very possibility, I asked your charming friend to pack your things for you. My zephyr is waiting to—"

"No, Mr. Durrant. I won't be going with you tonight. I will go with my parents when they come to see me. I would like to say good-bye to some of my teachers as well. Another day will not change the outcome."

Mr. Durrant looked puzzled. "I thought we might surprise your parents before they arrive on the morrow. If you came with me this evening, we could be back at Lockhaven before morning. It would tilt things to your advantage. Show that you are in control of yourself and not subject to your parents' whims."

"But I am still sixteen," Sera answered. "And I am subject to them for two more years. I would like you to return to Lockhaven and await our arrival." Sera glanced at Cettie and then back at her advocate. "Oh, and Cettie *will* be coming with me."

Mr. Durrant's brow wrinkled. "I don't think that is wise, ma'am."

"I know. But it is not your place to countermand me. Go make the arrangements. Since my parents no longer live together, I plan to stay with my mother in the home she is renting." There were too many dark memories in her childhood home.

Mr. Durrant took a sip from his steaming tea and then set down the cup. "I agree with your choice. Your mother is paying for my services, after all, and I had intended you to stay with her all along. Shall I advise the privy council that you wish to meet with them?"

"Yes, please. The day after tomorrow if you can arrange it."

"I am yours to command. I had hoped for better company on my return trip, but advocates are the lonely sort, and while deprived of your excellent companionship, I will further my work on your behalf along the journey." He sighed. "Can I not persuade you . . . ?"

"No," Sera answered firmly.

"Very well. Ere I depart, I will consult with the Aldermaston about the stranger spying on you. It makes me uneasy to have you here so unprotected, even for one more night."

"Really, Mr. Durrant. I don't much like it either, but what would you have me do? Don a hooded cloak and sneak out a back entrance? I have Cettie here with me, and no one can enter this home without our permission. The Leerings prevent it. If the Ministry of War has left a spy, then let him grow bored and cold in the bushes. If it makes you feel better, mention it to the Aldermaston, but I'd rather not raise a fuss."

"I intended to talk to him about it whether or not I had your permission," Mr. Durrant said. "It never harms to be prudent. Until our next meeting, I will bow and bid you a fond farewell. Miss Cettie, a pleasure as always." He doubled the bow to her and then departed.

Sera gazed longingly at the hearth, which crackled with flames from the Leering. The wistfulness of leaving home mingled inside her with the anticipation and excitement of returning to the seat of power. Once again, her life was about to change in a dramatic way. She saw that

Cettie had put out another teacup in anticipation of her arrival. Her friend was always so thoughtful.

"We're going to miss Muirwood," Sera said, casting her eyes around the small room. "But we will return to take the Test. And we'll be able to see Fitzroy more often at Lockhaven. I'll miss Anna and Adam most of anyone. There are good memories here. But at least we'll bring them with us."

When she looked at Cettie again, she saw that her friend's countenance had fallen. A shock of fear suddenly gripped hold of her heart. "What's wrong?"

"I'll be staying here. I won't be going with you."

This was the one possibility she had not anticipated. "You must come with me, Cettie. I need you."

Cettie sighed and shook her head sadly. "I've made my own choice, Sera. I shouldn't go with you. I know how your parents feel about me. They're not the only ones. I would be miserable in Lockhaven. I don't belong there."

Sera couldn't believe what she was hearing. Her friend wasn't just saying she wouldn't come with her now . . . she was saying she wouldn't come at all. Had this been her intention all along? Had Sera been so wrapped up in her own plan that she'd refused to see it? "It will be different. Cettie, you *must* come! Can't you see that I want to change the way things are? I want to repair the breaches in our society. You can help champion this change with me. If I become empress—"

"Even if you do become empress, things wouldn't change overnight. Every time you are away from me, people treat me horribly. I'm snubbed and reviled almost every day."

Sera started to say something, but Cettie waved her off. "I don't care about how they feel toward me, but don't you see? Those changes you want to make will be so much harder if I'm with you. And I would be miserable besides."

"But you've worried about what you will do after the Test," Sera said. "You don't have to worry. You will always have a place with me. I'll be able to keep my own household soon, and I would never bring on anyone who would ridicule or mistreat you."

"I'm not coming, Sera. I can't."

"But what will you do?" Sera asked. "You're not adopted yet. You cannot inherit any of the money Fitzroy wants to give you. You need to belong somewhere, Cettie. Make changes with me. All the things you've told me about the Fells, about life in the poorest areas here on the surface. We can change that, you and I!"

But Sera could see that Cettie's mind was already made up. Her friend acted more on principle than sentiment, and she stuck to her decisions once they were made. There was nothing equivocal about her.

"I don't want to hurt our friendship, but I've made up my mind on this," Cettie said after a long pause, confirming Sera's thoughts. "I ask you to please respect my decision."

Sera felt such a throb of loss and regret that tears threatened to spill from her eyes. "You've really been treated so poorly here? You never told me."

Cettie looked down. "I'm grateful to even be here. I've learned so much, and my friendships with you and Adam and Anna have meant the world to me. But the divisions between the classes are harsh indeed, and there's a lot of anger toward anyone who rises above their perceived station. I don't know how you managed to escape it, Sera . . . I'm just grateful that you did. Our friendship is important to me. I don't want to lose it."

Sera marched up and took her hands and squeezed them hard. "Do you think that there is anything you could do that would spoil our friendship? That I could stop loving you as I would a sister? Cettie? Surely we know each other's hearts better than that." She squeezed her hands again and then kissed them. "You are precious to me. I would do anything within my power to save you more pain."

The two embraced, and Sera let the tears fall. Why had she let herself believe that Cettie would always be with her? Why had she persuaded herself that she could change her social class's deep-rooted beliefs by a mere command? Cettie was right: it would take time. It would take years to overcome the corrosive traditions that their ancestors had allowed—nay, encouraged—to fester. Well, she might not be able to revoke the past, but Sera could do something about the future.

"I would never want to damage our friendship," Cettie said, pulling away enough to look at her. She was crying too; they both were. "You will do so much good for the people. You've been as dear as a sister to me as well. I'm so grateful that you chose me as your companion. I love you, Sera. I love you with all my heart."

It was a tender moment and one Sera knew she would always look back on. And it gave her strength to become the kind of empress that she knew she had to be.

Sera had not seen her father very often since coming to Muirwood. Time had bludgeoned him into someone completely altered from the strict, though occasionally warm, father she remembered from early childhood. She barely recognized him when he walked into the Aldermaston's office. Father's secretary, Mr. Case, had entered the room first, whereupon he'd announced Sera's parents. Without his intervention, she might not have placed him. His hair had receded, and long streaks of gray now frosted it. He was overweight and had a look of feverish intensity—could it be illness?—in his eyes. His costume was expensive and decorated with medals of honors he had been given, and she couldn't help but wonder how many of them had been earned. He had not succumbed to wearing a wig yet, but Sera felt it was only a matter of time. Mother looked less decrepit, but she had dropped any fastidiousness in her personal habits. It was clear she didn't much care what she looked like. Although they came in the same tempest, Sera suspected that they had not spoken two words together. She glanced at the Aldermaston, but his grave expression had not altered.

"It is my pleasure, Aldermaston Thomas," Mr. Case said, "to reintroduce you to the prince regent. I believe you were a teacher here when he was a student."

"I remember him," the Aldermaston said with a slight bow.

Father looked uncomfortable as he gazed at the ceiling and wrinkled his nose in distaste. "It is a bit dark in here," he said in an annoyed tone. "Darker than I remember. Seraphin, be so good as to brighten the room."

Mother's eyes flashed. "This is the Aldermaston's manor, Richard. That would not be appropriate."

So he was testing her already. She was not going to fall for the bait. "I'm glad you have come, Father. Mother. I have missed you both. What tidings bring you to Muirwood? You know I would have come had you summoned me."

"Your grandfather has passed," Mother said.

"I will speak," Father interjected quickly. He looked offended by her words. "The privy council must needs decide on a new emperor, as you undoubtedly know. There is also a delegation coming from the court of Kingfountain that I insist you—"

"I already know these things," Sera said brightly, hands behind her back. "I'm prepared to come with you."

Her father looked at her in surprise. "How did you . . . ?"

"That doesn't really matter, does it, Father? I am very well informed regarding the state of the empire. I have a meeting with the privy council tomorrow."

"The privy council?" said Father, perplexed.

Even her mother looked surprised, and Sera relished it.

"Oh yes. I look forward to it. I appreciate you coming all this way to get me, but it was unnecessary. I planned on coming regardless. I'm especially concerned about the cholera morbus disease rampaging the City. I'll be interested in hearing the council's report on what they have done about it so far. Shall we go?"

In her mind, she asked if the lights would please brighten. With the Aldermaston standing nearby, she felt confident they would obey her. She didn't struggle so much. As Sera walked toward her parents, the lights within the chamber began to beam brightly.

The look her father gave her wasn't one of tenderness from father to daughter. It was the scrutiny of a rival plotting her fall.

There was, in his wrinkled brow, a look of determination that she would not be allowed to speak to the privy council.

CETTIE

In days of old, every abbey had someone designated as its defender. This person, chosen by the Aldermaston, was allowed to bear arms and evict those who would violate the peace. It has been several generations since that practice was abandoned. The closest person to that role that I now have is the pilot of the abbey's zephyr. His name is Mr. Neal. Per the advice of Sera's advocate, I asked Mr. Neal to look around the village for evidence of a newcomer, a stranger in the village. Many have seen this scarred stranger and wondered at him. No one knows where he is staying or why he is here. I fear the abbey's defenses may have been breached by an agent of one of the ministries.

—Thomas Abraham, Aldermaston of Muirwood Abbey

CHAPTER NINE

ALONE

After Cettie's last class of the day, advanced mathematics, she remained behind to help tidy the room. The melancholy of Sera's departure the previous day had tormented her keenly. It was expected that her friend would be gone for a week or two before returning to take the Test, and so Cettie had the small dormitory to herself. She resolved to seek out Anna and spend more time with her almost-sister.

"You are so good to stay and help," said Mrs. Romrell in a kindly way. She had been teaching at Muirwood for many years. Her husband also taught in the Mysteries of Wind, and Cettie enjoyed both of their classes.

"I'm glad to do it," Cettie replied as she straightened the stools beneath the desks. The other students had already left, leaving the two of them alone.

"I am going to miss you when you leave," Mrs. Romrell said. "I thought you might have left with Miss Fitzempress, yet you stayed." It was phrased as a statement, but there was a tone of curiosity in her voice.

Cettie glanced her way, feeling her cheeks grow warm. Mrs. Romrell was the kind of teacher who treated all students equally, regardless of their background. It was one of the many reasons Cettie admired her. "I don't really belong at Lockhaven" was all she said in reply.

Mrs. Romrell went about her work quietly for a while, arranging her notes in her leather satchel. "Cettie," she finally said. "Do you have a place to go after you finish here? I don't mean to pry, and I'm sure Minister Fitzroy has already arranged things for you . . . I just hadn't heard."

Cettie bit her lip. Her cheeks were flushing even more. She didn't know what to say. The only arrangement was for her to return to Fog Willows indefinitely. That would leave her alone with Stephen and Phinia, and she had never grown close to either of them. What would Cettie do there? How would she fill her days? She longed to take the knowledge she had gained and put it to use somewhere.

"Have I upset you?" Mrs. Romrell asked.

"No," Cettie stammered hastily. "My situation is complicated. I do not have a place arranged for me yet, Mrs. Romrell."

Her teacher looked sympathetic. "I wondered if that might be the case. Cettie, you are one of the most capable and gifted students I've ever taught. One of my past students is a young mother living in a floating manor in Wellton. Her husband works for the Ministry of Wind and travels frequently. She is in need of a governess, someone who would be patient with her small children. I've had several students in mind for the position, but your name kept coming to me. I don't wish to intrude on your affairs, but if you would be interested in learning more about it, I believe the position is still open." She gave Cettie a hopeful smile.

Gratitude swelled in Cettie's heart. Someone she valued had noticed her need and offered to help. She pushed in the last stool and blinked quickly, trying not to weep.

"Thank you, Mrs. Romrell. It means so much to me that you'd . . . that you'd consider someone like me."

Mrs. Romrell approached her and touched her arm gently. "I don't mean to overstep, Cettie. Perhaps the minister has something in mind for you. This epidemic is keeping him a very busy man, no doubt. I just wanted you to know that you have impressed me and other teachers here. We all want what is best for you. Remember that you have friends here. I could even see you teaching at Muirwood someday. Once you have gained some experience in the world, you might find yourself back here to teach others."

Cettie gave her a hug and offered her thanks again. "I will talk with my guardian about it."

"You do that," Mrs. Romrell said, patting her shoulder. Cettie's heart felt lighter as she left the classroom. She was needed, wanted even. It was a delicious feeling, the butter on a hot bit of toast. As she left the wing of classrooms, she took a moment to admire the iron-framed windows, the stubby shingles that crowned the roof. The grounds were also full of students relaxing and wandering the extensive yards. Oh, how she would miss it. Cettie decided to visit the apple orchard, and she'd started that way when she spied Anna and her friends coming toward her.

"Cettie!" Anna said excitedly and rushed forward to give her a hug. The two embraced, and the warmth in Cettie's heart began to overflow. No matter how alone she had felt today, it was only a feeling, not the truth. Anna squeezed her tightly and then turned to her friends and waved them away. "Go on without me. I need to talk to my sister." Turning back to Cettie, she added, "Can I walk with you? Where were you going?"

"The cider orchard," Cettie said.

"Let's go together."

"Are you sure?" Anna's friends had walked off, but a couple of them were still throwing disappointed glances back at them.

"We don't spend nearly enough time together anymore. And now that Sera is gone, you're all alone. Come, there's much I wish to tell you."

Anna's long, wavy blond hair fell down her back. It looked like it had been spun from sunshine, and, indeed, being around Anna felt like sitting in the sun on a cool fall or spring day. Of all the Fitzroy children, Anna was the most like her parents.

Arm in arm, they walked briskly toward the walled area surrounding the cider orchard, talking all along the way.

They'd almost reached the orchard when Anna asked, "Do you think Phinia likes Adam?"

Cettie was startled. "What makes you ask that?"

"Maybe I'm being suspicious. She keeps asking me if I'm worried about him going to the Fells to work as a doctor. She gets so frantic about it."

"Aren't you worried?" Cettie asked.

Anna looked at her quizzically. "Adam Creigh is brave and compassionate. You know I admire him for wanting to help people. It has always been his dream to go to the Fells. Why would I hesitate or interfere in that? Let him pursue his dream. I have every faith he'll make a difference. He's such a hard worker."

Cettie could feel Anna's devotion to him throbbing in her voice. It made her uneasy, and not only because of the secret feelings she bore for Adam. She couldn't imagine Anna living in the Fells. Apparently Phinia felt the same way.

"I think she's worried about him for your sake," Cettie said.

"Do you really think so? They are the same age, and he's always so courteous to everyone. I just wish I knew . . ." She scrunched up her nose and fell silent.

"Knew what?"

"I wish I knew if he even cared for me," Anna said softly.

Therein lay the problem. Adam would never say something to commit himself unless he really felt it. He was gregarious and pleasant to all, but he was not flirtatious. To her knowledge, he had never overtly expressed interest in any young woman at the abbey. His focus had always been on his studies.

"He hasn't said anything to you?" Cettie asked softly.

Anna shook her head. "No. But he wouldn't do that, would he? I know he needs to be strict with his studies because he has to make a living. It's disgusting how wasteful some young men are. Many of them would rather gamble the day away than study or learn. Adam is quite serious in comparison."

"He isn't going to inherit a fortune," Cettie said. "He doesn't have the luxury of being idle or unwise."

"Like Stephen," said Anna disparagingly. "He keeps pressuring Mother to let him change the library into a small theater. He wishes to bring in performances and actors and actresses. To throw balls and galas." She winced. "Father has said no, of course. But he is often gone, and so Stephen keeps wheedling Mother. I'm sure he's a bitter disappointment to them both. His only ambition is to spend what others have earned. It's not right."

It did not require a storm glass to see this unpleasant weather brewing. Cettie sighed. "He's twenty years old. He has too much time and energy."

"I know," Anna said. "Father wants to see him try a profession. Even something that requires money, like being a part of the parliament. Father would gladly pay for it. But the stage? Balls?"

"It's a wonder that you haven't fallen prey to the same spell."

Anna shrugged. "Is it really? Mother is different than her sisters. She is very different than her brother who was so seduced by wealth that he disowned them all. I'm grateful that Father has set aside money for each of us to inherit. Even you, although Stephen and Phinia likely resent it. Why they should, I don't know, because you have helped increase our family's fortunes tenfold! They'll get more because of you. I wish they could see that."

"I really didn't do that much," Cettie demurred. Still, there was no denying the other Fitzroys' attitude toward her rankled.

They held hands as they walked through the doorway leading to the orchard. A few families were working the corkscrew cider presses along the inner wall, and wooden tables loaded with buckets full of apples had been set up near them. Some young men stood on ladders to harvest the apples from the higher branches.

Muirwood cider was the sweetest thing Cettie had ever tasted, and the orchard was one of her favorite places on the abbey grounds. Whenever she was there, she felt connected to something larger than herself, to the history of this great place.

She and Anna kept talking as they wandered through the lines of trees together.

"What do you think Father will do about Stephen?" Cettie asked.

"I don't know," Anna replied sadly. "Just because he is the oldest doesn't mean he will inherit the manor. Father will decide who he thinks will manage it best. And that won't happen until he dies . . . years from now. I'm afraid the tension between them will only grow."

"What if he chooses to give Fog Willows to you, Anna? The law allows him to decide, just like it will allow the privy council to decide which of the emperor's heirs will replace him."

"I don't know what he will do," Anna said, shaking her head. "I don't think I'm any more worthy of it than Stephen or Phinia."

"Which is another reason he might choose you," Cettie said with a smile. "I think Father will give Fog Willows to the person he trusts the most to look after it the way he does."

"That means he should give it to *you*," said Anna wryly.

"He can't," said Cettie, brushing away the compliment. "I'm not his daughter. I may never be."

Anna pulled Cettie closer. "If there is a way, Father will find it. Don't give up hope yet. We will become sisters in truth. Now that

Sera is gone to Lockhaven, you're all alone in your dormitory. I think I should stay with you. Will you let me?"

It was another kindness she did not feel she deserved. "Anna, you are so sweet."

"I don't like the idea of you being alone." She gave Cettie a loving look. "When I was frightened of the dark, you stayed with me. You tried to protect me when Mrs. Pullman sent that awful ghost to attack us."

"It's only going to be a short while, Anna. Sera will be coming back to take the Test."

"But it may take longer than she expects. I see you are hesitant. Perhaps you were longing for the quiet?"

Truthfully, Cettie was looking forward to it as much as she was dreading it. Sera was more like Anna, more prone to talking and sharing feelings. Cettie was more private and reserved, and she had a lot of thinking to do these next weeks.

"Say no more," Anna said, squeezing her hand. "But I will come by and visit you more often than I have lately. Summer is nearly here, and we'll be back at Fog Willows before you know it. We can share a room then."

"I would like that," Cettie replied. "But there is a chance I may have another opportunity. I only just learned of it."

"Do tell!" Anna said with eagerness.

The almost-sisters spent a delightful afternoon and early evening together and then shared dinner at one of the inns in the village. Several times Anna had tried to circumvent Cettie's defenses to see if there was a young man who interested her. Each time Cettie had deflected her away from that sensitive topic. There was only one young man she admired in that way, and she couldn't bear to tell Anna about it. Not when they loved the same person.

The cook at the inn had done a wonderful job of searing the pork chops, and the spiced rice was so flavorful and delicious that both had eaten their fill before they devoured some of the fresh apple crisp that came straight from the ovens. The harvest had produced copious amounts of apples that year. There was just a little chill to the air as they walked arm in arm back to Anna's home, where they exchanged hugs and kisses. After the door closed behind her, Cettie walked down the street to her own dwelling. There were some students about still, but lights beamed merrily from the windows of many of the little cabins.

When she arrived at her little gate, she opened it and reminded herself to tend to the lavender bushes the next morning. She approached the door and willed the lock to open, which it did, and then the Leerings flared to life in a warm glow. For a moment, she expected to hear Sera bustling around, but the room was still. The feeling of emptiness began to nudge her feelings away from the contentment of the afternoon.

She decided to read a book by the window seat as she usually did in the evening. With a thought, the hearth fire lit, and the flames began to dance and weave within it. Cettie walked to the window seat and found the book she'd discarded that morning. She picked it up, turning it over in her hands.

It was then she sensed the presence of someone else in the room.

The Leerings should have warned her at the front door. They should have prevented the person from entering. That they hadn't caused a stab of fear in her heart.

Cettie turned her head and instantly saw the dark-haired man she'd observed in the street. He was already halfway across the room.

He'd made no sound.

CHAPTER TEN

BREATH

Terror struck Cettie down to her bones—immediate and instinctual. Her mind froze with the panic, her muscles locked, and her knees began to quake. In just a moment, her entire body had seized against her will. The strange man should not be in her room. It wasn't possible. Yet there was no denying it was happening.

"How did you get in?" Cettie asked, her voice trembling as much as her legs. She was trapped against the window, far from either door.

In the soft light from the Leering lamps, she saw him better. Saw the sweat trickling from his brow. Saw the almost feverish look in his eyes, the shadowed smudges of sleeplessness beneath his eyelids. The scar that ran down the left side of his face was long but not jagged; it looked like it had been made by a saber slash or a knife. His hair fell just past his shoulders. He wore a merchant's outfit, but his bearing was militant.

"Look at you," he said with an angry voice. "Look at you now."

"Who are you?" Cettie demanded, experiencing a strange swelling inside her heart. There was something familiar about him.

"I'm taking you away from here," he said with determination. "You don't belong in this place. I'm taking you home."

Cettie began to control her breathing, just as Raj Sarin had taught her years ago. She was frightened and weak, but her body was under her control. With determination, she exhaled slowly and then breathed in through her nose. Her mind sought out the Leerings in the room, and she willed them to brighten like noonday. She hoped the change in lighting would serve a dual purpose: that it would both call attention to her plight and blind him enough for her to rush past him.

The Leerings obeyed, and suddenly the room was blazing. She heard and felt a hissing sound of agony and pain. Cettie knew the room by habit and instinct. She could travel it blindfolded. Squeezing her eyes shut, she rushed to the man's left, moving as fast as she could.

The room was plunged into darkness as another will overpowered her control of the Leerings. She collided into his body and fell to her knees. Panicked again, she opened her eyes. The only light in the room now came from the window. The man looked down at her coldly. She clenched her hand into a fist and struck him in the side, trying to knock him off balance.

A deeper darkness crept into the room, one that pulsed with dread and despair. She tried to get back on her feet, but her captor pulled her up and threw her roughly against the small sofa. The room was spinning, and the feeling of darkness grew more and more terrible. She looked up and saw that the intruder's eyes were glowing silver.

And she heard a voice inside her head say, *She is the one. Bring her outside.*

Horror broke through her will. She recognized the sound of that voice, that whispered thought. It was the tall ghost, the one with no eyes. The one that had tormented her at Miss Charlotte's hovel in the Fells and again under Mrs. Pullman's reign of tyranny at Fog Willows. For nearly four years she had escaped it, and she'd thought Muirwood would protect her. Until now it had. The creature was still hunting her. It was still seeking her.

Cettie screamed. Yes, she was terrified. Yes, she was weak. But she would use what weapons she had to escape.

The man's silver eyes flashed, and suddenly her scream was silenced, her speech robbed from her throat. He rushed forward and dragged her off the sofa. She struck the edge of her hand against the underside of his arm, knowing there was a painful nerve there, but the man merely grunted and then wrestled her arms behind her back. She thrust her head back into his face and felt it strike. His grip on her released as he reacted to the pain. She no longer thought of running. No, her blood was enraged now. She would bite and claw and attack him any way she could. She would attack this man who had brought the ghost back to her.

Suddenly she was on the floor, facedown, her arm torqued back into an agonizing hold. Her shoulder seared with pain. She heard him breathing hard with the exertion.

Bring her now. Before they come!

Cettie swung her other elbow back and struck some meaty muscle. Her time at the archery butts had increased her strength. He was using all his force to try to still her—there was still hope she could escape. She jerked her elbow at him again, only to find his arm suddenly clamped around her neck. She dug her nails into his wrist, knowing this hold would send her tumbling into unconsciousness in a matter of seconds. Tugging on his arm proved fruitless, and her chest began to hunger for air. She elbowed him in the ribs again, multiple times, earning grunts from him as he wrestled her into submission. White spots began to dance before her eyes, but she bucked against him, unwilling to yield. She reached her fingers for his face, trying to get his eyes and finding only hair.

There, there, there, there . . .

She felt the tall ghost's glee at her weakness. She felt its presence, felt its touch through his.

Cettie tried once again to claw his face, and then her strength failed her completely.

Cettie was roused by the swaying motion of being carried. She was slung over the man's shoulder, her face thumping against his back. Blood had rushed to her head, and her cheeks and neck were throbbing. She opened her eyes and saw the cobblestone street. They were still in one of the thin alleys in the village. The light from the town square was fading in the distance, but she could still sense the Leerings of the fountain.

He hadn't tied her hands. His urgency to leave had made him careless.

Although she was still weak, she felt her strength returning quickly now that she could breathe. She didn't know precisely where she was; some of the alleys led to porter doors that exited the village grounds. It was forbidden for students to leave without permission, but she and Sera had occasionally left to wander through the countryside. She knew how vast it could be.

Fighting this man had proven useless. She reached out to the nearest Leering.

Aldermaston. Can you hear me?

She felt his response immediately.

Cettie, where are you? We are searching for you.

A thrill of relief coursed through her. She was still bumping roughly against her attacker's back but managed to strain her neck and gaze down the mouth of the alley.

Someone is taking me. We're off the main square. She took a long, deep inhale. *I smell the butcher's shop.*

We are coming that way now. We are coming, Cettie. Don't be afraid.

I am afraid. I don't want to leave.

We are coming. Be ready to flee.

"Stop it," the man grunted to her, jostling her. Had he heard her thoughts too? She'd done her best to mask them from him.

When they reached the end of the alley, her attacker shrugged her off his shoulder and set her down against the wall near the porter door. She wanted to scramble back away from him, but there was only stone behind her.

"Why are you doing this?" she whispered. She had her voice back, but her words were rough and throaty.

He knelt, his face near hers. His eyes were no longer glowing, and his breath was hot against her skin. He looked enraged.

"Because I'm your bleeding father, and I'm not going to let them turn you into a heretic!"

Her insides shriveled. "You are not my father," she whispered.

He sneered at her. "You think George Pratt is? Oh, he doesn't know the first thing about you. Yes, you are my blood, and I am yours. You don't belong here. You don't belong in this world at all." He turned his head, hearing noise coming from the head of the alley. He pitched his next words as a whisper. "This isn't the time or the place. I'm getting you out of here. They've no doubt warped your mind, but there's hope for you yet. Now run with me to my ship, and I'll tell you all. Come, Daughter. I can't carry you all that way." He rose and held out his hand to her.

Aldermaston? Cettie pleaded with her thoughts.

We are coming down the alley now. I see you through the Leerings' eyes.

"What is your name?" she asked the man. She wanted to delay him any way she could.

He looked back down the alley, his face scowling. "I don't have a name anymore. Call me Kishion." He put his hand against the door and bowed his head. His eyes began to glow silver once more. She felt the Leering resist him. She sensed the Aldermaston's presence, felt his mind begin to overpower the door. Cettie joined her power to his.

"You cannot get out," Cettie said, starting to push herself up. "You cannot leave these grounds. Please, come with me to the Aldermaston's manor. We can talk there. Please, Kishion. I want to know who you are."

There was a crack and a zipping sound as a ball ricocheted off the stone frame of the door. Cettie flinched.

"Hold fast, man," ordered a voice from the alley. "The next one won't miss. Step away from the girl."

"Step away, step away," her attacker muttered darkly. She felt the throb of the ghost's power inside him.

He reached into his belt and withdrew a small handheld arquebus. Before Cettie could act, he aimed and squeezed the trigger. A loud explosion came from it with a flash of brilliant fire that blinded and stunned her. She had seen the shooting ranges at the abbey for the students who studied the Mysteries of War. *Their* weapons were quiet, the shots coming out with a hissing zip. This was unlike anything she'd experienced. Smoke filled the air, flavored with something alchemical, and her ears squealed loudly.

She felt the Aldermaston's command of the Leering fail. Cettie shoved the stranger aside and bolted from him, running down the alley, fleeing toward the light.

She didn't look back, but she heard the door groan as it opened. Her attacker was fleeing.

I will find you again, she heard the voice promise her.

There were two men lying on the street. She thought she recognized one of them as the Aldermaston's pilot, the one who flew the abbey's zephyr. He was groaning, clutching a huge red stain on his shirtfront. Blood was spreading on the ground beneath him as well. The second man who had fallen was the Aldermaston. Adam Creigh knelt by him, examining the red welt that had bloomed on his front. The young doctor's face was transfixed with a mixture of horror and determination. He applied pressure to the wound, trying to stanch it, but there was so much blood . . .

Cettie gazed at the Aldermaston, taking in his waxy pallor. His spectacles had fallen off and lay broken in the street. Her ears were still ringing from the blast of the pistol. The smoky haze filled the alley, its acrid smell clinging to her clothes, her skin. What could it be from?

"It went . . . it went through me!" gasped the pilot, disoriented. He tried to sit up and couldn't. His body started to convulse. He groaned with pain. Had one ball truly wreaked this much damage?

"Cettie, get help," Adam said, looking at her in desperation. His hands were wet with blood. "I think the Aldermaston is dead."

CHAPTER ELEVEN

ROGUE

When the door swung open, Cettie stopped her frantic pacing. She was still in the care center, unable to leave until she knew what had happened. The expression on Adam's face as he entered her room was guarded as she searched it for information. The first blush of dawn was appearing, turning the sky to an impossibly vivid shade of blue, a color that seemed to mock the dreadful terrors of the night preceding it. For hours she had paced and prayed and worried that the Aldermaston had passed on to another world. It was her fault. If she had gone with the villain who had tried to abduct her, this wouldn't have happened. Surely her life was not a fair exchange for Thomas Abraham's.

"I thought I might find you sleeping," Adam said with a weary sigh. She finally noticed the splotches of blood on his jacket, vest, and sleeve.

"How could I sleep without knowing?" Cettie answered. She was weary to her bones, but she had to know. "Is he still alive?"

"His breathing is shallow still. Too shallow." Adam raked his fingers through his hair. "I wish I could do more to help. Doctor Redd has been teaching here for ages, and he's performed more surgeries than he can count. This was the first time I got to help with a real one. The doctor has a special power with the Mysteries, and he can sometimes heal with his touch. But no such miracle happened this night." Adam shook his head, his eyes looking sad. "I don't understand why. The Aldermaston is a good man. Why wouldn't he be healed?"

"But he's alive," Cettie said in relief. "That's better than you feared last night after he was shot."

"True," Adam said with a tone of defeat. "Mr. Neal bled to death while we carried him to safety. The ball punctured his spleen, damaged his liver, and severed a major artery. If he had not stepped in front of the Aldermaston when that killer raised his arm, then Thomas Abraham would certainly be dead right now instead."

A chill shot down to the soles of Cettie's feet. This man, this *monster*, who had claimed to be her father had tried to kill one of the most revered men in the kingdom. His actions had been devoid of respect or deference. Hadn't he called Cettie a heretic?

"Well, it is a blessing Doctor Redd came so quickly," Adam said, drawing nearer. He touched her arm. "Thank you for what you did. If you hadn't kept your wits about you and run for help. Well, it may have been too late."

Cettie was close to weeping, and his praise only added to her guilt. Why was it that she seemed to attract such darkness? What if that man really was her father? Did that mean her blood was bad? Spoiled?

"I did very little," Cettie replied, staring down at the floor, trying to keep tears from spilling out.

"Come into the light," Adam said worriedly. Gripping her arm, he led her to a chair near the window and then helped her sit in a beam of sunlight. The cushion felt good, but uncomfortable awareness shot through her as Adam knelt in front of her. "You have bruises on your neck. May I?"

Her feelings of self-consciousness increased dramatically, bringing a wave of confusion because she heard herself saying "Yes, of course," before realizing what that meant.

With gentle fingers, he touched her chin and tilted it to one side, exposing her neck to the light. His touch brought intense jolts to her skin, and she felt her heartbeat begin to thrum erratically. He'd never touched her like this before . . .

"Did he . . . did that man choke you?" Adam asked, his words throbbing with anger. "Look, there's an abrasion on your temple as well."

"Yes," Cettie murmured, her hands in her lap, her skin tingling as he continued to examine her.

Then his hands touched hers on her lap, his fingers gently lifting hers. He was looking at her nails, which was how she finally noticed the blood beneath them.

"You scratched him, didn't you?" Adam said with a flush of respect. Then his eyes hardened into stones. "Did he . . . did that man—"

"No!" Cettie interrupted, her cheeks flaming as she realized what Adam was likely alluding to. "He didn't . . . assault me, not in that way. No, he tried to abduct me and was surprised that I fought back." She'd not told anyone what her attacker had said to her. The knowledge that he might be her father weighed heavily on her heart.

"You clearly *fought* him," Adam said with an approving grin. "And hurt him too, I'd say. He probably has some gouges in his skin that will pain him greatly. Good. Did you manage to throw him, Cettie?"

She flushed even more. "I don't think so."

He chuckled again and then shook his head. "He must have subdued you with a choke hold. That's the most effective way to render someone unconscious. Or kill them. But why did he attack you? Maybe someone hired a ruffian to abduct you in the hopes of stealing the secrets of your storm glass? It makes no sense to me, but some people do become desperate."

Cettie licked her lips. He'd finished examining her fingers, but he was still holding her hand. She had never told him about her ghosts, especially the one that had tormented her in the Fells. She already felt awkward enough around him, and if he knew all her ugly truths, surely he would think worse of her.

"Has someone told the prime minister, do you think?" she asked. "About the Aldermaston?"

"Yes, he has been apprised of the situation. I'm expecting to see Fitzroy at any moment. No doubt he'll come immediately to make sure you are well." He finally released her hand and lifted his to brush some stray hairs back from her brow. He was looking at her cheek.

"There's something else," he said. With the back of his fingers, he nudged her chin again. "The skin is pink here. Like from a sunburn."

Her cheeks were already flaming, making her feel even more awkward.

"It is a burn, isn't it? Is the skin sensitive when I touch it?" he asked, grazing his finger lightly across it.

"A little," Cettie answered, swallowing. For more reasons than one.

He came close to her, so close their cheeks were almost touching, and he sniffed. "Curious. Your hair and skin have an acrid odor . . . like brimstone, though not as pungent. It's definitely alchemical." He drew closer again, his thumb still pressed to her eyebrow, and examined her face closely.

"Did you see what he was holding? Was it an arquebus?"

"A small one, a pistol," she answered. "But it exploded from his hand. There was fire and then smoke."

"That explains the soot on your shoulder and sleeve," he answered, drawing back. "You were very close when he fired. It was deafening from my end of the alley."

Her ear had rung for a long time afterward. She nodded.

"Is there anything else you remember about him? Any details that might be helpful? It's best to revive as many memories as you can now. Those clues may help us find the man."

Cettie wasn't about to tell him about the man's claim of parentage, but she remembered something else she could share. "I don't know how he got into my dormitory."

"He was *in* your dormitory?" Adam asked with startled surprise. "I thought he'd attacked you in the street."

"No, he was waiting for me. I had dinner with Anna last night," she added, "and he was already inside when I came back. The Leerings didn't warn me as they should have. I just . . . sensed him. You know, sometimes you can feel it when someone is behind you or watching you."

"Go on," Adam said encouragingly.

"I tried to summon the Leerings to come to my defense, that's how I got those burns, but he overruled them. I don't know how."

"Was he a trained maston, then?" Adam asked with disbelief.

"No, I don't think so. When he attacked me, his eyes began to glow."

"What do you mean?"

"They turned silver and glowed," Cettie said, "and then the Leerings obeyed him."

"And you don't think it was a hallucination? Brought on by fear?"

Cettie shook her head and looked down. "It was real. I've never seen anything like it before. Not even in the Fells."

He put his hand on her shoulder, and she looked into his eyes again. "I believe you, Cettie. I wasn't trying to sound doubtful. This just sounds like one of the Mysteries. One we haven't been taught yet."

The hallway door opened, and Mr. Skrelling came barging into the room in a disheveled state. Upon seeing Adam kneeling on the floor in front of Cettie, he immediately pinwheeled his arms as if he'd collided into a wall.

"Well! I'm . . . pardon . . . I see!"

Adam gave him a sidelong look, but he immediately backed away. Cettie could tell that he appreciated, as she did, that the situation might give a misleading appearance.

"Mr. Skrelling," Adam said, rising to his feet.

The young advocate in training was tugging down his vest front. Cettie noticed that the buttons were mismatched. He'd clearly donned his apparel in haste. "Forgive the intrusion. I should have knocked first."

Adam shook his head. "There is nothing untoward occurring, Mr. Skrelling. I can assure you of that. Miss Cettie was attacked last night, and the Aldermaston was critically injured. I was attending to her injuries after helping Doctor Redd in surgery all night."

"You are hurt, Miss Cettie?" Mr. Skrelling asked, his voice dripping with concern. He edged closer, his body rigid, his movements awkward.

"I'm feeling a little better," she answered, hands folded primly on her lap.

"Was it . . . was it that fellow I warned you about, miss?"

"Indeed it was, Mr. Skrelling," Cettie said. She was so tired she didn't want to deal with him. "I did want to thank you for the warning."

"If I can ever be of service to you, Miss Cettie, I will, of course, do what I . . . as of course you already know . . . would do you the just honor to be of whatever service that you may . . . in time may indeed be . . . and, *ahem*, well—"

"Thank you, Mr. Skrelling," Adam said, walking toward him with palms extended, as if he were determined to push the young man backward out of the room. "Miss Cettie has been up all night and needs her rest."

Cettie was grateful for the interruption because Mr. Skrelling's little speech was becoming more and more insensible the longer he attempted to make it.

"Of course," Mr. Skrelling said, stepping awkwardly back. "I wouldn't . . . far be it from me to . . . I'm glad to see you are . . . *ahem* . . . still so . . . well." A look of mortification crossed his face, and he turned to leave—only to walk into the door that he'd closed behind him. He fumbled with the knob and then hastily exited.

Adam had an amused smile as he turned and looked at her.

She wasn't sure what to say after such an uncomfortable interruption. Thankfully, Mr. Creigh spared her the agony of breaking the silence.

"You do need rest, Cettie. I don't think you should go back to your dormitory. Not without an escort, and it wouldn't be proper if . . . well, now I'm tongue-tied." He sighed. "I think you should rest here, in the hospital, for now. I heard that Captain Hallstrom rounded up some cadets to hunt for the intruder."

"I'll be fine in here," Cettie said, stifling a yawn. "You should get some rest yourself."

Adam shrugged. "I may join in the hunt," he said. "A doctor is used to being deprived of sleep. And I don't think I'll rest very well until we've found the man who hurt you."

It was not easy finding rest in a hospital, and Cettie lay awake for a long while, seeing in her mind the attacker's face—his dark stringy hair, his cruel expression. Eventually, despite the light and the constant low buzz of noise in the hospital, she fell into a fitful sleep.

She awoke sporadically, feeling sluggish and weak, until she roused to find her guardian sitting in the chair by the window, observing her. At first she thought it was a figment of a dream, but when she lifted her head, he smiled, and she instantly came up the rest of the way.

"Father!" she gasped and flung herself at him as he stood from the chair. He held her, gently stroking her hair.

"Having adventures, are we?" he asked in a tender way. He looked down at her and then cupped her face in his hands and kissed her forehead. "I'm so relieved you are safe."

"The Aldermaston?" Cettie asked worriedly.

"Still unconscious. He lost a great deal of blood. What has surprised us all is that he *could* be shot. The pilot as well. Both were mastons."

Cettie nodded. "I've been wondering that myself. In my Ministry of War classes, they teach that officers cannot be shot down. One of the Mysteries, I know, and one only revealed to students of War. I wasn't sure if the Aldermaston would share that immunity, but I did wonder."

"The Aldermaston should have been protected from such a wound. Do you recall when I shot Lieutenant Staunton with an arquebus after he betrayed us? It did not kill him or even injure him overly much. What happened to Mr. Neal and the Aldermaston was entirely different. Adam said the pistol caused a plume of smoke and belched flame. That is not something I am familiar with, and I served in the Ministry of War for many years. No, what attacked you last night was something new. Something rogue."

"How long have you been here?" she asked him. "Judging by the light, is it noon?"

"It is," he answered. "I've been here an hour or so. I didn't want to wake you. Adam said you didn't sleep last night."

"I'm glad you're here. Did they find the man?"

He shook his head no. "Not yet. The Ministry of War has issued orders, however, and a full investigation is underway. There are people searching your dwelling as we speak. The prince regent and Sera only arrived this morning to Lockhaven. The privy council has grave concerns that the intended victim was supposed to be *her*. Trust me, my dear, this incident is being treated with the utmost seriousness." He sighed. "I wish Captain Hallstrom hadn't sent cadets into the woods surrounding the abbey. They aren't adequately trained, and I'm afraid they've made a mess of things. They meant well, anyway."

"Did they find the man's tracks?" Cettie asked.

"They did. The attacker beat a hasty retreat. Unfortunately, the trail has been trampled by now. It led to shore on the east side and then vanished. He probably had a zephyr hovering there, waiting to take him away. If it came in at night, it wouldn't have been seen."

Cettie shook her head. "But the man first appeared when Minister Welles came to see Sera. What if he works for the Ministry of War? Asking them to investigate this could make it only too easy for them to disguise the evidence."

Fitzroy looked at her in concern. He put his hand on hers. "He is a politician, Cettie. I'm not ignorant of that. But let us reason this through. An attacker shot and nearly killed an Aldermaston. He killed the man's pilot. This is outright murder we are talking about. No politician would risk being so blatant. Minister Welles was startled to hear the news. He took prompt and decisive action as if reacting to a crisis he was hearing about for the first time. I've observed men under pressure before. He acted exactly as I would have in the same situation. If this man was seeking Sera Fitzempress . . ."

"He wasn't," Cettie said in a low voice. "He came for me."

Fitzroy's brow furrowed with consternation. "What do you mean?" he said gravely.

"He said he had no name, but to call him *kishion*. Have you heard that word before, Father?" she asked him.

His eyes widened with shock.

CHAPTER TWELVE

THE FIRST EMPRESS

"The look in your eyes worries me, Father," Cettie continued, her heart sick. "I can see that you have. Please tell me. My attacker claimed to be my real father. He came for me, not for Sera, to take me away before I could take the Test. He said it was a heresy."

"A heresy?" Fitzroy exclaimed with alarm. She watched his hands go behind his back, where he began to wring them as he started pacing. "The situation is far more grave than I realized. You never heard the word 'kishion' before last night? Never in the Fells?"

"Never," Cettie answered. "He said he didn't have a name anymore. As if it had been robbed from him."

Fitzroy's frown went deep, as did the furrows in his brow. "I'm perplexed. Does this mean that Mr. Pratt is not your true father? That the records and evidence my advocates have assembled these last years were all collected in vain? The truth will out, as I've said. But this one seems to be buried under layers of deception. Describe the man, if you please."

"I will try. He had a dark countenance. A look of distrust and anger . . . maybe I should call it resentment. His hair was black, darker than mine, and he was very strong. He was disguised as a merchant.

And he had a quiet step. There was a scar on his face here," she added, running her finger down her own cheek.

"Thank you," Fitzroy said. "That is sufficient. I will give your description to the captain in charge of the hunt and encourage him to use caution. The man who assaulted you is very dangerous. I thought all the kishion had been eradicated long ago. It is important that he be captured, and, if possible, we must determine where he was trained."

"Why have I not heard of them before?" Cettie asked.

"Very few know of their existence, and it is by design. Curiosity can bring untold mischief. There was a time, long ago, when those who sought personal power enlisted the aid of unscrupulous servants to achieve their ends. The men in this order are trained to know the vulnerable parts of the body. They are adept at using poisons and disguises. They infiltrate supposedly secure places to gain access to people of consequence." His eyes narrowed. "They kill without mercy. There are some ancient tomes, Cettie, that describe in rather obscure ways their methods. They would sooner quaff poison than reveal their secrets to the world. They have secret signs and passwords to distinguish one another. Any betrayal of the order is met with tortured death. To become one of them, it is said, a man must renounce family and allegiance. He must *murder* a close family member in secret. They are only loyal to their secret brotherhood after this. Thus even their *name* is anathema to them. They are called kishion. I do not know the origin of the term. What I do know is that they were stamped out and exterminated by order of the first empress, Maia Soliven, long ago."

Cettie's blood had turned cold. Was her birth father a murderer? The thought filled her with horror. Once again, she could not help but wonder if there was darkness in her blood, if her destiny was not in her own hands.

Fitzroy gave her a sympathetic look and came over and touched her shoulder. "None of this is your fault, Cettie. In the days before the first empire, the kishion were more common. They were used to hunt down and destroy the mastons, and certain ruthless kings would use them to increase their power. Princess Maia was assigned a kishion as a bodyguard, a protector. She saw firsthand what they could do. Her protector was eventually killed, and after she became empress, she ordered that the band be rounded up. It was a costly and perilous task. It took stalwart persistence to weed them out. Some she offered a pardon if they chose to forsake the order, but many of those who did were found dead, mangled and brutalized. But even stone will crumble under constant pressure from wind and rain, and because she was persistent, the location of their training school was eventually discovered. And destroyed. It was an awful war, and her husband was critically injured during the final attack, but the war was finally won. It became a crime punishable by death to knowingly support or engage in the hire of such men. Do you see why I am so alarmed by your news? If this man operates in secrecy among our society, then it is a sign that the corruption Empress Maia snuffed out has returned. Of course, he could also have come from another world to sow mischief among us. The court of Kingfountain, I know, has a similar breed of assassins, only they are called poisoners. Any civilization that supports such people is doomed to recurring civil war."

"I'm frightened, Father," Cettie said, coming off the bed. The possibility that she could be related to such a man made her question everything she'd thought she understood about herself.

"So am I, Cettie. So am I." He embraced her and held her close. "If the man's truly a kishion, I don't think one of the ministries is behind it. I cannot believe any of the ministers would stoop to such a thing. Or that they could convince someone to keep it secret."

"Maybe it's not one of the current ministers," Cettie answered. "Maybe it is someone who wishes to become one."

"A weed can thrive at the edge of a garden better than in the middle where all can see it. It would take someone with power or influence. Or this man could be a poisoner from Kingfountain sent to meddle in our affairs. He may not be your father at all. It's possible he merely said that to mislead you. As you know, the prince is looking for a bride. Someone could be deliberately sowing dissension between our civilizations."

He pulled back and looked into her face, his arms still wrapped comfortingly around her. "You mentioned the word 'heresy.' As you know, each world has its own version of the Mysteries. In Kingfountain, it is enshrined in the dogma of the Fountain. They are just as committed to their beliefs as we are to ours, even though they're similar in essence." He paused. "Cettie, the word 'heresy' comes from an ancient word, *haireisthai*, which means the inborn ability to choose. That means you get a choice regardless of your parentage. Only you can decide who you will be. This is what makes me wince at my eldest son's choices. Yet I cannot deprive him of his responsibility to choose for himself, as much as I've tried to teach him by example. You see, our parents may try to mold us after their desires. But your own *haireisthai*"—he tapped her forehead—"will always supersede it."

His words, which directly spoke to her greatest fears, brought her a measure of comfort. She hugged him again, pressing her cheek against his chest. He always knew what to say to make her feel better. Regardless of who had parented her, Fitzroy was the father she chose.

"I have one more bit of news for you," he said after a pause. "Anna has offered, of course, to be your companion now that Sera is in Lockhaven. I applaud her bravery, especially in light of what has happened, but there is someone else who would be a safer choice."

Cettie looked up at him. "Who? Raj Sarin?"

He shook his head no. "I have asked my wife's sister, Juliana Haughton, to come."

"Aunt Juliana?" Cettie said with surprise. The woman was one of the few female captains of a tempest.

"The very one," Fitzroy answered with a smile. "I see that you approve. She said she would be on her way immediately, fair winds or foul. You'll be staying on her tempest, which will be moored within the abbey grounds." He pinched her chin. "I take my responsibility to protect my family seriously. Raj Sarin taught her the Way, just as he has taught you. I will feel safer knowing you're with her."

Juliana was her favorite relation through the Fitzroys.

"I would like that very much," Cettie said. "It's been two years since we last saw her." Then she remembered something that she knew she should tell him. "Father? Mrs. Romrell told me that she knows of an open post to be a governess."

His eyes crinkled. "Did she? That was very thoughtful of her."

"I have been considering it. I would like to hear your opinion on the matter."

"Well, I'm gratified you would ask for my opinion. Not all of my children do."

Cettie smiled. "Of course I would. I trust your judgment. You want what is best for me. If you thought I shouldn't consider it further, I would refuse without asking questions."

He smiled again, pleased by her compliment. "What is best for us isn't always easy. You'd make an excellent governess. I would recommend you to any family Mrs. Romrell would suggest. She is a capable teacher, and I admire her. But I hope you know, Cettie," he added with that twinkle in his eye, "that I have far bigger plans for you."

After getting some rest, Cettie felt well enough to attend her final classes that day. While the bruises on her neck and arms were evident and sensitive, her muscles were sore in the way they always were after strenuous activity. It was difficult to concentrate in her classes because her mind kept wandering back to the startling events of the previous night. Fitzroy pledged to stay at Muirwood until Aunt Juliana arrived, and with the Aldermaston still gravely injured, she did feel the need for his calming influence. Anna and Phinia probably did too.

Word of her attack also brought unwanted attention to her. The usual teasing and spiteful comments had stopped, but she felt like everyone was staring at her injuries. A few girls asked if she was all right, and even some of the ones who had been cruel to her ventured to ask her about it. No doubt they wanted something to gossip about. She thanked them for their concern and left it at that, denying them the fuel they wanted.

After her last class, she wandered the grounds, enjoying the freedom of being out-of-doors. She had not seen Adam Creigh since morning, but she caught herself turning every time she glimpsed someone of his stature. He was likely working alongside Doctor Redd, trying to save the Aldermaston's life. Her mind jumped, and she imagined him carrying a leather satchel and a wide-brimmed hat as he hurried down the ramshackle streets of the Fells, hastening from one home to the next. There were so many sick, so many who would need him there. No doubt he'd return home to a small tenement each night, exhausted but satisfied at a hard day of work, pleased to have relieved some little suffering in the world. It made her want to smile, but it also made her sad, seeing him—alone—in that little vision in her mind.

Fitzroy had said he had plans for Cettie following the Test. He hadn't said what they were, however, and he'd asked her not to speculate because he didn't want to distract her from the final weeks of study. Could he have plans for Adam too? Something that would prevent him going to the Fells, going to a place he was determined to go? Cettie felt that wouldn't be fair. Adam *wanted* to go, and he should be allowed to pursue his dream. Yet if he did make his life there, she knew she would worry about him. Worry that one of the street gangs would attack him. Worry that a boy like Joses used to be would pick his pocket to steal money to feed himself—a well-intentioned theft that would nonetheless end in someone going hungry. Why was there so much misery in the world?

She gazed at a set of buildings and the gardeners working the shrubs, trying to *listen* with her eyes. She had always been adept at studying people, at understanding the subtle motives that drove them. Sometimes, she could even hear what they were thinking, whether those thoughts were directed at her or not. Cettie knew her powers were unique . . . they set her apart from the other students who attended the school with her. She'd been taught that some powers and especially an *affinity* for the Mysteries were inherited. What impact did her parents' blood have on her abilities? Would she ever know who they really were?

The truth will out, Fitzroy liked to say. But would knowing the truth make things any easier? Even if he was right about her ability to choose for herself, there was no denying that some hurtful truths ached to the core.

As her mind wandered into morose thoughts, she observed a sky ship coming from the direction of a great hill called the Tor. There was a path that led up to the summit, which boasted a stone tower, and she had climbed it with Sera on several occasions. The sky ship was large—a tempest . . . the very tempest they were anticipating. Immediately the dark thoughts began to dwindle in anticipation of seeing Aunt Juliana again.

If thoughts were a special kind of alchemy, she wanted to be sure she chose to foster the very best kind.

SERA

Some knowledge we only gain through much suffering. Some knowledge comes only after death. For three days and three nights, I passed in and out of the shadow of the next life. Each revival brought physical agony; each breach into the Beyond brought additional understanding.

The abbey itself is a symbol of the doorway to what awaits in the Beyond. Power immeasurable. Power transcendent. In the past it was believed that only those with the blood of ancient families could be worthy enough to handle it. But we came to learn this was not true. While an individual with the fortunate birthright of such a lineage can be taught the principles early on in life, the same ends can be achieved by anyone who has carefully guarded their thoughts and submitted to the same requirements. I have learned from the Beyond, from the Knowing itself, that our civilization will suffer for deliberately preventing those without lineage from learning its ways. The cholera morbus is such a punishment. And it is only beginning.

—Thomas Abraham, Aldermaston of Muirwood Abbey

CHAPTER THIRTEEN

THREAT

The tempest was called the *Royal Gale*, and as it began its descent to the floating city of Lockhaven, Sera gazed down in awe. Though she had spent most of her life living in the floating collection of manors held in the sky by the powers of the Mysteries, she'd rarely seen it from this vantage point. The fog that usually masked the City beneath was gone, and the sprawling metropolis extended for miles beyond the portion covered by Lockhaven's immense shadow. There were waterfalls that plunged from gardens and secret streams and descended as mist onto the denizens below. She could not imagine what it would feel like to live beneath such a massive structure, one that blotted out light half the day and turned the alleys and byways into a sprawling den of tenements and moldering factories. There were well-to-do estates down below, to be sure, and their turrets and parapets often broke through the fog that usually reigned supreme. Did they live with the oppressive fear that the power holding up Lockhaven would someday fail and the floating citadels would come crashing down? Surely they must. Yet shacks and homes and mansions had all been built there, and lotteries were held for those living below, to grant access to the manors above in the thousands of positions available to the ambitious and the brave.

Her mother was in her stateroom, so when Sera heard the footsteps coming up behind her, she thought it was an officer come to warn her about leaning too far over the railing of the tempest. What would it feel like to fall from such a height? She was always fancying such strange things. Well, let him scold her if he wished. She was a Fitzempress and would not be told what to do.

"Careful, Seraphin," said her father, startling her. "There is no one who could catch you from such a fall."

His words evoked memories of her childhood. Once, she'd almost fallen from her favorite lookout tree. She could almost hear the cracking sound of the branch before it gave way . . . her father had rushed forward and saved her. He'd been worried and solicitous. But the look in his eyes at the moment couldn't be more different. It indicated that he was, perhaps, resisting an urge to end their rivalry then and there in an "accident." What had he become?

She backed away from the railing, feeling part of her soul shudder. "I'm not a child anymore, Father."

She saw the subtle flinch when she addressed him that way. Good. She looked back over the City, her eyes drawn to the tendrils of smoke rising from thousands of chimneys. The sky was a crisp blue, and nary a cloud marred the expanse.

"Your mother and I have spoken and feel it would be best if you remained with her during your stay in Lockhaven," her father said. His voice was measured, guarded.

She had already decided as much herself, of course. Her father did not consider her his true daughter, and she didn't trust him with her safety. "That is acceptable."

"I have made arrangements for a companion for you," he went on. She frowned, feeling resentment and rebelliousness flare up inside her. No doubt he'd hired someone to spy on her.

"I do not need one," she quickly countered.

"If you wish. Then I will send Baroness Hugilde away . . . again."

"What? No!" She turned to face him and realized that he had out-maneuvered her. A subtle, mocking smile turned up his mouth. He arched his eyebrows at her. "I mean, thank you for sending for her. I haven't seen sweet Hugilde in years."

"I thought it would please you. If you do end up going to the court at Kingfountain, I thought it might be more agreeable to you to bring a familiar companion."

She swallowed her pride. This game they were playing was under-way, she reminded herself, and those she knew and loved would suffer if she did not win. Well, he had attempted to outflank her before and had failed. She would not allow him to get the best of her this time either.

"When does the delegation from Kingfountain arrive?" she asked, trying to shift their interactions to business matters.

"Soon. As I'm sure Mr. Durrant explained, the delegation will be looking for suitable maidens. The selection process for the queen will take several years, no doubt. There are certain laws and covenants—I won't bore you with the details—that require hostages—"

"Hostages?" Sera asked with alarm.

"That is a technical term," he explained with a tone of exasperation. "One cannot take someone between worlds without leaving another in their place. You know the concept of equilibrium, I assume, from your studies?"

"Yes, I do."

"Good. So if, for example, four girls are chosen from our court to attend theirs, then four of their maidens will remain here during the term of the covenant. It's a simple matter. You won't likely be chosen, Seraphin. I wouldn't get your hopes up." He said the last words with a derogatory sneer. He was trying to goad her.

"Who else has been chosen to come?"

"Lady Vextel's daughter. I think she is the oldest at eighteen. Then there is Lady Telephina, Lady Simprose, and Lady—"

"My lord!" the captain of the tempest shouted as he hurried up to them.

Father looked annoyed at the interruption. "What is it, Captain?"

Once he reached them, he pitched his voice low. Sera was close enough to hear everything. "There was an attack, last evening, at Muirwood Abbey. The Aldermaston has been shot and is seriously injured. His pilot was killed outright. It's believed the intended victim of the villain was Miss Fitzempress."

Sera's stomach lurched with dread and fear. "The Aldermaston is hurt?"

"Severely, ma'am. He may not survive the day. Word has come that a stranger was seen lurking in the village."

"Cettie saw him," Sera stammered, feeling her insides quailing. She had told her friend it was nothing to concern them. "By the Mysteries, what is this news you bring?"

"I was given word by the prime minister himself," said the captain to her father. "The privy council is awaiting your arrival to discuss the possible danger. I hate to think what disaster may have happened if we hadn't come to fetch her."

Father looked genuinely surprised by the news. Did that mean he was innocent of any involvement? He glanced at her and then nodded. "Hasten to court, Captain. This must be addressed at once. An Aldermaston! Who would dare such an outrage!"

"I don't know, Prince Regent. The Ministry of War sent sky ships to the abbey immediately. I heard even a hurricane has been summoned for support."

"This will not go unpunished. Get us to the landing yard of the privy council at once."

"Aye, my lord," said the captain, who saluted smartly and then turned away.

The look on her father's face showed that he, too, was reeling from the shock of the news. He turned to march away, and she thought she overheard him murmur under his breath, "He wouldn't have!"

The court palace was decorated with several paintings that dated back to the rule of Empress Maia. As Sera walked urgently down the marble-tiled corridor, paying little heed to her father and the servants sent to escort them, she glimpsed one that she remembered from her first meeting with the privy council years earlier. The painting was of the empress at her first privy council meeting. Sera had been fascinated by the image and had wished keenly that she could step into the painting hanging on the wall to observe the events portrayed in the image. What would it have been like? Maia had been the first female sovereign of Comoros, the one destined to rule over a massive empire.

The privy council chambers in Lockhaven were not as opulent as those portrayed in the picture, which had been located on the land far beneath the present one, down by the river. The two doormen outside the chamber stamped their staves and opened the doors for them. Father strode in ahead of her, his longer stride easily outstripping hers. The room was paneled in decorative wood with crown molding on every aperture. Several tall bronzed pillars stood along the walls. A host of dignitaries surrounded the long rectangular table centered in the middle of the room. Each had his or her own private secretary prepared to scrawl notes documenting the event. A huge overstuffed chair waited empty on a dais at the head of the table, and Father strode up to the chair and seated himself. All the others in the room were standing. She saw uniformed officers from the Ministry of War, representatives from Law in their fancy waistcoats and jackets. After looking for Fitzroy, she was surprised to see he wasn't there. The prime minister, identified by his green sash of office and black velvet cap, looked to be suffering from gout and hastily sat after her father did. The others began to sit as well.

Sera was pleased that many members of the privy council were women. Most were stately older women, many of them widows, who had vast experience in the dealings of the empire. By her rough guess, they composed a third of the council. From Mr. Durrant's reports, she knew their empathy for her had made a great deal of difference in her prospects.

"Miss Fitzempress, if you would take a seat over there," said the prime minister, gesturing to a smaller chair beside his. She saw some small pillows had been arranged at the foot of the chair, in case her feet wouldn't touch. She bit her lip and choked down the affront as she deliberately slid the pillows to the side with the edge of her foot before sitting down.

"Prime Minister," Father said angrily, "what more have you learned about this outrageous attack on the abbey?"

"Details are sparse presently, Prince Regent," he replied in his nasally voice. "We await word from Minister Fitzroy. His ward was injured during the attack."

Sera leaned forward, eyes blazing. Cettie was hurt?

"Is she all right, Prime Minister?" she blurted out.

"I don't know, ma'am," he answered, shaking his head. "She was your companion. Naturally you would fear for her well-being."

"I wish to know of her condition straightaway," Sera demanded.

"Of course. We are only too grateful that *you* were not injured. Thanks to the prince regent's foresight"—here he nodded his head in respect to her father—"you were brought here before the attack. No doubt this blackguard, whoever he was, intended to do you harm. His goal may have simply been to prevent you from being considered for the throne."

It made Sera sick to her stomach to think that the man had been watching her dwelling for several days. That she had so flippantly ignored the warnings. Her father's muttered comment on the deck of the tempest had stayed with her—it was like a splinter that chafed and bothered her. Did he know the attacker?

"What is being done?" Father demanded.

"The Ministry of War was authorized to dispatch investigators to—"

"I know this already. What *else* has been done? Has the royal surgeon been sent?"

The prime minister looked uneasy. "Doctor Redd at the abbey . . ."

"Is quite capable. But send the best to the abbey. The very best. In the meantime, what is the Ministry of Thought doing to replace the Aldermaston?"

Another man at the table stood. He had snow-white hair and a matching goatee. "No replacement is being contemplated, Prince Regent. The extent of Thomas's injuries is still unknown."

"But there are so many students who need to take the Test," Father said. "Including my own . . . including Miss Fitzempress. This must be seen to at once. Cannot another Aldermaston from another abbey be sent for in his place? See to it, sir. And what of the Ministry of Law? Someone must have procured a sky ship to reach the abbey. It is surrounded by water. I want an investigation started immediately to discern how the attacker made it to Muirwood. Have your advocates research all possible short-term and long-term deeds."

"But that could take months, Prince Regent!" complained Lord Halifax, the Minister of Law.

Father shot him a withering look, and he promptly went quiet. A hush fell over the room.

Her father looked very regal in the chair, despite his ill health. He projected an aura of decisiveness and confidence that made her feel very young. "I will not have it said, ladies and gentlemen, that I took this threat on Seraphin's life lightly. That I dismissed it as of no worth. An Aldermaston lies dying. This assault must be treated with the greatest seriousness and discretion. If the investigation does not yield results, then it is likely—if not probable—that this action emanated from among our ranks."

At that moment not a sound could be heard in the room. A queer, sick feeling bloomed in Sera's gut.

"If so, we will still discover who did it and why. And a house will fall because of it."

Sera was impressed by her father's bold actions, his leadership. As she looked around the room, she could see that same look in the eyes of many members of the privy council. What had she said or done to contribute? What suggestions had she to give?

Nothing.

CHAPTER FOURTEEN
The Tyranny of the Past

The privy council had been kind and courteous to Sera. Unfailingly polite. But when she left the council room with the charge to return the next day and appear before them, Sera already felt like a failure. She was frustrated with herself for not speaking up more and worried that her poor performance—and her ready accessions to her father—would jeopardize her future.

Her mother was leasing a manor house in Lockhaven called Castlebury, and they were brought there by zephyr immediately following the meeting. Because her parents were estranged, the privy council subsidized the rent on the Castlebury manor out of the allowance the prince regent was given. Mother had her own inheritance as well, which Mr. Durrant had managed to apportion, and so when Sera arrived, she found a beautifully appointed residence. It was on a street with thirteen other homes, which shared a common landing area. As Sera walked into the manor and observed the servants busily at work, she felt herself a stranger and longed for the simple dormitory at Vicar's Close.

Mr. Durrant was pacing the foyer energetically as he awaited their arrival. The moment she entered, he walked up to her with a worried look. But she gazed around him and saw Hugilde waiting with the keeper of the house. Sera practically squealed and rushed past Mr. Durrant. Her former governess had aged quite a bit over the last four years. She had more wrinkles and was gaunter than before.

"Hugilde, sweet Hugilde!" Sera gushed, hugging her and kissing her. Her cheek smelled of peppermint.

"There's my little Sera," Hugilde said with tears in her voice. "My, how you've grown!"

"I've not grown at all," Sera said, pulling back and wiping her eyes with the back of her hand.

"But you have. Yes, you have. What a beautiful young woman you've become."

Sera was conscious that her mother was watching them, but she could not restrain her effusiveness. Hugilde had been more of a mother to Sera than anyone else. She had put up with Sera's tantrums and stubbornness, always, and while her governess had become exasperated with her at times, there had never been any doubt as to her feelings.

"I want to speak with you. To hear about where you've been, what you've been doing. Can you wait for me in my rooms, Hugilde?"

"Of course, Miss Fitzempress," the older woman replied lovingly.

"Yes," Mr. Durrant interrupted. "You can save the gushing for later. Sera, we need to talk. And not in the hall in front of the servants. Madame, may we retire to your library?"

"Of course, Mr. Durrant," said Sera's mother.

Sera gave Mr. Durrant an arch look. "I haven't seen her in four years, Mr. Durrant." She squeezed Hugilde's hands and kissed them. "I need not make excuses to you."

"Yes, Sera. Nor do I wish to hear them. I am relieved to see you are well. The rumors coming from the abbey are truly disturbing. If we may retire?" He gestured her toward a hallway door.

"I will come presently," Sera promised, giving Hugilde another hug. Then she followed her mother and Mr. Durrant into the study. A tray of fruit had been arrayed on a nearby table, and Sera suddenly realized she was famished. The melons were cubed, and she bypassed the little silver pincers and began plucking fruit from the tray.

"Where are your manners, Seraphin?" Mother scolded.

"It's all right, madame, we are in private company," Mr. Durrant said. "When word came of the attack at Muirwood, I feared the worst and cursed myself for not insisting more strongly that you leave with me. If I had realized the extent of the danger, I would have forcibly removed you."

Sera was touched by the look of alarm and worry on his face. Or perhaps he was merely reacting to the fact that his fortunes were tied to her success. He had made enemies supporting her cause.

"As you can see, I am uninjured," Sera answered. "I'm more worried about the Aldermaston. He's gravely hurt, and his pilot was shot and killed."

"His pilot?" Mr. Durrant asked with astonishment. "But he's a maston. How could that be?"

"No one knows. Lord Fitzroy is investigating the matter. The Ministry of War has sent in people as well. It is still too early to be certain of anything."

Mr. Durrant still looked agitated. "And you went straight to the privy council upon your arrival? How did that fare?"

"I would like to know that as well," said her mother, who hadn't been allowed in that meeting. "Your father looked smug afterward."

Mr. Durrant turned to Sera with a concerned look. "That does not bode well."

"Indeed, and it didn't go well," Sera said, feeling anxiety spread in her chest like a disease. "I was . . . too subdued. The news caught us all by surprise. I was so stunned I didn't know what to say. Father came across as decisive and concerned."

"Did he seem surprised by the news? This might have been set up by the Ministry of War."

"I don't think so, but I cannot be certain. By the end of the council meeting, they dismissed me and said they would summon me tomorrow for an interview. I was almost an afterthought."

"You should have spoken up!" her mother said worriedly.

"Please, madame!" Mr. Durrant intervened, holding up his hand. "I think Sera is fully conscious of any mistakes she may have made. It does no good to litigate evidence in a case already determined. Of course your father handled the surprise better. He may or may not have been previously informed. And he has certainly gained experience in the role of leadership over the last four years. The timing of the events is entirely too suspicious however."

"I agree," Sera said. "The man who attacked came around the same time as the ship from the Ministry of War. And if they are conducting the investigation on the attack *and* are the ones behind it, then we won't see an honest result."

Mr. Durrant pressed his fingers together as he paced. He was deep in thought. "There are multiple strategies at play here, Sera. It is critical to unravel them quickly. First, your grandfather died, likely of natural causes, and his death has set in motion irrevocable events. A new emperor must be chosen. Because your grandfather did not—nay *could* not—name an heir, it is up to the privy council to decide. Of the possible Fitzempress heirs, you and your father are unequivocally the most suitable, due to your uncles' mismanagement of their funds. One of them could be behind this, trying to discredit the both of you and claim the rewards that will come with the office. Their creditors, surely, would wish this. Second, we soon receive a delegation from the court of Kingfountain. A match between our two worlds would be unpopular, but it may improve our relations with that world and put an end to the hostilities between our peoples. There are undoubtedly some factions in Kingfountain that would not want this to come to pass. They may also be behind it."

"Do not forget my husband's ambition," Mother said flatly, her eyes like daggers. "He covets the throne. He feels entitled to it, I assure you of that, Mr. Durrant."

"His ambition is naked for all to see," Mr. Durrant scoffed. "And the privy council knows it. Which is what gives Sera the advantage in this case. There is a reason that the rights of inheritance no longer pass directly from the father to the eldest child. Sometimes they are the least qualified to assume the burdens of state. Your father's brothers stand testament to the wisdom of this policy. History is replete with examples of the misery that can follow the rule of an evil man or woman. Power does corrupt, that much is blatant. No, Sera, do not fret over your performance today. You will not be judged by a single incident. The privy council is wise on the whole. They want to choose someone who will protect and preserve the empire."

"But does that mean, Mr. Durrant," Sera asked, "that they would also want to preserve the social hierarchy? You know I intend to make certain changes."

"Of course!" Mr. Durrant beamed. "And I have ever been your most ardent admirer. These past years, I have done my part to curry favor with Lord Welles. I've already told you how influential you may be to his success. I've also done whatever I can to inform the people of your intended policies. Believe me, you are well liked down in the City. And there is great suffering. The cholera morbus is a terrible blight. No one is safe from it. Why, just last week it struck another manor here in Lockhaven. The entire household was banished to the City, and those who took them there have been refused permission to return until they can prove they are not suffering from the contagion. Your father has had no success in solving this epidemic."

"Surely it's not his fault," Sera objected.

Mr. Durrant shrugged. "The people don't care whose fault it is. He is a ruler, and so he is blamed."

"And so would I be," Sera said with exasperation, "were I in charge. It's irrational, Mr. Durrant."

"People are irrational," he countered. "They make decisions every day that are against their own self-interest. And let's not forget the people of Kingfountain and their water rites! How quick they are to consider *us* a threat to *their* way of life. We cannot change that aspect of humanity. But I believe, and I know that you do too, that if we spend some energy alleviating the suffering of the poor here, if we can forge a season of peace with our enemies, then you will go down in history as one of the most benevolent monarchs of all time! The laws of the empire favor the wealthy minority. They were established to ensure the hierarchy."

"It was established with good cause," Mother said in a warning tone. "You toy with it, Mr. Durrant, at the peril of us all. Change must be made wisely or not at all."

Sera clasped her hands and tapped her lips with her joined forefingers. "I have studied history in Muirwood, Mother," she said, giving her a sharp look. "You speak of the revolts. The rebellions. The wars with other worlds."

Her mother nodded firmly. "Kingfountain wants to rule us and liberate our people from our authority. And our own poor would probably celebrate the savages. They are both different than us."

Sera shook her head no emphatically. "They are *no* different than us, Mother. Consider how our own decisions have brought this upon us . . . how badly we have dishonored Empress Maia's vision. She wished to give all of her people the opportunity to study and learn the Mysteries. The schools were founded for that very reason, but in the end, we took that right away from them. They built her seat of power in the sky to keep it safe from invaders; we've imitated that with Lockhaven to separate ourselves from our own poor."

"Well said, Miss Fitzempress." Mr. Durrant clasped his hands behind his back. "A speech like that in the privy council tomorrow will find favor with many, I assure you. There will be some who will be offended by it, but it will make an impression. Each ministry has struggled with the others for supremacy. When business flourishes, the Ministry of Law blooms. When there is an invention, the Ministry of Wind excels. But the interplay between the two always leads to conflict . . . to disruption. And then the Ministry of War takes power. And after War? The Ministry of Thought comes to achieve the promise of peace. It's like the four seasons, only they do not rotate every year. These seasons can last for years. Decades even. It is past time for a season of change. A time to break the molds. A time to end the corruption. Only the younger generation can achieve this." Here he gave her a cunning look. "Because they alone cannot see something difficult as impossible. They've not been jaded by the failures of the past." He gave a sidelong look to her mother. "Do not let anyone force you to marry, Sera. You must be different. You must seize what opportunities you can. The rules do not apply to you. You are the maker of them!"

Sera felt a part of her buzzing inside. Mr. Durrant's words had reawakened her self-confidence. Her courage to defy the odds and claim her birthright.

"You swell her head with all your pretty talk, Mr. Durrant," Mother said warily.

"I trust her enough to take that risk," he replied evenly.

＝

When she finally went to her rooms after the long conversation with her mother and Mr. Durrant, Sera felt like resting. But she was too eager to see Hugilde, whom she found doing needlework on the small sofa. In an instant, it felt like she had shed years and was once again a little girl seeking wisdom from her governess.

Hugilde looked up from her work. "There you are. Quiet as a mouse. I almost didn't hear the door open."

"Are you tired, Hugilde? Do you need to rest?"

"What? Is Sera concerned about an older woman's aches and pains? You have changed."

Sera shrugged. "I'm not as selfish as I used to be. It's so good to see you, Hugilde. How I've missed you. You went back to Hautland, didn't you?"

"Yes, to my own people," she answered, setting the needlework aside. She rose and came to Sera and took her hands. "It was not easy finding work after your father dismissed me. He forbade me to contact you. His advocate sent for me, saying that I might be able to regain approval in the eyes of the prince regent if I came to serve you again." She lowered her lashes. "In another realm."

Sera felt a sickly feeling in her stomach. "Another realm?"

Hugilde shuddered. "I have been living very humbly, Sera. Last winter I feared I might die of cold." She looked into Sera's eyes. "Your father's advocate offered to pay me a sizable sum if I would persuade you to seek the prince's affections. He seeks to use me to manipulate you. I agreed to come, agreed to do his wishes. But only so I could warn you. Your father seeks your downfall. That man is determined to ruin you."

CHAPTER FIFTEEN

MINISTRY SECRETS

Lord Prentice, the prime minister, met Sera outside the privy council chamber the following day. A large block-shaped man with an expressive face and prominent forehead, he had light brown hair that had receded far back on his scalp but still grew long at his ears and the nape of his neck. He had a cunning look that immediately put Sera on her guard. She had come early and worn her violet-and-silver frock. Hugilde had braided her hair in a regal style and had applied some subtle embellishment to her lips and cheeks, which made her look older than sixteen.

"You are early, Miss Fitzempress," Lord Prentice said. "I was told you'd just arrived."

"Early is on time," Sera answered with a nod. "I'm ready to see the council."

"Not all the members have assembled yet," he answered. "Would you walk with me around the corridor for a turn? There is something I would like to show you before the meeting starts."

"Oh, and what would that be?"

"Something you will be intrigued to see, my dear. You have been at Muirwood for nearly four years, so you have learned that each estate contains a room that controls all of the Leerings throughout the place. I would like to show you this one."

He was right. Sera was intrigued. But there was a reason he had offered to do this. This man had been selected by her father over Lord Fitzroy, which had opened the position of Minister of Wind to Cettie's guardian. Sera was certain that Prentice supported her father. So why would he attempt to do her a favor? She would have to be on her guard, but she wanted to see what he was about.

"Thank you, Lord Prentice. Shall we see it now, then?"

"Of course. Follow me."

He escorted her down the corridor and around the bend. It would be easy to conceal a door since there were so many throughout the palace, each with a little bronze plaque with a number etched into it. He brought her to the one marked 117.

"Curious that there is no one guarding it," Sera said as he fished in his vest pocket for the key.

He gave her a knowing smile. "The guardians are *behind* the door," he said. "Otherwise it would be too obvious that this room is important. Ah, here we are." He produced the key, which was an iron key of ancient make, the metal mottled with rust stains. Rather than insert it in the lock, he merely held it near the handle. She felt a throb, and then the door opened of its own accord.

As she entered, she saw two men in uniform, their rank symbols showing one to be a lieutenant and the other to be a captain.

"Prime Minister," both men said in unison, bowing stiffly.

"Good afternoon, gentlemen," he answered, slipping the key back into his pocket. There were no couches or other furniture in the room, just the two men and a very large mirror at the end of a short pathway. She sensed a Leering embedded into the frame. It probed her thoughts, giving her feelings of disquiet for a moment, but the anxiety was quickly followed by a sense of calm.

"This way, Miss Fitzempress," he said, gesturing to the mirror.

As Sera approached it with curiosity, she felt a strangeness about the room. It was akin to the feelings she had when passing the abbey itself at Muirwood. There were definitely Leerings here, ones she could not see, beyond the mirror.

The prime minister waved his hand in front of the mirror. Again she felt a pulse against her mind. The glass of the mirror shimmered and disappeared, exposing a corridor lit by Leerings. He stepped inside the frame, and Sera followed. There was no dust in the corridor. Her shoes tapped against the stone tiles and echoed down the hall. As she walked, she felt the mirror re-form behind them. Her heart leaped with the sensation, and she looked back and saw that the mirror exposed the two soldiers in the room. But she had a feeling that they could no longer see her.

"It is a solemn privilege to guard this room," Prentice told her in a low voice. "There must always be two guardians. No man is ever left alone. They rotate the watch every few hours and assign new soldiers to the duty routinely to keep anyone from becoming too familiar. It is a strict precaution."

"Against what?" Sera asked. The echo of her voice sounded strange in her ears.

"You will see." When they reached the end of the hall, there was a stone door blocking the way. A man's scarred face was carved into the door, the eyes blank, the hair pointed like quills. It was a fearsome countenance.

"This Leering was carved in the likeness of the first empress's bodyguard," Prentice said. She felt the pulse of a command emanate from him, and then the stone door slid open.

Behind the door was an atrium. A brilliant glow emanated from the ceiling. At first Sera thought it was open to the sunlight, but she realized that the rectangular opening was lit by a powerful Light Leering that only resembled daylight. Stone pillars surrounded a shallow pool of still water, and a couch sat near two of the pillars. The water was clean and translucent, and she could see the black and white marble tiles that lay beneath it. Across from the couch stood a round pillar, about waist height, supporting a Leering carved in the likeness of a familiar woman. Her expression was peaceful, her eyes slightly downcast.

"Empress Maia," whispered the prime minister in a reverent tone.

Colorful tapestries decorated the walls, full of images celebrating the past, but the focal point of the room was undeniably the pillar with the Leering on it. Sera felt a strange tugging sensation at her heart.

The prime minister walked around the circuit of the room and then paused by the pedestal. "You understand, no doubt, the importance of keys and what they symbolize?"

Sera knew the answer well enough. "They are symbols of trust and the delegation of authority."

"Precisely, Your Highness." There was something odd in his voice. She was still on her guard. It was just the two of them, and she felt a twinge of vulnerability. Perhaps it had not been wise to follow him here. "Power is derived from the Mysteries. You will understand this better after you have taken the abbey's Test, but some power is hereditary. Some is earned. Yours, for example, is the hereditary kind. You have the *right* to rule because of the lineage of your ancestors. I do not. My power, as prime minister, comes from delegation of authority. Once I am removed from office, my key will be given to another, and I will never be allowed to enter this room again. I will not miss it, for it is a heavy responsibility. A burden, truly. Those who serve grow weary in the service."

He didn't sound weary at all.

"What does this one do?" she asked, nodding toward the Leering with the empress's face. "All Leerings do something."

"Empress Maia had a special gift. It was called the Gift of Invocation. She had a special affinity toward Leerings. To her, each one had its own chord. They were almost like music." He gave her a piercing look. "Do you hear the music that fills this room, Seraphin?" He gazed up at the illusion of the skylight.

Sera felt the power of the Mysteries in the room. But it did not strike her as music. It struck her on a more visceral level, one that made her slightly afraid, like one would feel in the presence of a lion or another savage animal.

She wasn't about to answer his question. "Why did you bring me here, Prime Minister?"

He gave her a shrewd look.

"Empress Maia was warned by her grandmother, a harbinger, that a foreign power would attempt to invade her empire by sea. She built Lockhaven to master the air. But being so high above the City, she feared losing touch with the common people and their needs. She maintained a spy network, of course, as most rulers do. But she did not wish to rely on their reports alone. The lifeblood of any civilization is its water. People need to drink, to bathe, to grow food, to wash. Water is paramount. Within the City below, there are dozens of fountains that provide fresh drinking water through Leerings. The people are ignorant of how this water comes to them, of course, but the fountains were a gift from the empress. The people had their water, and the empress could watch over them from this room. Here, put your hand on the stone, and I will show you. You will see what your father has often seen. Are you brave enough to face it?"

So it was a test of her courage, was it? What grisly scene might unfold before her? What horrors did he intend to show her?

"Thank you, Lord Prentice. I would be glad to see my subjects." She steeled her resolve, stepped forward, and put her hand on the stone.

At first, she felt nothing but the smooth texture of the rock on her skin. The air smelled damp. Then the prime minister joined his hand to the Leering and invoked it. She felt the power surge inside of her, and then the waters of the pool began to ripple. As she watched in fascination, the ripples calmed, and the pool no longer reflected the light beating down on it from above. It showed her a scene from one of the many fountain squares in the City below. People had gathered around the fountain—washerwomen scrubbing laundry, some carrying pitchers to tote water back to their homes. The square down below was grimy and noisy. She could hear the nicker of horses and the clatter of wagon wheels on cobblestones. She heard arguing and some women shouting at each other in anger. All her senses fired—in addition to seeing the scene, she could hear it and smell it as surely as if she were standing in their midst.

"This is happening right now," Lord Prentice said. "See how they scold and yell at one another? Do you see the urchin, that little girl, reaching her grubby hand into the filthy water to steal a drink? See the washerwomen. Listen to them reproach her." Sera heard it even as it happened. "Even though they've dirtied the water, they still prize it."

Sera's heart panged as she watched one of the washerwomen seize the little girl and cuff her on the ear and yell at her to go away.

"Sometimes, like during the Whitsunday festival," he continued, "people climb into the fountains and dance in them with their muddied shoes. They *profane* what gives them life. But of course, people will profane anything when they are drunk, and the people in the tenements drink constantly. They do it because they suffer, and they believe inebriation will quiet the ache in their hearts. But that ache is caused by the debauchery of their lives. You may as well prick a finger with a sharp needle and beg it not to bleed. They cannot see the true cause of their suffering. No, they blame it on us. And those in Kingfountain consider these abominations an utter sacrilege."

"That's not true," Sera answered, her feelings becoming more and more riled as she watched the village square. She spoke her words vehemently. "They are oppressed. And *we* are their oppressors."

"I agree with you," he answered, which startled her. "But not in the way you are thinking. We oppress them because we show them there is a higher way to live. They want what we have. But they don't want to get it the way we have gotten it. They'd like it to be given to them."

"Some do," Sera countered, thinking of Cettie.

"Of course," he said placatingly. She could hear the condescension in his voice. "There will always be exceptions . . . like your *friend*. But let me tell you the truth of things, Seraphin Fitzempress. It is a truth that even Empress Maia, who once shared your idealism, came to realize. Only a small portion of the people will ever reach their true potential in life. Because it is difficult. Because one must pursue excellence with unwearying vigilance. And that, my young friend, is beyond the capacity of most of humanity. People like to believe that success is merely the product of hard work. But it isn't. The secrets of the Mysteries aren't yielded to hard work alone. We are all tested by the Knowing, every single day. These people living in squalor are tested! Will they put another's interest above their own? Will they speak kindly instead of screaming? Will they let themselves be cheated without growing resentful? Do you see them, Miss Sera? Are they even capable of it?"

Sera's anger was blazing now. She stared at him across the pool. "Are they given the chance?"

"Of course!" he replied with scorn. "The Ministry of Thought is constantly teaching these principles. Yet, sadly, the teachings are almost universally ignored when it comes to the drudgery of daily life. They sit in a stupor on their holy days, anxious for the meetings to end so they can get back to work and earn a few pents. The men beat their wives, and the wives scold their husbands. They both *torture* their offspring in ways that would disgust you were I to share even a portion of what I've seen."

Cettie had begun life as an urchin, a poor and helpless soul mired in the drudgery of daily life in the Fells, and she had become . . . spectacular. No one at the abbey had more talent than she. Then there were plenty of other cases of the rich and powerful, of the mastons, squandering the gifts they'd been given. Stephen wished only to enjoy his wealth and prestige. Her father, the prince regent, wanted only power. And there was a very good chance someone in the highest echelons of the government had arranged for the attack at Muirwood. No, the prime minister was simplifying things. He wished for an easy answer, and so he'd found one that assuaged his guilt.

"You are wrong, Prime Minister," she said, her voice trembling with emotion.

"Am I? Have I not risen to the pinnacle of power because I have harnessed the power of Thought? I tell you, Miss Sera, that thoughts can be as contagious as diseases, like the cholera morbus. You wish to build a bridge down to the City to enlighten them. A noble cause to be sure, but most of the drudges who live down below lack all self-control. You, my dear, would bring the diseased to us to infect us with their spores. And by doing so, you would cause Lockhaven to come crashing down into the planet's tender crust."

The image shifted to another. This one was a windswept prairie full of boulders. No . . . the crumbled ruins of a fallen manor. The grassy valley was in the midst of a crater the size of a lake, and Sera gasped when she saw the devastation. If a single manor had caused so much damage, what would Lockhaven do if it ever fell?

"You are gazing from the eyes of a Leering set by the Ministry of Wind to study the healing process of the land," he explained dispassionately. "It took years before plants would start to grow again in that pit. The blow was so deep that jets of noxious gasses were expelled from the slits and seams in the earth. It is quite a fascinating study."

"Why are you showing me this?" Sera challenged, gazing back from the wreckage to his cunning eyes. "Do you hope to change my mind? To persuade me to abandon the very hope that drives someone to succeed? That would be hypocritical of you, Prime Minister."

He removed his hand from the Leering and stepped around the pool. He didn't alter his tone or try to sway her. "No, Seraphin. Because I wanted it to be very clear in *your* mind why I will oppose you."

CHAPTER SIXTEEN

SHIFTING LOYALTIES

If Lord Prentice had intended to rattle Sera with his declaration before the meeting, he had only succeeded in making her more determined to overthrow him. She was beleaguered by the privy council's questions, but she had done her best to project confidence and self-assurance. That her goals would, in the long term, benefit soldiers and statesmen, bankers and borrowers alike. They had wandered off the path Empress Maia had set out for them, but it was not too late to return to it. No doubt her mother and Mr. Durrant would be eager for her to recount the meeting, but she needed some quiet, some time to think. At least she would have a few moments to herself on the zephyr back to Castlebury.

She didn't notice that she had attracted an entourage of a dozen soldiers from the Ministry of War until she boarded the zephyr. When her zephyr rose into the air, four other zephyrs and a tempest, which loomed overhead, immediately surrounded it. She craned her neck, seeing the military insignia on the great ship's hull.

"We're getting an escort from now on, my lady!" the captain shouted down to her above the thrum of the wind. "Compliments of the Minister of War!"

The shadow of the tempest sky ship reminded her that her life was in very real danger. That there might be a faction inside their own government, or perhaps an external enemy, that did not want her to ascend to the throne. She had always wanted to experience something truly exciting, however, and couldn't deny that the risk brought a certain element of thrill.

When they arrived at the landing pad, the pilot's declaration from earlier was confirmed. A squad awaited her arrival on the street. Each soldier had an arquebus strapped to their shoulder, and they stood at fixed attention as her sky ship landed. The feeling of excitement intensified as she wondered if Will might be one of them. He *had* said he would soon be in Lockhaven. She leaned over the rail and examined their faces, but they were a good distance away, and each was wearing a hat as part of their uniform.

She descended the gangplank into the yard, and the two columns of soldiers snapped to attention and hoisted their weapons. Strolling confidently ahead as if this kind of reception were ordinary for her, Sera clasped her hands before her and discreetly examined each soldier's face. Some were young, but most were seasoned and experienced. Will was not among them. It would seem her speech had at least impressed Lord Welles.

When she reached the doorway, it was opened by her mother's butler, who greeted her and directed her to the study. Mr. Durrant, her mother, and Hugilde awaited her with cups of tea.

Mr. Durrant sized her up. "Well, she still *looks* regal. They did not flatten her like a pan of potato hash at least."

"Welcome back, Daughter," her mother said primly, but her eyes were eager for news.

"There are guards in front of the house," Sera said. "And we were given an escort from court."

"Yes," Mr. Durrant said flippantly. "I had to prove my credentials before they would let me into the house. It's a necessary inconvenience.

Lord Welles must prove he is taking his duty seriously. A captain is quartered inside and is interrogating the servants to ensure none of them poses a danger. This is serious business, Sera. But, back to the matters at hand. How did the privy council go?"

"I have a pounding headache if that's any indication," Sera answered. She saw a pitcher of water and poured herself a glass. Her throat was parched, and the water tasted delicious. Then she remembered the display from earlier that day. She remembered the little girl getting slapped.

"Council meetings can be arduous," he said, raising his eyebrows questioningly.

Sera set down the glass and turned to face them, more determined than ever. "It went as well as could be expected. Before the meeting started, Lord Prentice took me to the secret room that controls the Leerings of the court. He made it very clear to me that he opposed my ascension. In the council meeting, he kept harping on my youth and extreme inexperience. He made it clear that if the council chose me, he would demand there be a regency so that I could learn, more slowly, how to take on the reins of government."

Durrant started to massage his own temples, as if her headache had proved contagious. "Well, that was bold of him! What game is he playing, revealing the valuable Dominion cards in his hand so quickly? I thought Prentice was more clever than that. He must be overconfident that he can win the set."

"He lectured me," Sera went on, trying to bridle her temper and failing, "on my interest in helping the downtrodden. He all but confirmed that they are deliberately suppressed to prevent their lower thoughts and ways from 'infecting' our way of life. He warned that mixing with them would cause calamities that could rupture the earth. No one could ever accuse the prime minister of being too understated."

Her mother's expression indicated she agreed with the prime minister's outlook, something Sera had long suspected. It was the one thing her parents agreed upon. "But surely, Seraphin, it would be wise to proceed with caution . . ."

"Please, Mother," Sera said, cutting her off. "I'm not in the mood for a lecture. Consider the adage we're all taught in school. Isn't it true that we reap what we sow? Lord Prentice gave me a glimpse of the misery and suffering down in the City. And what I saw only confirms what Cettie has told me the last four years. Our problems impact their lives, just as theirs impact ours. How many have died from the cholera morbus within Lockhaven itself? It takes effort and labor to maintain a garden, even more so to maintain an empire, but we've let the garden run wild for years. Building a higher wall won't keep us safe, nor will it solve anything. I tried to explain this to the privy council. I know it will take time. Yes, the work will be arduous and difficult. But I am determined to see it done."

Her mother looked as angry and out of sorts as the prime minister had an hour ago. Mr. Durrant, on the other hand, looked pleased by her little speech.

"Well said, Sera. A bit idealistic and simplistic, but the argument is sturdy. I'm sure you studied the faces in the room. It's not important that you delivered a decent speech or upheld your high principles. Were you convincing? How many looked at you skeptically? Do you know their names? How can we, through careful coaxing, win more to your side? This is the art of politics, my dear. They all have concerns about having a young woman rule over them, and some of their concerns are bigger than others. You are much younger than Empress Maia was when she ascended to the throne, and she had already proved herself by managing a rebellion and then a war."

"I know the history, Mr. Durrant. And yes, I did try to see who was engaged and who was disinterested. I am tired, however, and I'd rather not spell it all out right now."

Mr. Durrant sighed and nodded. "Very well, Sera. Maybe I'll go to court and gauge the mood for myself. I'm confident Lord Fitzroy is still on your side. I am also inclined to believe that Lord Welles can be swayed. Personally, I think he detests your father. The Ministry of Law, which favors the status quo, will of course side with your father. That leaves the Ministry of Thought. The Aldermaston of Muirwood has always spoken highly of you, but he's not the minister. You are a chaste, exemplary young woman. If three ministers support you, I don't see how you can lose. The rest of the privy council will take their cues from them."

"But the prime minister is still powerful," Sera said.

Mr. Durrant shrugged. "Prentice is. Everyone knows that Fitzroy would have been a better choice. It was your father's resentment that prevented it. Many still see that as a flaw in your father's judgment. I have high hopes for you. Well, why don't you get some rest? I will return this evening for dinner to tell you what I've learned."

"Thank you, Mr. Durrant," Sera said with a sigh of relief. "I would appreciate that. We will see you tonight."

He bowed to her and offered a pleasant farewell to Sera's mother before departing.

Sera chafed her hands, wanting to be alone. "I'm going to my room, Mother."

"Sera," said her mother worriedly.

A sigh escaped Sera's mouth. "Yes?"

"I know you're tired. But please . . . there is some truth in what Lord Prentice said. You have not taken the Test yet. There are some Mysteries you still do not understand. If you do become empress, and I hope that you do, you will choose wise men and women to advise you. I would ask, I would hope, that you would permit *me* to serve on the privy council. I would be a devoted ally for you. You know you could depend on me. I hope you will consider it?"

Sera had thought about it, and, in truth, her mother was the last person she would consider for such a position of trust and responsibility.

She never spoke of the people, only of herself and the injustices done to her.

"I really must rest, Mother," Sera said, her voice falling.

Her mother's countenance fell when Sera didn't immediately give her the reassurance she desired. There came into her eyes a look of accusation, a look of grievance, a look of bitterness.

Without saying another word, Mother turned and left, the door striking shut harder than usual.

Sera's insides twisted with the conflict. Had she just made another enemy?

"Shall we go to your room, Sera?" Hugilde asked softly, coaxingly.

"I should enjoy that," Sera said. There were so many worries plaguing her that she hadn't taken time for her practice with the Leerings. The changes that had come so suddenly had nearly made her forget that she still had to pass the Test, or the privy council might not even consider her.

Arm in arm, she and Hugilde walked up to her room together. From the window, she could see the soldiers milling on the street below. Lest one of them should look up and see her, she took a seat in the chair by the mirror, out of sight from below. Hugilde started to unbraid her hair while she sat still, gazing at her reflection, seeing the little smudges on her face from the embellishments Hugilde had applied that morning. Had she pretended to be someone she wasn't today? Would the people even want someone like her, someone so unable to concentrate and remain focused?

The black thoughts invaded her mind, gaining traction because they were at least partially true. She knew she lacked self-discipline. She knew her mind wandered too much.

Hugilde finished the unbraiding, then took a brush and started to work the kinks out. Gazing at her reflection, Sera saw only the flaws. She knew she was pretty, but why was her nose shaped just so? Did her rounded cheeks make her look a little plump? Why couldn't she tame all these random, harmful thoughts? The first one seemed to have loosed a cascade that would drown her.

"You're so beautiful," Hugilde said admiringly as she worked the brush through Sera's hair. "I always thought you were a pretty child. But you are radiant now."

"You're saying that because you used to be my governess," Sera said, trying to dismiss the compliment. "Most people think I am only fourteen."

"No, Sera. I said it because it's true. Your biggest problem isn't that you're small in stature. I fear the prince from Kingfountain is going to *want* you to be his bride. And you'll start a war by turning him down!" She smiled with affection and squeezed Sera's shoulder.

"Some men will use any pretext at all to fight," Sera replied lightly, but she appreciated the compliment. It made her feel a little better.

"Something came for you today while you were gone," Hugilde said cautiously. She reached into her dress pocket and withdrew two sealed letters. "The first is from your friend at school. The second, well I . . . I didn't open it, Sera, even though I suspect who the author might be. You're sixteen now and nearly a woman. But I still want what is best for you. Did . . . Mr. Russell correspond with you while you were at Muirwood?"

Sera's heart lurched when she saw the letters in the mirror. Being away from Cettie for so long had caused an ache in her soul, like a festering bruise. Hearing news of her troubles had made her frantic for more information. But she also saw a little flush come to her cheeks at the mention of Will Russell. "No. Well, he did send me a letter recently, but it was the first I'd heard from him."

Hugilde handed both letters to her. "I know I should tell your mother it came. She is the mistress of this house. But that will be your choice to make. Not mine. You should be making your own choices now."

Sera's hair fell well past her shoulders, and some of the ends teased the paper. She recognized Will's handwriting from the letter

Commander Falking had delivered to her at Muirwood. You could tell a thing or two about a person by their style. Will was conscientious and confident.

She slid her fingernail under the hard wax, breaking the seal, and opened the paper. Her hands were starting to tremble, but she forced them to be still as she anxiously read on.

Dear Miss Fitzempress,

I am uncertain whether or not you received my previous letter. My apologies for being bold in this request, but I have heard that there may have been an attempt on your life at the abbey. It has vexed me to think that some blackguard tried to harm you. May the cholera take his life. I hope you are well and not terribly frightened. You were always so fearless when we were young. I've always admired you for that.

If you have not received my previous letter, then I will use this opportunity to repeat the information previously conveyed. I will be coming to the City in a fortnight or less to receive orders for my first duty. Your father has done all in his power to hinder my career, and I fear that I may be banished to the far reaches of the empire or even a more miserable post on another world. He has recently renewed his efforts to force me to hand over the letters. Although they are innocent, as you well know, I fear he may use them against you. If I can possibly improve my fate, and yours, by surrendering the letters to you instead, then I am willing to part with them. I will bring them with me and offer to give them to you in person, save one, which I hope to keep as a memento of our childhood friendship. Not that I seek to boast with my crewmates, of course! Never would I desire to do anything that would cause you grief, Miss Fitzempress.

My greatest regret is that I could not bid you good-bye when I was expelled from your father's house. I will meet you anywhere you choose if you can do me the honor of sending an invitation. Without one, it would prove impossible to get past the hosts that separate us. I will be stationed at the garrison at Whitehead in the City while I await orders. If I do not hear back from you, I will not think any less of you. Perhaps my letters have been intercepted by others and will not reach you. But I must at least try to see you again.

Your fellow conspirator of the hedge maze,
William Russell

CETTIE

It has been said that pain is a teacher. The lessons I have learned from clotting blood, black sutures, and near-constant pain have given me compassion for those who cannot escape the ghosts of hunger, disease, and fear. We must all of us confront our own ghosts and gain mastery over them. This is the essence of the Test. Some students cannot face their demons. And by not facing them, they remain trapped in ignorance and fear of the unknown. It is always easier to face our shortcomings sooner rather than later. If we do not, interest comes due, and it is a terrible foe.

I fear we have procured a lofty sum in our society today. A sum that will not be repaid without much loss of blood and treasure.

—Thomas Abraham, Aldermaston of Muirwood Abbey

CHAPTER SEVENTEEN

SERPENTINE

Juliana Haughton had always defied tradition and convention with a mischievous smile. While Fitzroy didn't fall sway to the dictates of fashion, his sister-in-law snubbed them outright. Lady Maren's younger sister wore breeches like a man, high leather boots, and a leather corset and had two daggers buckled to her belt, as well as a pistol strapped to her thigh. Her lips were always painted bright rouge, and while her curly hair was similar to her sister's, she'd been sailing the skies for so long that it was perpetually windblown and only half tamed by a black ribbon. Juliana was full of energy and life and had no intention of following normal womanly pursuits.

She had earned her way up the ranks of the crew by being smarter, a harder worker, and more cunning than any of the sailors she worked alongside. Of course, she also had the advantage of being trained by Raj Sarin, the Bhikhu, and had proven she didn't need to rely on the protection her relationship to a vice admiral naturally bestowed.

After her older brother disinherited the women in the family, Juliana went to live in a village beneath Gimmerton Sough with her sisters until Fitzroy and Lady Maren married. She had then lived in Fog Willows until she was of age to study. As a youth, she spent each summer away from school at Fitzroy's mine in Dolcoath, working hard to learn how to transport valuable commodities by sky ship. When she finished her training, Fitzroy had offered her a job piloting one of his ships, but she'd refused to take what she had not yet earned. She instead joined the shipping trades overseen by the Ministry of Law. Her ship, her source of income and freedom, had earned its name—*Serpentine*—delivering serpentine stone from a minefield on another world. She'd earned her captainship by navigating the *Serpentine* safely back to the empire after the original captain was killed in a skirmish.

Juliana had not gained her reputation or position by staying still, and after her arrival at Muirwood, Cettie spent her afternoons not wandering the grounds wistfully, but learning how to knife fight, how to negotiate with dishonest men, and—most excitingly—how to pilot the *Serpentine*. And she'd been encouraged not only to pilot it, but to test the ship to its limits.

"You're still too high, Cettie!" Juliana shouted above the roar of the wind as the tempest swept down a hillside within the marshland known as the Bearden Muir. "Closer to the trees!" The wind whipped Juliana's runaway hair, and the excited gleam in her eye showed how much she was enjoying the exercise.

Cettie gripped the spokes of the helm that connected her to the Leerings on board. She'd tied her hair back in the same fashion favored by Juliana so it wouldn't blow in her face. Some of the sailors were gripping the rails and casting nervous looks at one another.

"How close?" Cettie asked, feeling the power of the ship's Leerings thrumming inside her. They were a league or so away from the abbey and coming up fast on the Tor, the lopsided hill topped with a tower.

"You can see through the Leerings on the hull. Frighten me."

A sky ship, especially an unloaded tempest, could do some amazing, heart-pulsing stunts . . . and now she had permission, no orders, to indulge in them.

Sinking deep into herself, Cettie connected with the Leerings on board. She sensed the threads of magic that wove through the *Serpentine*'s timbers. Sensed the nails and rivets, the caulking, the planks and seams. She could see in almost every direction through the eyes of the Leerings on board. It was so easy to lose herself in the ship's magic . . .

She made the tempest lurch lower suddenly, causing grunts from the surprised crew. Gripping the helm spokes, she felt the power surge inside of her, raw and menacing as the vessel came so low it felt like they were sailing the treetops.

"That's it! That's better!" Juliana crooned.

Cettie felt the ripples in her stomach as she guided the vessel up and down, matching her rhythm to the natural rise and fall of the landscape. The rush of energy inside her was dizzying. They raced over pools of stagnant water, which rippled in the wake of their passing, and birds scattered to get out of the way. The *Serpentine* had yielded to her thoughts completely. In her mind, she controlled its functions, and it responded to her thoughts without hesitation.

Ahead, she could see the Tor rising in the distance and felt the uneasy urge to send the ship upward at once, but she knew Juliana wouldn't allow it. A sky ship would shatter against a mountainside. If she stopped the ship too quickly, the crew could be vaulted overboard. There were so many risks to manage, but the thrill of piloting the craft pulsed through her. A brazen smile rose to her face.

"Captain!" one of the sailors shouted worriedly. They trusted their captain. Cettie hadn't fully earned their respect yet.

She noticed the zephyr a moment after the sailor did. A huge oak tree in the midst of the woods blocked their current path, and a zephyr had just lifted above it.

"It's a ministry ship," Cettie said, feeling the thrum of magic coming from it.

"But we're bigger," Juliana said with a laugh. "Don't veer. He'll get out of the way."

Having two ships in proximity to each other was especially dangerous. An error in judgment could wreck both.

The zephyr was coming straight at them, and Cettie's heart pulsed with fear. She wanted to veer away. Why was the ministry ship acting so strangely?

"He will move," Juliana said. "Stay on course. He's testing you."

Cettie bit her lip and increased the ship's speed. The vibrations within the tempest shook her wrists and arms. Her legs felt weak from the stance she held. There was no time for her mind to wander, to worry about whether the kishion had commandeered a ministry ship. She trusted Juliana's instincts, which had been honed over years at the helm.

Obey orders.

The zephyr peeled away and began racing toward the Tor.

"Don't let him beat you there," Juliana said with a snarl. "Park us on top of the tower first."

A zephyr was more maneuverable and faster, so it was an unreasonable order. But Cettie was determined to follow it. Her heart was pounding in her chest as she tried to imagine how to perform the maneuver. She only had moments to decide on her strategy. The zephyr zipped upward toward the hilltop. Cettie could see the students climbing the steep stone steps to the summit. Some were pointing at the approaching sky ships, watching the race unfold before their eyes.

She increased the speed, and the thrumming started to rattle her teeth. The tempest convulsed at the order. If they'd been heavily laden with a shipment of stone, the cargo would have burst loose of its confinement. Sailors hunkered down, gripping the rails, and she could sense their fear. Juliana wasn't afraid. Nothing made that woman afraid. Some instinct also told her that this was a deliberately staged race. Juliana had arranged it to test her skills.

She had the speed she needed. The zephyr continued its ascent up the Tor, aiming straight for the tower. It began to slow so that it wouldn't overshoot the mark. In order to get there first, Cettie would need to uphold her current momentum yet still slow the ship enough to land precisely at the top of the tower—without knocking it over of course! In her mind, she imagined the maneuver from beginning to end. The answer came to her in a trice. The hull would need to pivot around so that the ship climbed the mountain rear first. Exposing the broad side of the tempest to the wind would help slow it down naturally while it gained altitude. She could picture it in her mind, an almost corkscrew ascent, each round dropping speed and bringing the ship higher until they were level with the tower.

It felt feasible. It wasn't overly dangerous, assuming the zephyr didn't suddenly get in the way. The Leerings on board understood her intention. And they obeyed.

The crew groaned as the tempest swung sideways. The motion of going forward and suddenly backward would have made less experienced passengers violently ill. Cettie kept her thoughts focused on executing the maneuver, willing the Leerings to do it quickly and safely, but she also looked out for the zephyr, trying to ensure that they wouldn't collide. Juliana gripped the support ropes tightly, an enormous grin on her face. Cettie continued the turn until the tempest was fully backward and then willed it up around the hill. The zephyr had not altered its approach—it was still slowing down as it made a straight ascent toward the mark.

The timbers of the tempest shuddered and moaned, but Cettie felt the sturdiness of the vessel as it climbed higher up the hilltop. Dizziness washed through her head and stomach. She could see how close they were to the Tor, the wind whipping the blades of grass down below. Some of the students were cowering as they watched.

The tempest finished its final turn just as the tower loomed in front of it. The tempest shot up vertically now, stopping only when it was parallel with the top of the tower. The final rotation set the bow over the top of it, blocking the space so the zephyr could not land there.

It was over. The *Serpentine* had won.

Cettie was exhausted from the strain of the journey. Her throat was parched, and her ears were ringing. She felt as if she'd run all the way up the Tor without stopping. Her shoulders sagged as she leaned against the helm and panted.

"Well done!" Juliana shouted warmly, coming over and patting Cettie's back.

"I wasn't sure . . ." Cettie said, gasping, "it would work."

"If I hadn't been sure," Juliana said, "I would have countermanded your plan. These ships really are remarkably maneuverable. Before the *Serpentine* was used to haul rock, it was a ministry ship that had seen some action. Most cargo ships aren't designed to suffer the kind of abuse you put him through."

Cettie looked at her. "I thought ships were feminine. Named after ladies."

"They are if they're piloted by *men*," she said with a wry smile. "Ah, here is your victim come to complain."

The zephyr pulled up alongside the deck of the tempest. There were three soldiers aboard, all dressed in the regimentals of the fleet—dark coats fixed with two columns of brass buttons up the front and some along the folded cuffs.

One of them, a darkly handsome lad of perhaps eighteen, wore a lieutenant's hat.

"Permission to come aboard, Captain!" he shouted while perching on the railing, elbow resting on his knee.

"Do you intend to scold me for reckless piloting?" Juliana answered back.

"Of course not, ma'am!" he countered.

"Then permission granted," she answered, folding her arms.

The zephyr edged closer to the tempest. Two of Juliana's crew began to unhook the boarding plank from its cradle when the lieutenant jumped the distance instead. Some of the crew gave him a look as if he were mad to attempt such a thing. It showed a marked self-assurance.

"Captain Juliana, your reputation is certainly well earned," he said with a charming smile.

"What reputation is that, Lieutenant?" she answered innocently.

"A daring one, I should say. I'm pleased to meet you in person." He offered his gloved hand, and she shook it with hers.

"Cettie, this is Lieutenant Russell," Juliana said, gesturing to make the introduction formal.

It struck Cettie forcibly that she was standing in front of the young officer that Sera admired so much. He fit her description precisely. He removed his tall hat, revealing a head of dark curly hair, tucked it under his arm, and then bowed to Cettie.

"Cettie of Fog Willows?" he asked with growing interest.

"I am," she replied, feeling as if she knew him already because of all the stories Sera had told her. "Is your given name William, by chance?"

"It is," he answered with a smile. "So. You are Miss Fitzempress's friend?"

"Her companion and her friend," Cettie answered. His demeanor quickly transformed to one of delight.

"And the one who piloted the *Serpentine* on his most recent voyage," Juliana added.

"That was you?" Will said with surprise.

Cettie felt her cheeks start to flush. She nodded.

"With such daring, I had assumed it was Captain Haughton. I am astonished. You are Miss Fitzempress's age, are you not?"

"Yes," Cettie answered meekly, wishing his attention were turned elsewhere.

"And she's accomplished a great many things already," said Juliana. "I'm going to try to persuade my brother-in-law to let her join the trade routes. Despite her course of study at the abbey, I think the Ministry of Law would be ideal for her."

"Miss Cettie would excel wherever she went, I am sure," Will said with a gallant bow. "When you asked me to wait at the sentinel oak, I hadn't expected this encounter. Next time I will be more prepared."

Cettie had suspected as much. She grinned at Juliana and gave her a knowing look.

"Tell me, Lieutenant," Juliana said archly, "how goes the hunt for the intruder?"

"That information, of course, is not public knowledge," he said evasively. He looked at both their faces. "But since you are relations of Minister Fitzroy, I shall assume you're in a position to learn any details you desire?"

"We expect him back from Lockhaven soon," Juliana said. "But go ahead and tell us now." Cettie saw that Juliana was determined to get her way.

Will looked hesitant a moment, as if he were concerned about displeasing a superior. "The investigation is certainly troubling. I'm not privy to all the latest information, but my captain tells me that the various manifests all checked out. Even the Minister of War's ship was investigated, and every member of the crew was interrogated in front of Leerings that forbid lying. Lord Welles volunteered to submit to questions, not being above the law himself. The intruder did not come aboard his ship. Or any other that was chartered to arrive in Muirwood."

"I suppose he must have come from a private zephyr, then," Juliana said, arching her brows.

"It seems likely, ma'am," he answered soberly. Then he turned to Cettie. "Many of us who haven't received orders yet were sent here to provide security, but I am leaving soon for Whitehead in the City. I hope to see Miss Fitzempress . . . soon." He gave Cettie a hopeful look.

She would do nothing to betray her friend's feelings. Will Russell was a very handsome young man. But looks and charm could conceal ambition and ill intentions. She thought again on the letter he'd written to Sera. The tone of it had troubled her, and though his every action seemed affable and well-intentioned, she worried about his eagerness.

"I'm sure you will, Mr. Russell," Cettie answered, keeping her expression neutral.

Will gave her a self-deprecating smile. He was hoping for something. But what?

CHAPTER EIGHTEEN

REVIVED

After her first encounter with Lieutenant Russell, Cettie did not cross paths with him again for another two days. The seasons were starting to change before her eyes—the rich greens of the hillsides beginning to turn pale brown. The apple trees of the cider orchard were done producing luscious fruit, and fewer bees hovered around the lavender bushes. More and more students were seeking refuge in the shade between classes. They were overdue a spring storm, and Cettie continued to check the storm glass she'd brought to her cabin on the *Serpentine*. The quicksilver was placid and had not budged.

The second afternoon after her race with Lieutenant Russell, Cettie made her way back toward her aunt's tempest after her advanced mathematics class, musing about what Sera would think of the man. He was handsome, agreeable, and seemed destined for great things . . . unless Sera's father was determined to keep him down. Her thoughts so distracted her she didn't notice Mr. Skrelling's approach as he fell in next to her. Finally, he had to cough into his fist to get her attention.

"*Ahem*, Miss Cettie, how are you?" He cleared his throat noisily.

Although she was startled by his sudden appearance, she concealed her alarm. "I am well enough, Mr. Skrelling. It's a pleasant afternoon."

"A bit warm for my taste," he answered, tugging at his high collar and the knotted tie. He was perspiring copiously, but she judged it wasn't altogether due to the temperature.

"What class did you have just now?" she asked, trying to be pleasant.

"Advanced rhetoric," he answered promptly. "That is a required course for one seeking a profession in Law. I intend to resume my employment at Sloan and Teitelbaum following my studies here, but ultimately, I think it would be more beneficial to open my own practice. I am a man of no small ambition."

"I could tell," Cettie said, keeping her voice neutral.

"And of course, I would never consider leaving Sloan and Teitelbaum until your case is satisfactorily resolved. I was only suggesting what my plans are for the future. The Law can be quite profitable." His voice was nervous, his tone slightly agitated. He was working up his courage to tell her something. Cettie dreaded what it might be.

"I imagine so," she answered softly. Some other students were smirking at them.

"Do you, *ahem*, have plans for after you leave Muirwood? Will you be a governess, perhaps?"

She gave him a bold look. "How did you know about that?"

He looked startled by her suspicious tone. "I didn't know, not exactly. Just a rumor I'd heard. I have a knack for remembering details, which is a good attribute to have in an advocate, I'd remind you." His tone was defensive. "I confess I employed a trick of the trade, as they say, in getting you to confess. I knew your reaction to the rumor would either confirm or deny it. In this case, it confirms it."

"That is rather underhanded, don't you think, Mr. Skrelling?"

"Underhanded, ma'am?"

"Dishonest. Why not just ask me about the rumor directly? And why should it matter to you in the least what I do after leaving Muirwood?"

"I'm ashamed that you took my intentions in such a way, Miss Cettie," he said hastily, trying to rectify the situation. "I was practicing a skill that is admired in my field of study. I had no intention of being offensive. I beg your pardon a thousand times. I am truly, truly sorry."

His rush to apologize mollified her a little, but she was still on her guard with him. They walked alongside each other in silence. She was hoping he'd excuse himself and go another way, but he seemed determined to be her shadow.

"As to why I was beseeching such information, Miss Cettie," he continued after the uncomfortable pause, "I wanted to know how to communicate with you after we part company. There are only a few days left before we take the Test, and the end of the year can be full of commotion."

She gave him a wary look. "You already know where I reside, Mr. Skrelling."

"Yes, Fog Willows, if that's what you mean. But if you were, for example, a governess at a certain manor belonging to an ex-student of Mrs. Romrell, it would take much longer for, say, correspondence to pass from me to you. You could be away from Fog Willows for some time, and I wouldn't want to incur Lord Fitzroy's displeasure should he find himself needing to pay additional postage fees to forward my communications to you."

"Are you saying you wish to write to me after we leave school?" she asked him.

He coughed into his hand again, looking uncomfortable and excessively hot. "I . . . I would, Miss Cettie."

The furtive look he gave her said much about his intentions, but she thought it best to keep everything in the open between them. She wanted no misunderstandings.

"What are your intentions, Mr. Skrelling?"

"Intentions? Toward . . . ?"

"Toward me, naturally. Speak plainly, if you please."

A rosy flush came to his cheeks. "I . . . well, I had thought to put it more delicately, in a letter, which I could compose and choose the words . . . you know . . . in a more precise and direct manner."

"Does not an advocate need to be extemporaneous at times?"

"Indeed! Surely!" He looked embarrassed and flustered. "Well, that is entirely true, Miss Cettie. You have great understanding of the profession. Very great. What I am trying to say—what I would have said in my first letter—is that I intend to ask your permission—naturally I would want to seek that first—to begin to . . . court you, following our studies." He let out a giant sigh of relief.

"Thank you for speaking plainly, Mr. Skrelling. Permit me the opportunity to do likewise."

"Of course!"

"Mr. Skrelling, I am sixteen years old. My future is anything but certain. But while that may be true, my feelings are very certain. I would save you needless pain and expense. Before I seek a suitor, which I have no intention of doing anytime soon, I require friendship above all. Your manners toward me, so far, have given me some cause to distrust you. You've watched me. You've sought information about me without asking for it directly. I'm afraid you've conjured some fantasy in your mind that is entirely one-sided."

As she spoke, she watched his expression begin to wilt. He listened to her, but the flames in his cheeks grew even brighter. She'd struck the mark in the center with her arrow of truth.

"Now, Mr. Skrelling," she continued after a short pause. "Your feelings may change after learning how forthright I can be. I will not begrudge you if they do. If they do not, and you seek to develop a friendship with me, then I will accept your letters on the condition that they remain on those terms. I do not know where I will be after I take the Test. I honestly do not. Mrs. Romrell was so kind as to offer me a position, but nothing has been decided. You may correspond with me, if you wish, at Fog Willows. If my situation changes, I will notify you of where I may be reached. Is that satisfactory?"

"Yes," he said in a choking voice. He looked humbled and mortified.

"I apologize if I've embarrassed you, Mr. Skrelling," she said. "I think it for the best if you depart and compose your feelings."

He tried to say something, but the words wouldn't come. Then he nodded and cleared his throat again. He gave her a piercing look, one of agitation but also appreciation. "Thank you," he said hoarsely. "For your honesty, miss." He then bowed his head and veered away from her, head still lowered in shame. There was, nonetheless, determination in his gait.

The heat of the day was oppressive now. Had she done the right thing in being so direct with Mr. Skrelling? When she looked ahead toward her destination, she saw Anna and Adam approaching her, arm in arm. Seeing the two of them connected like that gave her a visceral reaction. Was Adam just being a gentleman with Anna? But how could he not be charmed by her? Anna's hair shone like the sun, and her expression was just as light and charming.

As they approached, Anna gave her a probing look. "We saw you walking with Mr. Skrelling a moment ago," she said. "I suggested to Adam that we intervene to spare you, but you said something that chased him away. What did you do? Did you scold him?"

Now it was Cettie's turn to feel uncomfortable. "No, not really," she answered, aware of Adam's eyes on her face. She felt her own cheeks starting to burn.

"Well, he walked away like a whipped puppy," Anna said.

"Was he impertinent to you?" Adam asked with a tone of concern.

"No," Cettie replied, shaking her head. "I would rather not talk about it."

"Maybe later," Anna suggested. "Maybe we can have dinner together on board the *Serpentine*. All of us!" she added suddenly, tugging on Adam's arm.

"I was seeking you," Adam said to Cettie, "but I—"

"It's good news," Anna interrupted. Cettie was grateful because her heart had given a sudden lurch. She'd had enough dark feelings for one day.

"The Aldermaston has revived," Adam went on. "He's eating some broth and little bits of bread. He's very weak and still lacks the strength to speak, but he's scribbled some short messages on paper. Today, his strength began to return in earnest. Doctor Redd feels the worst is now behind us, that he will recover from the internal bleeding."

Cettie clasped her hands and pressed her knuckles against her lips. "That *is* good news."

"Not many in the school know about it," Anna said. "But Adam goes there every day and consults with Doctor Redd. He's been more than useful. I'm sure Doctor Redd thinks so."

Adam looked abashed. "We all care about the Aldermaston. I'm just grateful that I was able to help in some small way."

Cettie admired his humility, how he deflected Anna's praise.

"If you hadn't been there the night he was shot," Cettie said, "he probably would have died."

Adam shrugged, but the corner of his mouth twitched upward.

"Tell her!" Anna said forcefully.

"Ah yes," Adam answered, shaking his head. "The reason I was looking for you. The Aldermaston wants to see you, Cettie. Right away."

"Me?"

"Of course!" Adam said. "He wanted to be sure you were well. I went to the *Serpentine* to find you and found Anna instead. She said she'd help me hunt you down."

"Since I wasn't invited to see the Aldermaston, I'll wait by the tempest for you," Anna said.

Cettie nodded and then felt her throat tighten when Adam offered his arm to her next.

The Aldermaston was in his bedchamber. The curtains were pulled open, and the chamber smelled of dried lavender, which Cettie saw hanging in clumps from strings. Doctor Redd was washing his hands in a bowl of water when they arrived. His white hair was disheveled, but he had a radiant smile.

"Ah, the lost lamb," he said with a twinkle in his eye as Cettie entered. "I thought I might have to go after you myself, but I shouldn't have worried. Mr. Creigh is ever so diligent. That young man will do great things, mark my words."

The Aldermaston was resting on the sofa, wearing a dressing gown covered by a shawl and holding a cane. His cheeks looked gaunt and his skin sallow. He had shrunk since his injury, but it encouraged her to see him out of bed. He watched them but said nothing as he adjusted his spectacles over his nose.

Doctor Redd stepped in front of her to examine her brow, temporarily blocking her view of the Aldermaston. "Your own injuries have mostly healed. Just a few scabs on your brow. The body is one of the most amazing Mysteries of all! Without any orders, without any command, the different cells in your body went about healing themselves. How is the bruising at your neck?"

"It has faded," she answered.

"Good, good," Doctor Redd said. "Well, now that Mr. Creigh is here, I can go to the kitchen for a mug of cider. If the cook comes in with a quince pie, send her away immediately. I'm sure the Aldermaston's appetite is returning with vigor, but we should be sensible and let the repairs continue. It's good to see you again, Miss Cettie." He squeezed her arm and then nodded to the two men and departed.

Adam silently gestured for her to approach the weary man. As Cettie came near, she saw a look of relief bloom in his eyes. He set down the cane and reached out for her hands. Despite the heat in the room, his hands felt cold to the touch. She was so accustomed to people avoiding her bare skin, especially men, that it felt like a gesture of deep trust. Of connection. She trusted and admired the Aldermaston almost as much as she did her father.

"I'm grateful to see you so much improved," she said, coming down on her knees before him.

"And I am grateful to see you here," he whispered hoarsely. "I feared my summons would come too late."

She blinked in surprise. "What do you mean, Aldermaston?"

He took a deep breath, clearly in great pain. "Your attacker is on the abbey grounds at this moment. In the daylight. No one can see him, but I can sense him and feel his malice. He was waiting for you near the ship just now. I saw a vision of sorts. I saw him smother something over your mouth and then take you into the grove."

Adam closed the distance between them, his eyes full of white-hot fury.

"It was a vision given to me to act upon," the Aldermaston said. "I feared that it would be too late, but the warning from the Mysteries came to prevent your abduction. I am grateful." He looked up at Adam. "Thank you, my boy. Thank you for seeking her promptly."

"You didn't say why," Adam said in a controlled manner.

"I know. I didn't want to spread my concern to you. Bring the officer on duty to me at once."

Cettie turned to Adam, horrified by a sudden thought. "Anna went back to the sky ship."

Adam's face blanched with worry, and he bolted to the door.

CHAPTER NINETEEN

HUNTING A KILLER

The officer on duty was summoned, and the Aldermaston gave him orders to hunt down the threat and secure the safety of the students on the grounds. Guards would also be stationed at the manor itself to protect the Aldermaston and Cettie, though very few people knew she was there.

The knowledge that Adam had rushed ahead into danger made her feelings twist into knots of worry and dread. If anything happened to him or to Anna, or even Aunt Juliana, it would bring her the darkest misery. This was her fault. This attacker had sought her out. He was still seeking her.

"It is a natural impulse to pace and fret," the Aldermaston said softly. Cettie stopped midstride and wrung her hands in agitation.

"What can I do?" she asked. "I don't want anyone else to be hurt. Not because of me."

"Do you suppose that you are any less worth saving because you're from the Fells? Come and sit down. Brooding only yields bitter fruit. We have done what can be done. We will do what must be done. And we will trust that the warning I was given has served its intended purpose."

Cettie bit her lip and hesitated. She didn't feel like sitting. There was too much frantic energy inside her. But she obeyed and took a seat in a stuffed chair near the Aldermaston's sofa. She gave him a hesitant look. "Why is it that you cannot see the intruder?"

He gave her a bemused smile. "I don't know. Let us reason through it together."

His words surprised her. "What could I—"

He held up his hand to forestall more words. "I shouldn't need to remind the inventor of the storm glass that she can be of use. Have we not taught you repeatedly at school that when two or more minds are brought together in harmony, they draw on a greater power? This is the Knowing. While this can happen in solitude, it happens most often when individuals counsel together. There is so much we can learn from one another." He touched his palms together, looking at her intensely. It felt as if he could see right through her. "So there is a man who can shield himself from the gaze of the Leerings. He is at large here on the grounds."

Cettie licked her lips, thinking about the situation. "He did the same at the dormitory. He made it through the Leerings there, which should have stopped him."

"Indeed. The Leerings that protect the abbey grounds are even stronger. Yet he continues to subvert them."

"When he attacked me," Cettie said, "his eyes began to glow silver. The Leerings obeyed him when that happened."

The Aldermaston nodded. "Yes, Lord Fitzroy mentioned as much to me in a letter. Mr. Creigh spoke of it too. I am familiar with this practice. Before Empress Maia took her crown, the world was under the sway of a group of men who used amulets capable of controlling the Leerings. That twisted form of magic hasn't been practiced in centuries, and it is not something we teach in the school. No Aldermaston would dare share the knowledge of how it is done with a student for fear of igniting their curiosity. Yes, that would explain how he can get Leerings to obey him. But my authority here is paramount. I hold the key to this abbey. It can only be held by one man at a time. This man's dark power should not be able to thwart it. Yet it does. How?"

Cettie was equally baffled. "I don't know." Worry for Adam and Anna pulsed through her.

"Don't be troubled, Cettie. The Mysteries warned us of the danger for a reason."

She looked at him worriedly. "But they didn't warn you that you would be injured. They didn't warn me that there was an intruder in my dormitory."

"You misunderstand their purposes, child," he said patiently. "While they *can* prevent suffering, they rarely do, in part because of what we learn from experiencing those difficulties. Cettie, I am a new man because of my injury. I have had visions of the suffering of the people who live in the Fells. Most of all, the Mysteries . . . the Medium . . . the Knowing—they will not supersede our innate gift of choice. They cannot. And when they nudge events in a certain direction, they do so for a greater purpose, a larger good that we can neither see nor understand."

"You're right," Cettie said, shaking her head. "I don't understand it."

"I have found, more often than not, that clarity comes with hindsight. By looking back at an event much later. That is when I see the guiding influence best. In the present, I am like a blind man groping, but my eyes have been opened, Cettie. I am acutely aware of the suffering of our people. The grievous slavery of deeds we have imposed on the populace of our world. We have committed a horrible crime, and the natural consequences of it are playing out in our lives."

His words triggered something in her. A memory from her encounter with the kishion. Had she shared it with Fitzroy? She couldn't remember if she had. It was like a ray of light shining in from a slit in a curtain.

"Aldermaston," she said uneasily.

"Yes?"

"I don't think I have told anyone about this. Or maybe I have, but I've forgotten. The man who attacked me, he was a kishion, and Father told me what they are. Well, this one, he . . . he had a ghost inside of him. A ghost that I recognized. You see, it's been haunting me my entire life. A ghost with no eyes."

He stared at her, caught off guard by her words. His eyes bored into hers as his splayed fingers touched each other just over his massive beard. Silence stretched between them, making her feel more and more uncomfortable.

"Tell me more of this ghost," he said solemnly. "When you first came here, Minister Fitzroy told me that you had been plagued by them in your childhood. That you could even see them."

A dark shard of fear, buried deep in her heart, began to throb. *You're abnormal. Wrong. You attract dark things. Bad.* "I've always been able to."

"They cannot come into this manor," the Aldermaston said firmly, "unless I permit it. And I do *not*." He lowered his voice. "Normally, I make a point of not speaking of them. To do so invites them for reasons you will soon understand when you take the Test. But tell me of this particular ghost."

Cettie swallowed and nodded. Just thinking of it made her cold. "I've always been able to sense them and see them. Even when I was very little. I don't remember feeling threatened by them until after I was eight years old. I think that was around the time. I noticed that they never bothered little children, so I used to surround myself with the little ones to keep them away. But there was always one . . . one that would find me again no matter where I went. It even found me at Fog Willows because Mrs. Pullman let it in."

"It is persistent. That's not a good sign. You mentioned it has no eyes?"

Cettie nodded. "But it could still see. I don't know how to explain it. I could sense a difference between it and other ghosts. It was taller and more powerful than the others."

She saw a little crinkle in the Aldermaston's brow. "Ah," he said gently. Then he murmured, under his breath, "That kind does not go out but by vigil."

"But what does that mean?" she asked.

He nodded his head. "The meaning will become clear to you soon enough. It is troublesome that this creature has marked you as its victim for so long. And it used this man, this kishion, to get closer to you." Then he smiled. "But do not fear, Cettie. You will be taught to defend yourself."

"I am cursed," Cettie said with a shudder.

The Aldermaston shook his head. "Quite the contrary, my dear. It is singling you out because you are a *threat* to its kind. Otherwise, it wouldn't be trying so hard. No, Cettie, you are full of promise and goodness. Beings of darkness cannot abide bright light. It seeks to smother yours, that is all." He leaned forward, his face calm and peaceful. He didn't look frightened by her in the least. "As a child, you experienced something very rare. It's quite uncommon, but it is not unheard of. I've heard of other instances of the sight. One of your parents, maybe even a grandparent, might have been especially sensitive to the Mysteries. If there is evil in your family, perhaps you have been chosen to break the mold. I'm not sure. But it is not a curse. Please believe that."

Did he know what the kishion had claimed? Once again, she decided it would be best to be straightforward. "Did my guardian tell you that the kishion claimed to be my father?"

The Aldermaston nodded. "He did. It may be a lie. It may be the truth." He pointed at her with both index fingers. "But whoever your father really is, whoever your mother is, you—Cettie Saeed—have a choice about who *you* will be. And from what I have seen of your character, you are an honorable young woman who will do great things."

She looked at him with tenderness. He had always made her feel safe and appreciated.

"I'm still frightened," she said. "I don't want anything to happen to the people I love. I . . . I can't help feeling they'd be better off, safer, without me."

"That is always our deepest fear, I think. But remember, this second life is not the end," he said, shaking his head. "Why, it is only a mirror gate, as it were, to a much larger existence. What is the chief tenet of the Mysteries of Thought? What do we read over and over in the books you've studied? *Fear not.* A strange injunction, don't you think, in a world overflowing with violence, poverty, and despair? But, my dear, where else would we be able to practice that tenet but in such a place as this?" He winked at her.

His words did make her feel calmer. So did the conviction in his eyes. He truly did intend to take action. Wasn't it unfair, though, that the ones who were taught such things were rarely forced to confront those very evils? The gulf between the two worlds could not have loomed larger for her than it did in that moment. She was grateful to have learned at Muirwood, but so many others needed—and deserved—that same chance.

"So," he continued with a sigh, "you are plagued still by a creature that has long hunted you. You are stalked by a trained killer. Your companion has left you to fight for a throne she may never sit on. The odds seem risky indeed, don't they? But I would put my trust and faith in your future, Cettie Saeed. You came to this world to do some good. I am certain of that."

"Thank you, Aldermaston," she said.

"And you are not without benefits. Your guardian, your *father*, is Brant Fitzroy. Your sister Anna cares about you. And so do others here at the school. You are apt when it comes to the Mysteries. I've not seen your equal in this school." He paused, then added, "I'm grateful we had a chance to speak."

So was she—everything he'd said rang of truth—but she still couldn't shake her worry for Adam and Anna.

He raised his cane and tried to stand, but his legs were trembling so much he couldn't. Cettie rushed to him and gripped his other arm to help him up.

"Thank you," he offered, breathing heavily and wincing with pain. "I am starving. Some broth would do me good. If you can help me to the table?"

"Of course," Cettie answered. With her help and that of his cane, he made it there. She quickly arranged for a servant to bring a bowl and spoon and set about serving the Aldermaston when the sustenance arrived.

"My mind is cast back on a memory," he said wistfully as she worked. "There was an Aldermaston who served here long ago by the name of Gideon Penman. I read his tome when I was much younger. The man had a fascinating mind, and he lived in dangerous times. Back then, the mastons were outnumbered and hunted, but he had access to a device called a Cruciger orb. It could lead to something that was lost. Something hidden could be found. I wonder . . ."

She could see an idea sprouting in his mind as he gazed absently out the window. She set the bowl of broth and a heel of bread before him.

"Is it lost?" she asked him.

"Hmmm? The Cruciger orb? No. It can only be used by someone who is very strong in the Mysteries. I believe it's being kept at Billerbeck Abbey. Perhaps this is part of the solution we need. It was the use of such a device that helped Empress Maia hunt down the kishion of the past and eradicate their order. Approval must be given by the privy council, of course, but perhaps the Cruciger orb can lead us to him. And if we capture him, perhaps we can learn where he comes from."

Cettie heard the noise of steps coming toward the study. The Aldermaston was about to take a bite from the bread when a knock sounded on the door. It opened before Cettie could reach it, revealing a soldier.

"Aldermaston," the man said with a foreboding countenance. "The intruder was on the *Serpentine*. The captain was drugged and is being revived. He took Lord Fitzroy's daughter. We have men searching the woods now. That young doctor is with them."

CHAPTER TWENTY

CRUCIGER ORB

Commotion at the abbey increased tenfold following the latest attack. Word was sent to the teachers that a dangerous man was afoot on the grounds. Students were hurried back to their dormitories to wait for the crisis to pass while the Ministry of War responded to Anna's abduction. News was sent to Fitzroy immediately, as well as to the privy council.

Cettie stayed at the manor, worried sick about her friend. Her aunt had been brought to a guest room to be treated, but she refused to settle long enough for the doctor to examine her. Although she had a large bruise on her forehead, she was spoiling to join the hunt for her abducted niece.

"Now, if you'll be patient, ma'am," Doctor Redd said, trying to smooth away her hair to see the bruise better. Cettie had managed to coax her into a chair, but she was jiggling a leg impatiently.

"Patient, Doctor?" Juliana said. "My niece has been taken by a vile man. How can you expect me to be patient?" She swatted his hands away.

Cettie knelt by her and took her other hand. "Do you remember anything that happened?"

"Like how you got that bruise?" the doctor added, looking into her eyes, one at a time.

"I remember falling after a hand clamped over my mouth with some noxious odor. Before I could do anything, my legs gave way. I don't remember hitting the floor, but I clearly did. He left me there in my cabin."

"You are fortunate to be alive, Captain," the doctor said. "He could have killed you. Do you have any other injuries?"

Juliana stretched out her arm, testing her muscles. "No. Are we done yet, Doctor? I want to get back out there. I refuse to sit here idly while Anna is in danger."

"I think it might be wise if you did," Doctor Redd said. "The ministry is—"

"Hang the ministry," Juliana snapped. "I'm going back out there. Every set of eyes will be useful. Now stand back, sir."

The doctor, seeing the pointlessness of arguing with her, retreated a few paces. "A blow to the head can be dangerous, Captain."

"I know. I've been hit before, Doctor. The dizziness was caused by the cloth. I'm feeling much better. I don't know how he got on my ship without me knowing, but I intend to find out."

"He got into my room the same way," Cettie offered. "The Aldermaston said he can blind the Leerings. Do you think . . . do you think he might still be on board?"

"I hope so," Juliana said angrily. "It would entitle me to give him justice. I've wasted enough time as it is. I'm going."

"I clearly cannot stop you," said Doctor Redd with a sigh.

"No, you cannot. Cettie, come with me."

Cettie cringed. "I don't think the Aldermaston would—"

"Hang the Aldermaston!" Juliana barked.

Doctor Redd covered his eyes, shaking his head worriedly. Cettie felt conflicted, but she couldn't deny the urge to look for Anna . . . to do something. She obeyed her aunt's order, and the two left the room. The hall was crowded with people in uniform, teachers, and even a few students. It was mayhem. The bulk of the crowd was gathered outside the door of the Aldermaston's sickroom, down at the other end of the hall. Juliana gripped Cettie's arm and pulled her in the direction of the front doors.

"Should we be doing this?" Cettie asked worriedly.

"The longer the delay, the harder it will be to find her. If that villain takes her off the grounds, he probably has a sky ship waiting."

"But it's not her that he wants. It's *me*."

"I know. I'm not going to trade you, Cettie. You're my niece, too, no matter who birthed you. But if he is this desperate to take you, he's clearly not above murdering someone to get what he wants. We must make sure that doesn't happen. If the entire Ministry of War possessed more than an ounce of brains collectively, they would have found him already. I'm not afraid of facing that blackguard up close. In fact, I'm looking forward to it."

It was rash and reckless. Cettie was just as worried about Anna as the rest of them. But charging into a situation without thinking it through seemed more than unwise. It was foolish.

Then, through all the fussing and shouting and murmuring that filled the hall, she heard a sound off in the distance—almost as if orchestra music were being spouted from a Leering. Only this was different. This was the music of the Mysteries, and it compelled her to seek it out.

"Wait," Cettie said, touching Juliana's arm and stopping. She let her senses drift a bit, and then she was able to feel where it was coming from. The sound grew louder, and the strange music changed timbre.

"Cettie, it will be all right," Juliana said.

"No, it's something else," Cettie replied, trying to place the source. "This way."

She led Juliana down another corridor that was less crowded. The commotion in the hall behind them began to fade. The music continued to gain strength as Cettie rounded another bend in the passageway. As they went down the hall, one of the panels of wainscoting suddenly opened in front of them. Juliana started in surprise as several men stepped out of the secret passage, one of them in a soldier's uniform.

One that was not in uniform wore the coat and vest of the gentry. He was tall and strong, and the sound of the magic was coming from *him*. In fact, it emanated from a pure gold sphere he cupped in his bare hand. It was a curious-looking device, the likes of which she had never seen before. There was some sort of ornamentation on the top, and gold stays that converged to that point. It was about the size of an orange, and it radiated power like a potent Leering. But whereas Leerings tended to emanate a single tune—one that could summon light, or water, or fire, or what have you—this device was a nexus of some kind, one that drew upon multiple powers at once.

"Who are you?" Juliana demanded of the men in the hall.

Cettie's gaze had been riveted on the orb—clearly it was the Cruciger orb the Aldermaston had told her about. How many hours had passed since the Aldermaston had told her of it? Was this the man who had been summoned from the distant abbey in the north? How could he have arrived so soon?

"Pardon me, ma'am," the officer said in a disgruntled tone. "But what business is it of yours?"

Cettie gave the newcomer a closer look. He didn't look like someone from the Ministry of Thought. Most vicars performing their office wore a fringed gremial beneath their waistcoats; this man was dressed in browns and greens, but he did have a gold ring on his right hand. He was probably thirty years old, a little younger than Aunt Juliana, and his thick, dark hair had streaks of copper in it.

"I'm Caulton Forshee, at your service," he said, addressing Juliana respectfully and bowing his head.

"Oh, you must be the captain of the *Serpentine*," the officer said with a huff. "I haven't met you yet. I'm Captain Harrowgate."

"You're Forshee, then," said Juliana, ignoring the officer completely. "That sphere in your hand. I've never seen a Cruciger orb before. Are you the one who can use it to find my niece?"

Cettie didn't know the lore about the device. Some Mysteries were tightly controlled by their respective ministries, and people were only introduced to them on an individual basis. If this orb could help them find someone who was lost, however, it was powerful magic indeed.

He gave a modest frown and shrugged. "Perhaps. I came as soon as the Aldermaston sent for me."

"Can it be used to find her?" Juliana asked with a tone of challenge.

He shrugged. "It's working now."

"Then we're coming with you," Juliana demanded.

The officer, whose face had been getting redder every moment Juliana ignored him, looked incensed. "You have no right to interfere . . ."

"I have every right. It's my niece who was taken. The man may still be on board my ship."

"He's not," Caulton said. Then he gave Cettie a long, piercing look. "It's all right, Captain," he said to the officer standing next to him. "They *should* come with us."

Several more soldiers joined them as they walked together across the grounds, and it became obvious to Cettie that Caulton was following directions he was receiving from the Cruciger orb. He gazed at it from time to time and altered his direction slightly. She could still sense the music coming from it, a strange and interesting tune. As she listened, she began to pick the sounds apart, almost like they were layers of music. It was divining intentions and alternatives. This device was much more complex than most of the Leerings she'd encountered. Zephyrs zoomed overhead, and the captain of the soldiers would periodically raise his wrist, exposing a band around his arm with a stone fixed into it. Its purpose was obscure to her. He didn't say anything, but Cettie could perceive the flex of his thoughts.

"Daylight is ebbing," Caulton said in warning. "We will need some sky ships to fly overhead and provide us with light, Captain."

"Of course," replied the officer.

The orb led them into the cider orchard. The ladders used to harvest fruit had been abandoned, for all the groundskeepers had been summoned back to their dwellings. Cettie noticed soldiers with arquebuses were moving ahead of them, to the sides, and behind.

"Why don't we take a sky ship?" Juliana asked brusquely.

"If that were the best way, it would have told me," Caulton replied patiently.

"You keep altering your path," Juliana said. "Are you following the trail they took? You're not even looking for tracks."

"No, I am not," Caulton agreed. When they reached the edge of the orchard, he paused and studied the smooth surface of the orb. Cettie heard a subtle whirring emanating from the orb—a completely new sound—and felt a strange accompanying sensation. It looked as if some odd writing had risen to the golden surface, but she was not close enough to read it. Caulton frowned and gazed ahead into the woods.

"How far are we, Forshee?" the captain asked him, wrinkling his brow.

"I don't know for certain. He carried her to this point. Then they started walking together. She was terrified." He sniffed. "I can almost smell it. This way."

Leaving the orchard, they started across a field of deep grass. At the far end, there was a wall of trees and hedges marking the boundaries of the abbey grounds. Cettie knew they would have to leave, and her skin began to crawl. The sun was going down, but no one showed any signs of relinquishing the search. She didn't wish to stop, either, and yet . . . nighttime was when the ghosts came out. That was when their power was the strongest. And they would be outside the protections of the grounds.

She wrenched her thoughts away from the ghosts and gritted her teeth. Thoughts were powerful, she reminded herself. Thoughts could invite the very demons she wanted to shun.

"Are you all right?" Caulton Forshee asked her in a low voice. She hadn't noticed him slow down to walk alongside her.

"Are we going to be leaving the grounds?" she asked him, trying to control the throb of worry in her voice.

"Most certainly," he answered. "The trail clearly goes beyond them. You are nervous about leaving the borders, aren't you?"

"I am," Cettie answered, keeping her voice pitched low.

"Well, my father always taught me this. Maybe it will be helpful to you. Face your fear. Do what makes you uncomfortable. Lean into the discomfort instead of shunning it."

"That sounds like something the Aldermaston just said to me," Cettie said with a smile.

"Indeed?" He radiated strong self-confidence. Another zephyr whooshed overhead. "Captain," Forshee said, nodding to the sky. "Have them start circling the northern borders while we go east. It will make them think we are searching over there. I don't want our foe to know we are coming quite yet."

"If you say so," replied the captain.

After they closed the distance to the trees, Cettie stared at the shade and shadows that were gathering on the horizon. The sun would last awhile longer now that it was nearly summer, but she knew they were about to enter a place of danger. She steadied herself, heeding his advice, and rubbed her arms. She felt the boundaries of the abbey, a tightly woven mesh of magic that stretched from Leering to Leering. But there was something there, a disruption. When they reached the boundary line and paused, she felt it. There was a gap in the magic now. As if the mesh had been tugged aside and fixed. Caulton Forshee stood right at the opening and stared at it inquisitively.

"How curious," he murmured.

"What's curious?" Juliana asked, hands on her hips.

"The boundary was lifted," Cettie heard herself say.

All of them looked at her. She flushed with embarrassment. "I-I don't know how he did it."

"But you can sense it, can't you?" Caulton said, eyeing her again. "You have interesting gifts. This explains how he got into the grounds undetected. The wardings aren't broken. Let's close the open door, shall we?" He looked at Cettie. "Would you like to do it?"

"I don't . . . really . . . know how," she said anxiously.

"Just try," he coaxed.

Cettie moistened her lips and took a deep breath. She walked up to the edge of the boundary and tried to sense the strands of magic holding the barrier open. Again, it was like listening to music. The sound of the Cruciger orb was distracting at first, but as she fell deeper into herself, she began to sense the different layers of magic comprising the protection spell. The disruption was beautifully woven and incredibly subtle. It blended in with the harmony of the magic so perfectly it almost slipped her notice. Someone very canny and powerful had done this. Someone who had not wanted to leave a trace.

"Did you find it?" Caulton asked her softly. "One part not quite right?"

Cettie concentrated on the part that felt wrong, and then in her mind she commanded it to cease. The barrier drifted back down into place, fusing the hole shut. She felt a little dizzy, but it was a pleasant feeling.

"Well done," Caulton said. He glanced back down at the orb. "The hunt continues. Into the woods then, Captain? They are still several miles ahead of us."

The soldiers with arquebuses had assembled nearby.

"Move out," the captain ordered, and the soldiers began to stalk ahead into the forest, arms at the ready.

Caulton glanced at Cettie. "Stay near me."

They went together past the warding and entered the woods on the east side of the grounds. The languid, warm air had not one bit of chill to it, yet Cettie felt a shiver tear through her. As soon as she left the borders of the abbey, she felt a blackness begin to weigh on her. She heard every night insect's click, every crack and snapping of twigs and fallen detritus.

She sensed it in the woods. The presence that had always haunted her. *I knew you would come, child. I've been waiting for you.*

CHAPTER TWENTY-ONE

LEGION

The ghosts began to close in as the group continued to make its way into the woods. The buzzing that always preceded the ghosts filled the air, and Cettie glimpsed them in the shadows with her peripheral vision. Night was coming. Their power was growing.

Should she say anything? Before she could decide, Caulton Forshee slowed and then stopped, gazing down at the orb.

The captain on duty sniffed and looked around uneasily. "I've never cared for the woods around this abbey."

"Why did we stop?" Juliana asked, her hand resting on the stock of her pistol. She looked eager to continue the hunt.

"It's not the woods that brings you disquiet," Caulton said. He turned and looked at Cettie with open curiosity. It wasn't an accusation. "They're drawn to you."

"What?" the captain demanded.

"Can't you feel them?"

Cettie started to tremble, and her cheeks burned with shame. She should not have left the abbey grounds. Her instincts warned her to flee.

"We are all mastons here," Caulton told her gently. "You are not the only one who senses them, although you do not understand truly what they are." He put his hand on her shoulder. "Anna needs our help. She's not that far. Will you come with us?"

"They've always come for me," Cettie said, folding her arms, trying to quell the shaking in her body.

"I can see that, but they will not get past us. You are safe as long as you stay in the middle."

There it was again. Her source of protection lay in others. Although she was frightened, she nodded.

"Thank you," Caulton said.

"What is your plan, Forshee?" Juliana asked pointedly.

"Don't you remember the maston test?" he replied, arching his eyebrows. "There's a way to banish them."

He started walking again, increasing the lengths of his stride. The others followed, including the armed soldiers, who exchanged nervous looks as they moved forward. Cettie had no problem keeping pace, but her anxiety increased as she watched the sunlight fade faster and faster. The droning, buzzing noise followed them. Her enemies were near, prowling like wolves, but she steeled her heart and summoned her courage. She would face the ghosts for Anna, just like she had at Fog Willows.

A raven croaked overhead, startling her. Suddenly, the Cruciger orb lit up in Forshee's hand. It emanated a soft glow, just enough to spread a ring of radiance to guide their steps.

"He'll see us coming," the captain warned.

"He already knows we're coming," Caulton answered seriously. "He's waiting."

"We're walking into a trap, then?"

"You could say that," he replied.

"You are not a military man, Forshee. We need a strategy and a plan. He's got a weapon that belches fire and can kill a maston."

"I know," Caulton answered. "He shot the Aldermaston. How have your strategies worked thus far, Captain? You have the men, you have the zephyrs. I was brought here because I have the ability to find him. Trust me a little further."

The captain looked angered by the rebuke. "With all due respect, Lord Forshee, I outrank you. What we are doing is folly. We need to flank him, to—"

Caulton's eyes blazed with sudden anger, but he held it in check. "Captain," he said softly. "They can *hear* you. Have a little more confidence in me."

"At least tell me what your plan is," the captain snarled.

Caulton shook his head no. "If we do not act now, there is a strong likelihood she will be killed."

"Captain," said Juliana curtly. She gave him a warning look and a shake of her head like he was being a daft fool.

"Thank you," Caulton told her. He kept going without a backward glance, and everyone else followed.

The night air was getting colder, but their rapid pace kept Cettie from being too cold. She could still sense the ghosts, but most of them were trailing the group. Only the tall one lurked somewhere ahead. There was a sense of giddiness about it, as if the creature were savoring an upcoming victory.

It attempted to torture her with its thoughts, but she focused her memory on some of the passages she had learned from tomes during her stay at Muirwood. The mind could only think of one thing at a time, and she had every right to control what those thoughts would be.

They were far from the abbey now, deep in the heart of the woods. She knew the abbey was surrounded by water, that they would eventually reach the shore, and as she recited the quotes in her mind, she listened keenly for the sound of water lapping.

Caulton looked down at the orb once more and stopped short. "He's left her."

"What?" Juliana demanded.

"It tells me she is one way, and he is another. He's reacting to our movements." He paused, gazing intently at the surface of the orb. Once again, Cettie could see a strange script scrawled across it. "Captain, send half of your men into the woods that way." He straightened his arm and pointed to his left. "He's circling around to come up behind us. Have them wait to ambush him. He may be invisible. Listen carefully. Use your instincts. The rest will rush ahead to rescue the girl while she's alone. Summon the zephyrs to us. We're ready for reinforcements."

"It's about bloody time," the captain snarled, raising his wrist to his mouth. Then he selected six of his men to make the attack. "Capture him if you can. Your orders are to kill him otherwise."

"Where's Anna?" Juliana asked Lord Forshee.

"This way," Caulton said, and started to jog. The captain went with them, along with the rest of the soldiers.

The light from the orb grew brighter as they ran. Cettie could feel the ghosts hissing, shrinking back from the brightness that tortured them. There was pain in their thoughts, and Cettie felt a gush of vengefulness in her heart. She stayed near Juliana and Caulton, surrounded by the soldiers and their weapons. There would be violence soon. She sensed it, felt the wind hold its breath in anticipation.

"Over here!"

It was Anna's voice.

Caulton led them straight toward the sound. The clack and clatter of branches obscured their way, but Cettie batted the limbs aside in her eagerness to get to her sister. Then she saw the golden hair, the filthy dress. Anna cowered at the base of a tree, shielding her eyes from the brightness of the light. Something felt wrong. A warning pulsed inside of Cettie's heart.

"Anna!" Juliana called in relief.

They rushed up to her, the light from the orb blazing like the noonday sun. Cettie looked around for signs of Anna's abductor. The soldiers had their arquebuses aimed into the woods as they encircled the girl.

Caulton knelt beside her. She wasn't bound or tied by anything. Cettie rushed forward to hug her, but Anna shocked her by lunging forward and grabbing Caulton by the throat.

Her eyes were shining silver, and a snarl of hatred twisted her pretty mouth.

At that moment, an explosion blasted in the woods, followed by a sharp cry of pain from one of the soldiers.

Anna rose and threw Caulton into the tree with inhuman strength. As soon as he struck the wood, he dropped the Cruciger orb. Everything went dark except for Anna's eyes.

"You bring six against a legion!" said the tall ghost, speaking through Anna. Its voice echoed strangely, making Cettie's skin crawl. Anna struck the captain as he whirled around to look at her, and Cettie heard his jawbone crack with the blow. The soldiers turned their weapons on her.

"Don't!" Juliana shrieked.

Cettie had only been this afraid twice before. The first time was when she'd entered the grotto near the Dolcoath mines. Her presence had awoken a horrible beast that lurked there—and it had reached out to her, tried to control her. The second was when Mrs. Pullman had brought the tall ghost into Anna's room at Fog Willows.

She couldn't move, couldn't think—she was blind and mute once again.

Anna let out a screeching sound and ripped an arquebus out of the hands of a terrified soldier before clubbing him with it.

"Anna, stop!" Juliana screamed. Then she rushed at her, ducking beneath the arquebus and using the technique of *butterfly hands* to strike her in the middle. Juliana didn't stop there. She'd been trained by Raj Sarin to attack with her hands and her feet. She struck Anna three or four times in a blur before getting struck by the butt of the weapon and knocked down. There was more commotion in the woods as the kishion attacked the soldiers who had been left behind.

A wave of fear spread from Anna. The soldiers standing nearby looked terrified, even though they were the ones holding weapons. Should they shoot Minister Fitzroy's daughter to save themselves? Could they bring themselves to harm an innocent being controlled by an evil entity?

Light. Light held the ghosts at bay.

Cettie searched the area, even though she still couldn't turn her head, until she saw where the Cruciger orb had fallen—its music now silent.

Instinctually she knew it would obey her. She needed to lunge for it, to pick it up. But fear had frozen her in place. Fitzroy wasn't there to save her this time. She couldn't move!

Then a memory from long ago surfaced. Back at the grotto, it was Adam who had saved her from the beast's call. She remembered the sound of his voice, his coaxing way. He had pulled her from her own grasping fear. In her mind, she saw his smiling face. It was a vision that stabbed into the darkest part of her soul. Just one of his smiles could do that to her.

Adam had saved her then. It was Adam she wanted now, in this moment of fright and uncertainty. If only he were here and not with the other soldiers from the ministry.

Cettie.

She felt the distant pulse of his thought. They were far enough away from each other that it startled her, but something had connected them.

Cettie, where are you? You're in danger.

She felt his worry, felt his concern. And then suddenly she could move.

Anna flung the arquebus at another soldier, striking him in the head and knocking him down. The soldiers who were still standing eyed each other with uncertainty, and one of them took a step forward. There was no time to dally. Cettie lunged for the Cruciger orb. As soon as her fingers touched it, light exploded from it, blinding her with its radiance. Anna screamed in pain as if a thousand knives had cut her at once. The ghosts were still everywhere around them, but they scattered like black leaves in a storm. The woods were flooded with light again. A keening noise came in her ears.

"No! No!" Anna screeched in her otherworldly voice.

A hand gripped Cettie's wrist. Caulton was on his knees beside her, blood streaming from a cut on his brow. He looked intense and committed. His eyes were fixed on the blinding-white orb.

"I name you, *Ashphodel*, depart!" he said boldly.

Another scream.

"I name you, *Havilah*, depart!"

"You cannot command me!" Anna shrieked.

"I name you, *Belkin*, I name you, *Crizznen*, depart!"

The scream that followed drowned out Caulton's words, but still he spoke, naming the ghosts one by one. Anna's body started to convulse and shake, her eyes rolling back in her head. She began to tear at herself with her own nails. Cettie cringed and gaped, horrified by the sight of her lovely, radiant sister doing herself injury, but she joined her power with Caulton's, and the light only grew brighter. One of the soldiers dropped his arquebus and fled into the night.

"I name you—!"

"No! No!"

And then Anna crumpled to the forest floor, pale as death, bleeding from the wounds she had scored in herself.

The ghosts were all gone.

In the light of the Cruciger orb, Cettie watched as the man who'd claimed to be her father strode forward, his face full of enmity. Caulton struggled to his feet, and Cettie came up with him.

There were only two soldiers left, and the kishion struck them both down with well-aimed jabs. Juliana stepped in front of him, drawing her blades.

"You cannot have them," she spat at him.

The kishion looked at her coldly, his scar twitching as he frowned. He drew his pistol and aimed it at her face. "I have come for what is rightfully mine. You will not corrupt her. Stand aside."

"Do as he says, Juliana," Caulton said warningly.

"I will not," she answered, her voice throbbing.

"Juliana, please," Caulton said. "Trust me."

"I'll go with him," Cettie declared. "Please. Don't hurt anyone else."

She heard the music again. It was rising inside of Caulton as he stared at the kishion. He still had a firm grip on her wrist, and she sensed that he had no intention of letting her go.

Trust me, he thought to her.

Juliana, gazing down the barrel of the pistol, slowly stepped aside. There was nothing between them now.

"Die, Maston," the kishion said coldly. His look hardened. Cettie knew he would pull the trigger.

The kishion was plucked off his feet. There was a groan and the crackle of branches. It was as if the tree had suddenly come alive and seized him. The kishion was immediately obscured by the leaves and limbs, and he grunted in surprise at the realization that he was well and truly entangled.

"Get Anna!" Caulton shouted to Juliana as he pulled Cettie away from the tree, which continued to whip and flail around. She felt the power course through his body as his grip tightened on her wrist. Juliana scooped up Anna's prone form as the captain and several of the wounded soldiers crawled away. The pistol belched fire, and a ball zipped past them. Smoke and stinking fumes came next, reminding Cettie of the night the Aldermaston had been shot. The kishion thrashed against his confinement.

Lights from zephyrs started to shine from overhead.

The captain couldn't speak, but he raised his wrist to his mouth. More light began to shine down, and Cettie's heart filled with hope.

The kishion let out a roar of rage, and suddenly the entire tree was engulfed in flames.

"Back, farther back!" Caulton warned.

It was a frightening sight, and the waves of heat blasted Cettie in the face, singeing her. One of the soldiers caught fire and began shrieking in pain.

The kishion emerged from the fire unscathed, his eyes glowing silver.

Caulton met his gaze with a look of determination. Suddenly another tree wrenched its limbs around and tried to grapple the kishion. The man dived to the side in time to escape its embrace, but the whole woods swayed. The fire from the one tree was spreading to others.

"I have the whole grove to command," Caulton warned.

A zipping noise sounded, and a ball tore through the trees, landing by the kishion's foot. He glanced down as more shots began to rain down. He looked at Cettie in rage and desperation. But even he knew he was outmatched as the zephyrs and their soldiers closed in. The kishion shook his head at her, as if *she* were making a grievous mistake, and then he turned and bolted into the woods, dodging the trees that tried to grasp him.

Juliana set Anna down safely away from the burning trees, fingers touching the young woman's scratched-up throat. A look of fury and resentment crossed her face, and then she charged into the woods after the kishion.

SERA

At Muirwood, as at other abbeys of learning, we teach truths that will unlock the power of the Mysteries in our students' lives. A first-year learner is taught that everything begins with a thought. They begin a regimen of study and meditation to gain control of their own minds. Second-year learners are taught that their thoughts, mixed with strong emotions, begin to awaken the seeds of connection to the Knowing within them, and some begin to see evidence of growth in their lives. A third-year student is taught the importance of their interactions with their fellow creatures, how slights and insults can permanently harm others' thinking, as well as how praise and cooperation can achieve matters of great significance. Some students, especially the proud, are quick to exploit this knowledge for ill. The fourth-year learner is taught the importance of time—the law of the harvest—and how certain powers only unlock after much dedication and effort. Some powers require years to master. Others require a lifetime. But an acorn will never produce an apple tree. All these teachings prepare a student to face the final Test, to learn a Mystery that is concealed from the world at large. In doing so they face a deep fear. It masters them, or they master it.

Words are but symbols. Harken then to words of the ancients, words that every first-year learner reads, but only one in ten thousand ever puts to use: "We search the tomes, and we have many insights and even a share of the Gift of Foretelling; and having this guidance, we obtain power by hope, and our faith becomes unshakeable, so much so that we truly can command the very trees to obey us, or the mountains, or the waves of the sea."

—Thomas Abraham, Aldermaston of Muirwood Abbey

CHAPTER TWENTY-TWO

PAVENHAM SKY

Sera had never been invited to Pavenham Sky before, and she was nervous about the visit. Hugilde had fussed over which gown she should wear and how to arrange her hair. It was common knowledge that Lady Corinne set the fashions in the realm. When she chose a new dressmaker, that person became a celebrity, and every other fashionable woman sought to imitate her choices. She was the wife of the wealthiest man in the empire, Admiral Lawton, though some argued that Lord Fitzroy was quickly gaining ground because of his and Cettie's miraculous invention. The ability to predict storms was certainly a profitable endeavor.

Pavenham Sky was a floating manor above the western coast of Comoros. It was the largest manor in the realm, with extensive grounds and tiered parks. Of course, the Lawtons also had a manor at Lockhaven, but it was Pavenham Sky that was the envy of all other elite families. There was no other place like it, and Sera leaned over the balcony of the tempest as it made its approach, anxious to catch her first glimpse of it. She wished Cettie were there to see it as well, to share the experience. Surely her friend deserved some relaxation after the upheavals at Muirwood. She would have suggested it, if only Lady Corinne were not so averse to people from the lower classes. *Or to people in general,* she thought with disdain.

The day of Will Russell and the hedge maze, she'd witnessed a private meeting between her father and Lady Corinne. Though she did not understand how, the meeting had resulted in a rift between her parents. Of course, it was out of the question to ask Lady Corinne about it. Mr. Durrant had warned her to be cautious about what she told the powerful woman. Her influence ran deep.

"Not so close to the railing, Sera, the wind will whip your hair loose." Hugilde was always worried about appearances.

"Then you can fix it," Sera replied, not budging. They'd been on board for several hours as the tempest cruised swiftly over the valleys and hamlets. They would arrive in time for a luncheon. Sera knew she was to be introduced to Lady Corinne's set that day, along with all the other young ladies under consideration to be married to the Prince of Kingfountain. Some of the girls, Sera had heard, were regulars at Pavenham Sky—which was how they had come to be considered for such an opportunity.

Although Sera was eager for the visit, she couldn't shake a feeling of uncertainty. The Lawtons had a reputation after all. The admiral was a shrewd man of business. He had left the Ministry of War at the age of forty and married a much younger woman, Lady Corinne. Some said she was an heiress who had brought part of the fortune herself. Others said that it was merely her beauty that had entranced him. Everyone agreed that they had found, in each other, a partnership and companionship that had catapulted Admiral Lawton to his great success. There was no end to his ventures. He never lost in a speculation, either, having the uncanny ability to invest early to his gain and to divest before trouble started. Pavenham Sky was the symbol of their wealth and glory. It was unsurpassed, even among the sky manors.

"What do you know of Lady Corinne's background?" Sera asked Hugilde after realizing her mind had wandered quite far afield.

"Only what I've already told you, Sera," Hugilde said with an exasperated smile. "I don't know the true story. I don't know that anyone does."

"Do you remember that day at the hedge maze?" Sera asked.

Hugilde's look darkened. "I think of it every day, Sera."

"I came upon Father talking to Lady Corinne. She had come by to see him, to share some news. I thought it strange, back then, that Father was meeting her so privately. I wish I could remember what they'd talked about. Whatever it was, it made things worse between my parents."

"I wouldn't put anything past her," Hugilde said. "I've heard that earning her disapproval is a costly mistake . . . one that can have repercussions that last for years."

"I know," Sera said. "Lord Fitzroy's wife, Lady Maren, was such a person . . . all because she was upset when the young man who was courting her chose another. I think it's sad that one woman can tarnish someone's reputation so easily. Don't you think it is strange that she hasn't reached out to me before this?"

Hugilde shook her head, folding her arms. "I don't think it strange at all. She doesn't want you to become empress."

Sera looked at her in surprise. "Why do you say that?"

Hugilde arched her eyebrows. "Because if you become empress, my dear, then ladies will look to *you* to set the fashions of the future."

That was an entirely new way of looking at the situation. Sera had never considered the possibility that Lady Corinne might perceive her as a threat to her power and station. The insight gave her an added measure of self-confidence.

"Oh, I think I see it!" Hugilde said excitedly. "Look!"

Sera turned back to the railing and caught her first glimpse of the famous manor. "Oh my," she gasped in wonderment.

While it certainly did not rival Lockhaven in size, the monstrous rock supporting Pavenham Sky was the largest Sera had ever seen under a single sky mansion. But it wasn't just one floating mountain; there were several, linked together with giant iron cables. Most of the lower ones featured sculpted gardens, but some had elegant servants' quarters too. There were multiple tiers, ending on the ground, and Sera saw zephyrs floating up from the gardens to bring guests to the main island in the air. The main manor was huge, the structure four stories high with a triangular facade on the front with parapets. The landing yard in front of the entrance held no fewer than seven tempests, each one hovering in place with room to spare. As they neared, Sera gaped at the admiral's private hurricane moored to the side with a giant chain. There must be an army of servants to work the grounds, she realized.

"Look! The sea!" Hugilde's voice showed how impressed she was.

Sera saw that the manor was moored in the sky above a long stretch of cliffs that joined with the sea. Waves crashed on the immaculate beaches beneath the edge of the manor, offering a grand view. The grounds on the cliffs were all sculpted with lawns and hedges and pathways. There were people walking down below, but no homes or dwellings, just private gazebos and benches. It was the most picturesque place Sera could imagine. Everywhere she looked, there were exorbitant displays of wealth, from the bronzed shingles of the main estate down to the lampposts on the stair rails leading to the beaches.

"This is why she is famous," Sera breathed. "Who wouldn't want to live here? Or visit?"

"Do you see the fog?" Hugilde asked. "Look, it's almost like a wall of it is being held back."

The bank of fog was restrained by some force to provide a perfect view of the land below. Instantly, she felt the desire to live at such a place, to be surrounded by such luxury. She had never understood covetousness before—there'd been no need—but the feeling was powerful. How strange that just seeing something grand could trigger such urges.

Their tempest slowed its approach as it descended to the main manor. The manor looked to be at least a century old, if not more. But the outer buildings all looked younger. Much of the growth had happened during the admiral's rise to power.

Sera nearly asked Hugilde how she looked, but she caught herself in time. Confidence. Confidence was key. Lady Corinne was worried about *her*. How was that even possible?

The pilot of the tempest swung lower yet, easing down to an open position at the end of the line. The other tempests were all likely owned by the families of the other girls chosen to represent the empire to the Prince of Kingfountain. When had the others arrived?

Her stomach was doing somersaults, but she tried to exude calmness. The breeze was pleasant with a savory smell of the ocean at its tip. The only smells wafting up to Lockhaven from the City were sulfurous ones. She could hear the crash of the surf in the distance, the sigh of the waters receding. Such heavenly music. Then she noticed there was also music piping from the main house.

The crew lowered a gangplank since it would be unladylike for her to climb down a rope ladder. Sera descended to the landing platform, careful not to trip over her long skirts. Her silk gloves went up to her elbows. She had chosen not to wear jewelry because the event had been described as an afternoon excursion, not a state ball.

A handsome middle-aged man met her at the bottom of the ramp wearing an expensive uniform comprising a coat, a buttoned shirt, breeches, and boots with too many buckles.

"Welcome to Pavenham Sky, ma'am," he said with a charming smile. "I am Lord Lawton's butler, Master Sewell. Your Highness, you do us great honor in accepting the mistress's invitation. Was the journey from Lockhaven pleasant?"

"Indeed, Master Sewell," Sera replied. He offered his arm to escort her, and she placed her hand on top of his forearm, as was the etiquette for such an occasion. Hugilde followed behind, along with some of Sera's bodyguards, but they joined the other servants and remained behind. Sewell, who led the way for Sera, was all grace and wit. He complimented her on her gown, her hairstyle, and even her smile. All words designed to put her at ease and make her feel welcome and comfortable. The intent was likely to manipulate her into lowering her guard. She was having none of it.

They passed the tempests floating at their respective berths, each one containing crew that had not been invited to join the festivities. Sewell then led her to the triple arches that fronted the estate, and when they passed beneath the shadowed lip, she felt the presence of the Leerings hiding there. It gave her the sensation of being watched, but then the Leerings always made her feel that way. The path opened to a courtyard as soon as they passed through the arches, revealing a massive square of gray stone. There was a fountain in the middle, beyond which twin stairs zigzagged up to a massive double door that was probably eighteen feet tall. It was capped by a triangular casement level with enormous windows. Indeed, windows gazed down at her from almost all sides. The patio had been swept recently, and their shoes made stuttering clicks as they walked.

Sewell escorted her up the stairway to the right, and when they reached the top, the massive doors swung open. The sound of the instruments grew much louder, and it only took her a moment to realize why—there was a full orchestra on display. The music at Pavenham Sky wasn't teleported in by Leering. No, they had their own music made there.

Sera tried not to stare as she entered the massive hall. The columns, stairs, railings, and banisters were ornate and decorated, some even sheathed in gold. The wealth on display was staggering. It was difficult to wrap her mind around the idea that Lord Lawton had earned the bulk of his fortune through speculation. Most men were ruined by excessive speculation, but his had earned him this. Uniformed servants dressed like the butler stood at attention along the main gallery. Sera was escorted down the long hall, but she saw a woman approaching her before she reached the double doors at the end.

It was Lady Corinne herself.

Sera guessed her to be in her midthirties. She had obviously been a very young woman when Lord Lawton had married her. What little of her hair that could be seen beneath her fancy hat was brown, but it was her face that intrigued Sera the most. Lady Corinne was pretty, but not in a particularly exceptional manner. She had a proud mouth, one that seemed to rarely smile, with just a touch of pink applied. Her eyes were grayish green and deeply serious, showing a keen intelligence. She was not flighty. If anything, she looked a little underwhelmed by the sight of Sera. If Sera had been concerned about her lack of jewelry, Lady Corinne wore only two dangling earrings of modest fashion.

As she drew close, Lady Corinne stopped and made a gracious bow. Now she did smile, just a little lift to the corners of her mouth, and she inclined her head in greeting.

"Your Highness, welcome," she said.

Sera recognized her voice, having heard it once before on that fateful afternoon.

"Sewell, if you would introduce us to the gathering please."

"As you will, mistress," Sewell replied with a bow, and quickly walked ahead.

Lady Corinne came and took Sera by the arm, not in a possessive way, but so she could speak to her in a confidential tone and be heard.

"I'm grateful you came, Miss Fitzempress."

"Thank you for the invitation," Sera replied.

"We may not have another moment to speak privately," Lady Corinne then said, dropping her voice even lower. They had just passed the gaze of two servants, and now no one stood between them and the rich maple-colored doors that Sewell was preparing to open.

Sera's unease grew even keener.

"Would you be so kind," Lady Corinne asked in a whisper, "as to return these letters to your father? I have not opened them. I do not want to know what is written in them. If he wishes to communicate with me, please inform him to send a note through my husband."

From beneath her vest, she carefully slipped out three folded letters and handed them to Sera. The scrawled directives on the envelopes were indeed in his handwriting. The seals were all still intact.

As Sera took them, Lady Corinne gave her an imploring look. "We have been an ally of your father's for many years. But this . . . these signs of familiarity must end. If you please, Miss Fitzempress. I would appreciate you returning them to him with my message."

"I-I will," Sera stammered. The letters were burning in her fingers.

Mr. Sewell pulled open the doors.

CHAPTER TWENTY–THREE

DEED OF SERVITUDE

It was almost impossible for Sera to focus on the conversations happening that afternoon in Lady Corinne's sitting room. She had tucked the letters away, but she quivered with indecision about what to do with them. Yes, she had said she would return them to her father. But she was keenly interested in opening them and learning their secrets. Was her father trying to instigate something untoward with the lady of Pavenham Sky? And if he was disrespecting her in such a way, would his behavior disqualify him for the throne?

Sera felt little loyalty to the man now, so she was primarily concerned with her own self-interest. He had tried to convince the world that Sera wasn't his true offspring. This could be an opportunity to get revenge, to humiliate him. That alone was tempting enough. But Lady Lawton had clearly intended for the indiscretion to be concealed. Making an enemy of such a powerful woman would be fraught with its own risks. Was Lady Corinne testing her? Sera's instincts were so knotted up and twisted that she couldn't begin to unravel them. Cettie would have known what to do. She was always so clearheaded. How she missed her friend . . .

Then there was the strangeness of this invitation to Pavenham Sky. Why gather together the rivals for the Prince of Kingfountain's affections? What did the lady stand to gain or lose from the arrangement?

Lady Corinne led the conversation, directing questions toward each of the young ladies present. Some of the questions were political. Which ministry would rule next? How did they feel about the trade disputes between such and such realms? What speculations were they involving themselves in? Others were more personal, like amounts they would inherit, other lands they had traveled to, their choice of study in school.

Sera waited for a question to be directed at her, but so far Lady Corinne had exempted her from the conversation. The mistress of Pavenham Sky never revealed what she thought on any of the subjects, and Sera believed this was done on purpose. It helped the lady of the house maintain her privacy and superiority.

Each of the young ladies was very wealthy and established. Most had finished their schooling the previous year and had passed the Test. One or two were on the cusp of finishing, though Sera was easily the youngest of them all. And the smallest.

While she listened to the questions, she observed the servants coming in and carefully and quietly replacing trays of food and drink. They were all uncommonly handsome young men dressed in uniforms that matched the chief butler's. Mr. Sewell remained in attendance for the entire event, giving directions with discreet gestures of his hands and fingers, sometimes just a nod. He was always attuned to Lady Corinne, watching her closely, as if trying to anticipate what she might desire.

After an hour or so passed thusly, Lord Lawton entered the study and was announced. Lady Corinne gave him a private smile and joined him before introducing him to each of the young ladies assembled. He was kind and gracious, and Sera noticed how Lady Corinne doted on him, watching his every move, just like the butler did for her. She clung to his arm, smiled when she spoke to him, and caressed his sleeve. It was plain for all to see that Lady Corinne admired her husband, and he treated her with respect and tenderness in return. It was an unfamiliar sight for Sera, a sharp contrast to her own parents' dynamic.

A sudden clattering sound jarred the tranquility. One of the servants had fumbled a tray. It didn't fall, but the contents had rattled and drawn attention. Mr. Sewell rubbed the bridge of his nose, clearly displeased by the disturbance. The servant was a young man, probably no more than twenty. He was the only one who wore his hair in a queue, tied in the back with a black piece of ribbon. Like the other servants, he was exceptionally well built and handsome, and he looked chagrined by his mistake. Sera felt a throb of pity. He wasn't reprimanded, but the mood in the room altered slightly at his gaffe—the only imperfection that had infiltrated the event—and Sera noticed some of the other young ladies smirking in derision. Mr. Sewell approached the young man and whispered something in his ear. The young man nodded and hastily lifted the tray to carry it out.

"And this is Miss Seraphin Fitzempress, of course," Lady Corinne said, startling her. She hadn't realized she'd been so distracted by that little scene.

Lord Lawton stood before her. This was not the first time they had been introduced. Although he was not a member of the privy council, his presence at court was not uncommon.

Sera rose and bowed to him while he did the same. "Lord Lawton, it's a pleasure to see you again. I think it has been a year, has it not?"

"It was the twenty-seventh to be exact, one year ago," he replied smoothly. He was one of the most mild-mannered men she knew, rivaling Lord Fitzroy in his gallantry. "My condolences about your grandfather, young lady. He was an honorable man."

"Thank you, Lord Lawton," she replied. "This is my first visit to Pavenham Sky. It does you credit, sir. I hope we have an opportunity to explore the grounds this afternoon."

"Most of our visitors desire that," he answered with another bow. "I would recommend seeing the cliffs at sunset. The view is quite stunning. There have been no portents of a storm either. It should be quite safe."

"That would be delightful," Sera answered, pleased.

"Miss Fitzempress," Lady Corinne said with a sly air, "has always wanted to visit the poor, have you not? Why, I believe your companion at school was from the Fells. What did you learn from that experience?"

Sera suddenly found herself the focus of everyone's attention. Was the question innocent? There was something in Lady Corinne's tone that suggested it wasn't. No, her host had excluded her from the previous questions to put her at ease, to put her off her guard. Now she would strike and see how Sera reacted.

Sera's courage rose to the occasion.

"I adore her completely," Sera said effusively. "She is probably the best student at the school. What do you think, Lord Lawton? Should knowledge of the Mysteries be kept secret except for those of privilege? Or should they be opened to all who have the aptitude to master them?"

She shifted her focus to him and saw Lady Corinne's eyes narrow just a little in her peripheral vision.

"It is a complex issue surely," he replied evasively. "What do you think?"

It would be easy to state her own opinions on the subject. She held strong ones. But she recognized this game they were playing. She would let them win if she revealed her own position before requiring them to reveal theirs. So often people spurted their own ideas without learning from others. Asking good questions was the key to wisdom.

"I am only sixteen, Lord Lawton," Sera replied with a sad shake of her head. "You have lived longer and have seen much more of the world. I would value hearing your insights on the subject. If you please?"

Lady Corinne's eyes narrowed a little more.

Lord Lawton was nonplussed. "It has been my experience that the prejudices of those living below preclude them from having the clarity of mind necessary for the rigors of mastery of thought."

She was grateful to have had Mr. Durrant as her advisor for so many years. She was used to language that concealed. The Law had always been something she'd excelled at.

"What you are saying then is that they lack the rigid self-discipline required or attained by patient study and determination?"

"Quite so," he answered.

"But if they do not lack rigid self-discipline or determination, should they be precluded from harnessing the gifts they possess and enlarging them as we do?" Sera was going out of her way to use the fanciest words she could summon to mind.

A wry smile came to Lord Lawton's face. "Every person is capable of enlargement. Most decide against it."

"What is your reason for thinking so?" She was beginning to enjoy herself despite the silent pressure of Lady Corinne's cold, assessing gaze.

"Because effort is anathema to them. Most people stay at a task longing for it to end. A man will work twelve hours at a factory each day because he knows when the whistle blows that his labors will no longer be required. They do as little as possible and nothing more. They endure the toil only because it is fixed, and they shirk and slouch and wait until their overseer's eyes are turned away before halting their efforts entirely. A reprimand is preferable to arduous work. That is my experience, Miss Fitzempress, with those who dwell below."

Almost timed to his words, the servant who had been surreptitiously trying to exit the room with his tray collided with the door. The tray, the goblets, and the dirty dishes all came smashing down at once with a dreadful clamor. Everyone turned their heads at once, and the young man, who now bore a smear of white sauce across his black-and-gold jacket, went instantly scarlet with humiliation. Lord Lawton's eyes became like flint, but he said nothing. Mr. Sewell rushed to the scene and scolded the young man in sharp undertones, his nostrils flaring.

The young women in the room began to titter and laugh, and some of the other servants broke their composure as well.

Soon the room was in an uproar.

"I don't recognize him," Lord Lawton said to his wife. "Is he new?"

"Very new, Husband," she sighed. "My apologies."

He shook his head curtly. "He will learn. Don't let Mr. Sewell dismiss him. It's just a mistake."

The poor young man's embarrassment was evident. He knelt on the floor, trying to pick up the broken pieces with his white gloves as the butler continued to chastise him for causing a scene. Sera was not laughing. She glanced around at the other young women, taking in their looks of disdain and mockery. *They* had never carried a heavy tray in their lives. Sera could not imagine doing so herself without fumbling. The injustice of their behavior made her blood seethe.

She was impulsive. Probably *too* impulsive. But she could not sit quietly and abide their laughter. It grated on her and made her rage inside.

"Excuse me," Sera said to the Lawtons. She quickly strode up to the young man kneeling in disgrace and bent down and started collecting the broken pieces.

"I'm so sorry this happened," she said to him in a kindly way. The laughter in the room ceased immediately as if the surf from the cliffs below had suddenly risen and drowned everyone. She would probably be shunned from Lady Corinne's inner circle forever because of her bold act. She didn't care.

The young man looked at her in startled surprise. He probably knew who she was. She picked up a few more pieces and hurriedly set them on the tray.

"It was just a little mistake," she said, trying to laugh. Everyone was staring at *her* now. Her fingers felt like they belonged to someone else. She could imagine the looks coming her way, but she refused to glance backward. She was shaming them all by helping him. Suddenly there were three more servants crouching nearby, their eyes wide with shock as they quickly collected the broken fragments together.

A stab of pain in her index finger told her that she'd cut herself on one of the slivers. She bit her lip and clenched her fist. The glove was made of silk. Of course it hadn't protected her from the shard.

"Did you cut yourself?" Mr. Sewell asked in her ear. "Let me see it."

"It's nothing," she replied, coming to her feet. The scraps were all collected on the tray, and another servant carried it swiftly from the room.

Mr. Sewell shot a look of daggers at the young victim who had caused the scene. "Go change at once," he hissed.

The young man bobbed his head. "Yes, Mr. Sewell. Of course." He was much taller than Sera. He had warm brown eyes and an embarrassed smile. "I'm sorry, Mr. Sewell."

"Just . . . go," said the butler, straining to be civil.

Sera watched him leave, noticing again the black ribbon tying back his queue. The room was no longer silent. She heard the murmurs and whispers from the young ladies gathered there. Sera felt the sting on her finger still, and when she looked at it, she saw her glove was stained with a splotch of red, right at the knuckle. She looked back at the young man who had reached the door. He'd opened it but paused at the threshold to look back at her. The embarrassed smile was gone. He was grinning at her, positively grinning. The sheepish look was gone. She saw keen intelligence in his eyes. He gave her a small nod and then left.

It was then she heard a whisper in her mind. It was so faint she wondered at first if she'd imagined it. It was like a flash of insight, a nudge to her thoughts.

The Prince of Kingfountain.

Of course he was. What other servant would be allowed to make such a fumble at Lady Corinne's notoriously perfect manor? As the idea bloomed in her mind, she realized that their arrival at Pavenham Sky was more than just a social call. They were all on display for him.

CHAPTER TWENTY–FOUR

The Cliffs

After the experience in Lady Corinne's sitting room, Sera immediately began to doubt the premonition she had received. Did she simply have an overactive imagination? None of the other young ladies seemed the least aware that the bumbling servant was anything out of the ordinary. None of the ladies behaved in a very friendly way with one another. They were rivals, after all, and that put them all on insecure footing.

After the refreshments and discussion ended, Lady Corinne announced that they would be visiting the lavish gardens of the estate together, culminating in a walk along the beach at low tide. Everyone seemed eager to participate.

The manor had a fleet of zephyrs, and the girls were to be sent to the lower gardens in groups of five or six. Sera shared a bench with Lady Wilkins's daughter, Penelope, whom she greeted warmly.

"If you don't mind my asking, Miss Fitzempress," Penelope said, "why did you stoop to help that clumsy servant? It wasn't your fault he spilled the tray."

"Does it matter whose fault it was?" Sera answered, not caring for the girl's reproachful tone. "He was made into an object of ridicule."

"Yes, but he is only a deeded servant. I should think you wouldn't have done that in the prince regent's household."

"Perhaps. But I haven't lived in my father's household in quite a few years," Sera answered.

"Oh," said the other girl in an obnoxious tone. "I'd quite forgotten. He tried to disown you. Really, Miss Fitzempress. Let the servants alone. Your attention to their station does them no good. It does you no good either."

"What do you mean?" Sera asked, trying to control her temper.

Another girl sitting across the aisle spoke up. "You would make them equal to us?" she said. It was Lord Mortenson's daughter, who had vast wealth and high connections.

"Your assumption is," Sera countered, "that because of the privilege of your birth they are not already equal."

"There is no chance or coincidence," she answered haughtily. "We were born in our station and they to theirs."

"But is it not possible for even *your* family to fall, Miss Mortenson? Is there not a chance of that happening?"

The girl gave her a sulky look. "For every speculation to succeed, someone must fail. There is a winning side and a losing side of every bet. My parents are betting that your father will be chosen as the new emperor. I think they are right."

Sera felt her cheeks begin to flush with heat. "If they are wrong, you've chosen your words unwisely."

"I don't really care," Miss Mortenson replied stiffly. "Soon I'll be living at the court of Kingfountain. I think it will suit me better."

"You are so vainglorious, Ingithe," teased another girl. "The prince will not choose you. He will choose *me*."

Sera thought about the young man who had dropped all the dishes. She kept her feelings to herself.

⌐‿

The gardens of Pavenham Sky were wondrous, and each had a different style and variety of vegetation. From one level, Sera could look over and see the next, farther below. Some were even joined together with floating boulders connected by iron railings or bridges so that guests could walk from one to another. The variety of flower breeds was astonishing, and they were distinguished by painted placards identifying them. It was whispered that the gardens were Lady Corinne's legacy, that she painstakingly directed the gardeners on how to arrange them.

During their walks, each of the young women present sought an individual audience with Sera, and it emerged that they were evenly divided in supporting her and her father. Again she thought of the letters she'd been given and wondered how their contents might sway the vote in her favor.

She would feel better about making her own decision if she better understood Lady Corinne's motives. In watching her, Sera tried to understand her personality and her character. The lady was intensely focused, and while she did possess deep knowledge of the gardens, she revealed very little about herself, choosing instead to draw out the girls she'd invited to the event. All except for Sera.

After visiting the gardens, they took the zephyrs down to the cliffs and walked along the well-tended footpath. It led to a stone pavilion where there was seating and a giant ring of fire fueled by four smaller Leerings. The flames rippled and danced in the wind from the cliffs. Near the dining area, there was a small kitchen and serving area where the servants had gathered to prepare the evening's meal. Sera spied the servant from earlier among them, his uniform clean. He watched the procession go by but avoided her eyes. Was that deliberate?

At the crook of the trail, a stairwell of timber slats had been built into the cliffside. It was very steep, and despite the iron rails lining the stone, some of the girls were unsure of themselves and their footing. Sera had climbed the Tor many times at Muirwood and found the descent easy. The sun was descending on the western horizon, lowering above the flat gray waters that extended into the distance. When they reached the beach, there were officers from the Ministry of War stationed there as bodyguards. Some of the young women teased and flirted with them, but the soldiers remained focused on their duty. Seeing the uniforms made Sera think of Will Russell, and her heart fluttered. How soon would he arrive at the City with the batch of letters? The irony of that thought made her sigh.

Piles of bleached driftwood were gathered against the walls at the bottom of the cliffs. There was so much of it that others had used it to build makeshift structures like benches and huts. The gentle shushing of the waves came and went, and Sera's eyes were fixed on the moving waters when she caught sight of something that made her gape in surprise. The beach had collected another piece of driftwood that was impossibly huge.

"Look! Look at that!" said Penelope Wilkins in wonder.

It was a tree, massive and tall, that had been uprooted and washed ashore who knew how many years before. The bark had all been stripped from it, giving it the same bleached look as the other trees. The root ball was five times taller than a man, a mass of tentacles frozen in rigor mortis. The silvered trunk tapered away from the root ball, but it was easily two or three times as wide as a human was tall. As Sera stared at the fallen tree, an intense craving to climb it seized her, flooding her with memories from childhood.

"I have never seen a tree so big," said Miss Mortenson. "It's gigantic."

"It came from that outcropping of rock," explained Lady Corinne, joining the group assembled on the beach. She gestured toward a small mountain jutting up from the waves farther along the beach. The cliffs were all scarred and battered by the surf, but the crown of the hill was green and covered with tall evergreen trees. None was so massive as the one that had fallen.

"Did it really?" asked Miss Mortenson with interest.

"You can reach that mound by sky ship," Lady Corinne answered. "There is a crater where it grew before."

"Can we go there next?" asked another girl excitedly.

"No, there are no trails there. It is very rugged and dangerous. The best view is from here on the beach."

"What is that tree called?" asked another girl, knowing Lady Corinne was an expert on all the names.

"It's called a *Shui-sa*. The Bhikhu named it. It means 'water fir.' They only grow on the coast or high in the mountains. If you were to cross the waters to the north, you would reach the principality of Pry-Ree. The trees come from there and are very ancient. This one fell long ago, and the waters washed it up on shore. It has settled in the sand and has never moved since. The trunk is nearly petrified now. Come feel it."

All the girls, including Sera, were eager to do just that. They joined together at the fallen tree and explored it while Lady Corinne watched them with interest. Sera grazed her hand along the silvery trunk. What she wouldn't give to have seen the mighty tree fall from the cliff and land in the water. There were still some broken limbs that would have made good ladders, and she found herself longing, again, to climb up it. It was clearly wide enough for her to walk down the length. Shoving the impulsive thought away, she walked into the shadow beneath the trunk and admired the mass of roots. The sand near the cluster was compact and wet, showing that part of the roots would be submerged when the tide was up.

She definitely had enjoyed the gardens and the beach more than the sumptuously decorated manor, which she couldn't currently see because of the cliffs. The beach was a treasure, owned by one family. Enjoyed by one family and those whom they invited to visit. It was a shame to guard such a secret.

The group of ladies lingered on the beach until the sun set, something they watched together. It was a unique moment for Sera. She'd never seen the sun get swallowed by the sea in quite such a manner.

When it was gone, a zephyr came off the mountain and joined them on the beach.

"The tide will come in soon," said Lady Corinne. "It is time for our dinner at the cliff."

Many of the girls looked relieved at the sight of the zephyr, which meant they would not need to climb back up the steep stairs.

"I should like to walk back up, Lady Corinne," Sera heard herself say. Mr. Durrant had always taught her to demand what she expected instead of ask for it.

Some of the girls gave her offended looks. Some admiring ones.

"By all means," Lady Corinne said. "The guards will see you up."

One of the girls, Miss Gentry, seemed eager to go with her, but she lowered her head after glancing at the other girls. No doubt she was too worried about their opinion of her to risk it.

Sera nodded to Lady Corinne and then started back up the beach. The cliffs did look imposing, but she knew she could handle the ascent. The cove had a magical air, and she regretted that she could not stay down below to watch the tide come in. The others gathered into the zephyr, which instantly lifted them up to the height of the cliff, and Sera began walking up the pathway. Two soldiers led the way.

The climb was indeed a bit strenuous, but Sera was grateful once again for the view and the opportunity to linger. She would never forget Pavenham Sky, and she could only hope to return one day and climb that tree. But not with anyone watching.

By the time she reached the top of the cliff, her legs were sore, and she was sweating and a little out of breath. She was also very thirsty. The others had assembled at the stone pavilion and were chatting gaily with each other. Servants with trays brought them drinks, and the light of the fire revealed their animated faces. As Sera drew closer, she heard music emanating from one of the Leerings.

A servant approached her with a tray, and she recognized him instantly. There was a single chalice on it, which he offered her with a slight nod.

"Thank you," she said, taking it. Her throat was parched, and she took a long draft of the sweet-flavored nectar. It was a blend of different juices. Very subtle but refreshing.

He bowed again and turned to leave without saying a word.

"What is your name?" she asked him, and he startled a bit.

"I am known as Trevon Wyckford, if you please, ma'am," he answered meekly.

"And where are you from, Trevon Wyckford?" she asked, again as he was about to leave.

He paused again and turned to look at her. "I'm from the north."

She took another sip. "Dundrennan, perhaps?"

She was hoping that her reference of a duchy in Kingfountain would stir a reaction from him. His eyes crinkled around the edges. "No, ma'am."

"Your name isn't Trevon," she said softly. "'I am known as . . .'" Then she offered a little chuckle. "You won't lie outright. That's good news. Your Highness," she said, inclining her head to him.

He was struggling not to smile.

"What gave me away?" he asked in an almost whisper. "Did someone tell you I was here?"

"No," she answered, shaking her head. "Just a feeling."

He pursed his lips. "Indeed? Are you going to reveal me in front of the others now?"

"I assume Lady Corinne knows?"

"Of course. The disguise was my idea. You get to know a lot about someone from how they treat others. Especially from how they treat people lower than themselves. You are the only one who thanked me for the drink, by the way."

"Your accent is impeccable," Sera said. "I always heard that our languages are very different. Though I've never met someone from Kingfountain before."

"Thank you, but I cannot take credit. Language is a Gift from the Fountain. Our cultures are similar in some ways. But they are also very different." He glanced back at the pavilion. "And I see we're attracting too much unwanted attention. So, do you plan to reveal me, Miss Fitzempress?"

"I can keep a secret," she answered, taking another sip from the chalice.

CHAPTER TWENTY-FIVE

TESTIMONY

Sera secretly enjoyed herself as she watched the prince in disguise serve each of the young ladies gathered around the fire pit. Some hardly paid him notice at all, taking what refreshment they were offered without even looking at him. Others seemed to recognize him as the disruptive servant from earlier in the day and gave him a slightly curled lip and a look of disdain. Miss Mortenson's reaction was especially hostile, and Sera had to shield her face, for she nearly burst out laughing.

Sera honored her word, however, and did not reveal the young imposter. Yes, he was getting a fair assessment of each young lady. The tide came in, and soon the waves were crashing against the wall of cliffs beneath them. A cool breeze followed soon after, but the warmth from the fire Leerings drove away the chill. A few young ladies took the opportunity to talk to Sera again, which she recognized as an attempt to curry favor, but if she'd learned anything from her visit to Pavenham Sky, it was that she had not missed much in terms of friendship by being kept away from these young ladies when she was younger. Her parents, flawed as they were, had at least shielded her from the pretenders who would puff up her feathers and the more competitive girls who would seek to best her at every turn. The encounters she had with the others made her even more grateful for her relationship with Cettie. She wondered how her friend would have been treated in such a gathering. Probably not very well.

Several hours after the gathering had started beneath the pavilion, Sera noticed the butler, Mr. Sewell, approach Lady Corinne and whisper something in her ear. The man had a concerned look, and Sera shifted forward in her seat, but she was unable to hear any of the words.

Lady Corinne's expression changed to one of concern. She nodded, touching the butler's arm, and then rose and quickly approached Sera. The conversation in the pavilion abruptly ended, and all watched to see what would happen.

"Your tempest has been put on alert," Lady Corinne said in a quiet way. "The privy council has called an emergency meeting, and your presence is required."

The news made Sera's heart beat faster. "Do you know what it is about?"

Lady Corinne shook her head. "Your sky ship will come down here to whisk you back to Lockhaven. The word just arrived. I am grateful to have met you, Miss Fitzempress. Thank you for coming to Pavenham Sky."

The other girls began to murmur to each other in low voices, no doubt speculating what situation could have demanded Sera's immediate return.

The tempest descended from the upper heights of the estate and came down to meet her on the grassy knoll by the cliffs. Sera saw Hugilde on board, leaning over the railing, as she approached the ship with Lady Corinne and Mr. Sewell, who personally escorted her.

"Have a safe voyage," Lady Corinne offered.

"Thank you for your hospitality," Sera replied.

They lowered the gangplank, and Sera strode up the steep ramp until she reached the ship. One look at Hugilde told her that her old governess was worried but didn't know anything herself.

Before she could ask, Hugilde said, "I don't know, Sera. A message came through the Leering from the Minister of War himself, ordering the tempest to fetch you and bring you back. Something has happened, but not even the captain knows what."

Sera didn't like being kept in the dark. She walked to the edge of the rails and watched as the gangplank was raised back on board. The tempest lurched, making her sway and catch herself on the railing bar. The small gathering of young women and servants quickly rushed away, and she thought about the young prince in disguise. Although she was more intrigued by him than she'd expected to be, she still felt her duty and her destiny was toward her own people, not his. But then she saw him standing amidst the dispersing crowd. He was the only one watching her sky ship rise. Their eyes met for a brief moment.

The speed of the sky ship increased, and from her vantage point, she could see the surf crashing below and could even spy the huge fallen tree amidst the waves. She wondered if she would ever return to the famous manor. And if she did, would it be as empress?

The tempest reached Lockhaven by morning. Sera had managed a few hours of fitful sleep in her stateroom on board, but she was drowsy and a little short-tempered when Hugilde helped her into a new gown and redid her hair for the meeting with the council. Looking at her own reflection in the mirror, she saw the gray smudges beneath her eyes and frowned at herself.

There were many tempests moored at the docking yard, but they were all military save one. It was a merchant vessel bearing the name *Serpentine*. The moniker sounded familiar to her, but she could not place it. After disembarking from the ship, she approached the entrance to the palace. Mr. Durrant awaited her at the opening, looking disheveled and wary.

"Do you know what this is about?" Sera asked him, and he quickly shook his head no.

"I do not. Whatever it is has been declared a state secret, and only members of the privy council are to be told. A merchant ship arrived before yours, and some people were ushered into the palace, a man and a woman. That's all I know. This way!" He took her arm and started to tow her toward the privy council chamber.

"Mr. Durrant, I have a question for you," she said as they walked swiftly.

"I will do my best to answer it," he replied.

"When I was visiting Pavenham Sky, Lady Corinne took me aside. She gave me several letters, still sealed, from my father addressed to her. She asked me to return them to him. I have them with me now."

His eyes bulged with surprise. "Did she indeed? Have you opened them?"

"No, of course not."

"'Of course not?' Why not? They could contain information that could ruin your father's credibility with the privy council." He chuffed, shaking his head. "If you have qualms about reading them, I certainly do not! A decision is likely to be made very soon. This could be just what we need for victory. May I see them?" he asked eagerly.

Sera still felt rather unsure about the situation. She'd been wrestling with her conscience all day. And yes, had she not constantly been in the company of others while at Pavenham Sky, she likely would have opened one by now. She'd been sorely tempted during the journey back to Lockhaven but had decided to ask the advice of Mr. Durrant and Lord Fitzroy before she did so. It was evident what Mr. Durrant's opinion was.

"We will discuss it after the privy council meeting," she told him.

"But, Sera," he urged, "I can read them and think of a suitable plan while you are *in* the meeting."

"Later, Mr. Durrant," she said firmly.

"Of course," he demurred. But she could see the sign of resentment in his eyes.

Some servants and military men were gathered just outside the council room. Sera was always one to look at faces, and she stopped suddenly when she recognized the Prince of Kingfountain's face amidst those gathered there. It startled her to see he'd somehow beaten her to the meeting. How was it possible? He met her gaze, and a half smile came to his mouth when he realized she recognized him. This time he was disguised as a soldier. She gave him an accusatory look, but then she was ushered into the room. She looked back at him, trying to untangle what was going on, but then the door was shut behind her, and she saw that the privy council had gathered and had been waiting for her.

Lord Fitzroy was present this time, conferring with two people she had never met before and who were not part of the council. Her father was in his usual seat, but there was a guilty, worried look in his eyes rather than his usual blustery confidence. Did he know about the letters? Had Lady Corinne told him that he would be getting them back?

Neither Mr. Durrant nor Hugilde had been permitted to enter, so she quickly came around and took her seat near her father's. The room came to order immediately.

"All right, Fitzroy," her father said grudgingly. "She's here now. I can't believe we've had to wait this long."

Although her father's tone was condescending, Fitzroy would not be ruffled. He looked haggard and weary, as if he had been up all night, but he spoke calmly in reply.

"I appreciate your patience, Prince Regent," Fitzroy said. "And to avoid taxing it further, I will be to the point. Yesterday, the privy council authorized the use of the Cruciger orb to hunt down the kishion who shot the Aldermaston of Muirwood. This man beside me is Caulton Forshee, a teacher at Billerbeck Abbey and the operator of the orb. The woman is my sister-in-law Juliana Haughton. I will summarize the events of last evening, and then they will answer any questions you may have. Agreed?"

"Get on with it, then," said Sera's father impatiently.

Fitzroy's eyes narrowed at the show of disrespect. He clasped his hands behind his back and then faced the rest of the council. "As you already know, my youngest daughter was abducted by this kishion last night. She was dragged outside the abbey's boundaries of protection."

"How is that possible?" interrupted Lord Welles.

Fitzroy glanced back at Mr. Forshee before returning Lord Welles's gaze. "The boundaries were tampered with. The kishion is clearly in possession of a kystrel. He bore the marks in his eyes. He caused a rift in the boundary. One that didn't trigger the Leerings."

A few muttered gasps filled the air. Sera had no idea what a kystrel was, other than a breed of falcon she'd heard about in her studies. But their reaction to the word and its dangers was pronounced.

"They were escorted by several armed scouts and followed their quarry into the woods. They found my daughter, but she was possessed. You could almost say she was infected by multiple entities of great power. In the commotion, several of the scouts were killed, the captain of the company was injured severely, and my daughter nearly died. If it were not for Mr. Forshee's gifts with the Mysteries of Thought, they might all have died last night."

"One correction, Lord Fitzroy," said Mr. Forshee. "Without your ward's help, it could have ended in even more deaths. She's exceptionally gifted."

Sera felt a rush of pride in Cettie and smiled.

"Noted," said Fitzroy. "Thank you. After they confronted the kishion and tried to restrain him, he escaped again into the woods. Juliana pursued him."

"That wasn't very wise," said one of the councilwomen, and a few others murmured similar comments.

Juliana smirked but said nothing. She didn't look the least bit chagrined. Sera had heard multiple stories about Cettie's aunt Juliana who piloted a tempest and worked in the trade routes. The woman certainly met her expectations.

"If I may continue?" Fitzroy said, clearing his throat. The room quieted again. "Thank you. Several zephyrs had been summoned by the captain on duty and were converging on the scene from above. Plenty of men to apprehend such a dangerous individual. He led Juliana on a chase through the murk before reaching the water's edge. As you know, the abbey is surrounded by water. They expected to find a zephyr hidden in the woods. They were prepared to intercept it. What she found is the reason this privy council was summoned. Sister?"

The quiet in the chamber became even more pronounced. It was then that Sera noticed the bruise on the woman's cheek and mud stains on her knee-high boots. She and Mr. Forshee stood near each other, both weary and unkempt. They must have flown to Lockhaven straightaway.

"I caught up with the kishion twice," Juliana said in a firm, steady voice. "We fought each time that I did, and he got the better of me both times. But I continued to pursue him out of vengeance for what he had done to my niece. The zephyrs had encircled us by then, and they all shone light down on the area. Some of the dragoons took shots at him, but he was fast, never standing still for very long, and he used the trees as cover. He reached the water's edge, and the water parted for him. Like he repelled the water in a way I don't understand. And he didn't slog through mud, as you'd expect on a lakeshore. He marched right down into the waters on dry ground. There was a ship waiting for him that had been submerged. He opened the cockpit. I only had a quick glimpse, but the hull was made of stone or some sort of marbled metal. After he entered the ship, the waters flooded back, and I could only watch the ripples as it moved away. It was completely underwater. I've never seen a zephyr do that before. Our ships are designed to float and ride out a storm, not travel underwater. What little I saw of its shape was completely foreign to me. Caulton arrived shortly thereafter, having used the orb to track me down. He didn't see it. Only I did."

"Thank you, Juliana," said Fitzroy. "I'm grateful you're safe."

"As am I," replied Juliana with a laugh, earning a spattering of chuckles from those assembled. "I've never seen a ship like that. And I've spent my life traveling."

"What does this mean?" the prince regent asked. "Lord Welles, what does it mean?"

Lord Welles rose from his seat and put his knuckles on the table. "I spoke to the prime minister before this meeting. I had already heard the report, and I'd like to add that the zephyr crews near the scene also saw something glowing beneath the waters. The craft sank lower and lower before it disappeared. I think this craft, this 'sea zephyr' if you will, is not from this world. As we all know, the world of Kingfountain uses a water-based form of magic. Though it has the same source as our own, they have rituals and customs that are very different than ours. Our superiority in the air is unmatched, but we know from our network of spies that their fleet of water-bound ships is vast and powerful. Their *navy* is unmatched. As we've learned from fighting them in the past, they can strike our ships in the air just as we can strike theirs at sea. We have been in balance. But this . . . this development is alarming. If they have invented ships that can travel beneath the waves undetected, then we will have no warning if they should decide to attack us. Hence the secrecy of this meeting.

"This overture of marriage may be nothing more than a pretext for another invasion. This offer to trade sciences may be only a distraction. Why buy what they can take? We already know many of their people consider our use of the Mysteries an affront. Heresy even. They have tried, over the centuries, to convert us to their ways with logic and pleading. More often with force. Some of our citizens have deliberately abandoned the empire to join in their ways. Some have returned disillusioned. Some were not permitted to return at all. Perhaps they have invented new weapons they wish to keep secret?"

He sighed and looked sternly at those gathered. "Ladies and gentlemen, we may be on the eve of war."

Lord Fitzroy shook his head. "Why would they send their prince to us to negotiate the marriage proposal himself?"

Sera had been wondering the same. "Maybe we should ask him?" she suggested.

The prime minister turned to her. "Miss Fitzempress, he is not at Lockhaven presently. He is staying with one of our illustrious families and learning more about our customs."

"He was at Pavenham Sky last night," Sera answered, ignoring the surprised looks on their faces. "But I tell you, I just saw him outside those doors dressed as one of Lord Welles's soldiers. Bring him in here. Let's ask him directly."

She could tell by the startled looks on their faces that they hadn't known he'd returned. Or how.

CHAPTER TWENTY-SIX

LOCKED DOOR

Lord Welles stood abruptly, his face twitching with anger. Several of the council members had turned to give him distrusting looks.

"That is a bold accusation, young lady," he said. "I would have been told if he were en route back to Lockhaven. Perhaps you are mistaken."

"There is one way to find out," Sera answered. "Open the doors."

"Welles, how could she know this?" her father demanded suspiciously.

"I don't know, Prince Regent," he said through gritted teeth. "But as she said, there is one way to find out." As he pushed away from the table, Sera rose from her chair and followed him. Lord Fitzroy's eyes had narrowed as well, and he cast a warning look her way. The council members began to chitter among themselves in disbelief.

She ignored them all and continued to make her way to the doors. Lord Welles reached them at the same time, his displeasure evident in his scowling mouth. His eyes stared into hers for a moment, almost accusatorily, before he pulled the door open.

The cadre of guards was still in place, including the young man she had met the night before. She saw that Welles recognized him instantly.

"Would you join us, please?" he asked, his tone rigid.

The prince touched his chest in surprise, and Welles nodded firmly. The young man's demeanor immediately turned defensive. He noticed Sera standing at Welles's elbow and shot her a look of confusion, but he did not hesitate. He nodded and then warily approached the council room door.

There was a collective gasp of surprise when the prince entered the room. The young man looked chagrined at the reception, but he strode in purposefully, one hand clasped to his wrist behind his back. His bearing and demeanor took on a more regal attitude, even though he was dressed as a soldier.

Sera's father had come to his feet and was trembling with rage. "Back so soon, Your Highness?"

The prince gave the prince regent a cool, studied look and then shifted his gaze for a moment to Sera. "I was made aware at Pavenham Sky that there had been some trouble. I thought it expedient to return quickly."

"How?" asked Lord Welles flatly, arms folded.

The prince swallowed but maintained his composure. "I elect not to answer that question."

"You are here as an invited guest," said Sera's father. "We have kept all of the terms of the negotiations thus far, and you have been granted unfettered access to our realm. The hostages were exchanged in good faith. But your welcome is not without its limits. You have violated our trust."

"How so, sir?" the prince countered.

"If I may, Prince Regent—" Fitzroy interjected.

"No, you may not," interrupted the prime minister. He, too, had risen. "Is it true, Your Majesty, that your nation has access to ships that sail underwater? That can be completely submerged without sinking? Be wary how you answer us, young lord. No falsehoods may be uttered in these chambers."

"Is this a trial?" the prince replied, still patient, though clearly ill at ease. "Am I not entitled to counsel from an advocate before answering?"

"Is your arrival here but a pretext for *war*?" the prime minister nearly shouted at him.

The feeling of animosity and anger in the room was powerful, and it made Sera cold and fearful. This animosity must not go unchecked.

The prince's lips were a firm line of disapproval. He was offended. He was vulnerable. "Do you think my father would have sent me here if he were planning duplicity?" he finally asked in a cold, measured tone. "Do you think him capable of such a breach of integrity?"

Sera's father's look was full of withering contempt. "You did not answer the question. A question put to you directly."

The prince glanced from face to face. "That you *asked* it at all says much. I don't know what game you are playing, Prince Regent—"

"Game?" her father snarled.

"Please," Sera said, finding her voice at last. She stepped forward. "Can we not all be civil? These accusations do nothing but churn the waters, making it difficult to see."

The prince looked at her. She couldn't understand what his look meant, but he finally said, "An apt metaphor, Miss Fitzempress." She realized he was probably referring to his belief in the Fountain. That had not been her intent.

"We are not the ones playing games, Prince Trevon," her father said angrily. "One of our Thought leaders was shot by an assassin. The kishion order was wiped out in our realm centuries ago, yet your world is renowned for its poisoner school. He uses obscure and improper magic to control water, and he then escaped in a ship that went underwater. Should not these facts cast doubt on your intentions? Was your arrival to woo one of our daughters merely a pretext? Or maybe you will say the Fountain commanded it. As if that absolves you from using your free will."

Prince Trevon's face grew pale with rage. Sera saw his hands clench into fists behind his back. Father had mocked his religion and his people. Deliberately.

"I think it is past time that I returned to my world," he said evenly.

"Not until you have answered some of our questions," Lord Welles replied in a dangerous tone.

The prince turned and looked at him with contempt. "I begin to see your end game, Lord Welles. A bold move."

"Surely," Sera said, coming closer to the prince, "we can resolve this peaceably. If you would but explain yourself, defend yourself."

The prince shook his head, and she fell silent. "I had hoped to make a peace between our peoples. To end this cycle of war. But this *machine* your ancestors invented—this business of despair you call your government—knows no other way. It corrupts everything it touches. It won't be stopped. It *cannot* be stopped unless it is broken. I'm sorry. I should like to have known you better."

"It's not too late," Sera implored. To her surprise, she felt a strong connection with him, an understanding of sorts, and he seemed on the verge of an irrevocable decision.

"Sit down, Seraphin," her father commanded.

Anger flashed through her. "And your hasty words are helping?" she shot back. Then she turned to the prince, extending her open palm. "Please, Your Highness. You have the power to put an end to this. Speak the truth. I will believe you."

"You do yourself credit," he answered. But he still looked wary, distrustful. "Yet I see where the true power lies." He turned and faced Lord Welles. "You forget, Minister, that my people have been playing a game called Wizr for a very long time. These machinations for power are not foreign to us. I see your move, and so I will counter it."

"I think not," the prime minister said. "We have you as a hostage to ensure good faith, and you've broken it."

"*I* think not." The prince repeated him archly. "Good-bye."

244

He jerked his arm away, revealing a flash of gleaming brass in his hand. It was a small device, no larger than a small baton, encrusted with jewels. It had clearly been concealed up his sleeve.

One moment he was standing in front of them; the next he was gone.

Over the course of the following hours, the empire switched to a posture of war. The privy council was angered by the prince's sudden and inexplicable departure from the center of the council room. Clearly the other kingdom's magic outstripped their own in some ways. The sky manors had been a protection for centuries against the seabound fleets of Kingfountain. But if the prince could come and go of his own accord, the safety they had enjoyed was now over. Despite Sera's pleading for a coolheaded response and an examination of the facts, she saw the council's blood was up. Lord Fitzroy also tried to argue for peace and the further use of diplomacy to resolve the crisis. But logical arguments did little to quell the council's wounded pride and even less to combat their fear. The empire was vulnerable against a threat that had powers they did not understand.

Lord Welles was given increased authority to prepare the defenses of the empire, especially the cities along the coasts, which were deemed the most vulnerable to a surprise attack. Conscription orders were given to bolster the military—workers would be taken from the factories and pressed into service—and the Ministry of Wind was ordered to screen each new candidate for signs of the cholera morbus. One infected soldier might kill an entire crew. The wheel of commerce would be changed into a wheel of war.

The prince regent's bellicose words helped inflame the situation. He hungered for the coming conflict. And Sera saw that many on the council looked to him for leadership and strength. Her impassioned words had not won her any support. If anything, they had harmed her position.

She returned to Castlebury, her heart full of anguish at the prospect of the impending conflict. Two days passed, and from her window she could see the hurricanes arriving to defend Lockhaven. No doubt her father was acting as protector of the empire. She chafed at her feelings of helplessness. In her mind, she repeated her encounters with Prince Trevon over and over again. She could not believe that he had deliberately taken part in some ruse to infiltrate the empire, but how could she prove it?

Somehow she had seen through his disguise. Had the Mysteries finally spoken to her? If so, why hadn't they also told her what to say to sway the council's decision? She wrestled with her feelings of helplessness. She knew she needed to take action, but she had no notion of what to do.

It was on the third day that Hugilde came to her with another letter from Will Russell. Preoccupied as she'd been with the war preparations, she'd almost forgotten about missives. As she broke the seal and scanned the letter's contents, she remembered the letters that Lady Corinne had given her to return to her father. She'd been meaning to talk to Lord Fitzroy about them and ask his opinion, but her ability to focus had been seriously compromised.

Will's letter was short and to the point. He was in the City down below. He'd been assigned as a dragoon on the hurricane *Vigor* and would be deployed the next afternoon to the massive ship that would be sent to defend the empire. He asked if she could meet him that evening at Commander Falking's home in the City. He provided the street name and described the house. He would return the letters to her then.

"What did he say?" Hugilde asked her with a tone of concern.

Sera sighed and read it over a second time. "He's been assigned to a hurricane. He leaves tomorrow. This is the only night he can meet me." Sera bit her lip. "Hugilde, it feels as if we are truly going to war. And

Will is part of that ministry. He could die. So many men and women will lose their lives because of this conflict. Why can't I stop it? They want to fight. Do we not have troubles enough without creating more?"

"What do you want to do?" Hugilde asked.

Sera turned the paper over in her hand. She dug her fingernail into the broken wax seal and picked it off. "I would like to go see him, but there is so much commotion everywhere. How would we get to the address he gave us?"

Hugilde shrugged. "That's a safe neighborhood, Sera. The officers don't live in the barracks. Any zephyr pilot worth his salt could find it in a trice."

"But it is in the part of the City that lies beneath us," Sera said. "Father never once let me go down there. What will Mother say?"

"Your mother's been invited to a society function with Lady Corinne tonight," Hugilde answered. "I heard her mention it at breakfast. Didn't you?"

Sera had been daydreaming about the prince and the coming conflict. In truth, she rarely listened to her mother's announcements. She shook her head, and Hugilde smiled patiently.

"What I'm saying is . . . tonight would be ideal. I could arrange for the zephyr."

Sera's eyes brightened. The thought of the small adventure, and the accompanying departure from her problems, was undeniably appealing. "I could wear a servant's gown as a disguise."

"Exactly," Hugilde said. "I won't tell your mother, Sera. And getting those letters back is for your own good, after all, especially if your father still intends to get his hands on them and use them against you. Best to get them back and squash the potential harm. We should go after your mother leaves."

"Wi—Mr. Russell wanted to keep one of them," Sera said worriedly.

"I wouldn't advise it," Hugilde replied with a sigh. "Maybe you can convince him to part with them all."

The rest of the afternoon, Sera prepared herself for the jaunt to the City. She had always wished to see it, and the prospect of seeing Will on the eve of his departure only added to her excitement. Mother was thrilled about the invitation she'd received to Lady Corinne's gathering at her Lockhaven house. It wasn't a ball, but such gatherings often lasted past midnight. Sera wondered why Lady Corinne had invited her mother. She wasn't aware of any sort of friendship between the two, but maybe it was a signal of a change in favor?

"Will you and Hugilde be all right?" Mother asked after dinner, accepting Sera's kiss on the cheek.

"Oh, don't worry about us. We're old friends," Sera answered innocently. "Have a delightful evening."

She watched as her mother left, and then she went back to her rooms, where Hugilde was waiting with a different dress for her to wear. Sera quickly changed and donned a cloak with a veil, which was how many servants traveled at night. Nervous energy thrummed in her heart as they carefully descended the steps and slipped out the back into the gardens. None of the servants saw them leave. Hugilde, casting careful glances around them, led her around the gardens to the gate leading to the front of the manor. She paused there, and Sera felt her use a small pulse of power to dim the eyes of the Leering there. The gate lock clicked, and Hugilde pushed on the bars, opening it. No soldiers had protected the house for a few days now, as all of them had been summoned for duty elsewhere. Only two bodyguards had been left, and they were stationed inside the house.

They walked side by side, cautiously and quietly, and crossed the small courtyard to the outer gate, where Hugilde repeated her efforts to disable the Leering. Beyond, they found a darkened zephyr parked on the street.

The pilot was slouching, but as they approached, he snapped to attention. "Good evening, Madame Hugilde. At your service. Have an errand to run in the City tonight? Should be down and back in no time. If you'd like to come aboard?"

"Yes, please," Hugilde said, pulling her cloak tighter. The pilot opened the side gate of the zephyr and lowered it, revealing a set of small steps leading to it. Hugilde went first, as if she were the important passenger, and Sera followed meekly. The pilot gave her a grin before following her up the platform. She nestled quietly on the small wooden bench next to Hugilde.

"Rowe Street it is," announced the pilot. "Bit of fog tonight, my ladies. But you trust old Hamblin, and he'll see you through it. I know the best ways up and down."

He started to hum to himself, and the zephyr came alive and began to hover. Sera's stomach lurched with a thrill as the sky ship raced away from their dark and quiet street and passed over the rooftops of the neighboring houses. She looked back a few times to see if any other zephyrs were following them. There were none she could see.

"I told you there was fog," the pilot said as they reached the outer edge of Lockhaven. The City was smothered in clouds, the thick, impenetrable kind that Sera had so often witnessed from the walls of her childhood manor. Only a few ghostly lights could be seen through them. The weather was ahead of the calendar—it already seemed like summer, and nightfall had only come an hour or so before. A few turrets poked up through the clouds, and Sera pointed at them and whispered to Hugilde. "What are they?"

"Some are manors," her old governess explained. "Some are hotels for the wealthy who cannot find a place in Lockhaven. They want to get as close as they can and see the view at least from beneath."

Sera nodded and felt her stomach lurch as the zephyr plunged into the bank of fog. Little droplets of water collected on her veil and began to drip down. She was overly warm in her gloves, cloak, and gown and wanted to whisk away the veil and feel the mist on her face. It had a hazy smell, the pungent scent of withered flowers.

Her excitement continued to grow, but she was nervous too. What if Mother returned suddenly to find her gone? Hugilde would get in serious trouble again. It would not be the same as before, when Sera had been little more than a child. The stakes were higher now. But her friend had accepted the risk. In fact, she'd arranged for the transportation on her own. And what they were doing was perfectly sensible. Getting the letters back from Will was a smart thing. Those thoughts helped assuage the nervous feelings twisting in her stomach, but they didn't banish them.

The journey lasted no more than half an hour, and soon they descended through the mist to Rowe Street. Leering lamps lit the way, but there were very few people around. The cobblestones were slick and wet. The buildings were five, maybe six stories tall, fronted with stone, and quite stately. The roofs were sharply pointed, and lights glowed from windowpanes set into wooden beams. The zephyr alighted on the landing yard for the street and soon settled into place.

"I'll wait right here," Hamblin said with a smile. He helped them down the squat steps of the ladder one at a time.

"Which one is it?" Hugilde asked, looking at the various doors facing them from both sides of the street.

Sera had already memorized the address in the letter. "See the iron bell? It's that one," she said, pointing. Now that they had arrived, her anxiety pressed against her mind. She overruled it, eager to get the business done with.

Hugilde led the way, and Sera followed, their shoes scraping against the wet cobbles. It felt like they had crossed into another world because the stones up in Lockhaven had all been dry.

Hugilde mounted the steps to the door and firmly knocked. It was a narrow-looking place—most of the homes were—and the color and form of the bricks were different between each of the homes on the streets. Though Sera was surprised at the variety in style, the differences were not as major as she had supposed they'd be. This was still very much a part of her world, her empire. Sera bit her lip in agitation and eagerness. Footsteps could be heard from inside, followed by the jangling of the door handle, and then there was Commander Falking on the landing, not a hat to be seen on his graying hair.

"Ah! You've arrived! Thank you, madame, for the note earlier. We were expecting you. Come in, come in!" He smiled broadly, though he cast a nervous glance over the street before ushering them in. "Was the fog much of a devil to you on the way down? You had a good pilot, I hope?"

Hugilde glanced around nervously. There were no servants inside the house, and it felt still and empty.

"He was very good," Sera said, answering for her. She lifted the veil. "It's a pleasure to see you again, Commander."

He gave her a strange look—neither fully a smile nor a wince—and bowed. Then he gestured for the hall. "Well, the lad's been a bit nervous, to speak truthfully. This way. This way." He began to walk down the narrow hall toward the sitting room doors. There was a small, well-lit study off to the side, but Sera couldn't see if anyone was in there. She heard no noises, no footfalls except their own. The house was dead quiet. Falking must have dismissed his servants for the night in anticipation of their arrival. The fewer witnesses, the better, right?

Why then did she feel as nervous and out of sorts as Hugilde looked? Had this been an error in judgment?

When they reached the study doors, Commander Falking opened them. Will was pacing inside. She recognized him instantly, although he was much taller, more muscular, and even more handsome than she remembered. He was wearing his regimentals, and his gloves were stuffed in his belt. The buttons on his jacket gleamed like huge bronze coins. His rank insignia, lieutenant, was on his shoulders.

When he caught sight of her, he immediately stopped pacing. His mouth was so serious, as if he were indeed very nervous. He had transformed since their last meeting. He was a man now. And she felt very much as if she were still a girl of twelve.

Sera tried to master her flurrying feelings. She strode into the chamber, extending her gloved hand. Why wasn't he wearing gloves? Aside from Minister Fitzroy, the only people she knew who regularly shirked them were Adam Creigh and Cettie. "Mr. Russell, it's so good to see you again," she began, in a formal but cheerful way.

Then she heard the door shut and lock behind her.

CHAPTER TWENTY-SEVEN
THOUGHT MAGIC

The sound of the lock was subtle but unmistakable. Sera was alone with Will. For a moment, she could not think beyond the shock of the situation, then she began to feel her legs tremble because it felt as if she'd been caught in a trap. Being alone with a young man was against the mores of her world. This was a social violation of the highest order.

"Thank you for agreeing to see me," Will said. "I thought it might not happen in time, but I was relieved when I received word from Falking that you were indeed coming."

He took her hand in his, and she realized she was still extending hers. Discomfort roiled inside of her. He did not seem so nervous now. A hint of a smile toyed with his mouth.

"Why did they shut the door?" Sera asked haltingly. "H-Hugilde should be with us."

"You didn't seem to mind when you charged into the hedge maze with me," Will answered with a chuckle. When he rubbed his thumb across her knuckle, she extricated her hand.

"I'm . . . I'm here to get the letters," Sera stammered, cursing herself for having agreed to this outing at all. Once again, she'd been too hasty. She was certain her cheeks were pink, and her ears were quite hot. The way he looked at her, the handsome smile, the look of familiarity, showed that he was expecting something more than exchanging letters. Her throat tightened into a knot as tremors shook her body. Cettie had warned Sera that her heart might be more involved than she realized. How wise her friend had been.

"I know," he answered smoothly. "But I get to keep one of them. Remember?"

"Yes, yes, I do remember that part." The room felt as if it were shrinking. There was a slight buzzing sound in her ears. She felt completely vulnerable, but she tried to rise above it. Only there was one thought she couldn't shake. Why had Hugilde left them alone? She listened for a sound from the other side of the door, but she could only hear their mingled breaths in the room.

"You know," he said in a half-serious tone, "I believe all the things they taught us at school about thoughts and destiny. It's true."

She looked at his face, and again her body started to shake. Something felt off, unfamiliar . . . dangerous. She had not been summoned here in earnest. "Where are the letters?" she asked. Would her voice not stop trembling?

"I have them here," he said, patting the pocket of his jacket. He slipped his hand into it and withdrew a bundle tied with a green ribbon.

Seeing them made her feel a bit of relief. Perhaps she'd misinterpreted the situation, and there was nothing to worry about after all. His brown eyes looked deep and earnest in the dimly lit room. The only source of illumination was a single Leering set above the fireplace. She was tempted to snatch the letters from his hand.

"May I have them, please?" she asked, holding out her hand.

"Of course, Sera. I brought them for you. But it pains me to part with them. All but one. I want something in return. If I give you what you want, then you should return the favor." He slid the bundle back into his pocket.

Sera's heart was pounding faster than horses now. She knew what he wanted without him asking. The image of them kissing came unbidden to her mind. Her mouth went dry, and fear and guilty excitement did battle inside her. She'd thought of kissing him, many times. She'd never had such an experience before, and Will was an exceptionally attractive man. And yet, this was wrong. They didn't feel alone, even though they were. Her thoughts were like moths trapped in a jar—she could hardly make any sense of them.

"Don't be afraid of me," Will said softly, shaking his head. She saw his hands were trembling. "Before I go . . . I had hoped . . ." He struggled to find words and failed.

Part of her wanted to rebel against the rules, and yet . . .

"Will," she said, not sure what to do. Her feelings told her one thing. Her sense told her another.

He stepped even closer. "Yes?"

"I don't think we should," she said thickly.

"You can think right now?" he said with a suppressed chuckle. "I've imagined this moment for the last four years. An opportunity to be alone with you. With *you*, Sera Fitzempress. I've wanted to see you again since that day your father forced me to leave you. How I wish we could have studied at the same school. Seen each other every day." He shook his head, his eyes blazing with emotion. "He robbed that from me. From us. I don't have any expectations from you, Sera. Just give me a memory that I can take with me into battles that are coming. If I'm to die on an airship, I want that memory to linger on my mouth. Please, Sera." He turned his head slightly, his voice husky and earnest. "Please."

His words had a calming effect on her. Instead of the frantic beating of the surf, her heart now felt like a bird trapped in a cage. The panic was receding. Calm assurance was replacing the disquiet. She did ache to touch him.

He took another step closer. They were so very close . . .

"Please," he whispered again.

The cravings inside her were so intense she could hardly breathe, let alone speak. She wanted the memory too. Lowering her lashes, she nodded to him.

She had already lifted her veil after coming into the house. His fingers traced the edge of it near her face and brushed it slightly back. The tips of his fingers grazed her cheek, sending a jolt of awareness through her. He leaned down, pausing a moment, and she smelled his breath. It had a pleasant fragrance. The light from the Leering exposed the slight blush on his face. Suddenly, she couldn't bear the thought of the stone statue staring at her. In her mind, she commanded it to go dark.

The light from the Leering shrank until it disappeared entirely, leaving them both in deep shadow. There were three large windows on the far wall, veiled and curtained. There was only one source of light—the lampposts from the street behind the house. It illuminated the room just enough for them to see each other.

"You like that better?" he asked her in a gentle way.

Again she nodded, and then she leaned up on her tiptoes to press her mouth to his. When they kissed, her mind swooned from the warmth and passion and energy of it. His arms wrapped around her shoulders, and he pressed against her. She held her hands in front of her, not able to succumb so fully to the moment, as if she knew she should push him away. A feeling of delicious warmth soaked through her. The hunger in her grew into a lion's roar. He was kissing her mouth and then her cheek and then her neck. Each press of his lips made her more and more uncomfortable, more dangerously delirious.

"Will," she breathed, pushing against him.

His hands came up and untied the veil and hat, which dropped down her back.

"Will, stop," she said, trying to push against him again. Her voice sounded weak in her own ears.

"Sera," he breathed, and then he was kissing her neck again.

Part of her begged her to surrender to him. Her passions were inflamed. *This* was the reason that propriety was so strict. Her willpower shriveled in the face of such heat, such passion. But she would not compromise her standards even further.

"No, Will. No," she said, feeling anger replace the flush of desire. This was more than a kiss farewell. This was a greedy demand, an urge he was satisfying for himself. He didn't care about her feelings. Only his. She pushed harder, and he finally backed away.

His knuckles came up and rubbed his bottom lip. He didn't look wounded or hurt. He looked almost gleeful.

"Give me the letters now," she said, feeling more in control of herself.

He smirked and fished them out of his pocket again. "How about we read them again first? The ones I sent you were all destroyed by your father, I know. But these . . . these are precious to me."

"Give them to me," she insisted.

He shook his head. "You can't leave so soon, Sera. I just need to entertain you a little longer. There are *other* ways we can do that, of course, ones that are more interesting."

"How dare you," Sera said indignantly. A sudden rush of anger restored her strength.

"Oh, I dare much," he answered, his tone growing colder. "It won't be long now. Your mother was forbidden entry to Lady Corinne's party. In fact, she was never invited. No doubt she's back home by now, and you aren't there. Has the panic settled in yet? Where is her daughter? Where did she go? Who is she with?"

Sera realized with dread that it had been a trap after all, one that had been carefully orchestrated. And she, gullible and naïve as she was, had walked into it.

"I'm sorry," he said with an unapologetic shrug. "I had hoped for a little more fun before you realized what happened. What you'll be blamed for." He reached for her hand and brought it up to his mouth.

She slapped him with her other hand, rocking his head back.

"I'm going, Mr. Russell," she said with blistering rage. "Letters or no."

She strode to the door and knocked on it firmly. No one answered. There still wasn't any sound on the other side. Had Hugilde betrayed her too? The thought sickened her.

Will put his hand on her shoulder. "They're not coming," he said coaxingly. "We are truly alone in an abandoned house. You need to be here just long enough for suspicions to firm. For your reputation to be irrevocably damaged."

"How could you do such a thing?" Sera said, whirling around and hitting his chest with her fists. The thought of being caught alone in a home with him . . . well, there was no doubt what the privy council would think. This would disqualify her from becoming empress, certainly. Wasn't that the point? Vast sums were betting on the outcome. Yet, like everything else, the speculation had been rigged by one more of the players. And she had unwittingly become an accessory to her own downfall.

"I am being well rewarded for spending this time with you," he answered, jerking back when she tried to hit him again.

She turned and yanked on the door handles, but they were locked and wouldn't budge.

"Please, Sera. You're not going to break down that door. I doubt even I could."

"You are a scoundrel and a rake," she said, turning on him venomously.

"And you are the daughter of a selfish puppet," he shot back. "One who punishes those who do not deserve it. A hypocrite and a fool."

"I thought better of you, Will Russell. I was wrong."

"You're wrong about a lot of things," he said. "And even if you got out those doors, where would you go? The zephyr isn't waiting for you. And you have no idea how the world down here works. We're both of us caught in a cage." He shrugged. "We wait now for the jailor to arrive." He began to unbutton his coat.

"What are you doing?"

"It needs to *look* convincing, Sera. Maybe a few loose buttons on your gown?"

A blinding white heat seared her mind. "If you touch me again, I swear I'll—"

He chuckled, raising his eyebrows. "You think a threat will work in such a moment as this? I'm a dragoon, Sera." He finished unbuttoning his jacket and then tossed it on the floor where it lay in a heap.

Sera turned around and pounded on the door again. "Hugilde! Hugilde!" she shouted.

Will came up behind her and, seizing her around her waist, pulled her from the door. "I'm not going to hurt you, lass. But I won't have you causing a racket."

"Let go of me! Let go!" Sera struggled against him, and he released her, sending her away from the door. She rubbed her arms, trembling all over. She wanted to scream at him. To rage against the injustice he'd visited upon her.

He leaned back against the door, arms folded, eyeing her. She backed away from him toward the curtains, feeling sick to her stomach. Why had she even left Muirwood to begin with? The Aldermaston had admonished her to stay. Why hadn't she listened to his wisdom?

Will tugged loose the collar knot of his shirt and flung it onto the floor. "Come, Sera. No matter what you do, you'll be blamed for an indiscretion. The least you can do is earn it."

"Is that supposed to convince me to go along with this?" Sera asked furiously. "How do you know you'll be paid for this, Mr. Russell? The same people betraying me will turn on you. You know too much. If you can be bought once, you can be sold twice. Don't you understand? Do you even know who is behind this?"

"Do I care?" he shot back, growing flushed with anger. "My father was left penniless because of people like you. He was robbed. Just as you are being robbed. It was your fault that you dragged me into that accursed maze. Well, at least it will benefit me now."

"You're deceiving yourself," she said, backing farther away. She felt the fabric of the curtains brush against her back. "This won't end well for either of us."

"Well, you've certainly dashed *my* hopes thus far," he countered. "I thought you'd be more . . . willing to indulge."

Her mind was working furiously. The curtains led to windows and to a street. This wasn't the Fells. It was a respectable neighborhood, or at least she hoped so.

"How soon before they come for us?" she asked.

"Soon enough, darling," he answered spitefully.

Sera closed her eyes. Drawing on her fragile will, she summoned the Leering's light, needing it to help her see the window and its latch. It wouldn't respond to her at all this time, and her failure struck her as hard as a physical blow. But still she wouldn't quit. Turning, she shoved the curtain aside and tried to find the latch in the dark.

"What are you doing?"

She found it and torqued it open. The window was heavy, but it pushed outward.

"No!" Will shouted, starting to run across the room.

Sera got her foot on the sill, grabbed the frame with both hands, and pulled herself up. If she allowed him the opportunity, he would grab her again, pull her back into the room. He'd pin her on the floor if he had to. And so she jumped from the window without a second's hesitation. The cold, misty air rushed against her face until she struck the hard cobblestones with bone-jarring force. Landing on her forearms and knees, she got to her feet and started running down the alley. She didn't look back.

But she did remember, at the last moment, that her hat and veil had been left behind in the dark room.

CETTIE

The Test has evolved over the centuries because the conditions on this world have changed. Exposure to other worlds similar to our own has broadened our knowledge. Intelligent people can observe the same facts but disagree as to the interpretation of them. Such is the case with neighboring worlds. Such is the case among our own people. Each student at the abbey comes to learn the general principles behind the Mysteries, the power of thought and its alchemic effects. They learn that if they control their thinking, they may commune with the Knowing and harness knowledge capable of benefiting the various worlds. Then each student chooses a discipline and is taught the gifts that have already been bestowed therein—the varieties of musical instruments, the wonder that a brush dipped in paint can bestow, the laws of momentum and matter, the intricacies of deeds, and the stratagems of war and power.

All of these things are taught during their years of study here. But there are vital truths held back until the Test. Truths that must be experienced firsthand. For some students, these truths are terrifying. They go against their wishes, perhaps even their personal beliefs. But it is our duty and calling, as ministers of the Mysteries, to gather in every item of truth and reject every error. We must be willing to receive the truth, let it come from whom it may. Truth embraces all morality, all virtue, all light, all intelligence, all greatness, and all goodness. It introduces a system of laws; it circumscribes the theories of the day. If we understood, for example, the process of creation, there would be no mystery about it. It would be all reasonable and plain, for there is no mystery except to the ignorant.

—Thomas Abraham, Aldermaston of Muirwood Abbey

CHAPTER TWENTY-EIGHT

THE TEST

The day for Cettie's Test had finally come, and she waited nervously in the Aldermaston's manor. The sitting room was full of people she knew and cared about, for she and Phinia and Adam had been allowed to wait together with their visiting family, as was customary. Lady Maren had come earlier to help Anna recuperate from her harrowing experience, escorted by Stephen in the family tempest, and all three of them were present. He was currently teasing Phinia about taking the Test, telling her she wasn't prepared for it and would likely fail. His smirk revealed he didn't believe it, but it bothered Cettie that he would choose such a time to tease his sister.

If only Sera were there with her, they'd exchange a look, and both would know what the other was thinking. Why hadn't Sera returned from Lockhaven yet? The last letter she'd gotten from her friend was about her visit to Pavenham Sky. Surely it was a good sign that the Mysteries had whispered to her and allowed her to recognize the prince. Cettie had written back asking when Sera would be coming back for the Test and sent her a sprig of lavender. She'd gotten nothing in return.

She was worried about her. Perhaps, as a Fitzempress, she could take the Test at her own convenience, but even so . . .

Adam stood at the window, hands clasped behind his back, gazing out at the bright sunlight. His posture put her in mind of Fitzroy, a thought that helped calm her uneasy mind. She looked away from him when Lady Maren rose from the couch she shared with Anna and came over to sit by her. Putting her arm around Cettie's back and hugging her, she asked, "Are you nervous?"

"Of course she is. What student isn't?" Stephen quipped. "I'm grateful the Test is over. For me anyway."

"You are so rude, Stephen," Phinia complained.

"I don't know why they even bother with it," he said flippantly. "While I worry about Phinia passing, I have no doubt that Cettie will. I've heard good things about her progress. She's quite envied." Praise from him was rare, and Cettie felt her cheeks flush.

Lady Maren rubbed her back. "There will be much to think about. I didn't understand it very well at the time I took it. But I do agree with Stephen. You will do well. The vigil will help heighten your senses. It will make the experience more meaningful."

"And then we can all have a nap this afternoon," Stephen drawled with an exaggerated yawn. He had been less than pleased to sacrifice his sleep with them, as was customary.

Phinia swatted his arm. "And what about you, Doctor Creigh? Are you nervous?"

Adam looked away from the window. "Not in the least. I'm intrigued by it."

"Spoken with all the dispassion of a physician," Stephen said. His target's expression changed not at all. "I'm jesting, man. I have no doubt you'll pass."

A knock sounded on the door, and when it opened, Aunt Juliana entered with Caulton Forshee.

"Aunt Juliana!" Phinia exclaimed, rushing forward to hug her.

Lady Maren rose from the couch and embraced her sister next. "I didn't know you were coming back so soon."

"I didn't want to miss the opportunity to see them before the Test," Juliana said, smiling brightly. "It wasn't easy leaving Lockhaven."

"Who is this?" Maren asked.

"Caulton Forshee, at your service," he said, bowing to her. "I begged a ride from Captain Juliana."

Cettie noticed he was standing rather close to her.

"I'm grateful you returned," Maren said to him. "I wanted to thank you in person for saving my daughter."

"Your husband was gracious enough to already thank me back at Lockhaven, ma'am," he said with a reserved tone. "And truly, it was the Mysteries' will, not mine. The villain who attacked us has left these shores. It seems likely he returned to Kingfountain. I think that threat has ended."

"While another has begun," Juliana said. She frowned. "This incident won't end here at Muirwood. The council suspects Kingfountain is after a war, and the prime minister has ordered Lord Welles to put the military on high alert. All available young men are being conscripted." Her gaze flashed to Adam standing by the window.

Cettie saw a look of growing dread on his face.

"Truly?" he asked in a half whisper.

Juliana nodded. "All the graduates from this year have been given their commissions, but the Ministry of War is conscripting doctors to serve in the fleet. I'm sorry, Adam, but I've no doubt you'll be one of them."

His mouth turned to a frown as the disappointment came crashing down on him. His whole face twitched with emotion. Cettie's heart panged to see his hopes dashed so thoroughly—and right before the Test. She could only imagine how he felt.

"But the cholera morbus," he said with forced control. "We haven't learned the source or even the cure. If all the doctors are taken, many will die needlessly."

"The ministry is calling for strict quarantines," Juliana said. "The sickness comes and goes. No one knows why."

"I know," Adam said angrily. He clenched his jaw and started to pace. "Such are the vagaries of life. I've never had a desire to serve in the Ministry of War. None at all."

Lady Maren spoke what they were all wondering. "What about my husband?"

Juliana frowned and shook her head. "I don't know. I couldn't get anyone to tell me anything about it. He has served in the Ministry of War before. Maybe they'll ask him to relinquish his position and take a command."

It felt as though a cloud had blotted out the sun. War was truly coming. The cycle was repeating itself once again. Inexorable. Like time itself.

"Might I have a word with Cettie and Anna?" Caulton said in the somber moment following Juliana's pronouncement.

"Of course," Lady Maren answered, her face suddenly ashen. Her husband was being ripped away from her. Even Phinia looked shocked by the news, and Stephen had lost color—no doubt he was pondering his own fate.

Anna rose from her couch and then hurried over to sit beside Cettie. The two girls gripped each other's hands.

Caulton approached them there, and he squatted in front of them. "You look better than you did the other night," he told Anna. "But still shaken, I see. Still haunted."

"I am," Anna confessed. "It was a living nightmare. It felt like I was trapped in my own mind."

Caulton nodded. "I'm sure it did. I took the liberty of talking to your father. He said that you used to have night terrors in your childhood?"

Anna squirmed. "Yes."

Cettie remembered them well. Mrs. Pullman had had cruel ways of controlling everyone in the household who didn't meet her personal standards. Her thoughts turned dark.

"You still have two more years at school before you will take the Test. When you do, you will have a better understanding of what happened to you that night. What you need to know now is that it was not your fault. Not one bit. If I may, I would recommend that you consider the Mysteries of Thought as you continue your studies. The knowledge imparted in those classes may help you. I hope it does, and I truly hope you can leave what happened behind you. You were abducted. That would terrify anyone. But it doesn't have to rule you." He patted Anna on her knee and then turned to Cettie. "All I wanted to say to you, Miss Cettie, is that even though you've studied the Mysteries of Wind, you clearly have a talent for the Mysteries of Thought as well. That you could use the Cruciger orb at all is quite remarkable. I teach at Billerbeck Abbey. I should like you to visit me someday so we can talk further about your experiences in the Fells. There is much I would learn from you."

Cettie was taken aback by his praise and interest. She'd never imagined it was possible to do what he had done in the woods beyond the abbey. She would like to learn from *him*—and was honored that he thought he could learn from her too.

The door opened again.

The time had come.

All the students who had finished their fourth year were gathered into two groups, male and female. They'd all spent the night with their families in various sitting rooms at the manor. The teachers whom they had studied under then helped them into robes that fit over their regular clothes. The robes were light gray cassocks that extended down to their ankles, with hooded shawls that draped across their shoulders and could be lifted to cover their heads and faces. They were instructed not to look at the other students as they entered the abbey, which they would do from the outer doors. Mrs. Romrell helped Cettie into her robes and smiled encouragingly at her all the while. Before they were separated, Cettie gave Phinia's hand a reassuring squeeze. She looked very nervous—no doubt the product of her brother's teasing.

They were then escorted from the Aldermaston's manor single file and led down a small footpath to one of the abbey's arched doorways. Cettie looked up at the spire. The midmorning breeze caressed her face, carrying all the gentle fragrances from the grounds. For four years she had passed by this structure, feeling the strength of its protective Leerings. The music they made together seemed to thrum against her skin, giving her a feeling of awe. This structure had been built hundreds of years ago. The stone was flecked with lichen, but it had endured storms and ice for generations. It had endured wars too. There was comfort in that. She was not the first to take the Test. Nor would she be the last. This moment linked her to so many other moments that would come before and after.

As they neared the arched doorway, which was held open by two of the teachers, Cettie felt the Leering set in the keystone glare down at them. It exuded a powerful feeling of fear and dread. Cettie saw one of the girls ahead of her trembling with agitation, but she dared not comfort her. They'd been instructed not to speak to one another.

As they neared the threshold, the girl halted, quailing in fear. She stepped away from the line and started back toward the manor, tears streaming from her eyes. Cettie bit her lip, sorry for the girl who hadn't been able to tame the Leering. It was strange, but while she, too, could feel the warning and foreboding emanating from the Leering, it was more like the drone of a bumblebee collecting pollen than the warning of an angry wasp threatening to sting.

Cettie followed the other girls into the abbey. The walls shone with Leering light, and a feeling of intense peace surrounded her. Just past the doorway, two female teachers were helping the students remove their shoes. The girls continued in just their stockings.

The walls were intricately designed, she noticed. The trim was inlaid with gold leaf, and the polished stone tiles fit together at angles to form interlocking geometric shapes. It was like staring at an equation from one of her mathematics classes, and she was so distracted by the sight she nearly collided into the girl in front of her who had paused. The line led to a door, which in turn led to a stairway leading to a level below the abbey. They were surrounded by the deepest quiet, but Leerings were carved into the walls at regular intervals, and there were bouquets of flowers in huge stone urns. To Cettie, it felt as if she had come home.

When they reached the bottom doorway, it opened into a larger room full of heavy wooden benches. There were two sections, slit in the middle by an aisle, and Cettie watched as the young men in their robes filed in to the opposite side. They had entered the abbey from another door, but the destination was still the same. She tried to spot Adam, but instead caught Mr. Skrelling's eye. He quirked a smile at her and nodded. Cettie nodded back before taking her seat on the bench.

When all the students had entered, save those who hadn't made it past the first test, the teachers closed the doors and then stood in front of them as if guarding the gathering from intruders. Cettie waited in anticipation, feeling at once eager and nervous. She was sitting on the end of one of the benches, so she risked another glance across the aisle. Adam was sitting just across from her, head bowed in concentration. Seeing him so close made her wonder if fate had arranged it.

The Aldermaston of Muirwood entered from an alcove at the head of the room. His gray cassock matched theirs. He supported himself on a cane and winced as he ambled forward. One of the teachers came to help him, but he waved the man back. The sound of his shuffling steps and the thump of the cane on the tiles mixed with his labored breathing. The Aldermaston's face was strained, but he was clearly determined to perform his duty.

When he reached the front, he paused to catch his breath and supported his weight on the cane. His forearms trembled with the effort.

"My young friends," he said at last. "For many years I have officiated in this ceremony. I worried that I would lack the strength to do so this time. But I am supported by your kind thoughts and by the excellent teachers at this school. Forgive me—" He paused, wincing again, and waited a moment for the pain to subside.

"At this abbey you have been tutored in the Mysteries. We do not know them all, nor can we because of our finite human minds. You have learned how to listen for the whispers that connect us to the power and wisdom of the Knowing. Some of you have practiced this and gained wisdom. Some of you think it is a farce and have progressed very little. Some of you have used this power to persecute one another. You each have your choice. And you will reap the fruits you have planted by your industry . . . or your neglect."

He coughed, and then his voice became stronger. "When each generation builds on the knowledge of its forebears, the whole of civilization progresses. This ritual differs from bygone days because our knowledge of truth has so expanded. But there is something they knew that you do not. It is the Mystery I will explain to you now before you take the Test."

Cettie leaned slightly forward, attentive to his every word. She quieted her mind, trying to muster her courage and her belief.

"What I speak now is the truth insofar as we comprehend it. When our world was created and organized by the power of the Mysteries, it was not uninhabited. Before the First Parents were stationed in a garden of Leerings meant to protect and shield them, there were other beings who walked the craters and hissing storms of this planet. They were called the Myriad Ones, the Unborn. They had a queen, Ereshkigal, who persuaded the First Parents to partake of the fruit that made them mortal. It was her intent to forestall their progress, to prevent them from building cities of stone that would sail the skies and visit other worlds. For many thousands of years, Ereshkigal was successful in her quest to stamp out light and twist truth. Her goal is to turn this world back into ashes."

Cettie felt a shiver go down her back.

"But in the days of the first empress, Maia Soliven, Ereshkigal was trapped in a Leering, confined in a prison of stone. Her followers, those with mortal blood, were all hunted down and destroyed. The first empire grew, and with it came a season of peace and prosperity unlike anything our people had yet experienced. The Mysteries began to be revealed in numerous and advantageous ways. All because the people honored the truths that they had learned."

His brow furrowed, and he frowned. "But those are no longer our days. Prosperity and wealth have brought pride and cunning. In the past, the Myriad Ones feasted on the baser emotions of mankind. They marauded the world in the guise of animals and serpents. Now they walk among us. The people call them ghosts and believe them to be the spirits of the dead. But that is not the truth. They are still the servants of their dark queen, and they seek a way to free her. No one knows where the Leering confining her is located. For if it were known, there are those among us just cruel and selfish enough to seek to free her and unleash her terror once again on the world. These ghosts, these ancient demons, seek to possess our corporeal bodies. They do this through our hearts, our emotions, which they touch with their thoughts and even with their fingers."

His voice became grimmer, more solemn. "You may think I am jesting with you. I assure you, I am not. Since you came to the age of understanding, the age in which your minds begin to quicken, a wrestle started over control for your thoughts. You have been sought after by the Knowing, which has encouraged and whispered to you to seek out truth. And you have been seduced by the Myriad Ones, who wish to take possession of your thoughts, your very bodies, to do unspeakable evil. Some, a very rare few, are so sensitive to these creatures that they can actually see them with their natural eyes." He paused, and Cettie swallowed. "Most of us cannot, which makes it difficult to discern which dark thoughts come from them. You may believe you yourself are the source of all of your negative thoughts. This is not true. But we are, each of us, culpable for our actions. Our choices. To guard yourself from these beings and to remind yourself of what you have learned here, you will each be given a chain and a pendant, which you will wear close to your heart. This pendant will repel the Myriad Ones and prevent them from entering your body through your heart. If you ever take it off, you will be at risk to them."

Cettie blinked quickly, feeling tears prick her eyes. Could she be safe from her ghosts at last? A spark of hope brightened inside her.

"You may wonder why this knowledge has been kept as the final Mystery, why we allow others to suffer from these demons, these evils spirits. In the past, this knowledge was shared with all. Indeed, Empress Maia made provisions for everyone to learn. But some began to mock what they were taught. To doubt it and scoff at it. Visitors from other worlds called us heretics and built towers in an attempt to reach our floating cities.

"Remember, those who want to free Ereshkigal desire the world to burn, to revert back to its primeval chaos. The truth will always make the ignorant angry, whether they be ignorant out of choice or lack of opportunity, for the Myriad Ones despise truth and light above all. Your test, my young friends, is to face your fear and release a demon trapped in a Leering here inside the abbey. You will command it to learn its true name and then confine it again. It will try to possess you. Guard your thoughts. This is your test. Stand when you are called."

CHAPTER TWENTY-NINE

BANIREXPIARE

One by one the students were called forward and taken by a teacher into the alcove. Since none of them returned, Cettie assumed that they were permitted to leave when the Test was over. She was nervous. No, that wasn't even the right word to describe her feelings. Her insides were twisting into knots. All her life, these Myriad Ones, these ethereal beings, had tormented her. She was more than a little afraid to face them.

She glanced over to Adam and found his head bowed in deep concentration. Despite the news from earlier that he would likely be summoned to use his skills to aid the Ministry of War, he looked calm. His calm infiltrated her, giving her the peace she needed to face the test ahead.

Adam turned his head then, and their eyes met. He offered her a reassuring smile.

You can do this, Cettie.

She felt his thought brush against her mind. Smiling back at him, she gave him a small nod.

You will do well, Adam. I know you will.

She wasn't sure if he could hear her. He didn't react to the little thought push she sent him. But his little nudge of encouragement helped enormously. She waited, hands folded in her lap, and began to slow her breathing and calm her fears. In the abbey, she was safe. They would not give her an experience she could not handle. They wished for her and all of them to succeed.

Soon she was wrapped in a cocoon of magic. Her thoughts and fears had calmed. When they called her name, she rose steadily from the bench and passed the empty rows in front of her. To her surprise, it wasn't a teacher waiting for her at the alcove, or at least not one of *her* teachers. It was Caulton Forshee. He gave her a slight nod, and she fell in next to him as he escorted her through a gray-painted door. The corridor beyond was lit with Leerings.

"I begged permission from the Aldermaston," he said softly as they walked. "I wanted to be the one to introduce you to this Mystery. At Billerbeck, this is my favorite part of being a teacher. The most rewarding."

She gave him an inquisitive look. "Why is that?"

"All of your years of preparation and schooling will finally come to fruition. People have different experiences taking the Test. Some are terrified by it and never want to return to an abbey again. Others require years of reflection to understand the ritual. But still others, and I believe you might be one of them, are transformed by the experience. It starts them on a path to fulfill their destiny. I cannot take the Test for you, Cettie. But I will be close. You can do this."

She'd heard the same sentiment from Adam, and their faith in her comforted her all the more. At the end of the corridor, her way was blocked by a door made of stone with a Leering carved into it.

Caulton paused in front of the door and then turned to face her. "The first empress was powerful with Leerings. Her meekness was such that all Leerings desired to obey her. She had a Gift called Invocation, which enabled her to create them. She created the first Leerings that could bind the Myriad Ones, trap them into stone. When she began to do this, they fled from her and from her cities. Above all, they desire freedom of action, freedom of movement. They covet what *we* have and seek to force us to surrender our freedom of will to them. As you pass this Leering, you will walk down a corridor made of pillars, each with a Leering. Certain Gifts require covenants. You must agree to the terms to receive the knowledge of how to bind the Myriad Ones. From here, you are on your own, but I will be watching you. You are never truly alone, Cettie."

She gave him a nod of respect and appreciation, steeling herself to face the Leerings ahead. Otherworldly music spouted from beyond the stone door. Already she could sense it, feel it tingling against her skin. Powerful emotions surged inside of her. Not fear, however, but a feeling of certainty. Of welcome even.

"Go," Caulton said with a smile.

As Cettie approached the stone door, it opened at the slightest push of her thoughts. The stone door closed behind her. She felt and heard the Leerings before she saw them. It was a symphony of sound, but she could pick apart the various instruments easily. Each Leering represented an oath she must take, but these weren't requirements or restrictions. They were empowering. To revere and not profane the Knowing. To keep her body and mind chaste. To never pollute herself with any substance that would lessen her willpower. To speak the truth. To protect the innocent if within her power. To contribute to the feeding of the poor. To tame anger and malice. To willingly give of her means to allow others to be taught the way of the Mysteries. To never reveal the covenants she made to outsiders. There were nine in all, and she made them willingly, wholeheartedly, eagerly.

A thrum of approval came from the pillars as they fell silent. Two Leerings began to exude mist at the far side of the room. She felt she should walk into it, and so she strode down the corridor purposefully. The mist bathed her face, so thick that she could not see far ahead . . . and then she could see nothing at all. She put her hands forward to avoid bumping into something, but light appeared from another Leering just ahead of her. As she approached, she realized it was a pair of glowing eyes. This Leering was carved into a plinth, a polished sheath of stone that was sculpted into an obelisk, as high as her chest. The top formed a pyramid. The burning eyes of the Leering revealed a gold chain slung across the pyramid. The medallion threaded onto it was the eight-pointed star, the symbol of the mastons. She felt instinctively that she should put it on.

Cettie reached out and touched the necklace. It was warm to the touch. She slipped it over her hair and let the medallion dangle in front of her bodice. But that felt wrong. The Aldermaston had said it must be worn beneath her clothes. So she tugged at her collar and slipped it beneath her dress so that the medallion nestled on her chest. A surge of strength flooded her, making her fingers tingle. She wondered what to do next—should she leave the corridor?—but she felt a whispered command to put her hand atop the obelisk.

Gently, she set her palm down on the pointed tip of the obelisk. The chorus of magic grew louder, stronger, and suddenly the eyes of the Leering burned impossibly bright. She winced and closed her eyes, but even through her darkened lids, she could still see light from the Leering shooting through her hand.

In her mind she heard the words.

Your name is Celestine. Guard this name. Never speak it.

Another Leering beckoned to her from up ahead. Cettie ventured deeper into the mist as she approached it. The mist parted to reveal it to her. It was a kind she had never seen before. There were two face profiles, pointed in opposite directions, joined by a single head. Both faces looked sneering, angry, menacing. As she approached, she felt she should touch the stone, and as she did, she heard both of the faces mutter a different word.

Apokaluptis.

Banirexpiare.

The thoughts were spoken resentfully, almost angrily. She invoked the Leering again, and the faces repeated the words. She did not understand, so she kept her hand on the Leering and invoked it a third time. Again the words were spoken, but this time she understood the meaning. They were both words of power from an ancient language. *Apokaluptis* meant "to reveal that which is hidden or secret." To break past an illusion. The other word, *banirexpiare*, meant "to banish by royal decree." To speak it would be to leverage the authority of someone greater, like speaking in the name of the emperor.

Now she understood. One would reveal the true name of the Myriad One. The other would banish it. Both words could be spoken by the mind or whispered aloud. Because the beings could hear thoughts, they were affected by the words of power. She remembered when she had first met Fitzroy at the tenement in the Fells. He had driven away the tall ghost, the one without eyes, without saying a word, and only now did she understand how he'd managed it. It was because he had learned the ancient secret for banishing the Myriad Ones.

Suddenly the room went black as night. She couldn't see the Leering or even her own hands. The darkness was instant, impenetrable. It had happened so quickly that her first instinct was fear. But it made sense. She'd been told she would need to face and banish one of the Myriad Ones, and she knew from experience they could not abide light.

A buzzing sound came to her ears. The hair on her arms and neck stood on end. Images from her childhood began to flash vividly through her mind. Her heart raced, and she found herself breathing quickly, fearing the moment the being would enter the confines of the room. In her mind, she saw Mrs. Pullman's evil smile, saw her disdain and loath-ing. Cettie shuddered at the feelings coursing through her body. It was dark; she was alone and helpless.

Hello, child. Have you missed me?

Cettie's voice felt choked. She couldn't have spoken if she'd wished to, and her limbs seemed frozen in place. Panic welled up inside her.

Did you think that a few years would make you more powerful than me? Mrs. Pullman's voice sneered at her. *Only hate grows more powerful with time. Oh, how I* hate *you, child. What you did to me. It was your fault. You stole everything from me.*

Cettie didn't understand how Mrs. Pullman was there with her. But her voice was unmistakable, and it brought back all the emotions of helplessness and fear from her childhood. She was a little girl again, trapped in the garret.

I thought you were in prison, Cettie pushed out.

Prison? Is not this a prison, child? The mastons show no mercy, despite their boasts and claims of it. If you cross them, you are doomed forever.

Cettie felt the presence in the room begin to circle her. She could not see Mrs. Pullman, but she could smell her in the air. Was it a lotion she had used? Cettie didn't know, but the horrible familiarity of it ter-rified her even more.

Oh, and they tricked you, child. Just as I tricked you. It's all a web of deceit. They are corrupt. You know they are. They teach humility, but they do not practice it. The proudest of them rule. And you want to be one of them? You want to wear their yoke around your neck?

Cettie felt a wraithlike hand reaching for her heart. If she could have screamed, she would have. Once those ghost fingers touched her chest, they would sink into her skin. They would take something from her.

The fingers touched her chest, but a spark of magic sent them jolt-ing away. The pendant.

I wore one of those too. When it was yanked away from me, I finally understood what it all meant. How I had been their slave all my life. It was too late for me, child. I had sold my soul and now am forced to live in a body of stone. That will happen to you, too, unless you let me free you. Tell me your true name, and I will unlock your trap. Just think the name and I will hear it.

Cettie's mind was whirling with doubts and concerns. How was Mrs. Pullman here? It sounded like her, smelled like her. But could those senses be false? Was this not the very trickery the Aldermaston had warned her about?

You aren't Mrs. Pullman, Cettie thought angrily.

How can you doubt me? You know *me. You remember me. Of course I am, child.*

How long have you been trapped here?

She felt a hiss of anger in the thoughts. *You dare question me? Who are you, insignificant child? You mongrel from the Fells. That is where you truly belong. Why would they let someone like you in this place to begin with? You are never going to amount to anything.* He *will never love you back. Oh, you try to keep your secret from the world, but you cannot keep it from me. I know you've already given your heart to him. And who are you to deserve someone like him? Who are you to take what a Fitzroy wants?*

It was not Mrs. Pullman. Of course it was not. The Myriad One had latched on to her thoughts, her fears, and her strongest emotions. It spouted words that caused shame and self-doubt—a dark art it had no doubt perfected over its long, long life. Why was Cettie even listening to it?

Apokaluptis, Cettie thought.

Nooo! the evil being shrieked at her mind. The discordant rhythm grated down her spine, like the horrid squeal of violin strings.

The storm of rage went silent.

My true name is Tethera the Unborn.

Cettie felt the binding on her mouth loosen. Her legs and arms were freed as well.

"How long have you been bound, Tethera?" Cettie asked her, her voice shaking a little. "Speak truthfully."

Three hundred years, mortal. But I have always existed. As have you. There is darkness in you. I sense it.

Cettie had long struggled with feeling the darkness inside her. So she willed the Leering to brighten.

It began to glow, and the being known as Tethera shrank accordingly. Cettie saw it as a pale shadow, a being of energy that swirled like dust motes. The thing hissed and began to slink away from the Leering.

The light. It burns. Bind me!

The Myriad One couldn't escape the room. As the Leering grew brighter, its pain grew worse. It cowered against the wall, shrinking smaller and smaller. Cettie stared at it, feeling no remorse or compassion. It would have taken her over if it could. It would have claimed her body as its own. It would have ruined her. Memories from the Fells surfaced at that moment. The suffering that she and so many others had endured under the influence of the Myriad Ones. Most people had no notion there was a way to free themselves.

Banish me! Banish me, mortal! But we will be avenged. We will break free of this prison. The final end has not come. Our queen will be freed once more. Then we will have our vengeance. Vengeance on you all.

Cettie saw it shrink even more, saw steam waft from it. It was a being of pure hatred. There was no limit to its malice.

"Banirexpiare," Cettie said, and heard the screech of nails on stone as the Leering dragged it back inside the light.

The peaceful feeling began to return, but still she was shaken by the ordeal. It was only an imposter. They all were. But how quickly it had

deceived her and led her mind and thoughts down a dangerous path.
Cettie frowned and clenched her fist. She would allow these creatures
no more power over her. As her heartbeat slowed and she felt the relief
of passing the Test, she heard the Knowing whisper to her.

*You will leave the abbey grounds. Banish the Myriad One that
hunts you.*

CHAPTER THIRTY

EYELESS

The ordeal of the Test was over. Cettie returned her robe to the teacher awaiting her at the end of the passageway and walked briskly toward the sitting room in the Aldermaston's manor to rejoin her family. The mood on the grounds was subdued. She saw students hugging each other, many of them weeping loudly. She had imagined it would be a moment of celebration. Instead, it was a time of deep emotion and great solemnity. The abbey felt different to her now as she gazed at it. It was not just a beacon of light. It was also a prison for the unholy.

When she reached the study, she found Phinia in tears, her handkerchief damp with them. Stephen had a consoling hand on her shoulder, and Lady Maren was holding her hand. Anna wasn't there, which was confusing. Where could she have gone when all her family was here? Aunt Juliana paced the room and gave Phinia a reproachful look. Maybe she hadn't passed?

Cettie shut the door gently behind her, but even that quiet sound drew their gaze.

"Of course *she* passed," Phinia said, sniffling. It was said with resentment and misery.

Stephen gave Cettie a wary look, but he said nothing.

"There you are," Lady Maren said, coming away from Phinia and embracing Cettie. "I've been watching the door for you. It's over. You passed?" There wasn't a speck of doubt in her voice.

Cettie nodded but felt uneasy expounding upon her answer.

"It was *awful*," Phinia wailed. "How could they expect us to confront our fears like that? I'm never leaving the clouds again. Not in a hundred years. Not if we have to deal with those . . . those *things*."

Lady Maren turned and gave her daughter a reproachful look. "You have good reason to be upset, Phinia."

"But you have no one else to blame but yourself," Juliana said.

"Sister, let me handle this," Maren said.

"You are her mother. You are supposed to be gentle with her. I'm her aunt, and that entitles me to speak the truth for her own good. I love you, Phinia. But I'm not at all surprised you didn't pass. Ever since you were small, you've been more interested in dancing and balls than serious study. Well, you've reaped what you have sown. Some consequences come soon. Some come later. Better to realize your faults now and improve upon them."

Phinia's expression crumpled, and she buried her face in her kerchief and sobbed again.

"That didn't help," Maren sighed out.

"Maybe. But it felt good to finally say it." The two sisters looked at each other and shared a secret smile, though Maren was quick to drop hers.

"What does it mean for her?" Stephen asked, his arm coming around his sister protectively.

"It won't hurt her prospects very much," Lady Maren said with a sigh. "Our family has a good reputation and considerable wealth. She won't be ignored."

"But what will I *do*, Mother?" Phinia said through her tears. "I'm so ashamed. How can I face my friends?"

Lady Maren glanced at Juliana again. "Phinia, dearest. Most years, only half of the students pass the Test. You are far from the only one."

"Is that supposed to make me feel better?" Phinia wailed.

Maren approached her daughter again and cupped her chin. "I know it doesn't. I know your heart is hurting, and that grieves me too. But Aunt Juliana is right. For a long time, you've been more preoccupied with the wrong things. You weren't prepared for the Test. You know that. I don't need to say it. But it troubles me that you are only worried about the social consequences." She gave her a serious look. "Instead, you should be worrying about how to improve, how to better hear the whispers from the Mysteries, how to be more aware of the feelings of others. It's not impossible to take the Test again in the future. It's just that most people choose not to because they failed once. It makes them afraid to try."

Lady Maren bit her lip and then pulled Phinia into a hug. Phinia started to sob again from disappointment, and Cettie felt the room growing too stifling for her. She had been told to leave the abbey grounds, and she still hadn't obeyed. Her nerves were tightening with worry the more she procrastinated.

Juliana gave her a wink as she slipped out the door, unnoticed by the others, who were still carrying on over Phinia. Cettie smiled back.

She walked out of the manor and started toward the apple orchard. Summer was in full bloom early, but there was a chill in her heart as she acknowledged what she was going to do. She had not faced her greatest fear in the abbey. No, hers lurked beyond the safety of its borders.

As she tramped through the grass, she thought about what Lady Maren had revealed. Only half the students typically passed the Test. She had always assumed most of them did. Perhaps it was a carefully guarded secret, a Mystery itself. Certainly, knowledge of the odds would have increased the students' anxiety. Each person was given a chance. A choice.

Out of the corner of her eye, she saw Mr. Skrelling walking toward her. She was not in the mood to entertain his persistent advances.

"Good afternoon, Mr. Skrelling," she said curtly when he arrived. She didn't alter her pace.

"I heard that you also passed the Test, Miss Cettie," he said cheerfully. His use of the word "also" implied he, too, had been successful.

"Congratulations, Mr. Skrelling."

"Congratulations are in order for you as well. I also received the glad news from Sloan and Teitelbaum, *ahem*, that my employment with them has been secured. I will not be enlisted to join the war effort. I'm quite relieved."

"I'm sure you are," she said evenly, thinking of Adam and wondering where he had gone.

"I should hope to see you in the near future, if you'll permit me to call on you. At Fog Willows, as you said. I will continue to hunt for your mother. My determination is strong. And I am, if nothing else, persistent."

"Indeed, you are," she replied with a grudging smile.

"Where are you off to, if you don't mind my asking? Would you prefer to be alone?"

She was not about to tell him her mission. "I'd like to be alone," she agreed, not divulging anything more.

"Ah, yes. Well then. As you wish." He bowed his head, gave her a crooked smile, and then went the other way. His clumsiness and awkwardness were almost endearing. He wasn't a bad fellow, despite everything.

After he was gone, she reached the orchard. A little nudge to her thoughts sent her to the right. She followed the new path, and in the distance she could see the old abbey kitchen with smoke coming from the cupola. The look of the aged stone had always appealed to her. It gave the grounds personality, as did the street of Vicar's Close. From her current vantage point, she could also see the fields of lavender, the archery butts, the gardens. A feeling of sadness and longing welled up inside of her. She would be leaving Muirwood soon on a tempest, piloted by Stephen. The beautiful chapter in her life was ending. What she wouldn't do to bring the feeling of the abbey with her . . . touching her breast, she felt the edges of the maston symbol against her skin. In a way, she was bringing it with her. It had become an essential part of her.

The feeling guided her through a copse of oak trees that formed a little park. There was a walking path that led through it, and so she followed it to the lookout point where there were benches for resting and a Leering marking the edge of a cliff. She had been there many times before to enjoy the view of the small valley below.

She was alone. Students were packing their things and preparing to vacate Vicar's Close. Cettie's trunks were already packed and ready. No word had arrived from Sera, but Cettie had packed the rest of her things for her, missing her fiercely all the while.

Climb down.

The whisper brushed against her mind. She was a little confused by the impulse, but she obeyed it and walked toward the Leering at the edge of the cliff. It radiated its warning about the danger of the cliff, but she silenced it with a thought. Passing around it, she noticed a few jagged rocks that looked climbable. She stepped down on the first and noticed a second. Then she passed the second and saw a third. Soon she was low enough that she couldn't even see the benches above her . . . which was when she realized the boulder she stood on was hovering in the air. Her stomach thrilled for a moment, and she had a feeling of vertigo that made her sway. She touched the side of the mountain to center herself and then carefully climbed down to the next rock.

It took several minutes to climb down the cliffside, boulder by boulder, but the floating stones, held up by the Mysteries, were there to mark a path. When she reached the bottom, she was inundated with the noises coming from the woods. These were wild sounds, the chirping of loud insects, the squawk of birds. These were not the tame sounds of the vibrant gardens kept by the school. This was wilderness. It was like the woods she had crossed with Caulton Forshee and the Cruciger orb.

She hesitated, not certain what to do. There was a mound nearby, overgrown and full of ferns. A few stunted trees grew in it. She paused, and then she felt the urge to keep walking, even though there wasn't a path. She trudged through the undergrowth, snapping small twigs and feeling her hem catch on brambles.

The sensation of eyes following her sent a shiver down her back as she walked. The woods became thicker, a mass of unruly oaks. Squirrels chittered and seemed to warn her not to go. The air smelled strong and pungent, of dirt and detritus. She made a horrible racket as she walked, but she felt herself going a certain direction. No logical reason led her. Her heart knew the right path.

The shade became so deep that it no longer felt like afternoon but twilight. The eerie sensation of being watched lingered. She glanced back, feeling she wasn't alone, and the frantic chatter of the woodland creatures seemed to confirm it. Nevertheless, she persisted.

After a long walk, she discovered a huge oak. Its limbs were so heavy and twisted they rested on the ground. The behemoth was taller than the abbey itself, and she remembered seeing it from above while practicing her piloting skills with Aunt Juliana. What had they called it? The sentinel oak? She had traveled much farther from the abbey than she'd realized. A strange feeling swarmed her. Then, one by one, the noises of the forest began to hush until they were utterly silent. Not a bird sounded. Not a squeal or even the creaking of branches.

Her heart began to pound with fear. The tall ghost was stalking her in the woods. The one without eyes. She was alone in the woods, far from the abbey. Far from help. Doubts began to flicker to life in her mind. She had expected to confront it, but she was so far from everyone . . . so far from help. Why had the Mysteries led her to this place?

She touched one of the lumbering branches with her hand, feeling the jagged edges of the bark. From the wood, she felt music begin to stir. Tingles shot down her arm. Something about this tree seemed . . . familiar. She had been here before. Not above, flying over, but here . . . in this exact location. Her memories did not go back that far. But she was certain of it. She had been here. Maybe it was a dream she couldn't remember.

The silence in the woods became absolute. She couldn't even hear her own breathing.

The tall ghost entered the grove from behind her. She began to tremble as she sensed it, reliving the terrors of her childhood. *No, not a ghost,* she reminded herself. It was a Myriad One. And it had tormented her for what felt like forever.

You came at last. I knew you would come.

She felt a shudder ripple through her as it approached her from behind. Her mind went black with terror. All the memories of her childhood came flooding back to her. She felt like that little girl again, overcome by terror and helplessness. She was nothing. She was insignificant. No one loved her or cared for her. There was nothing but utter loneliness.

You seek the secrets of your past. You wish to know who and what you are. You are your father's daughter. You are bound to us, child of dark. You were born in sin. You will rule us all. You are Ereshkigal incarnate.

Suddenly Cettie's arms and legs began to tremble and convulse. She couldn't control them. She sagged down to her knees as if a huge weight had begun to crush her. The fear brought on by her memories and the present threat combined to drown her. Her voice was locked away, seized and broken. Breathing was impossible. This feeling was so much more potent than what she'd experienced with the false version of Mrs. Pullman. It was a hundred times worse. Had she been brought there to die?

You must become her, child. You were born to quit the light. Every king and queen, every empress and duke will bow the knee to you, child of the Fells. Remove it. Remove it. Remove it.

The urge to rip away the chain was overpowering as the Myriad One's thoughts hammered against her mind. Why had she come here? Why had she thought she could defeat a being so full of hate? One older than the world? She was nothing but a helpless little girl. She'd never had any power over this hateful thing, and she never would.

Help me, she pleaded silently in her mind. She could sense the frail thread of her faith, and she clung to it. *I don't want to be trapped in the darkness. Help me!*

You plead to it? the dark being mocked her. Soon it would be close enough to touch her, and then she knew she would be lost. *You whine and beg? Stand and act! It is your destiny to rule over* worlds. *Claim it! Your true father calls to you. Come to him. Join with us.*

Help me, Cettie pleaded again, trying to banish the dark thoughts from her mind.

A light pierced the grove, blinding her. It was the sun, breaching the maze of limbs at last. Cettie raised her hand to it as if she could grasp it and pull it. She felt power surge inside of her.

No! No! She is mine! She is mine!

Strength filled her body as she looked up, feeling the light bathe her face. It was too bright to see, and she had to shield her eyes from it.

No!

She could control her thoughts again.

Apokaluptis, she thought.

The word of power seized ahold of the tall one, making it hunch over and twist in contortions. She felt its intense agony as it was forced to reveal itself.

I am Istfar the Fallen.

It had spoken its true name. That gave her power over it. She felt waves of hatred billowing from the being. It filled her heart with darkness.

The pain of Cettie's past began to shed from her. She wasn't a child anymore. She wasn't an unloved waif in the Fells. No one could force her to do anything she didn't want to do. The choice was hers. Always hers. Cettie straightened herself, feeling the glow of light suffuse her. Somehow touching the tree had lent her strength. There was power in the tree—a strange power—and its music sang to her.

Banirexpiare, she thought to it, rebuking the creature, sending it away.

A wind rushed and shook through the woods. The earth trembled. There was a clash of thunder somewhere in the distance. Cettie steadied herself against the oak, her knees knocking together—and she felt part of the great tree *open.* The music of the Mysteries filled the air in triumph, almost loud enough to drown out the Myriad One's shrieks as the tree swallowed it whole. The rush of power ended, and Cettie felt as if she had climbed the tallest mountain and run out of air.

She collapsed, suddenly overcome with weakness. The noises from the woods returned as she lay panting, breathless. To move a muscle would have required more energy than she possessed.

There were crackling noises. The sound of shoes.

Still, she couldn't move. She was falling asleep, exhausted beyond her mortal strength.

Someone knelt and crouched by her from behind, causing the dry oak leaves to crackle. She could smell onions. A heavy hand grazed her head. As she sank into a hole, the sounds around her growing fainter and fainter, she just barely heard a throaty, thickly accented voice say, "I bestow on you the Gift of . . ."

SERA

For most, the Test marks a change in them forever. But that change can be for good or ill. It promises protection from the unseen evils of this land. But it also brings to sharper focus our differences with the rest of the fallen world. It invites persecution and mockery from other worlds that rival ours. Those who cannot endure the light of reason and knowledge are more comfortable living in the darkness of superstition. Light reveals. Darkness conceals. How quick we are to disbelieve what will hurt our view of ourselves. People, whatever their circumstances, struggle with being petty and jealous by nature. We are all, to some extent, selfish and self-absorbed. The Test tries to lift us above it. For some, it only makes it worse. Hence the ancient wisdom of days long past: "For in much wisdom is much grief; and he that increases knowledge increases sorrow."

—Thomas Abraham, Aldermaston of Muirwood Abbey

CHAPTER THIRTY-ONE
The Below

Sera kept glancing over her shoulder, expecting to see Will pursuing her down the dark street. She had stopped running only because she was so winded, and each gasp felt like it wouldn't be enough to sate her hunger for air. Where was he? Her ankles and heels throbbed painfully because her shoes were not designed for such hard walking or running. Passing under the glare of a Light Leering, she quickly altered course to plunge back into shadows.

"Sera!"

It was *him*. Her heart trembled in panic. Would he wrestle her back to the house? He was stronger than her. She hated the situation she was trapped in. Hated that she'd trusted the wrong people. The night air was cold, and mist wreathed the rooftops. Walking in the shadows, she felt frightened and determined and sick to her stomach. Shelter—she needed shelter soon. But where?

Turning another corner, which opened to a wider street, she saw carriages pulled by horses. It amazed her to see them, a sight she'd only seen depicted in gazettes, but the amazement withered when she saw there were steaming piles of manure in the road as well. More lights lit the way, and the street opened to shop fronts with soot-smudged windows revealing an assortment of bakeries, milliner shops, and confectionaries—each already closed, the insides darkened. Lights came from the windows above the shops where the owners had retired.

There were others walking around, so at least she wasn't alone.

"Sera!"

The sound was getting closer. Her sense of vulnerability was growing by the moment. She didn't know where she was in the City. Were there street gangs here like the ones Cettie had told her about in the Fells? Would some youth try to rob her, even though she had no money?

Mr. Durrant. He lived in the City. If she could find out where, she could perhaps get a message to him or have someone take her to him.

"Are you lost, miss?" said a man, deliberately blocking her way. He smiled at her, but there was something in his grinning expression that troubled her. He held a hand up in a friendly way, but she stopped and retreated.

"No, thank you," she said, moving around him.

"I can help, miss. Let me help you find your way."

His excessive zeal made her even more distrusting. Suddenly light from a zephyr streaked overhead, catching their attention. It was a military craft, and it was heading the way she had come. This was the evidence, had she needed it, that Lord Welles had played her for a fool. He'd brought Commander Falking and his letter straight to her in Muirwood. Perhaps he'd even played a role in the unfolding conflict with Kingfountain. He'd certainly seemed less than diplomatic in his dealings with the foreign prince the day of the privy council meeting. What better way to ensure his own power than to pursue a war that would elevate him to his former position . . . and who better to arrange for one than her own father? The gears in the machine were turning even now, and perhaps she had caught on too late to stop them.

Well, if Welles was involved, she wouldn't make it easy on him. Taking advantage of the distraction the zephyr brought, Sera slipped around the man and hurried down the street, ignoring the throbbing in her legs. Where could she go? How could she hope to find Mr. Durrant in this foreign place?

The noise of hooves coming fast behind her frightened her, and she lunged out of the way as another carriage roared past. The driver shouted a reprimand at her, and as she reeled with the reprieve from danger, she stepped into one of the piles of filth. It was disgusting, and she stamped her foot to dislodge the mushy, odorous cakes. Looking back, she saw Will coming down the street, looking from side to side. He was still searching for her, and if he caught up with her, all would be lost. All might already be lost. She had to get off the street quickly.

Ahead, she saw a row of houses with steep steps leading up to the doors. They were tall and thin, like the one she had just left, and there were lights shining within. She hurried to the first one and mounted the steps. The hair on the back of her neck was standing up, and a shiver went through her. She ignored the sensation—there was no time to seek out another doorway—and knocked several times.

There was the turning of several locks, and then the door opened, and a butler stood in the crack, eyeing her suspiciously.

"What do you want?" he asked sternly.

"Please help me," she said, glancing back down the street. Will was getting closer. "Can I speak to the master of the—"

The butler shut the door with a resounding thud, and he locked it up again. Angry, she fled down the steps and didn't bother with the other houses. There was darkness ahead, and she hoped to slip into an alley and wait for him to pass by before she went the other way. How could she have gotten herself into such a predicament?

When she reached the darkness, where there weren't any streetlamps, the houses were shabbier. This was a seedier neighborhood. But if she attempted to turn around, there would be no avoiding Will. Then she saw the kirkyard just ahead. The gate was shut, but the bars were quite wide. Could she squeeze through them? She increased her pace, intent on trying.

Weeds grew in the seams of the cobblestones. There was a small church beyond the kirkyard, and it was also darkened. Sera stepped through the bars and struggled through the opening because it was too narrow. She clenched her jaw and wriggled, trying to get through the cold, wet bars that were making a mess of her gown. The sound of Will's boots echoed on the street, closer, closer. Still, she wasn't fitting. Screwing up her determination, she twisted and squirmed, crushing her breasts in the process, but she made it through with relief, grateful that her small stature had finally proven useful. There wasn't a moment to spare. Stealthily, she crept to a larger headstone and then crouched behind it and held her breath, afraid Will might have heard or seen her.

A few moments later, she saw him walk by the gate. He stopped at it, gazing into the kirkyard. She ducked but couldn't see his face through the shadows. She heard him shake the bars, saw his face twisted with anger, but then he proceeded down the street, muttering under his breath.

Sera rested her forehead on the stone and trembled with cold. Then she turned and sat down, leaning her back against it, wrapping her arms around her knees. Her mother was probably frantic. Her father was undoubtedly gleeful at her mistake. There was a good chance he had helped orchestrate it.

Tears pricked her eyes, and she brushed them away angrily. Now was not the time to cry about her misfortune. Now was the time for action.

300

The air felt so much colder than before. Her legs were aching. How had she bungled things so badly? All her feelings of self-doubt came bubbling like water in a kettle. Who was she to think she could save the people of this world from their misery? Why should she even try?

She bit her lip, feeling so sorry for herself. Her reputation would be ruined forever over this one mistake. The people would be horribly disappointed in her. She was disappointed in herself. Why go back to Lockhaven at all? Why face the shame? No matter how she tried to defend herself, people would only believe the worst. People would want to believe the worst. It would give them something to titter about over their afternoon tea.

Those same young ladies from the gathering at Pavenham Sky would cluck their tongues and comment on her lack of character. Of course a young woman so sympathetic to the plight of the poor would make such an error of judgment.

Sera's anguish grew deeper and deeper. When had she ever felt so miserable? Why did she keep making mistakes?

It would have been better if she'd never been born.

The thought struck a chill in her heart. Coldness seeped inside her. There was a strange, twisted logic to her thought. What if she never returned? She could go back to the street, and when a carriage roared past, she could step in front of it. What a tragic end to the tale. Something sweet and delicious came with the image of her parents finding her crushed body. Then Will would mourn what he had done to her. He'd grieve the rest of his life. A hint of satisfaction bloomed. Yes, wouldn't that be a way to get—

It terrified her when she realized what she had been contemplating. She shook her head and blinked quickly. Her thoughts had completely run away from her. Why couldn't she ever rein them in? A queer feeling had come over her. It confused and sickened her.

Looking around, back pressed against the stone, she saw a small candle glowing from the window of the church. She hadn't noticed any light before. From the way it wavered and flickered, she knew it couldn't be a Leering. Slowly, Sera rose from her hiding spot. A carriage rattled in the distance, and the yearning to seek it out became overwhelming, but so did her curiosity about the candle. It seemed to be moving toward her.

She took a few hesitant steps closer, and then she heard footsteps from the church. The door opened, and a man stood beneath the awning, holding a candle. He was not an aged old thing, probably a man in his thirties. The vicar?

"Is someone there?" he asked in a wary voice, raising the candle higher.

Sera stepped into its circle of light. His eyes widened with surprise and a little fear.

"Can you help me, Vicar?" she asked.

"The vicar went home," he said hesitantly. "I'm . . . I'm the groundskeeper. What do you want? I don't have any money to give you. I locked the gate earlier. How did you get in?"

"I squeezed through the bars," she answered, wringing her hands. "I was attacked by a man. A soldier. He's looking for me right now. I need to hide."

"Are you alone?" he asked, raising the candle higher and gazing around her. He looked doubtful of what he should do.

"Yes," she answered. "Please, sir. Can you help me?"

He sniffed and wiped his nose on his arm. A scowl showed he was not thrilled with the idea. "You really shouldn't stay here, lass. It's a kirkyard."

"Yes, I know, but I need help. If you would—"

"No, lass. You don't understand. I just buried ten folk today. Two families. All of 'em died of the cholera morbus. You . . . you really shouldn't come near me. Don't know if I caught it too." He sniffed again, looking weary and fearful.

And she had been nestled in the ground behind a grave marker. Her insides twisted at the dilemma she was in. Now it was even worse.

"I'm sorry for disturbing you," she said miserably. She turned to leave.

"Wait," he called after. She hesitated. "I'll . . . let me unlock it for you."

She nodded, and he shuffled down the steps of the church, candle in hand. He sniffed and wiped his nose again on his arm. When he reached the gate, he withdrew a key from his pocket and fit it into the lock.

"There's lots who's died this time," he said in a melancholy way. "But I hear it's fewer and fewer cases these days. Many on this street fled to the north when it struck. Haven't been here in weeks. Folks die," he said, grunting as he jiggled the key in the lock, "are buried, then more die. Then, like a fever breaking, it's over for a time. No one knows how it starts or when it'll end." He pulled on the gate, and it squeaked as it opened. "My job is digging graves." He sniffed. "It's work. I'm luckier than many."

"Thank you," she said, giving him a nod.

"Do you have any parents, lass? Anyone you want me to send for?" he asked, hand resting on the bar. "You look awful young to be walking the streets. Awful young."

Then she realized that her appearance and story had given him the wrong impression.

"I have an uncle," she said. "He's an advocate. He would come get me."

"What's his name? Where does he live? The City is an awful big place."

"I don't know where he lives. I don't even know where I am. But his name is Mr. Durrant."

"Durrant?" said the groundskeeper with a whistle. "The famous one? The one who helps the prince regent's daughter? He's your uncle?"

"You know him?" Sera asked, hope beginning to stir.

"Everyone down here knows him." His countenance changed dramatically, turning much more cheerful. "Here, why don't you come with me to Billowby's pub? It's warmer there, and it's a friendly crowd. I know old Billowby. He'll send for your uncle. How's that?"

Sera smiled at him broadly. "Thank you. I can't thank you enough."

It was nearly midnight when Mr. Durrant arrived at the public house. Some of the patrons were still sipping the dregs of their drinks, and there was a strong yeasty smell in the air. But a fire crackled in the hearth—a real one, fed by wood, not by a Leering. The men in the tavern were a rough crowd, and more kept coming in by the hour to spend the humid night. The owner of the pub, Mr. Billowby, greeted each by name and offered them mead or beer or wine depending on their preference.

Sera sat at a table, and her new friend, Mr. Krant, sat across from her with a mug of his own. No one else had sat near them. Apparently being a gravedigger wasn't exactly a noble profession. But Billowby took his coins anyway.

Mr. Durrant arrived in a black cloak and hat, and when he saw Sera sitting at the table, he nearly lost all his composure. He tucked his hat in the crook of his arm and then hurried toward the table.

"Mr. Krant," he said to the gravedigger, reaching out and gripping the man's bare hand with his own gloved one. He pumped it vigorously. "Thank you for summoning me to find my *niece*." He gave Sera a scolding frown. "We will talk later, young lady. I brought a carriage. Thank you, sir. If you are ever in need of services from the Law, you know how to find me. Thank you."

"It's no trouble, Mr. Durrant. Your niece Sera is a nice lass. Probably fell in with the wrong crowd. It happens more often than it should, unfortunately."

"The wrong crowd indeed," replied the advocate with a hint of irony. "Well, your efforts tonight are appreciated. Come, *niece*." He bowed his head to the gravedigger, and Sera rose from the table.

"Thank you for helping me, Mr. Krant. I won't forget it." She gave him a kindly smile, knowing that she would see to it that he never had to dig graves again . . . if he'd manage to avoid the outbreak.

"G'night, miss. Best to you both."

Sera followed Durrant out of the pub to the carriage stationed in front of it. A pair of sturdy horses stamped and nickered, and the driver held his whip, ready to go.

Durrant opened the carriage door, and Sera climbed the small steps to the sheltered cab. A zephyr flew overhead, shining its light down on the street, and she stared up at it for a long moment. Was it another ship from the Ministry of War, looking for her?

"Quickly," Durrant urged, and she hurriedly entered.

Taking a seat on the cushion, she breathed a sigh of relief.

Durrant closed the door, seated himself, and then tapped the roof with his cane. He leaned back in the seat, his features haggard and defeated. The look he gave her was full of disappointment. Sera's relief wilted.

"How bad is it?" Sera asked him, bracing herself to hear his words.

"Tell me that you gave the letters from Lady Corinne to somebody. Anybody. Who has them?"

Sera's stomach dropped. "They're still in my room. I was going to show them to Fitzroy, but I never had the chance."

He closed his eyes and pinched the bridge of his nose with his fingers. The carriage jumbled and rattled down the street. He looked as if he were suffering from an intense internal pain.

"Never had the chance," he sighed. Then he shook his head, gazing out the window, looking anywhere but at her eyes. Disappointment was etched into the lines of his face. She could feel it coming off him in waves.

"Tell me," she asked meekly.

He was silent, composing himself, as if he didn't trust himself to speak. But he finally did, and his words tortured her.

"You went out tonight with your governess, a woman who has likely betrayed you, to visit a young man who, I've come to find out, has a reputation for seducing the fairer sex. Lord Welles was very concerned to learn from his commander that you'd left your mother's house to meet one of his soldiers. I learned several hours ago that you had disappeared, that you were probably having a little *chat* with your old flame in an abandoned house. I was notified by your mother. She thought you'd been kidnapped. The search going on right now . . . I've never seen the likes of it. Other than those who arranged it, everyone is afraid you've been abducted. But the truth, when it comes out—and it *will*—will bring you down. Will bring us *both* down. No doubt they searched your room first. And found the letters.

"Sera, it will look as if you and I were scheming to upstage your father. I knew about the letters. I cannot deny it in front of an Oath Leering. My dear, the cause is lost. There is no way the privy council will choose you now. None whatsoever. It's all . . . ruined." His face contorted into anger. He still wouldn't look at her. She saw his clenched fists tremble in his lap. He had tied his future to hers.

And it led nowhere.

The carriage pulled to a sudden stop, and the driver called out, "What is it, Officers?"

Mr. Durrant closed his eyes, leaning his head back against the head-rest in despair.

Sera saw a light shine in through the window, blinding her.

"We're looking for—" The man abruptly cut off his words. "Captain! Captain! She's in here!"

CHAPTER THIRTY-TWO

THE RISING

Sera's first foray to the world below had ended in an unmitigated disaster. It was a scandal. There was no other suitable word to describe the situation Sera found herself in when she returned to Lockhaven with a military escort. What troubled her the most were the looks of disappointment on everyone's faces. She had earned such looks from her parents when she was younger. Now everyone, including Mr. Durrant, looked at her as if they were terribly disappointed.

She was brought back to the palace before dawn, but wasn't permitted to speak to the privy council. Mr. Durrant tried to insist on it, to exercise her rights as a princess, but he was met with a stone-cold reproof, and the two of them were ordered to wait in a sitting room while the council met. Durrant had slumped into a stuffed chair and rubbed his eyes, for he had not slept most of the night. Sera paced in the room, glancing occasionally out the window to track the rising of the sun. Each hour they were made to wait was a new kind of torture. The suspense of not knowing what would happen to her made her imagination run rampant. She was already experiencing the effects of the shunning. When servants entered with the morning meal, they wouldn't meet her gaze or speak. Not a word. The tinkling of the silverware became deafening in the silence.

"At least have some potatoes, Mr. Durrant," Sera attempted in a lighthearted tone. He looked as if he had aged ten years overnight.

"I've quite lost my appetite," he said in a surly voice.

Sera had as well. The slices of fruit on the tray looked somewhat appetizing, but her stomach squirmed at the mere thought of food. No, she continued to pace, wondering how long the privy council would protract the torture.

"They haven't even asked to hear my side," Sera said forlornly. "I was duped. But I'm not wicked. Where is Hugilde?"

Mr. Durrant's eyes were narrowed with misery. "Who knows? Probably on a zephyr far, far away with enough money in the bank to live comfortably for years. You were alone with a young man, Sera. You were locked in a room with him. That alone may brand you for the rest of your life. Some of the ladies on the privy council were aghast at what you'd done. What you risked to reclaim letters. They thought the contents must be very bad indeed. And you'll not be surprised to hear the letters themselves have disappeared." His lip twitched. "You should have reached out to me. You should have confided in me. I was your advocate, Sera. Four years I've spent. Wasted. Instead you put your faith in a woman your estranged father had appointed to you."

His words stung her heart.

It was shortly after sunrise that a knock sounded on the door. Lord Fitzroy entered. Her insides coiled into knots, and she stopped her pacing, seeking his eyes. He looked tired but not accusatory. The corner of his mouth quirked into a little smile of familiarity.

"Please, Lord Fitzroy, out with it," Sera pleaded. "Don't spare me the worst."

"Miss Fitzempress," Mr. Durrant chided, rising from his chair for the first time. "Let him speak. You bear grave news, Minister. I see it in your countenance."

Fitzroy shut the door behind him and wandered over to the trays of food. "Our forces at Grishawk were attacked. The war has started." He said this as he gazed at the cantaloupe and the orange slices.

"Grishawk?" Durrant whispered in shock. "That's a coastal fortress."

"It's not a fortress anymore," Fitzroy said, looking at the advocate. "It's been reduced to rubble. Kingfountain has won the first skirmish. They have power we do not yet understand. Power to smash stone. The reports are still coming in. Part of the fleet was deployed to defend Grishawk. They say the enemy ships came out of the water without warning and launched some sort of fiery missiles at the fortress. One of the hurricanes was damaged when it dropped low to counterattack, and it had to retreat higher to the clouds to avoid foundering." He sighed. "So we are at war with Kingfountain." He gazed at her. "You can imagine what the privy council has decided in consequence."

Sera bit her lip, her heart full of anguish for the fallen soldiers. Yes, she knew. There wasn't another choice. "The decision has been made, then."

Fitzroy nodded slowly. "It has. The privy council has chosen your father as the new emperor. It is a pragmatic choice, under the circumstances."

Mr. Durrant stifled a groan, and Fitzroy shot him an angry look. Sera felt a spasm of pain at the words. Her hopes had all crashed to the ground, broken to pieces like the fortress of Grishawk.

"Did anyone speak for me?" Sera asked huskily, trying not to cry. "Was I condemned without knowledge of all the facts? I was duped, Lord Fitzroy."

Fitzroy turned and faced her, his hands behind his back. "I spoke for you, Sera," he said compassionately. "Even though I sensed the momentum of the situation was against you. Even though I knew it would be unpopular for me to speak in favor of you. But then, I've never much cared for others' opinions of me."

Mr. Durrant approached, his face angry. "Were you the only one who spoke for her? Was everyone else too cowardly?"

There was a glint of answering anger in Fitzroy's eyes. "Mr. Durrant, have a care. Are you so caught up in your own feelings that you cannot appreciate what Sera is suffering?"

"What she is suffering?" Durrant said, aghast. "I've given—"

"Four years," Fitzroy interrupted. "You speculated, like many others, that she would gain the throne. No doubt your losses are great, but they are not greater than hers. She had no money at play here. Only her future."

Sera turned and looked at Mr. Durrant. "You . . . you speculated . . . about me?"

"Everyone has!" he shot back. "It was always a long shot. But it is in those risks that great fortunes are won. Or lost." His voice was like a growl.

Sera put her hand on her heart. How many people had lost money because of her failure? It was obvious the depth of people's feelings toward her had been motivated by greed, not only her plans for the empire. She was like a racehorse who had foundered on the track. The thought disgusted her.

"Lady Corinne was behind this," Sera said angrily. "She and Welles were behind it. Like spiders. She gave me the letters. And I, like a fool, let them harm me."

"The letters you reference," Fitzroy asked for clarification, "are the ones found in your room?"

"Yes. The ones my father wrote to Lady Corinne."

Fitzroy's lips pursed. "They were unopened, if I understand things properly. They were given to the emperor after they were discovered in your room. I was told they were forgeries, written by a hand that only resembles your father's. He claims it was an attempt by you to blackmail him."

"That isn't true," Sera countered. "Lady Corinne gave them to me secretly when I visited Pavenham Sky. She asked me to return them to my father and to insist that he not send any more. She wouldn't read them because they didn't go through her husband."

Spiders, just as she'd thought, and she'd stumbled into their web without realizing it.

"Is that why you believe she orchestrated these events?" Fitzroy asked. "Such a serious accusation requires proof. She was named a member of the privy council last night."

"Lady Corinne?" Durrant gasped in surprise.

"Indeed," Fitzroy said. "Her husband has been called back to military duty. As have I. I'll be returning to Muirwood shortly to bid farewell to my family before taking my command."

"But you're the Minister of Wind," Sera said in surprise.

"Not any longer," he answered. "Lord Welles was named prime minister by your father in the meeting. Lord Prentice was forced to step down and has returned to his old post as Minister of Wind. Everything else remains as it was with one exception: Lady Corinne has joined the council. If you have any further information, Sera, I should like to know. I thought her above such blatant political scheming, but when such power is up for grabs, people will stoop low to snatch it."

Of course. They'd gotten everything they wanted. Power. Prestige. A war to distract the people from the cholera morbus. From poverty. From the divisions in their society. And presumably Lady Corinne's husband had made a neat bundle from speculating on it all. The people would suffer for this.

Sera clenched her fists, but her resolve began to founder. "If I had become empress, she would no longer have as much power. She controls fashion, she controls who is ostracized . . ." She regretted saying it, remembering that Fitzroy's wife had once been shunned by the lady.

If he was bothered by her comment, he didn't show it. "That is all probably true, Sera. She would have lost some of her influence. Unfortunately, it won't be enough to convince anyone that she was scheming against you." He sighed. "A very good friend of mine lost his estate, Gimmerton Sough, because of the machinations of the Lawton family. Now that he has prospered running my mines, he would like to buy the property back, but Admiral Lawton has refused to sell it. It's not about money. The Lawtons don't want my friend to get his estate back, even though it's still unoccupied. They consider him undeserving of his former position in society. Simply because they decided it was so."

Cettie had told her the story of the family's fall from grace. She'd felt the floating manor quake beneath her.

"I don't have any firm evidence," she admitted. "Just the suspicions I've shared with you."

"Best to keep those to yourself," he replied with a warning tone. "It would be fair to say that the Lawtons betted against you becoming empress. You are correct—they had reason to support your father as emperor. The incident last night made you lose favor with the council. For now. I'm hoping it's not lost forever. But it will take time. Trust is easily broken. Like a mirror. You cannot repair the cracks. It must be made over."

Sera nodded, feeling her shame flare up again. "I will do what I can to make amends. Just so you know, I didn't—"

Fitzroy held up a hand, forestalling her. "You don't need to tell me anything, Sera. I'm on your side still. Whatever happened. And those who are your true friends always will be." He gave Durrant a pointed look as he said this.

Sera sighed in relief. "Thank you, Lord Fitzroy. I'm sick inside that I was so foolish. What will I do now that Father is emperor? Can I go to Muirwood to take the Test?"

"Yes, what is to be done?" Durrant asked. He looked beaten down by Fitzroy's rebukes.

"I was not the only one who spoke up for you during the council," Fitzroy said. "While the Minister of Thought did vote for your father, he encouraged us all to be understanding of the foibles of youth. That we tend to be too severe. He said, and I will always remember this, that if the Knowing desired to put a forty-year-old's head on a sixteen-year-old's shoulders, it would have done so. Instead, the Knowing put a sixteen-year-old's head on a sixteen-year-old's shoulders, and we should all try to be more understanding. Sometimes we measure someone from the position of our own years and experience. We forget what it is like to be young. You made a mistake, Sera. What happened in that room will be speculated about. Gossiped about. Only you and that young man know the facts, and we can assume he was paid to embellish the incident. Perhaps it's not as serious as the rumors suggest, but it was still an unfortunate error in judgment. And when you lead people, when lives are at stake based on the decisions you make, the people must be able to trust you. To trust, too, that you can learn from your mistakes. This is your opportunity, Sera, to prove that you can."

She nodded vigorously. "I will do my best, Lord Fitzroy. So I am to go back to Muirwood, then? To spend another year as a learner? The Test was yesterday, was it not?"

He shook his head, and her stomach plummeted.

"What, then?" she asked worriedly.

"She'll be put in wardship," Durrant surmised. He clapped his hands together, his eyes intent. "Who? You?"

"I did request it," Fitzroy said, but the resignation in his voice told her that he had not been granted his desire.

"I think I see where this is going," Durrant said in despair.

Fitzroy nodded. "You will not be permitted to take the Test yet. Your father has asked the Lawtons to oversee the remainder of your education at Pavenham Sky. As a personal favor to him. I don't think Cettie would be permitted to go there. Your mother will be given the right to visit on a schedule."

Sera's eyes widened with surprise and shock. "Pavenham Sky?"

"And what's to become of me?" Mr. Durrant asked in desperation.

"Your services are no longer required," Fitzroy said flatly. "The emperor has banned you from returning to Lockhaven. With the privy council's decision, Sera is no longer in need of your services."

"But what about the Test?" Sera asked in desperation.

"You will be permitted to take it later, when the privy council feels that sufficient time has passed. I'm sorry, Sera. That is the will of the council."

She lowered her head and felt the burning tears at last.

CHAPTER THIRTY-THREE
WARS OF RELIGION

The days began to blur together for Sera as she prepared to depart for Pavenham Sky immediately following her father's coronation ceremony. The decorations in the palace were transforming it into some sort of fairyland of opulence. She hardly recognized the corridors or the mobs of servants working from before sunrise until well after sunset.

In all her dreams of becoming empress, she would never have imagined spending a fortune on the ceremony itself. Not when they were now at war. Not when there were people starving down below. She had seen the people's hunger, their resentment against those who lived in the clouds above them. She'd seen a glimpse of the true disease infecting her empire.

The palace kitchens never stopped working to feed the hosts of nobles assembling from their sky manors throughout the realm. Dignitaries arrived from distant shores to witness the event, and she was forbidden to meet any of them. For the most part, she was sequestered with two maids, both chosen by her father to keep watch on her. Neither girl attempted to befriend her. They seemed sullen and resentful that they were forced to be her chaperones.

News of the war with Kingfountain was slow to reach her. She'd always relied on Mr. Durrant to supply news and gossip, but now he was gone for good, ripped from her life. Mother was given permission to visit with her for just an hour each day. She bore a portion of blame for Sera's indiscretion. But if she were to be accepted as the emperor's consort, she had to acquiesce to his demands. Their marriage, everyone knew, was still a sham. But during a time of war, it was important to project the illusion of unity. Sera found it all rather sickening.

Her belongings were packed and ready to be loaded. She wore a ceremonial dress, too ostentatious for her tastes, but it had been provided for her, and she had been given no choice but to wear it. Her hair was coiffed, and her nails buffed and decorated. She would look like a princess, even though she wasn't permitted to attend the celebratory events following the coronation. Basically, she was a prisoner of the court.

A knock sounded on the door, and Sera instinctively braced herself for the visitor. Rather than the underling she expected, it was Mr. Case, her father's secretary. She despised the man, but she rose from her chair and greeted him with false affection.

"The emperor will see you now," he said, bowing to her.

Getting an audience with her father was a rarity, and it unnerved her. What demands would he make of her now? Was another privilege to be stripped away from her? What more could Father take from her? They were at war with a rival world, a world that shared some common beliefs but had very different traditions. A war in the name of religion. It filled Sera with foreboding.

She followed Mr. Case as he led the way to her father's private chambers. Again, the transformation of the corridor required them to move cautiously. The flowered garlands practically rained petals down on them, and there were servants with brooms and trays to sweep up the remains. The clamor of the workers made it difficult to hear.

When they arrived, the guards at the chamber parted, and the door opened. Her father sat at his breakfast table, the gazette at his elbow. He was chewing vigorously, though his appetite did not curb his animated conversation with Lady Corinne, seated near him. Sera recognized the butler of Pavenham Sky, Master Sewell, standing in attendance at a discreet distance.

"What of the cholera morbus?" Lady Corinne asked. There were remains of a meal on her plate. So, they had breakfasted together. Never had Sera felt more certain she'd been duped.

"Ah yes," Father said after clearing his mouth. "The doctors report that fewer cases are inflicting the City. Fewer corpses to bury. It seems that the fire has burnt out for the time being. There are certain quarters of the City that were abandoned after it struck. People fled to the countryside, those who could afford to at any rate. Some households were wiped out. Overall, the toll seems to be around twenty thousand." He shrugged. "It's not as bad as it could have been."

"That's a relief," Lady Corinne said. She glanced over at Sera, her eyes revealing nothing of her emotions. Neither satisfaction nor disdain. "And isn't it fortunate, my lord, that the outbreak has ended on the eve of your coronation?"

Father positively glowed at her attention. He wiped his hands on the silk napkin and dabbed some grease from his chin. "It is indeed," he said with real pleasure. "A sign from the Mysteries, I should think. The doctors were never able to determine the cause of it, but the current theory is the noxious miasma that persists down below. They have encouraged people to walk about with handkerchiefs covering their mouths. I've seen it through the Leerings." He wagged his own handkerchief at her playfully and then set it down.

Sera stared at the two of them, feeling anger start to ignite the blood in her veins. Whenever her parents breakfasted together, they always sat opposite each other, their mutual loathing obvious. Here was Lady

Corinne, sitting at Father's elbow, having a private conversation with him as he strutted like a peacock in front of her. As he mocked his own sick and dying people.

Father turned, and his look cooled immediately. "I said to bring her *after* breakfast, Case," he snapped petulantly.

Mr. Case looked mortified. "I'm sorry, Your Majesty." Sera could see that Mr. Case didn't even try to defend himself. His job was to weather Father's moods.

"Well, she's here at any rate." He coughed into his hand and then leaned back in the plush cushions of his chair. His look was that of a cat grown fat on cream. He lazily rubbed his finger around the goblet and then brought the cup to his mouth and took a sip. "You will be departing after the ceremony to Pavenham Sky with Master Sewell," he said firmly. "He will see that you are situated as due your station." There was something in his voice that warned her, chilled her. "Lady Corinne is part of the privy council now and will return to the manor following the next council meeting." He dipped his head to Lady Corrine respectfully. The lady's expression did not change. But she looked at Sera coolly, gloved hands clasped on her lap.

"I already knew that, Father," Sera said, struggling to maintain her temper. He still flinched subtly when she used that name for him. There was still a part of him that didn't believe she was his offspring. And following her disgrace and his ascension, he had little need to acknowledge her. The familiarity between Corinne and himself revealed much. Sera knew that Lady Corinne had no children of her own, and the lady was quite a bit younger than her husband. Who would inherit Pavenham Sky? Maybe she planned for it all to come to her. Maybe she had her sights set on replacing Sera's mother.

"Of course you knew it," Father said peevishly. "But that's not why I summoned you. I wanted to share other news with you myself."

Sera swallowed, feeling the room tighten in around her. "What news?"

319

"Be silent and I shall tell you. You've heard of the skirmish of Grishawk, no doubt. Yes, I see that you have. There was another battle fought yesterday at a mirror gate off the coast of Dahomey. Do you know what a gate—"

"They are the portals between our worlds," Sera interrupted. "How we have made trade possible with other worlds." She knew this from her studies at Muirwood. The portals were made of natural arches, stones that had worn away, leaving a hollow space within. Leerings were carved into them, which connected them to natural arches in other worlds. Some portals were formed by the erosion at sea. Some were made from rivers in canyons. Once they toppled, they could no longer be used. And depending on the size, ships could even be sent through them. They were rare and took thousands of years to form.

"Yes, well, the one at the shore of Dahomey was attacked. We have ships stationed at every one now, and we were prepared for the fight. It was a vicious battle, and our forces had to retreat. We lost a hurricane and twelve tempests in the fighting. They had an armada of sorts. Vicious fighting, as I said. There were many casualties. Many gave their lives trying to defend the empire."

His eyes glittered as he said this. For some reason, he was savoring it. He still hadn't revealed his purpose.

"That's awful," Sera said, her stomach churning.

"The carnage was immense," Father said. "They use some strange new weaponry. Exploding balls that wreak havoc on our hulls. They leave lots of smoke, make it difficult for our dragoons to find targets. Messy business. One exploded into the hull of the hurricane, and the bits of metal cut into the young men stationed there. Many fell to their deaths because they weren't roped in." He folded his hands in front of him. "Including one . . . Lieutenant . . . Russell."

Sera was horrified. Not just at the news but at the vindictive way her father had decided to reveal it to her. Her feelings for Will had certainly changed since his betrayal—her memories and fancies had altered irrevocably. But she hadn't wanted him to die, and the thought of him plummeting from a broken sky ship after being lacerated by an explosion made her tremble with sadness and regret. She would never see him again. He would never have the chance to gain the type of wisdom that only came with age. To right the wrongs he had done. His life had been snuffed out, among so many others. Grief and anguish flooded her.

War. Bloody and final. And it was just beginning. It was no cause for celebration, for speculation. Lives were on the line.

"That young man can tarnish you no more," Father said coldly.

"Did you . . . did you send him to his death?" Sera said with a trembling voice.

"Did I *know* that Dahomey would be attacked? Of course not! I'm no harbinger. I sent him far away so that you wouldn't be tempted by his ignoble blood any further. You shamed yourself, Sera. I would be angrier if it had not yielded the fruit I desired to taste. You are young and naïve, which the council took into consideration. I hope that you will learn from your mistakes. Always you were a headstrong girl, but perhaps shame will teach you prudence. As a personal favor to me, Lady Corinne has agreed to take you in as her ward. You've much to learn about the ways of society and the proper boundaries. I hope you will learn from her and adopt all that she teaches you. One day, if you prove faithful to me, you may yet be chosen as my heir." He shook his head slowly. "You are not entitled to it, my dear. You've done nothing that would entitle you to it. But if you are submissive and humble, if you bend to my will, your exile from court may not last more than . . . say . . . a few years?"

Sera was trembling. She wanted to lash out at him, to decry his hypocrisy and his machinations with Lady Corinne and Lord Welles. But she ruled her tongue and refused to let it run away. Her eyes felt hot, but she didn't cry. Not for Will. Not for herself. She would not cry before him.

"I see that stubbornness in your eyes," he said in a low, cruel voice. "How it disappoints me still. You've always been a disappointment to me."

His words drew blood. They always had. But she had learned that nothing she could ever do would please him. He wanted a mindless, obedient puppet that he could forever control. One that would submit to his whims just because he thought to entertain them. Approval was an enticement that most people responded to. Not Sera, however.

"I am grateful to hear that the cholera morbus has stopped its work of death," Sera finally said. "Thank the Mysteries." Her fingernails dug into her palms. But she hid her fists behind her back. Just like Fitzroy. She wouldn't let Father see how much he affected her. Even though the words would be sour in her mouth, she would taste them. "And thank you for the opportunity to better myself at Pavenham Sky. I will try to be a good student." Her heart ached with regret, with sadness, with the feeling of vulnerability. She would withstand whatever they had planned for her. She would bend. But she wouldn't break.

"Thank the Mysteries indeed," Father replied with a cynical smile.

CETTIE

Pain always leaves scars. Some can be seen by all. Others go unobserved. Those private scars are the most painful. But it is an eternal truth that a burden shared is a burden lifted. Solace comes when another shares our grief, our sadness, our scars. As I look at the scar from where the ball punctured my body, as I feel the lingering agony of that injury, I think of the pain that countless will endure in the conflict ahead. I knew the emperor would die before the year was out. I had no idea it would lead to war. A new man has tightened his grip on power. If nothing else, history cautions us about power and those who wield it. There is foreboding in my heart about what sort of man our new emperor is. What he may do.

So another school year has come to an end. There are garlands hanging in Vicar's Close to celebrate Whitsunday. The students will assemble to dance tonight. Families have come from all over the realm to take their sons and daughters away. Many sons will go to their deaths. Many young women will be bereft of husbands. All will bear scars after this night. One does not need to see the future to know this. And to grieve.

—Thomas Abraham, Aldermaston of Muirwood Abbey

CHAPTER THIRTY-FOUR

HARBINGER

When Cettie awoke next to the sentinel tree, she could not remember all that had led to her being there. She remembered the wicked spirit she had banished, but there was something that nagged her mind after that, something that wouldn't come to her. The memory was masked by the dream she'd had after passing out.

It was unlike any dream she had ever had before.

For her, dreams had always been snatches of things she'd experienced during the day, perhaps a fact about birds she'd learned in one of her classes. Or a calculation that Mrs. Romrell had explained. Or they were nightmares from her life in the Fells—dark memories of a childhood smothered in shadows. This dream had been more like a vision.

She had been standing on a cliff high above a scene. Only it wasn't a cliff at all but a shining sheet of gold high in the air. It was a whorl of translucent particles around her feet that dazzled and dizzied her. Down below, she saw an island jutting out of the waves of the sea. It was a craggy thing, the rocks black and speckled with all manner of life that she could sense from her golden perch. She could sense tiny sea creatures clinging to the rocks just beneath the surface of the crashing waves. They were creatures she'd never seen before, with hard, spiny bodies and strange geometries, yet she saw patterns in their forms.

Massive hurricane sky ships were moored in the air near the island. They were full of soldiers, men of the Ministry of War, some young, some seasoned. She felt their fear throbbing inside them, and she could name every man present. How could she see so much, know so much, in an instant? It was as if her mind had enlarged. She heard their voices, their murmuring words, the march of steps as they strode the galley ways within the hull. The vision swept her along, and she saw the commander of the fleet poring over a map with his aides. It was a war map, and she saw his finger pointing at a small island off the coast of Dahomey. The point was labeled "Dochte Ruins." She sensed the ink blots that formed the words, and for a moment she found herself sucked into them. She heard the whirring gears of the machine that had made the map, smelled the wet ink. Cettie pulled herself back, realizing that she could dive into any facet of the scene to learn its true source, its origin. Her mind reeled with the knowledge that flooded into her.

"They'll come through an arch on that side of the island," said the fleet commander gruffly, his gray sideburns twitching with worry. "That is the mirror gate. That is where—"

"Admiral!" shouted a man who barged into the room suddenly. Cettie could feel the fear throbbing inside him. His name was Decker. How could she know that?

"What is it, Captain Decker?" the commander said angrily. "You can't barge in—"

"Sir, they're through. They've appeared just beneath us, rising from the waves. We didn't see them cross the portal. They—"

His words were cut off as an explosion rocked the hurricane. Cettie was propelled outside the sky ship suddenly, and she saw a mass of ships rise from beneath the tidewaters. These were not ships with masts and spars, but sleek metallic vessels sculpted and angled and covered with runes. Burning orbs flew from strange turrets on the front end of the vessels and struck into the fleet of sky ships overhead. Smoke belched from the holes in the hulls. Men fell to their deaths from the gaps, and Cettie could only look on in horror. The chaos of battle filled the air as the hurricanes began to maneuver away from the trap that had sprung up beneath them.

Cettie's attention shifted to the island of rock jutting up from the sea. Around the far side, she saw that part of the island had worn away, opening a gap for the seawater to rush through. It was like a bridge made totally of stone, all craggy and uneven. Years and years of waves hammering against it had created the gap. From that gap, she saw ships sailing in, the traditional kind with sails and masts. It was strange because the ships just appeared in the opening. One moment it was simply sky and water, the next another ship sailed through. It was a fleet of vessels. But the metal ships had come as a surprise. Somehow, they had crossed underwater without being seen and had positioned themselves beneath the sky ships. They were much larger than the little one she'd been told the kishion had used to escape the abbey. The threat was much worse. Their enemy's inventions had changed. There were half a dozen or so, each firing burning spheres up at the hurricanes and tempests. There was mayhem. There were screams of death.

And then she woke up next to the sentinel oak, a twig hurting her cheek. She had no idea how long she had been passed out. But she could smell the scent of sulfur in the air, hear the screams echoing from far away.

Then it was gone.

Fitzroy arrived the day of the ball, the day before all the students who had completed their study of the Mysteries would return home. The celebration was being held at the Aldermaston's manor, which was open to the public for such an occasion, for it had the largest ballroom. The noise of the crowd intensified as the youths eagerly awaited the orchestra to begin playing. The buzz and whine of the strings brought an air of anticipation to the moment.

It was a day that the students looked forward to, but to Cettie it was bittersweet. Fitzroy had taken his family aside upon arriving at the event, and he'd told Cettie that Sera would not be returning to Muirwood. He'd also shared the story of Will Russell's betrayal, and her friend's subsequent disgrace. Cettie's heart ached for her friend.

She wished to tell Fitzroy about her vision, but there were so many people around there wasn't enough privacy. Although Phinia was still suffering from the humiliation of failing the Test, the ball had certainly improved her attitude. Anna wore a white dress with long white gloves, and her blond hair was done up in pretty ringlets. She radiated beauty, but there was a wariness to her now, a loss of innocence.

Cettie had never been comfortable in such fashionable or fancy clothes. Her frock was more simple, the collar tight around her neck. There was nothing immodest about the Fitzroy sisters' dresses, of course, but Cettie felt more comfortable with her own choice. Her dress was gray, not white, and very simple and plain. She did not wear gloves deliberately.

After the girls wandered off—Phinia and Anna because they were summoned by their friends, and Cettie because she needed some time alone with her thoughts—Cettie noticed Lady Maren and Fitzroy continued to talk quietly in the corner. Lady Maren looked worried and concerned and spoke in a low voice to him. Cettie knew she could commune with a Leering near them and listen in to their conversation, but it felt too intrusive, and she wouldn't do it, particularly since her guardian, who already wore his regimentals, was preparing to be deployed the next day. They deserved this time alone.

Then she saw Stephen charging toward his parents with a raging look on his face. Adam Creigh walked alongside him, much calmer in appearance. She'd rarely seen Stephen so angry, his eyes flashing with hostility. Normally he loved balls too. Something had surely set him off.

Adam slowed when he saw her. He, too, wore a uniform and would be departing for his vessel the next day. Some girls found a military uniform exciting, but it hurt Cettie to see him wearing it, knowing that his heart longed to help heal the sick and impoverished. The spread of the disease may have slowed, but there was still no cure.

"Let me catch up with you," Adam told Stephen. "I wanted to talk to Cettie."

Stephen, noticing her, flushed and scowled even more. "You can speak to whomever you wish." His nostrils flared, and he stalked off.

Cettie felt like she'd done something to offend him.

"What was that all about?" she asked Adam worriedly.

He clasped his hands behind his back and sighed. "Fitzroy is sending him to Dolcoath to run the mines."

"What about Sir Jordan?" Cettie wondered, but the answer came to her before he could speak. "Oh, he used to be in the Ministry of War. He was a captain, I believe. That makes a great deal of sense."

"To everyone except Stephen," Adam said wryly, a twinkle in his eye. "He's offended on many counts. He was expecting to rule Fog Willows in Fitzroy's absence. Instead, he gets sent to the mines. It's dirty work, but it will be good for him. I can relate, though. I don't get a say in where I'll go either."

"Surely the mines will be better than a warship," Cettie said.

"Indeed," Adam said with a shrug. "Well, the music is about to start. Anna made me promise to dance with her first. But I hope you will stay around?"

Cettie felt a shiver of gooseflesh go down her arms. It had been many years since she'd danced with Adam, and things had since changed between them. At least for her. "Yes. I will be here."

"Good. I didn't want you wandering off like you did the other day when we couldn't find you. I looked at all your usual haunts, but you weren't there. Skrelling said he'd spied you heading to the orchard, but you weren't there either."

Cettie hadn't shared her experience with anyone. It felt private. Something not to be shared lightly. "You went looking for me?"

"Of course," he answered. "Well, I should give this to you now. Before all the commotion starts."

A single piccolo started up, beginning the opening notes of the song "Sky Ship's Cook." The tune was as familiar to her as any of the others. It was a lively dance.

"Oh?" she asked.

From behind his back, Adam brought out a small worn book, one she had seen him studying. It was small enough to fit in her hand.

"I don't have much," he said with a sigh. "But this one has always been my favorite. It's a book of plants and birds. There are little sketches in it to help identify the different breeds. It's a little shabby, but it means something to me. I wondered if I might give it to you while I'm gone? I've scrawled some notes in the margins. It's silly, I know, but it pained me to have it tossed out as rubbish. Would you keep it for me?"

Her throat went tight as he handed it to her. She stared at the little gray binding, the corners bent slightly. Some of the pages were loose. There was something sticking out from the middle of the book. This was something precious to him, and he'd given it to *her*. As she took it, their fingers touched.

"I would be honored," she stammered, feeling her cheeks growing very hot.

"Thank you, Cettie. There's Anna. I must go. I'll look for you."

She nodded, giving him a hopeful smile as she watched him hurry to meet Anna. She didn't feel any jealousy as she watched them start to dance. How could she when she held something so precious in her hands? Then she gazed down at the book and flipped through a few pages. She recognized his handwriting, of course, and could imagine him sitting against a tree, observing a wren in the branches and writing what he saw. The sketches were done well and had different symbols of measurement and facts about the various creatures he'd observed. Oh, it was wonderful. The best of gifts. Poking out from the middle of the book was a sprig of lavender that he'd smashed into the page, flattening it. She brought it to her nose and smelled it, along with the scent of the old pages. For a moment, she thought the floor was spinning.

Then she carried the book over to Fitzroy and Lady Maren. Stephen had already stomped off in the distance.

"I wish Sera were here," Cettie said, glancing at the rows of dancers whooping and clapping in time to the music. "She liked this song."

"She'll be at Pavenham Sky soon," Fitzroy said. "She misses you dearly."

"I don't know when I'll see her again," Cettie sighed. "I imagine I wouldn't be very welcome there."

Fitzroy pursed his lips. "Well, there are other places you are more than welcome."

"Tell her, Brant," Maren said, nudging him. "You've waited too long."

Cettie looked at them curiously.

Fitzroy gave her a tender look. "As you know, I have tried these last four years to adopt you. Your deed is paid off, so you have no obligation to anyone. But adoption is another matter, as you know. Sloan and Teitelbaum are still working the case. Even though we aren't your actual parents, we feel as strong of a connection to you as we do to our other children. It pleases us to hear you call us Mother and Father. Well, I should just get to the point. Cettie, we've decided to name you the keeper of the house of Fog Willows."

Cettie stared at them both in shock and surprise. She was only sixteen. It was unheard of that someone so young be given such a responsibility. It was a position of enormous trust, one that usually had to be proven over years of faithful service.

"B-but Mrs. Harding," Cettie said, her voice trembling.

"Took the position knowing full well that it would be temporary," Maren said, smiling. "And she misses her family very much." She cupped Cettie's cheek. "You are incredibly strong with the Medium, Cettie. Stronger than I am. And I'll be there to teach you and to help you. Once Brant gives you the key, you will be empowered to act as if you were him. The estate will obey you in all things." She then linked arms with Fitzroy. "It will be a good experience for you regardless. A sign to others that you are trusted implicitly. It will raise you in society."

Cettie's eyes pricked with tears, and she rushed forward and embraced both of them, feeling so grateful for their love and their willingness to defy tradition. Feeling so grateful they'd given her a chance. Again. She nearly dropped Adam's book but kept her fingers firm on its binding.

"I don't know what to say," Cettie said.

"Tell us you won't accept Mrs. Romrell's offer to become a governess," Fitzroy said with a smile. "I told you that I had something else in mind for you. And it will give me peace of mind when I'm away from home."

Cettie pulled back, realizing there was another source of Stephen's anger. "Stephen knows."

Maren glanced at Fitzroy first and then nodded. "He's not pleased. We have tried to teach him that he must *earn* Fog Willows. It won't just be given to him. We are giving him an opportunity to prove himself elsewhere, and he sees it as an injustice." She was about to say something else but stopped and shook her head.

"What?" Cettie pressed.

Fitzroy was about to speak, but Lady Maren made a gesture to silence him.

"She should know, Maren. He suggested sending *you* to Dolcoath instead. It was petty and unjust of him to say that. A few years of real work will be good for that young man. It will temper his character. If he had taken any of the martial classes when he was studying here, beyond the required few, he may have been conscripted too. But poetry and dancing wouldn't serve the Ministry of War very well. He's luckier than he knows." His eyes trailed off, lost in sad memories.

"I will miss you, Father," Cettie said, giving him another hug. He patted her shoulders.

"We will also rely on you to keep storm glasses going. The information they provide will prove essential during a conflict. And you understand them better than anyone. Some will try to steal the idea while I am gone. You must safeguard it."

"I will," she promised.

"We knew we could count on you," Maren said. "We love you, Cettie." Then she looked up at her husband. "If they start 'Genny's Market,' you must dance with me."

He bowed to his wife, a pleased smile on his mouth. It was one of Cettie's favorites too.

She felt the sudden urge to tell them about her experience in the woods. It came as just a little nudge, a little push, the kind she was learning to heed. The song finished, and everyone clapped. It was time to exchange partners.

"Something happened to me the other day," Cettie said as the noise of the room intensified. "The day of the Test." She quickly related her experience to them. They looked concerned as she told her story. But then she related her vision of the strange battle she had witnessed off the coast of Dahomey. Fitzroy's eyes widened with surprise at that part. He was stunned by it.

Cettie bit her lip, gazing at him, wondering why her words had affected him so.

He pitched his voice lower, even though there was a ruckus among the cheerful students as they began to assemble again for another dance.

"Cettie. There was a battle fought yesterday at the ruins of Dochte Abbey in Dahomey. Just like in your vision. It is where one of the mirror gates between the worlds is located. It is a state secret you couldn't have known." His voice throbbed with concern, with wonderment. He looked at his wife, who looked equally transfixed by the news.

"Is she . . . ?" Maren whispered in awe.

Fitzroy nodded slowly. "I think she may be."

Someone approached to ask Cettie to dance. She turned, her emotions awash with the implications of their unspoken words. But she was eager to dance with Adam. She wanted to spend every moment possible with him before he was gone. Before he was taken away on a sky ship into battles far away.

It was Mr. Skrelling.

"If you please, Miss Cettie?" he asked, extending his hand.

AUTHOR'S NOTE

One of my favorite TED talks was given by Amy Cuddy. It was from that talk that I heard the term "imposter syndrome" for the first time. While I don't think she invented it, her powerful talk has made me think a lot about the little voices in our heads that whisper negative thoughts. I don't know anyone who has not felt them.

I have found similar anecdotes from my own life, from books, and from the lives of others I know. I struggled with them, especially one Christmastime years ago after self publishing the Legends of Muirwood trilogy. I felt tempted to quit trying to be a writer. Who was I to write books? Who would ever want to read them? I resisted the strong urge to quit and moved forward with more determination. Just a few months later, I was contacted by 47North, and the rest, as they say, is history.

As I've read many books on a variety of topics, I have seen the theme of imposter syndrome throughout. I've seen it in the eyes and heard it in the voices of other writers. I felt it at my job at Intel.

It is my hope that this book and this series will provide courage for someone to face their fear and attempt to live their dreams. Fear holds so many people back. A question I have been asked and like to ask others is "What would you dare to do if you knew you couldn't fail?"

I am living my dream right now. Every one of us who tries to live our dreams is met with setbacks and failure that make us want to quit.

I hope that something in the stories of Sera and Cettie will inspire you to challenge those persistent negative thoughts. There is a wonderful piece of wisdom that Aslan passes on to Lucy in *The Voyage of the Dawn Treader*: "Courage, dear heart." This is a quote I've always remembered, one that has helped me during many dark times. It is as appropriate in Narnia as it is in our world. And other worlds too.

Courage, dear heart.

ACKNOWLEDGMENTS

Life is full of rises and valleys. Sometimes it feels like a roller coaster. Things always change. I'd like to acknowledge Courtney Miller, from Amazon Publishing. As of this writing, she's well into her new job at Amazon, but she was instrumental in bringing *The Queen's Poisoner* into the Kindle First program, which really catapulted my career. She's a wonderful person, too, and I'm grateful to have worked with her. As always, I have a great team whose candid and insightful feedback helps make my books shine. To Jason and Angela and Wanda—I couldn't do this without you. To my first readers who suffer through withdrawals and emotional distress while reading or waiting for the next batch of chapters, thank you for your sacrifices and endurance. These include Emily, Isabelle, Shannon, Robin, Travis, Sunil, and Dan. Your words of encouragement and years of support are appreciated.

ABOUT THE AUTHOR

Photo © 2016 Mica Sloan

Jeff Wheeler is the *Wall Street Journal* bestselling author of the Kingfountain Series as well as the Muirwood and Mirrowen novels. He took an early retirement from his career at Intel in 2014 to write full-time. He is a husband, father of five, and devout member of his church. He lives in the Rocky Mountains and is the founder of *Deep Magic: The E-zine of Clean Fantasy and Science Fiction*. Find out more about Deep Magic at www.deepmagic.co, and visit Jeff's many worlds at jeff-wheeler.com.